continued . . .

D0441918

From
Hell with
Love

Simon R. Green

A ROC BOOK

ROC
Published by New American Library, a division of
Penguin Group (USA) Inc., 375 Hudson Street,
New York, New York 10014, USA
Penguin Group (Canada), 90 Eglinton Avenue East, Suite 700, Toronto,
Ontario M4P 2Y3, Canada (a division of Pearson Penguin Canada Inc.)
Penguin Books Ltd., 80 Strand, London WC2R 0RL, England
Penguin Ireland, 25 St. Stephen's Green, Dublin 2,
Ireland (a division of Penguin Books Ltd.)
Penguin Group (Australia), 250 Camberwell Road, Camberwell, Victoria 3124,
Australia (a division of Pearson Australia Group Pty. Ltd.)
Penguin Books India Pvt. Ltd., 11 Community Centre, Panchsheel Park,
New Delhi - 110 017, India
Penguin Group (NZ), 67 Apollo Drive, Rosedale, Auckland 0632,
New Zealand (a division of Pearson New Zealand Ltd.)
Penguin Books (South Africa) (Pty.) Ltd., 24 Sturdee Avenue,
Rosebank, Johannesburg 2196, South Africa

Penguin Books Ltd., Registered Offices:
80 Strand, London WC2R 0RL, England

Published by Roc, an imprint of New American Library, a division of Penguin
Group (USA) Inc. Previously published in a Roc hardcover edition.

First Roc Mass Market Printing, June 2011
10 9 8 7 6 5 4 3 2 1

PUBLISHER'S NOTE
This is a work of fiction. Names, characters, places, and incidents either are
the product of the author's imagination or are used fictitiously, and any resem-
blance to actual persons, living or dead, business establishments, events, or
locales is entirely coincidental.
   The publisher does not have any control over and does not assume any responsibility for author or third-party Web sites or their content.

Previously in the Secret Histories . . .

The name's Bond. Shaman Bond.

You can mention that name anywhere in the darker parts of London, and someone will smile ruefully, or nod knowingly. Shaman Bond is a well-known face—always turning up when things get dangerous or a little bit weird; always ready for action, intrigue and a little illegal fun. Always there on the edges, where the games get strange and the night people dance to their own peculiar piper. Everyone at work or at play in society's shadows knows Shaman Bond.

Except, they don't.

I'm Eddie Drood, and Shaman Bond is just my use name—a mask for me to wear in public, to hide who and what I really am.

I'm a field agent for the ancient and mighty Drood family. We stand between Humanity and all the dark forces that threaten. We defend you from aliens and

2 ○ Simon R. Green

elves, mad scientists and their monsters, secret organisations and ancient inhuman enemies. Ever since
my Druid ancestors first made contact with an other-
dimensional entity called the Heart, who made them
the protectors of Humanity by granting them incredible
golden armour.

It was only very recently that I discovered the awful
price my family paid for that armour, and was still paying, centuries later. I destroyed the Heart, to save my
family's soul. Now we have new armour, provided by
a new other-dimensional entity. Called Ethel. I really
don't want to talk about that.

I saved the family from itself, and for my sins they put
me in charge, but I was never happy with that much responsibility. First chance I got I dumped it all on someone else and went back to being just a field agent again.
One of the best, if I do say so myself.

But—the Man from U.N.C.L.E. had to contend with
agents of THRUSH. James Bond had SPECTRE. So it
really shouldn't have come as such a surprise to me, that
a family as ancient and powerful as mine might have its
own very dark shadow . . .

CHAPTER ONE

The Return of Doctor Delirium

I n the secret agent business, no one is necessarily who or what they say they are. It comes with the job, and the territory. Agents in the field collect names and identities the way normal people collect credit cards; and just like you, we all have to pay the cost when the bill comes due. Use names are common, if only to help us avoid the consequences of our actions. I'm Shaman Bond as often as I'm Eddie Drood. In fact, a lot of the time I think I prefer being Shaman; he doesn't have the duties and responsibilities of being a Drood.

And it's not just us poor bastards risking our lives out in the field—no organisation is ever what it appears to be, when seen from the outside. They all have levels within levels, inner circles and hidden agendas, and the left hand is never allowed to know who the right hand is killing. Like the onion, there are layers within layers within layers, and sometimes, just like the onion, we have no heart.

The Droods are a family, as well as an organisation. *Anything for the family,* we are taught to say, from a very early age. And if you can't trust your family, who can you trust?

It's always hot as hell in Los Angeles, but that's just one of the reasons why the natives call it Hell A. On the one side you've got Hollywood, where all your dreams can come true, including all the really disappointing ones; and on the other side you've got Disneyland, where dreams are up for sale, or at least rent. And in between . . . there's all the sin and avarice in the world, just waiting for you to put a foot wrong. Everyone who matters turns up in LA eventually, because LA is a city that deals in temptation. Especially for the kind of people who like to think they're above the laws and moral constraints that operate in the rest of the world. Las Vegas deals in money, New York deals in deals, but LA deals in sin.

Hollywood is the town where people will sell their soul for a three-picture deal; or a sit-down with a big-name producer; or just for a walk-on in a popular sitcom. Hardly surprising, then, that the place is full of people ready to buy as well as sell. You can buy anything in LA, if you're prepared to pay the price. Dreams come cheap in Hollywood, because there's a glut on the market.

I arrived in Los Angeles on a commercial air flight, under the Shaman Bond name. Business class, so as not to draw attention. You have to keep up the character, as well as the name, and Shaman Bond had never gone first class in his life. Ordinarily, I would have simply activated the Merlin Glass, and stepped from the family Hall in England to my destination in Los Angeles, but apparently using a major magical item that powerful would set off all kinds of alarm bells, among all the wrong people. And since I was supposed to be operating under the radar on this one, I did it the hard way. And made a point of keeping all my receipts. The family's been coming down really hard on expense claims recently; just because a few of us have been known to be a little . . . creative, on occasion.

And I am here to tell you, fourteen hours cooped up in a plane gives you a whole new insight into air rage.

To my surprise, Los Angeles turned out to look exactly like it does on all the television shows. Brilliant blue sky, towering palm trees, more fast-moving traffic than the mind can comfortably cope with, and a sun so hot it's like stepping into a blast furnace. My bare skin actually smarted from contact with the sunlight, so I grabbed the nearest taxi and told the very laid-back driver to take me to the Magnificat Hotel in Anaheim.

The driver just grunted, took a long drag on his hand-rolled, and steered the taxi straight into the thundering traffic with a casual disregard for road safety, and indeed survival, that took my breath away. The driver was big and black and uncommunicative. He'd covered the inside of his cab with assorted voodoo charms, pictures of the saints, and a whole bunch of severed chicken feet. More feathers and fetishes dangled from the roof. I would have settled for one of those little green pine things. I wondered whether I should inform the driver that I knew for a fact more than half his collection was complete and utter bullshit. I decided against it.

I was going to Anaheim, not Hollywood. Anaheim is on the whole other side of town, as far as you can get from the glamour and the ballyhoo and still be in the same city. There was a Disneyland park, which I hoped to visit if I got the chance. If only to chat up Snow

White. (Boyhood crushes are a terrible thing.) Still, despite all my best intentions, I was just a bit overawed at being in a city I knew only from films and television. We passed off-ramp signs, for places like Echo Beach and Mulholland Drive, names the whole world knew. It was like seeing road signs to Narnia and Oz.

I was in Los Angeles to meet up with the local field agent, Luther Drood. I didn't know the man, but then, it's a large family, and field agents by their very nature don't come home much. In fact, it's the reason why most of us become field agents. Luther had made Los Angeles his home for more than twenty years, and despite all the good work he'd done, there was always the chance he'd gone native. Nothing like being a big fish in a small pond to make you forget all about the sharks who operate in the larger world.

I was supposed to meet Luther at the Magnificat, the single biggest hotel in LA, opening tomorrow morning in a gala ceremony at nine a.m., sharp. But Luther and I had business to attend to in the Magnificat today, and how we got on would decide whether there would be any grand opening tomorrow. Whenever possible, I like to get in, do the job, and get out again without being noticed, but given the nature of the job, sometimes fire, general mayhem and extensive property damage are just unavoidable side effects.

The taxi driver fixed me in his rearview mirror with his calm, steady gaze. "So, man, are you an actor, or a writer?"

"Neither," I said firmly.

There was a long pause, as he tried to get his head around such a novel concept. "Hell, man, everyone here is either an actor, or a writer. Or a producer. Everything else is just what you do to pay the bills, till the big break comes around. You're a Brit, right? Love the accent. You guys make the best villains . . . So, are you a producer? Because I got this killer screenplay, guaranteed to do major business. All about this guy who can turn invisible, but only when he's naked . . . You don't like that one? Okay, how about this for high concept—James Bond meets *Alien*!"

"Been there, done that," I said. "Just drive."

And there must have been something in my voice, because he sniffed loudly, shut up, and fixed his gaze on the road ahead. He turned his music up loud, which seemed to consist mainly of bass beats, heavy grunts and extensive use of the word "ho." I didn't think it had anything to do with the song from Snow White. Unless one of the dwarves was called Shouty.

We hadn't been driving long before we hit hard traffic. Every lane was full, in every direction, and everyone had ground to a halt. There was a lot of bad-tempered horn abuse, and even more harsh language. My driver just sat back in his seat and rolled up another fat one, quite content to sit there as long as it took, and watch his fare rise. I wasn't. I had work to be about, and a deadline to meet. So I got out of the taxi, paid off the driver, (including a tip nicely calculated to spoil his whole day without inciting actual violence), and walked up the highway, strolling in and out of the parked cars. And no one saw me, because I had armoured up and invoked stealth mode.

The marvellous armour of the Droods flowed out of the golden torc around my throat, and covered me in a moment from head to toe, like a second skin. The awful heat was cut off in a moment, the unbreathable smog was filtered into air fresh as a spring morning, and I felt stronger, smarter, and fully alive for the first time.

And, more importantly, I was pretty much invulnerable to anything the world could throw at me. (I say pretty much, because no one's actually tested it against a nuclear blast, or a full-on faerie curse . . . but the family Armourer was working on that.) With the armour in stealth mode, I couldn't be seen by anyone or anything, including all kinds of electronic surveillance. (I've never been too sure how that actually works; presumably the torc rewrites the signal, to edit me out. The Armourer did try to explain how the strange matter in my torc works, and I had to go and lie down in a darkened room for several hours.)

I strolled in and out of the parked cars, resisting the urge to strike down some of the louder and more obnoxious drivers with an invisible fist round the ear, and quickly decided it was in everyone's best interests if I got out of there as fast as possible. So I broke into a run, moving faster and faster as the incredible strength of my armoured legs kicked in. The cars became just a blur as I got up to speed, shooting in and out of gaps in a split second, thanks to my speeded-up reflexes. I was laughing into my featureless golden mask now, arms pumping easily at my sides as I really hit my stride. The world was just a smear of colours, every sound dopplering down behind me, and I wasn't even breathing hard. My family has the best toys in the world.

Soon enough I was past the pileup that had caused all the congestion, and was sprinting in and out of moving traffic. Cars and trucks and bikes roared along, filling all the lane space available, and I had to slow down or risk running right over them. Reflexes are great, but they're no match for an idiot behind the wheel, of which Los Angeles has more than its fair share. I got fed up dodging drivers who changed lane with no warning and no signal, so I waited for a lengthy articulated to come along, raced along beside it to match speeds, and then jumped up onto its roof. My armoured legs sent me flying through the air, and then absorbed the impact on landing so completely the articulated's driver never even knew I was there. I struck a heroic pose that no one could see, just because, and surfed the articulated all the way to Anaheim.

I got hit by an awful lot of insects, but the armour just absorbed them.

When we finally got to Anaheim, I switched from vehicle to vehicle, riding the roofs as I followed the street map I'd memorised, and jumped off a block short of the Magnificat. I found a quiet side street, and armoured down when no one was looking. And just like that, I was just another tourist, wandering happily down the street. The air was blisteringly hot again, and so thick with pollution you could practically chew the stuff, but that's what you get for living in the real world. No one paid me any attention as I joined the throng in the main street, heading for the Magnificat. There's nothing memorable in my appearance. I've gone to great pains to appear to be just another face in the crowd. Field agents are trained to blend in, and not be noticed. It's a useful skill for a field agent, not looking like anyone in particular. The last thing you want in this business is to be noticed or remembered.

Even when I was still a long way off, I could see the Magnificat Hotel. It was the tallest building for miles, a massive steel and glass block that towered over everything else, effortlessly dominating the scene without a single trace of character or style in its appearance. The neon sign with the hotel's name was almost brutally ugly. Everything about the building shouted that it was there to serve a purpose, nothing more. All very efficient, but a total pain in the arse to look at. Ugly buildings are like ugly women—you can't help feeling someone should have made more of an effort. I said this to my girlfriend Molly once, and she hit me. I've got a lot more careful about what I say out loud since I acquired a girlfriend. I still think things, though. Sometimes very loudly.

Luther Drood was already there, waiting. He looked exactly like the photo in his file, except even more tanned, if that were possible. Luther was a tall, heavily built man in his late forties, wearing a baggy Hawaiian shirt over blindingly white shorts, and a pair of designer flip-flops. He had a broad, lined face, with close-cut grey hair and a bushy grey moustache. He was standing right in the middle of the sidewalk, staring at nothing, smoking a large cigar as though it was the most important thing in his world. But people just walked right past him, paying him no attention at all . . . because he had a mobile phone at his ear. Those things are a godsend to the modern agent—the perfect excuse for just standing around, doing nothing.

Luther saw me approaching, put his phone away, and nodded easily to me. As though he saw me every day of the week. Typical LA native: cool and calm and so laid-back it was a wonder he didn't fall over. I stopped before him, gave him my own very cool and collected nod, threw in a quick smile for good measure, and offered him my hand. He clasped my pale offering in his large bronzed hand, and gave it a quick meaningless LA shake.

"Hi," he said, in a deep and apparently sincere voice. "Welcome to LA. I'm Philip Harlowe."

I gave him a look. "Does that fool anyone?"

"Does Shaman Bond?" He allowed me a small tight

smile. He still hadn't removed his cigar from his mouth. "Everyone knows use names are fakes, but the kind of people we have to deal with are only ever comfortable with masques and illusions. So better a false ID you know is fake, than a seemingly real name you know you can't trust."

"But we're family," I said. "You're Luther and I'm . . ."

"Please." He stopped me with a raised hand. "Everyone in the family, and everyone in the field, knows Eddie Drood. Your reputation precedes you—like an oncoming missile." He took a map out of his back pocket, and unfolded it. "Look at this. It isn't important or even relevant, but maps make excellent cover. No one pays any attention to two tourists studying a map."

He had a point. I stood beside him, and looked at the Magnificat over the top of the map. Luther finally removed his cigar, just for a moment, and blew a perfect smoke ring. If my Molly had been there, she would have turned it into a perfect square, just to put him in his place. I settled for giving him a hard look.

"I thought tobacco was forbidden in this health conscious, zero tolerance paradise?"

"That's cigarettes," Luther said easily. "Cigars are different. Only important people smoke cigars, and no one bothers important people in LA. Even a complete health nazi will light your cigar for you, if they thought you could get them a meeting."

"My worst fears are realised," I said sadly. "You've gone native."

He raised an eyebrow. I'd never seen so much work go into the creation of such a bitingly sardonic gesture. I felt like applauding.

"At least I still serve the family," said Luther. "I've never tried to run it. Or run away from it."

I sighed, plucked the cigar out of his mouth, dropped it on the ground and stamped on it. Luther made a shocked, pained sound, as though I'd just shot his dog. I gave him my very best hard glare.

"Do you have a problem with my being here, Luther?"

He would have liked to glare at me, but his cool and laid-back persona wouldn't let him, so he settled for looking down his nose at me. There was a lot of nose to look down. Noses run in our family. (Old family joke. Really old. You have no idea.) Luther must have realised my attention was wandering, because he stuck his face right in close to mine.

"Just for the record," I said. "Second-hand cigar smoke is in no way attractive."

"This is my town," said Luther. "My territory. No one knows it better than me. The people, the organisations, the schemes and the hustles. They didn't need to send you. I could have handled this myself. I've handled a lot worse in my time, and never once made a ripple in the waters. I have a reputation for getting things done and keeping things quiet, and I don't want it upset. I operate without being seen, behind the scenes. I keep the lid on things, I defuse situations before they get out of control, and no one ever knows I was there. It's the only way you can operate, in a media-saturated town like this. The last thing I need is a show-off, grandstanding overachiever like you, coming in here playing the hero, overturning the applecart and then setting it on fire. I know all about you, Eddie. No gesture too dramatic, no action too violent. Well, you aren't going to operate like that here. We can't make waves; we'd be noticed. Even after everything you've done recently, we're still supposed to be a secret organisation of secret agents."

"After everything I've done?" I said, innocently.

He wanted to splutter and raise his voice. I could tell.

"I know your reputation," he said doggedly. "It doesn't impress me. You're impetuous, you're unnecessarily aggressive, and you're sloppy! How many times have you been seen in armour in public? That's not how we get things done!"

"I saved the entire world from the Hungry Gods," I said.

"And got a lot of good Droods killed in the process. You're not getting me killed, rushing in where devils fear to tread. This is my territory, and we're going to do things my way. Either you agree right now to follow my orders, or I'll kick you out of town and deal with this problem myself. And to hell with the Matriarch's instructions!"

I considered him thoughtfully. "If my girlfriend was here, she'd make all your pubic hair fall out, just by looking at you in a Certain Way. I'm not as subtle as she is. So either you agree to work with me, as a full partner . . . or I'll just punch you repeatedly in the head till your eyes change colour."

"You see! You see! This is what I'm talking about! You can't operate like that in a city like this!"

"Pretty sure I can," I said.

He glared at me for a moment, and then his face went studiously blank, his eyes cold and calculating. "Is it true?" he said. "Did you kill the Grey Fox?"

"Yes," I said. "I killed my Uncle James. And he meant a lot more to me than you do."

"I knew James," Luther said flatly. "Worked with him on a few missions, back in the day. He was a good man, and a real agent, and a credit to the family. I knew your mother, too. Your father, less so. They got themselves killed by rushing in without first . . ."

"Don't go there," I said, and something in my voice, or perhaps in my eyes, stopped him dead.

"Things were better the way they used to be," Luther said finally. "Back when the Droods were a real power in the world, and the world did what it was told. For its own good. Now, countries and governments and organisations all go their own way, and the Droods . . . are just one more force among many. Used to be, when we spoke people paid attention. Now all we do is run around playing catch-up, occasionally snatching victory from the jaws of defeat."

"We were never meant to rule the world," I said, just a bit tiredly. "Just protect people from outside forces and from themselves, when need be. I know things were easier for us in the past, but the price we paid was too high. Or have you forgotten that our old armour was made from the imprisoned souls of sacrificed Drood babies?"

"I haven't forgotten anything," said Luther. "But you have to admit, we did a better job when our hands weren't tied behind our backs."

"A better job?" I said. "Two World Wars and a decades-long Cold War, in the last century alone? No, we spent too long holding Humanity's hand; it's well past time they grew up and took responsibility for themselves."

"And how many of the sheep will die, because the shepherd won't intervene?"

"We protect them from wolves. Everything else is up to them."

"I didn't become a field agent to see people get hurt on my watch!"

"That's how children learn. We'll still be here, to pick them up when they fall."

"Nice words," said Luther. "Pity about all the blood and suffering and death."

"You've spent too long in Hell A," I said. "You've got far too used to being in charge of people. For their own good, of course. You're a bit old to be a field agent, aren't you, Luther? Most of us get called back in once we hit forty. And you're forty-nine. I checked your file. So what are you still doing here? Could it be you see them all as sheep now, unable to cope without your benevolent authority?"

"I have a good record here," said Luther. "Done a good job, down the years. I've made good local connections, carefully maintained and nurtured, with important individuals and organisations. In LA, and in Hollywood especially, it's all who you know. Who you can get to take your call, and then do what you tell them to do. The right names, the right relationships, can open doors here that would stay shut to anyone else. Even another Drood."

"I was right," I said. "You have gone native."

"Training a replacement, and rebuilding all the connections and relationships would take years! The Matriarch knows that. She's just . . . looking for the right man, for me to train. Besides, I'm not ready to give up yet. Not nearly ready to go back to the Hall, and sit behind a desk, pushing paper around. I've got years left in me yet! I've given my life to this job, to this town!"

"Doesn't mean you own the job, or the town," I said. "They survived before you, and they'll do just fine after you've gone. We go out into the world to serve the family, and Humanity, and when we stop forgetting that, it's time to go home."

"I've thought of nothing else, since they said they were sending you," said Luther. "They never sent anyone before."

"I'm not your replacement, Luther."

"No, you're my wake-up call." He smiled briefly, mirthlessly. "I'd miss the excitement of this place—all the larger than life people and places—but I have no roots here. No people who'd actually miss me if I disappeared tomorrow. We're not allowed to have friends or loves or real relationships, out in the field. Because the family doesn't allow it. That way your only loyalty is to the job, and the family. All these years I've fought being called back home, but I don't have anything here I couldn't pack into a suitcase."

"I know," I said. "That's why you need to come home, to the Hall. Because things are different there, now."

"I'm forty-nine," said Luther. "Old-school Drood. Different . . . scares me."

"That's good," I said. "That's how you know you're still alive."

"Spare me the platitudes," said Luther. "This is LA. I can get them wholesale here."

"Sorry," I said.

We stood together, hidden from the people passing by behind the protection of our unfolded map. Men and women went on their way and noticed nothing unusual, because Droods are trained not to stand out. Even when in the midst of an emotional crisis. It's not easy being a field agent. Or a Drood. But then, nothing worth doing is ever easy. Across the street, the Magnificat Hotel stared calmly back at us, smugly expensive and exclusive, ready for its Grand Opening tomorrow morning. It was a really big building. Just looking up at the top floor made me dizzy and unsteady on my feet, as though at any moment I might lose my footing and be snatched up into the sky, falling up and up into the endless brilliant blue. So I stopped looking up, and made myself concentrate on all the colourful bunting and banners that had been draped across the hotel front like so many ribbons on a present. Large signs proclaimed parties and ceremonies and even awards, along with the promise of various big stars and names and celebrities. None of whom would have been seen dead at a hotel opening if their careers were really going as well as their publicists said.

(Molly has an insatiable appetite for the glossies and the gossip rags. I have therefore acquired a certain amount of celebrity information through sheer proximity and osmosis.)

"We have to get in and out before the media coverage starts," said Luther.

"Oh sure," I said. "Plenty of time yet. Hours. I still can't believe we're here because of that loser, Doctor Delirium. You are sure he's here, in the city, waiting for his moment?"

"Quite sure," said Luther. "He's been keeping his head down so far, with about thirty of his people. I've got some of my people watching them. The Doctor can't make a move without us knowing. Why did the Matriarch send you in particular, Eddie? When has it ever taken more than one Drood to handle Doctor Delirium?"

"I have a history with the Doctor," I said. "I ran an operation in London, some time back, to deny him funding for some new scheme of his, but he got away. Reluctantly, I am forced to admit that I don't have nearly the financial acumen of the late departed Matthew Drood. He really knew the City. But, unfortunately, he turned out to be a part of the Zero Tolerance insurrection and a traitor to the family."

"So you killed him," said Luther.

"No," I said. "Though he'd probably have been better off if I had. Anyway, we still haven't found anyone to replace him, so I'm handling London all on my own. And without Matthew's insider knowledge, I betrayed my hand a little too early and it all went to rat shit in a hurry. Doctor Delirium set his mercenaries on me, and while I was kicking them around he made a swift exit. He always did believe in letting others do his fighting for him. We still don't know exactly what he was up to in London, or what precisely he needed so much new money for . . . He's never been short of cash in the past. Anyway, I was really . . . quite upset, when he got away from me, so when we learned he'd turned up here, I persuaded the Matriarch to let me come and assist you in taking the Doctor down."

"Ah," said Luther. "So this is nothing to do with me, and all to do with you. You're only here because the Matriarch favours you. Because she's your grandmother."

I had to smile. "Shows how little you know her."

I didn't take Doctor Delirium seriously. Nobody did. He had a secret base and a private army only because an uncle left them to him in his will. Ever since, the man who used to be a decent small-time research chemist has been hamming it up big-time as a mad science villain, Doctor Delirium, and building up his army with small ads in the back of *Soldier of Fortune* magazine. He's based somewhere in the Amazon rain forest, after being hounded out of every civilised country, and the Nightside, and spends all his time now plotting grand schemes and revenges against all of civilisation. A little man with lots of money and resources, and serious delusions of grandeur. Always a bad combination.

He might have become a real problem, if he hadn't been such a prat.

His usual modus operandi was to work up some awful new disease in his secret laboratories, and then threaten to unleash them on the world, if all the various governments didn't agree to pay him off, in rare postage stamps. I suppose once a collector, always a collector. But the Doctor was such a sloppy operator we always managed to find some weak spot in his organisation, and then we'd just squeeze the knowledge we needed out of some poor sod at the bottom of the food chain, get our hands on a specimen of his new disease before he'd even finished testing it . . . and by the time he got around to issuing his threats, we already had a cure or a vaccine. End of problem. On a few occasions, we have found it necessary to bomb his secret labs, but he always escapes and sets up somewhere else. The Amazon rain forest is a really big place.

"Who's the field agent in his area, these days?" said Luther.

"Conrad Drood," I said. "Good man, old African hand, very experienced. But he has a lot of ground to cover, and limited resources. And, he has to be very careful every time he ventures into the rain forest area; Timothy Drood's still in there somewhere."

"Tiger Tim?" said Luther. "That crazy bastard? He's still alive? Why hasn't someone killed him yet?"

"Because he's still a Drood, for all his many faults. And we are notoriously hard to kill. Talk to me about Doctor Delirium. How long has he been here? What do you know, about why he's here?"

"Not much," Luther admitted. "He's only been in town a few days, holed up in a motel with his mercenaries. Word is, he's here to attend a very private auction, being held on the top floor of this very hotel, tonight. Before it officially opens. It's hard to get any real information; my people are using every listening device and surveillance spell at their command, but the Doctor's defences are first class. But, it seems he's come all the way here, so far from his heavily protected comfort zone, because he's desperate to acquire one of the items at this auction. Doctor Delirium wants the Apocalypse Door."

"I read that name in your last report," I said. "There's no record of such a thing in the Hall Library, or the Old Library. Which would normally suggest it can't be anything that dangerous, or significant, because if it was we'd have heard about it."

"Possibly," said Luther. "But any use of the word Apocalypse has to be just a bit worrying."

"Either way, the Matriarch has decided that Doctor Delirium is not to be allowed to get his hands on this Apocalypse Door, whatever it might turn out to be. We are to put a stop to his efforts, give him and his people a good kicking, and then send him home with a flea in his ear. If only for being such a bloody nuisance."

"Why don't we just kill him?" said Luther.

"You've been in LA too long," I said sternly. "Watching too many cop shows. We're supposed to be agents, not assassins. Otherwise there'd be no difference between us and the forces we fight. It's enough that we protect Humanity; we don't get to bully them. Besides, Doctor Delirium really is a scientific genius, when he can be bothered. We might just need his help some day. Right now he's a menace, but one day he might be an asset. Droods have to take the long view. So, we spank him and send him home crying. Tell me more about this auction."

"On the top floor, strictly private, cut off from the rest of the hotel," said Luther. "One night only, before the hotel officially opens, very definitely By Invitation

Only. Lots of armed guards in place, security people everywhere, trespassers will be disappeared. The auction's being run by the Really Old Curiosity Shoppe people; long established firm, very good reputation. Of a kind. They specialise in acquiring rare and unusual items, with or without their owners' permission, and then offering them up at their very private auctions for the delectation of interested (and extremely wealthy) parties. No questions, no provenance, and absolutely no guarantees or refunds. But, they can get you things no one else can, things from the Past, Present and Futures. Sometimes things no one ever really thought existed, and a few that just plain shouldn't."

"I've heard of the company," I said. "Who runs things, these days?"

Luther shrugged. "No one knows, and the company likes it that way. I suppose it's possible someone in our family knows, but if they do it's way above my level." He looked at me thoughtfully. "You used to run the family. And you're still part of the Advisory Council. Are you sure you don't know who these people are?"

It was my turn to shrug. "The family as a whole knows lots of things, but at any given time we all only know what we need to know."

"Why are you just a field agent again?" Luther said bluntly.

"I prefer to maintain a comfortable distance from the family," I said. "Running it will do that to you."

Luther carefully refolded his map, put it away, produced an oversized colour brochure and handed it to me. "This is an advance copy of the auction catalogue."

I studied it carefully. Very expensive, stiff laminated paper, lots of colour photographs; images so sharp they seemed to jump right off the page. Which was actually quite disturbing in places, given the nature of the images. No suggested prices, or values, though. Probably came under the heading of *If you have to ask, you can't afford it*. I looked at Luther.

"How did you get hold of an advance copy? If they even suspect a Drood knows they're here . . ."

Luther looked at me pityingly. "This is my territory. I know people, and people who know people."

"Do any of these people know you're a Drood?"

"Of course not. I'm Philip Harlowe. Whoever he is."

I sniffed, and went back to studying the catalogue. Items up for grabs included a formula from thirteenth-century Venice to make your blood undrinkable by vampires; a spell from Old Moore's grimoire to make ghosts corporeal so you could have sex with them; a wristwatch that could show you the exact time in fifty-two different universes, to make dimension-hopping more exact; a crystal alien skull that when properly provoked would provide you with mental images of all the worlds its owner had visited; and a Word tattooed on the framed and mounted skin of a murdered priest, that when spoken aloud would blow this world apart like a firecracker in a rotten apple. Allegedly.

There were photos of a Martian tripod (some assembly required). a hard-boiled Roc's egg (double yolk), a Crystal Egg (see what the Curate saw), a Hellfire grenade, an Angel's tears preserved in aspic, and Baphomet's Engine of Destruction. Just looking at that last one made my eyes hurt. I handed the catalogue back to Luther.

"We need to take the Word back with us," I said briskly. "Can't have something like that running around loose. Besides, the Armourer always says I never bring him back anything fun."

"I also have a list of some of the Big Names and Major Players who are supposed to be attending the auction," said Luther.

I gave him another of my hard looks, though he seemed to be developing an immunity. "Any more useful information, or are you planning to keep on doling it out one bit at a time, in case I get overexcited?"

"No," said Luther. "That's it."

He handed me the paper, and I ran my eyes quickly down the list of names. I then resisted the urge to whistle, or indeed curse loudly. A whole lot of Very Important Personages, Complete Bastards and not a few Powers and Dominions. Not one of them the kind of people even Droods like to cross without heavy weaponry and serious backup.

Jerusalem Stark, the Knight Apostate, heretic and blasphemer. Used to be one of the London Knights, until he had a crisis of faith. Now he carries his dead love's heart in a silver cage on his belt, right next to the sword he used to kill the Man who would be King. Then there was Prince Gaylord the Damned, Nuncio to the Court of King Artur, of Sinister Albion. Aunt Sally Darque, current Witch of Endor, and banned from every coven and gathering in Europe after that nasty affair at the Danse Academy in the German Black Forest. Three Dukes of Hell, attending via the possessed; two living Saints (stigmata permitting); and a Name I didn't even want to think out loud, in case He heard me.

"What the hell does Doctor Delirium think he's doing, mixing with people like this?" I said. "He is not in their class. Nowhere near. He must know that. Hell, he won't even get through the first round of bidding . . ."

"There's no way we could hope to infiltrate the auction with so many Major Players around," said Luther.

"That's why I thought we should get here early, find a nice hiding place, wait for Doctor Delirium to show up, and then put the grab on him before he even enters the hotel. That way he doesn't even get within spitting distance of the Apocalypse Door. Whatever that might turn out to be."

"Strike your enemy down from behind, when he's not looking," I said cheerfully. "That's the Drood way. Though I think we'll be better off hiding inside the hotel . . . That way we can sneak onto the top floor, grab the Word and the Apocalypse Door, and anything else worth acquiring, before we go home."

"What if the auction people find out it was us?" Luther said carefully. "I have to live in this town, remember? And if they catch us actually burgling their items, there could be major firepower, curses for everyone, and blood and slaughter all over the shop."

"Well, let's not let that happen, then," I said.

We both looked the Magnificat Hotel over very carefully. To the everyday eye, it looked like just another really ugly, tasteless expensive building. But Luther and I are Droods, and when we choose, we can See the world as it is, and not as most people think it is. We both concentrated, and the torcs around our throats extended long filaments of strange matter, that shot up the sides of our faces to form really quite stylish golden sunglasses over our eyes. And through these special lenses we Saw the Magnificat as it really was—in every awful detail.

Major security defences surrounded the hotel on every side, roiling and spitting on the air in tight little bundles of spite and malevolence. Force fields, magic screens, avoidance spells and *Move along nothing to see here* influences. Floating curses, proximity mindwipes, soul scramblers, and bottle demons lying buried under the hotel patio like so many red-eyed trap-door spiders. Screaming ghosts with terrible teeth and claws, just waiting to be unleashed, and a whole bunch of really nasty transformation spells just waiting to be activated. All kinds of nastiness, spreading out from the hotel in overlapping layers of appalling vileness. And up on the roof of the hotel . . .

"Oh bloody hell," I said. "Luther, do you See what I See, up on the roof? Is that what I think it is? It is, isn't it? They've only got a bloody dragon up there!"

"And not just any old dragon," said Luther, craning his head right back. "Not one of those stupid and extremely ugly beasts the elves ride around on. That . . . is one of the Great Old Beasts of England. That is the Lampton Wyrm."

"You have got to be kidding," I said. "Really? Who'd be crazy enough to dig that old horror up, and let it loose in the world? Is it tied down? Tell me it's tied down! Tell you what, I'll start running and you try and keep up."

"Look at the rear left leg," said Luther, entirely unperturbed. "See the nice glowing chain? That's an elf binding. It'll hold, for the duration of the auction. After that, well, they must have some plan in mind."

"It's times like these when I wish I'd paid more attention in class," I said. "I know we covered Old Beasts, but I'm pretty sure there was a girls' volleyball match going on outside the window that afternoon . . . The Lampton Wyrm was the one where if you cut it up, the pieces just joined back together again, right? How did they kill it, in the end?"

"They drowned it. Dug a great pit, filled it full of water, dragged the Wyrm into the pit and held it under till it drowned. Of course it didn't stay dead, but they covered the pit over with a really heavy-duty seal, and locked it in place with really powerful magics. So the Wyrm just kept on waking up and drowning again, over and over, for centuries. Not that I feel in any way sorry for it; the Lampton Wyrm killed thousands of people before it was stopped."

"I think we can safely say it isn't in a very good mood, now it's out," I said. "I'm almost sure it's looking right at us and I do wish it wouldn't. How in hell are we supposed to deal with something like that?"

"Well, here's my plan," said Luther. "It's up on the roof, so let's not go up there. Let us not, in fact, go anywhere near the bloody thing."

"Good plan," I said. "I really like that plan. I want to marry that plan and have its babies."

"You're weird," said Luther.

We looked some more at the Magnificat Hotel. The strange matter sunglasses allowed us to See all four sides at once, in as much detail as we needed. And more and more defences kept popping up, revealing themselves openly, as though defying us to do anything about them.

"There are dimensional gates attached to all the outer doors," I said. "Preprogrammed to send you Somewhere Else if you open a door without the right passWord."

"Standard operating procedure, when you're running an auction half the unnatural world would love to gatecrash," murmured Luther. "Crank your Sight up to full, and take a look inside the hotel."

I concentrated, and the golden shades sent my Sight into overdrive. The outer façade of the Magnificat seemed to leap forward, filling my vision, and then I plunged through and in, looking around the deserted lobby. It was all very fine and luxurious, with no staff anywhere, and no security guards in sight. Presumably the auction people had a lot of faith in their outer defences. I would have. But there were no obvious guardians or booby traps, so I sent my Sight shooting up through the hotel, floor by floor. I spotted the odd group of security guards here and there, oblivious to my mental presence, all of them heavily armed but fairly relaxed. They weren't expecting any real trouble until the auction was up and running. But the sheer number of guards increased steadily as my Sight ascended, until finally I reached the top floor, and the site of the auction.

The function rooms had all been opened up and combined into one great display area. There were people everywhere, moving back and forth, transporting objects, and getting everything in order. The security guards just stood at their stations and watched them do it. Because the guards were alive, and the auction people weren't. They would probably have looked quite normal to the unaided eye, but Seen through my golden shades, they were quite definitely dead. Zombies. They hefted and carried, they set things in motion, they checked lights and items and cargo manifests, and not one of them had a soul. The did have quite colourful auras, which showed they were being remote-controlled by overseeing minds elsewhere. The Really Old Curiosity Shoppe people never appeared in public, even at their own auctions. All the staff, and even the auctioneer himself, would be dead men walking, remote-controlled from a safe distance through a series of cutouts, so none of the controllers could be identified or tracked down. And given that they were, when you got right down to it, just a bunch of thieves . . . it was basic common sense.

They only ever spoke through the mouths of the dead, so even their voices could never be identified.

"The security guards are all local boys," Luther's voice murmured in my ear. "Familiar faces, no one special. Guns and muscle, from off the rack. You can hire thousands just like these. Only here to place themselves between the more valuable items and any possibility of damage, even if the poor fools don't know it. Hmmm. That's odd. I can't seem to See any of the auction items clearly. Can you?"

"No," I said, after a moment. "Every time I concentrate on a specific item, it goes all blurry. Which means they're hidden behind stealth screens. Really powerful screens, if our Sight can't punch through. We can't even be sure the Apocalypse Door is in place yet."

"It's there somewhere," said Luther. "Or Doctor Delirium wouldn't have committed himself to a personal appearance . . . Wait a minute. Hold everything. Something's happening on the floor below."

I pulled my Sight down a floor to match his, just in time to see Doctor Delirium and his troops appear through a dimensional door. It wasn't much of a door, just a by-the-numbers rip in space and time, forced open through brute force and energy, but it succeeded where a more sophisticated gateway might not have. The Magnificat's defences were targeted at a much better class of intruder. This attack was so basic it sneaked in under the radar. The Doctor hurried through, followed by twenty or thirty heavily armed and armoured men from his own special fighting force. You could always recognise members of Doctor Delirium's private army, because he made them all wear his own special black and gold uniforms. They looked like escapees from a production of *The Pirates of Penzance*, if the costume lady had been on crack that week. Still, they established a perimeter and took up positions like they knew what they were doing, and they held their guns like they knew how to use them. A mercenary is still a mercenary, even if he is dressed like a dick.

The floor's security guards were no problem. A nerve gas grenade had preceded Doctor Delirium through the dimensional door, and the guards went down almost immediately, without managing a single warning shot. Presumably the Doctor had protected his people against the gas in advance. The man was a genius with chemicals, when he could be bothered.

"This is why the Doctor wasn't worried about being outbid on the Apocalypse Door," said Luther. "The sneaky bastard's come early, to grab it for himself. Why is he so keen on this item, Eddie? Getting the Really Old Curiosity Shoppe people mad at you is never a good idea, if you like having your organs on the inside. They have a bad temper, a long reach, and they bear grudges for generations. What is this Apocalypse Door, that Doctor Delirium's ready to risk everything to get his hands on it?"

"The clue's probably in the question," I said. "I'm guessing the Door is a lot more Apocalyptic than we've given it credit for. And the Doctor wants it because . . . he's not getting any younger. All his great plans have come to nothing, mostly thanks to us, and his name has become a joke. He's a delusional scientific mastermind, but he gets no respect. He's fed up being laughed at, he's mad as hell and he's not going to take it anymore."

"Midlife crisis, in other words," said Luther.

"Exactly. He has a scheme to rule the world, and all he needs to make it work is the Apocalypse Door."

"A real scheme?" said Luther. "One that would actually work?"

"Yeah," I said. "And if my arse had teeth it could play

the banjo. A real plan? Come on, this is Doctor Delirium we're talking about."

"Even an idiot can get lucky, if he has a powerful
enough weapon," said Luther.

"There is that," I said. "Hello, there he goes, up the
back stairs to the top floor, and the auction site. At least
he's got enough sense to let his troops lead the way . . ."

The black-and-gold-clad mercenaries moved silently
up the back stairs, moving with calm and sinister grace.
They'd clearly rehearsed this. One man went ahead
holding up a Hand of Glory, its dark magics defusing
the few security spells in the stairway. Another soldier
shut down the electronic surveillance systems with a
small localised EMP. The Doctor gave every indication
of actually having thought things through. Either that,
or he'd hired someone who knew what he was doing. I
knew which way I'd bet. The Doctor's troops reached
the top of the stairwell, and the man in the lead started
packing plastique against the closed door. Doctor Delirium really wanted his Door. And didn't care who got
hurt in the process.

I sighed heavily, and told my torc to pull back its extension. The golden sunglasses ran quickly down my
cheek, and back into the torc. The world seemed very
grey, and very empty, without the Sight. I looked at
Luther.

"We're going to have to get personally involved," I
said. "A hands-on practical intervention, with no holds
barred. If the Apocalypse Door really is as powerful as
the Doctor clearly believes it to be . . . he can't be allowed to have it."

"Unfortunately, I have to agree," said Luther. "It's
time to armour up and smite the ungodly with vim and
vigour. But Eddie, please, let's try and keep the collat-

eral damage down to a minimum. I have to live in this town."

"You suit yourself," I said. "Personally, I plan to beat the shit out of anyone that doesn't run away fast enough, throw the Doctor and his troops back through their own dimensional door, grab the Apocalypse Door and then leg it for the nearest horizon."

"A workable plan," said Luther. "And at least this way, we don't have to face the bloody dragon."

I subvocalised my activating Words, and my golden armour leapt out of my torc, insulating me from the world in a moment. I flexed my arms and breathed deeply, feeling strong and sure and more than ready to kick the arse of Evil and make it cry like a baby. Luther armoured up beside me, his golden form blazing brightly in the LA sun. For a moment he looked like the Oscar statue come to dangerous and vicious life, and then the armour shifted and stirred about his body, the strange matter flowing into new shapes and forms as he concentrated. The torc provides a basic suit of armour, like a second skin, and for centuries that was good enough for the Droods; but then a soldier from the distant future showed us how to reshape and personalise our armour, the better to strike terror into our enemies and suit our individual needs and capabilities. It takes a lot of concentration to make a new shape, and hold it, but we're learning by doing.

Given the shape of Luther's armour, it was clear he'd spent entirely too much time watching old *Transformers* cartoons. His armour was large and bulky, padded out with gun emplacements that might or might not actually do anything. I was ready to bet good money that his armour would revert to standard the moment the mayhem started, and he needed all his concentration for the fight. I still kept to the basic shape, just jazzing it up a little here and there. I favour the old knightly style, with hints of greaves and a breastplate. I still kept the featureless golden face mask. Nothing like a blank eyeless face to freak out the bad guys.

"So," said Luther. "A traditionalist. This is the city of the future, Eddie. Only the very best will do here. Try and keep up."

"Funny," I said. "I was about to say the same to you."

"*Oh shit,*" said Luther, abruptly.

Once again, he was staring up at the top of the hotel. I craned back my head and followed his gaze. Another dimensional doorway had opened up, hovering in the sky above the roof of the Magnificat. And this time, it was very much the real deal. A state-of-the-art, all-the-bells-and-whistles gateway; a perfect circle some hundred feet in diameter, with edges so sharply defined you could almost hear the air splitting as it hit them. I caught just a glimpse of a whole different sky through the circle, before it dropped down over the chained dragon. The Lampton Wyrm looked up, startled, its hideous gargoyle head rising up and up on its long neck, and the circle just sucked the dragon up off the roof and into itself. The circle then collapsed and disappeared, taking the dragon with it. All that remained on the roof was a short length of glowing chain.

"Happy as I am to see the dragon gone," I said, "I find myself seriously disturbed. That . . . had to take a hell of a lot of power. Which means . . . someone else has come early to the auction."

"Why does everything have to be so complicated?" said Luther, wistfully.

The dimensional gateway returned, just as large and twice as impressive, and a whole army of armed and armoured men fell out of it onto the hotel roof. They were all dressed in basic leathers and body armour, with no identifying patches or tags. They moved quickly to rehearsed positions on the roof, while a core group set up explosive charges.

"So, the Doctor goes in through the backdoor, and this bunch goes in through the roof," said Luther. "Should be interesting . . . Any idea who these new boys are, Eddie?"

"Not a clue. No one should have been able to organise an operation this extensive without our knowing something in advance. I shall have some serious words with the family pre-cogs when I get back."

"The new boys aren't local," said Luther. "Do we assume they are also here for the Apocalypse Door?"

"Would seem likely," I said. "Though I really hate the idea that there are two sets of people who know more about it than we do."

The new arrivals blew a hole right through the roof with a shaped charge, dropped a bunch of ropes through, and rappelled down into the top floor. And at pretty much the same time, Doctor Delirium's plastique charge blew the stairwell door clean off its hinges, and they all charged through into the auction site. Both sides took one look at the other, and opened up with all guns blazing. Bullets filled the air, mowing down the auction's security guards in a moment. The remote-control zombies were punched this way and that by the impact of the bullets, staggering back and forth, with dust and bone fragments erupting from their bullet-riddled bodies. One by one they went down as their legs were blasted out from under them, and they lay thrashing or crawling on the floor, ignored by both sides.

The two sets of soldiers dug in at opposite ends of

the auction room, using overturned furniture and the shielded auction items for shelter. The firefight was doing a lot of structural damage, but there weren't many bodies yet. Both sides were clearly professionals. The shooting gradually died down to occasional suppressional fire, as both sides considered what to do next. A remote control zombie rose up on one elbow, and denounced both sides with its dead voice. There was a single shot, and its head exploded.

"So much for our original plan," said Luther. "What do we do now?"

"We go in," I said. "We bestow beatings on one and all, take the guns away from both sides, and shut this nonsense down before it starts attracting attention. Then I will grab the Apocalypse Door and it's head for the horizon time."

"Shouldn't we take some prisoners, ask some questions?" said Luther.

"If you must," I said.

"I feel I should remind you, there are two private armies in there, going head to head with extensive firepower, explosives and nerve gas grenades," said Luther. "You really want to just charge right in?"

"Two armies; one for each of us."

Luther shook his head slowly. "There is such a thing as overconfidence, even for a Drood."

"First problem," I said. "Our armour should get us through the hotel's outer defences okay, but we are going to set off all kinds of alarms . . . The last thing we need is for the two sides to discover who's coming, and team up against us."

"Worry not," said Luther. "I've got a basic can opener and alarm-suppressor that the Armourer sent through, just the other day. For testing. He thought I might find a use for it, given that LA has so many secrets to hide, and so many different ways of hiding them. It should open up the force shields and the magic screens, while shutting down the alarms. Notice my emphasis on the word *should.*"

"The Armourer has always believed in the triumph of optimism over experience," I said solemnly. "It's not that his wonderful gadgets don't work; it's just that they will insist on working in unexpected ways. But you can't complain, or he sulks. All right; let's do it."

"Lock and load," said Luther. "And God help the guilty."

"Native," I said sadly. "Definitely native."

We moved forward, two golden statues striding across the plaza towards the Magnificat Hotel. No one noticed a thing; we were both in full stealth mode, our torcs transmitting telepathic *You can't see me!* commands to all the passersby. Luther pulled something that still looked half finished from inside his armour and pointed it at the hotel. Looking through my golden mask I could clearly See the hotel shields split and break and vanish, dismissed almost casually by the Armourer's new toy. Luther and I kept going, the last remnants of the more stubborn shields clinging and dragging at our armour as we strode through them. They broke and fell away like cobwebs, thrown off by the sheer power inherent in the armour. Shaped curses and proximity mines detonated harmlessly, and howling ghosts burst like soap bubbles as we marched right through them. Spirit bottles shattered under the patio, releasing their demons, and they reared up to grasp at our golden legs. We just kept going, dragging them along with us, and they soon broke up and fell apart, too fragile to last long outside their bottles. Defence magics shattered and spattered against our golden chests in rainbow bursts of dispersing energies.

I kicked in the front door, shattered glass falling like hail on my shoulders, and led the way into the lobby. Two armed guards opened up on us with automatic weaponry. The bullets stitched across the front of our armour, which absorbed all the impact and then swallowed up the bullets. We worry about ricochets, these days. This rather upset the guards, who turned to run. I picked up the nearest table and threw it at them, and it slammed the two guards against the far wall like a flyswatter. Luther looked at me.

"Now that's not fair. I never got to do anything."

"You can have the next two. Where are the elevators?"

"At the back. But they're all locked off, till the Grand Opening ceremony tomorrow. And you need a special key, to get you to the top floor. Watch and learn."

He moved over to the main desk, located the main computer, and instead of powering it up and using the keyboard, he just stuck one golden fingertip against the monitor screen. Golden filaments spread out from the fingertip, spiderwebbing the screen.

"I'm accessing the hotel's security protocols through its own operating systems," said Luther, quite casually. "I've unlocked the elevators . . . shut down the alarm systems . . . and turned off all the CCTV cameras. We don't want any record of our being here. The armour should render us electronically invisible, but this is LA—who knows what upgrades they've put in? Why take a chance you don't have to, especially when we don't know what the auction people have installed on the top floor?"

"You can operate a computer with your armour?" I

said, genuinely impressed. "I didn't know it could do that."

"Have you ever tried? Just send a filament of strange matter into the computer, and let the armour do the rest. It is just an extension of our will, after all. It does what you tell it to do. I've used it as a contraceptive before now . . ."

I held up a hand. "Far too much information. Let's go."

Luther pulled his golden finger out, and we headed for the elevator doors at the rear of the lobby. They opened automatically as we approached, and once inside I jammed a golden finger into the lift controls, and concentrated on the top floor. The whole elevator shuddered, the doors slammed shut, and the elevator headed for the top floor like something was chasing it. When we got there the elevator's doors flew open, as though it couldn't wait to be rid of us. We stepped out, the doors slammed shut, and it headed for the ground floor again, at speed. I think I upset it. I stepped forward, Luther right beside me, and everyone in the world opened fire on us.

It was an attack of quite staggering proportions. Bullets came flying at us from every direction, a storm so heavy and concentrated you could almost see it. Gunfire chewed up the walls on either side of us, and pockmarked the closed elevator doors from top to bottom. The roar was deafening, and smoke curled thickly on the air. Luther and I stood our ground as gunfire raked across our armour without doing the slightest damage. We didn't even rock on our feet from the impact, and the armour just swallowed up the bullets. Behind my golden mask, I was grinning. There's something really quite psychologically devastating about a foe who just stands there and allows himself to be shot, so Luther and I struck arrogant poses and made the most of it.

They tried explosives and nerve gas grenades, and neither of them affected us in the least. You'd think they would've known better; I mean, they had to know we were Droods. This kind of low-level assault was almost an insult. The only way to win a fight with a Drood is to not be there when we turn up.

The gunfire died away in spurts and coughs, and a slow, awful silence settled across the top floor. Armed and armoured guards peered at us with big eyes from behind various places of cover. There was a lot of looking at each other, and general shrugging. I could just make out the podgy figure of Doctor Delirium, peering out from behind the protective shield of some auction item. The shield glowed dully, like a silver smear on the air, hiding the nature of the item. It might have been the Apocalypse Door. It was big enough.

I moved forward, and again they opened up with every gun they had. I just walked right into the hail of bullets, not slowed or bothered in the least. Luther was right there with me. I had to say; I'd thought most of the soldiers would have had an attack of common sense and started running by now. That's the normal reaction to Droods in their armour. I looked at Luther, nodded quickly, and we both surged forward, into the gunfire. In a moment we were in and among the armed men and throwing them this way and that. They flew screaming through the air, tossed half the length of the room. Luther took the mystery group, and I dealt with Doctor Delirium's mercenaries. I was moving so quickly now I must have been just a golden blur to them, as I struck them down with my golden fists, for having the sheer nerve to try and kill me.

It took me longer than I thought to clear the floor, due to the sheer press of bodies. I had to force my way through a crowd of armed soldiers, knocking them down and throwing them aside. Some clung to my arms and neck, trying to drag me down through sheer weight of numbers. It took time to shrug and peel them all off, or slam them against the nearest wall. I wasn't trying to kill anyone, but they were, after all, killers for pay, hired thugs with uniforms. But eventually I ran out of people to hit, and looked around for Doctor Delirium. He was standing beside his auction item, crowing triumphantly. Somehow, he'd broken through the protective shield.

It looked like just an ordinary door: a tall wooden oblong with no handles, or knocker. Ancient and unfamiliar runes had been carved around its edges. It stood upright on its own, entirely unsupported. And there was something about it . . . Like the feeling you get when you stare into an abyss, and know that death is only one small step away. It was the Apocalypse Door, and just the sight of it chilled the blood in my heart. There was something *beyond* that Door, and it wanted out, in the worst way. Doctor Delirium ran his podgy hands over it, crooning in delight.

His crude dimensional door opened and swallowed up both him and the Apocalypse Door in a moment. Those of his men left behind, and still conscious, made a run for it. I had no time for them. I was trying to come to terms with the knowledge that for the first time in his life, Doctor Delirium was now a Major Player. And almost certainly in over his head.

The mystery group's soldiers hadn't given up, even with their prize gone. They were still firing everything they had. Luther raged among them, slapping guns out of hands, and striking the soldiers down with rough efficiency. I didn't have the patience for that, so I just picked up the nearest pieces of furniture and threw them at the thugs like missiles. Tables and chairs flew through the air, and struck down whole groups of men like the wrath of God.

A few kept moving, dodging from one piece of cover to another, sniping at me with more exotic weapons. They had science things and magic things, and even a few unfamiliar objects that might have been both or neither. They kept trying one thing after another, looking for anything that might pierce my armour. The fools. One of them actually produced a collapsible bazooka. He loaded up a silver shell wrapped in mistletoe, and fired it at me. I felt like showing off, so I just stood my ground and caught the shell in my arms. Didn't even knock me backwards. I hugged the shell to my chest, and my armour absorbed the whole of the blast as it exploded. When the smoke cleared, I was still standing there, completely untouched. The soldier looked like he was going to burst into tears. He threw the bazooka down, and stamped on it.

Another soldier stepped up, and stabbed an Aboriginal pointing bone at me. Now those are pretty serious magic; a shaman who knows what he's doing can kill you with a bad thought, throw your soul into the Dreaming, even rewrite reality itself on a small scale. Fortunately, most of that kind of magic has been lost, or forgotten. And this guy really hadn't done his homework. The bone's spell hit my armour, rebounded, and blasted the guy right out of existence.

Another armed thug, with more courage than sense, stepped forward and showed me the glowing metal glove on his hand. It looked a lot like the old Roman cestus, nasty things used in the Arenas by gladiators who liked to get in close and personal with their victims. This particular glove had been soaked in really nasty magics; it left long blazing trails on the air when it moved, as though just its existence stained reality. The poor fool using the glove clearly didn't know that just wearing the thing was more than enough to kill him.

Luther finished mopping up and stepped forward to face the boxer. The soldier struck a classic pose, and then lunged forward and punched Luther right in the throat. The glowing glove actually shrieked in rage and triumph as it slammed through the air, and then the awful sound was cut off abruptly as the glove hit Luther's golden throat . . . and was immediately swallowed up by the armour. It sucked the glowing glove right off the man's hand, absorbed it and made it nothing, nothing at all.

The soldier fainted dead away at Luther's feet. Though that was probably mostly due to the toxic radiations the glove had been giving off. I considered Luther thoughtfully.

"You're just full of surprises, aren't you?"

"Oh yes. Really. You have no idea."

We looked around us, taking our time. The long room was littered with unconscious bodies, and a dozen or so surrendered men, on their knees with their hands on their heads, looking very much like they wished they were somewhere else. There were a few dead men, which was a shame, but they should have known better than to attack Droods. I started rehearsing the questions I was going to ask, starting with *What do you know about the Apocalypse Door?* And that was when a dimensional gateway appeared above our heads, sucked up all the soldiers in a moment, the living and the dead, and then slammed shut again. I looked at Luther.

"You know, that is getting really bloody annoying."

"Couldn't agree more if you bribed me."

The dimensional gateway opened up again, and the Lampton Wyrm dropped out of it. The dragon was back from wherever the gate had taken it, and it clearly hadn't enjoyed the trip. It filled more than half the floor, fifty feet long from snout to tail, its great membranous wings unfurling angrily. Its ugly head rose up on its long neck and slammed against the ceiling. Streams of broken plaster and ceiling tiles rained down around it. The dragon's spiked tail lashed back and forth, destroying everything it touched, and sending shielded auction items flying through the air. Clawed feet dug deep furrows in the carpeted floor. The Wyrm snatched up one of the more intact remote control zombies from the floor, chewed on it for a moment, and then spat the bits out. The dragon roared angrily, and the ghastly sound shook the whole floor.

It smelled really bad—of blood and carrion, brine and seaweed, and an atavistic stench of ancient lizard.

I really would have liked to turn and run, but that option wasn't open to me. If the Lampton Wyrm broke free of the Magnificat and went on a rampage in Los Angeles, they'd be cleaning up the dead bodies for weeks. The Wyrm was one of the Great Old Beasts, a living god or devil, and though it was much reduced by time and age, there was still nothing in human science that could stop it. You could drop a nuke on it, and the Wyrm would just laugh at you from the depths of the atomic fires, as the mushroom cloud formed overhead.

"We've got to contain it," I said to Luther.

"Ten out of ten for ambition, Eddie, but this is the Lampton Wyrm we're talking about!" said Luther.

"You can't hurt it, you can't kill it, and I'm not even sure our armour can protect us!"

"Get ahold of yourself, Luther! You're a Drood! It's easy to be brave when you're facing something you know your armour can protect you against; it's times like this that we get to show what we're made of."

"By getting killed, dismembered and eaten? Not necessarily in that order?"

Luther gave every appearance of being severely shaken. He'd spent too long in a town where he was always going to be the baddest thing in it. I kept my voice clear and calm, whilst at the same time being very careful not to make any sudden movement that might attract the dragon's attention.

"It's been stopped before, remember? The Lampton family sealed it in a pit and drowned it. Does this place have a swimming pool?"

"Well, yes, but I don't see how we're going to drag the dragon down to it, hold it under and build a cover over it, without being reduced to small bloody gobbets in the process! We have to get out of here, and call for the cavalry!"

"We are the cavalry! Get a grip!"

"Sorry," said Luther, after a moment. "I've got a thing about dragons."

"Well," I said. "Who hasn't? Let's try the basics first. Hit it from two different sides, and tear it to pieces. If we can reduce it to small enough parts, and keep them from recombining . . ."

"There's that ambition again. But, for want of anything better . . ."

We hit the Lampton Wyrm from both sides at once, moving as fast as our armour could power us. I hit the dragon hard in its hideous head, my golden fist plunging deep through flesh and bone and into the brain beneath. I grabbed a handful of brains, yanked them out through the hole I'd made, and threw them on the floor. The massive head wound had already healed by the time I turned back. I grabbed great handfuls of dragon flesh, tearing them away by brute force, digging deep wounds in its sides, but they all healed in seconds.

Luther jumped on its back and punched viciously into the dragon's spine, to no better effect. And all the time the dragon was heaving and thrashing around, trying to reach us with its claws. The head swept back and forth on its long neck, snapping viciously again and again, while I used all my armour's speed to dodge it.

I ducked in under one carelessly wide swing, grabbed one of the dull green arms, and ripped it right out of its socket. The dragon screamed so loudly it hurt my ears, even inside the armour. The arm convulsed in my grip, still trying to get at me with its claws, and then suddenly it withered, and collapsed into dust. The dragon had grown itself a new arm. It lashed out at me. The claws skittered across my golden chest, raising a great shower of sparks. The claws couldn't penetrate the armour, but the sheer impact blasted me off my feet, sending me flying halfway across the room.

I hit hard, and stayed on my hands and knees for a moment, getting my breath back. Luther was still riding the dragon's back, hanging on grimly as it bucked and twisted. And then the Wyrm rolled suddenly over onto its side, pinning Luther to the floor with its great weight. With no leverage, he couldn't use his armour's strength to escape. I forced myself up onto my feet, charged forward and punched the dragon in the head again. My fist plunged into and through its right eye, and the dragon screamed like a soul newly damned to Hell. But when I pulled my fist out again, dripping with gore and pus and eyeball fluid, a new eye filled the bloody socket immediately. The Lampton Wyrm: the Beast that couldn't die.

Its jaws surged forward and closed over my left arm. The dragon's teeth broke and shattered as they ground against my armour, but they continually reformed, trying to gnaw their way through. The dragon swept its great head back and forth, shaking me like a dog shakes a rat. I grew golden spikes on my other hand, and pounded the dragon's head again and again, but it wouldn't release me. Luther had seized the opportunity to pull himself out from under, and he attacked its ribs, smashing them over and over again. The dragon's jaws gaped wide with pain, and I staggered backwards.

And then the dragon's jaws opened really wide, and it surged forward and swallowed me whole.

For a moment there was just darkness, and a sense of pressure from all sides. I couldn't even tell which way was up. I was battered from all sides, as a series of muscular contractions tried to force me down the dragon's throat and into its stomach. I concentrated and razor sharp blades shot out from every surface on my armour, digging deep into the throat muscles and holding me in place. The dragon screamed again, and it was even more painful hearing it from inside the throat. I lashed out with my bladed arms, opening up a long gaping wound in the side of the throat. Light flooded in, and two golden hands from outside quickly grabbed the sides of the wound and kept it from closing. Luther was on the job. I retracted my blades and forced myself out through the gap, and then Luther and I quickly retreated as the dragon thrashed back and forth, smashing everything in the room in its pain and fury.

Luther and I backed away some more. I was still thinking furiously. There had to be something, some way . . . The huge head swung round and fixed on me, studying me with its glowing eyes. It was really mad now. It wanted to take its time with us, make us suffer. And that . . . was when I got my idea. It was a really bad idea, based on a really old story, but . . . it felt right. I gestured to Luther.

"Get ready to back me up. I'm going back in."

"What?"

"I'm going back down its throat. I've got an idea."

"I don't think hoping it will choke on you is enough."

"I've got something rather more . . . extreme in mind. Once it's swallowed me again, you grab its head. Hold the jaws closed, so it can't spit me out. Got it?"

"No. But I've reached the point where I'm willing to try anything, including prayers and bribery. Go for it."

The dragon's head snapped forward, moving horribly fast on the end of its extended neck. I stepped forward to meet it, the huge jaws opened wide, and I threw myself into its mouth. The jaws slammed shut, and it swallowed automatically. And this time I didn't fight it. I curled into a ball, to make the swallowing go easier, and the muscular contractions carried me swiftly down the long neck and into the belly. I uncurled, and once again grew viciously sharp blades all over my body. And step by step, I fought my way deeper into the beast. I couldn't see where I was, or where I was going, but my Sight gave me a direction to follow. I fought my way into its stomach and on into its guts, its bowels, and all the way to the base of the tail. And once I was there, I grabbed it and with one good heave, pulled the tail inside out, so that it was in there with me.

You wouldn't believe how strong my armour can be,

when I really put my mind to it. Luther was right; it's an extension of our will. It does what we tell it.

The dragon really didn't like what was happening inside it. I've never heard screaming like it. I took a firm hold on the inverted tail with both golden hands, turned around, and step by step I struggled back through the body of the beast, from the rear to the front. And with one last effort, I hauled the tail up and into the mouth, punched a hole through the teeth from the inside, and marched out of the gaping jaws, dragging the inverted tail with me.

And that was how I turned the Lampton Wyrm inside out. It probably helped that the dragon was, after all, a magical creature.

Luther and I stood together, breathless and exhausted, and looked at the steaming, twisting mass before us. It smelled really disgusting.

"And I thought it looked ugly from the outside," said Luther. "Heal that, you bastard."

"Let's contact the family, and get some experts sent in," I said. "I think we've done all that can reasonably be expected of us."

And that was when the dimensional gateway opened above us again, and a whole army of heavily armed troops dropped out of it. They hit the floor easily, wrapped in glowing body armour and carrying a whole bunch of really nasty-looking weapons. They saw the inside out dragon, and paused for a moment.

"Oh bloody hell," I said.

The gateway snapped shut and disappeared. The armoured troop surged forward. And I . . . lost my temper. I'm usually a calm and reasonable sort of guy, but there are limits. I used my Sight to find a suitably weak fracture point in the floor, and hit it hard with my golden fist, with all my strength. The whole floor broke in half, and with a great grinding roar it collapsed, and we all fell through and down into the next floor, accompanied by several tons of assorted rubble.

Luther and I rose to our feet. No one else did. Mostly they just lay there, around and under the rubble, making low moaning noises and hoping that the ambulance wouldn't take too long to get there. It was their own fault. Never annoy a Drood.

"You might have warned me you were going to do that," said Luther.

"Oh hush, you big baby," I said. "I was almost completely sure we'd live through it."

I made my way through the mess, searching for a soldier who was still conscious. I wanted answers. I finally found one, pinned under a block of stone. He didn't look in particularly good shape. He raised a gun as I leaned over him, and I slapped it out of his hand.

"You know who and what I am, so answer my questions. Who are you, and who are you working for?"

He smiled briefly, revealing blood-smeared teeth. His face was white from pain and shock, and beaded with perspiration. He glared into my featureless golden mask.

"We're everything that ever scared you. We're the wolf in the fold, and the serpent at your bosom. We're the Anti-Droods. And we'll be at your throat till the end of time."

He bit down hard, and I heard a poison tooth crunch. He convulsed, his eyes starting from his head; and then he was dead.

"Fanatics," Luther said disgustedly. "I hate fanatics. What was all that Anti-Drood stuff?"

"Beats the crap out of me," I said.

And that was when one of the other fanatics activated a suicide bomb. I didn't see him do it, but there was a hell of an explosion, the floor opened up beneath me, and suddenly everything was falling again. It must have been a really nasty bomb, because it cracked the hotel open from top to bottom. I fell all the way down, crashing through floor after floor, thrashing helplessly, until finally I slammed to a halt back in the lobby, right back where I started. It took me some time to dig my way out of the tons of rubble, but eventually I emerged from the mess of what had once been a very large and expensive hotel. After a while, Luther emerged to join me.

"You know," he said. "We really don't appreciate our armour enough."

"Can you hear sirens?" I said. "I'm pretty sure I can hear sirens. And there are crowds gathering. I think we need to get the hell out of Dodge."

"Yeah," said Luther. "Let someone else sort this mess out."

"I think we've done all we can," I said.

"The Matriarch really isn't going to pleased with us, is she?" said Luther.

"Is she ever?" I said.

CHAPTER TWO

You Can Go Home Again, But Trust Me, You'll Regret It.

When it all goes wrong, when the mission's a failure, the bad guy gets away with the prize and you've just demolished a perfectly good brand-new hotel ... it's time to call it a day and go home. Secret agents can't really hang around to say sorry, and help fill in the insurance paperwork. So I headed for the airport and left Luther to talk with his people, make what excuses he could, cover up the rest, and generally stonewall any inquiry as to what actually happened. Let him make use of those important connections he was so proud of.

Cleaning up the mess afterwards is always the hardest part of any mission; so mostly I don't bother. Get in, get out, and then disappear while everyone else is still standing around waiting for the smoke to clear. I did offer a few possible excuses to Luther ... Gas explosion, that's always a good one. Or maybe a terrorist bomb, by the Aesthetic Liberation Army. On the unanswerable grounds that the Magnificat was just too offensively ugly to be allowed. Visual pollution, and a crime against the senses. I was just getting warmed up, when the taxi Luther had called for me arrived, and he picked me up and threw me bodily into the back of it.

I can take a hint.

When I got to the airport, I discovered my family was so eager to have me home again that they'd sent one of the family planes to pick me up. We use Blackhawke jets, lovely sleek black beasts, based around systems reverse engineered from an alien starship that crashlanded in a Wiltshire field in 1947. They can fly faster than any commercial jet, they're shielded from all forms of detection even when they're right on top of you and they can go sideways or even backwards, as required. And no, we haven't shared the technology with anyone else. Droods aren't big on sharing.

All our planes carry a big stylised Letter D. If anyone at an airport gets curious, we just tell them it stands for Dracula, and they go and find something else to get interested in.

I was the only passenger on the plane. Rows of empty seats stretched away before me, so I just chose one at random and settled down with a nice glass of pink champagne and the in-flight magazine. Even in a certain amount of disgrace, a Drood is still a Drood, and entitled to all the perks and courtesies. No stewardess, though. Droods don't believe in personal servants; they make you weak. The only human contact I had was the pilot's voice over the intercom. Iain Drood was almost unbearably cheerful as he grilled me for all the nasty details on my latest embarrassment. I could have lived without the word *latest*.

"An entire hotel!" Iain said gleefully. "Got to be a personal best, even for you, Eddie. You're not the most subtle of secret agents, are you? Or even the most secret . . . We can always tell where you've been, because suddenly most of it isn't there anymore . . . So, how was Hollywood? Did you meet any stars? Did you get any autographs?"

"I was in Anaheim," I said, at least partly in self-defence to stop him talking for a while. "That's right on the other side of Los Angeles. I didn't even get a sniff of anything glamorous. Now, if you don't mind, I have some serious brooding to be getting on with."

"Oh sure, don't mind me! Keep your seat belt on, help yourself to the complimentary peanuts, and if we hit any turbulence try and get some of it in the bag provided."

He finally shut up so he could concentrate on his takeoff, and I leafed listlessly through the in-flight magazine, the *Drood Times*. We have our own monthly magazine, never distributed outside the family. In fact, all copies self-destruct if anyone without Drood DNA even touches the cover. The current issue's headline was THE MATRIARCH'S BACK! AND THIS TIME IT'S PERSONAL! READ OUR BIG NEW INTERVIEW FOR ALL HER PLANS FOR A NEW AND IMPROVED FAMILY, EXTENSIONS TO DROOD HALL, AND HOW TO KEEP EXPLOSIONS IN THE ARMOURY TO AN ABSOLUTE MINIMUM. The *Drood Times* is rather like one of those long chatty letters people include with their Christmas cards, filling you in on all the latest news and gossip concerning people you really don't know or care about.

The magazine is bright and cheerful and almost unbearably glossy, contains no adverts, and yet still seems to go on *forever*. The Droods are a really big family, and the sheer amount of news, gossip, cheerful chatter and character assassination results in a monthly issue big enough to stun an attacking bear. I do flick through it, on occasion. We all do. If only to see if we're in it. There's nothing like living together in one big Hall to get on everyone's nerves; and if nothing else, the extremely lengthy letter columns do allow us to let off steam safely. I tend not to appear in the magazine much; except as a Bad Example.

Even when I was running the family.

I put the magazine to one side, and stared glumly out the window. We were already out and over the sea. I tried out a few excuses for size, but none of them seemed especially convincing, so in the end I just gave up and settled for my usual explanation: *Look, shit happens, okay?*

The pilot had been instructed to fly me straight home to Drood Hall, so I could make my report . . . but I overruled him. I wasn't ready to talk to anyone, just yet. So I broke into the cockpit, and told him he could either land at Heathrow in London or I could punch him twenty or thirty times in the head. Given my reputation, he believed me, which was just as well, because I meant it. And I think he was just a little thrilled to have an excuse to disregard the Matriarch's orders for once, even if only by proxy.

We have our own private landing area at Heathrow, as at all major airports across the world. We have agreements in place with all major governments, organisations and significant individuals the world over. They let us do what we want, and we promise to leave them alone. No one ever says anything, but if questions do get asked, they're usually slammed down with the magic words *National Security*. On the unanswerable grounds that it's Droods who keep nations secure. It helps that our Blackhawke jets can't be filmed or photographed. One really fanatical plane-spotter did get uncomfortably close a few years back, so we just put him in charge of airport security. Turning poachers into gamekeepers is an old trick.

I told Iain that he could give my excuses to the Matriarch, or not, as he wished, but that I'd report in at the Hall when I was good and ready, and not before. He said he thought he'd take the long way home, round both poles, so he wouldn't have to touch down at the Hall until after I'd decided to show up. Potentially bright lad, I thought.

I took a taxi back to my new flat in Kensington. The traditional black London taxicab made a nice change from its LA equivalent. A little ganja-smoking voodoo fetishist goes a long way. The driver here did try to be chatty, but I wore him down with a series of low growls. In revenge he turned his music on high, and it was *The Carpenters Greatest Hits* all across London, the bastard. I slumped in the back of the cab, tired in body and spirit. I really needed some downtime, before I had to face my family again. The mission had gone quite spectacularly wrong. I should have reported in right away. But . . . it was only Doctor Delirium. How important could it be?

I looked out the taxi window, and the familiar London streets rolled past. Places I knew, locations I remembered, all of them looking safe and secure. And all the ordinary people, going about their ordinary business, with no idea of who and what they shared their world with. I could have raised my Sight, and looked on the world as it really was, but I didn't. Sometimes I just liked to pretend that this was it, that this was all there was. At least I have the privilege of choice. These people, with their everyday jobs and ordinary lives, keeping the machinery of the world turning, were my responsibility. My job, to stand between them and the dangers they didn't even know existed. As Droods, we're encouraged to see the world's populations as our children, who must be protected. And if we do our job right, they'll never have to know their nightmares are real.

Until the day they finally grow up enough that we can trust them with our knowledge. And then we'll all get together and kick the Bad Things right off our world. On that far future day, we'll all be Droods.

When I gave up the leadership of the family, and went back to being just a field agent again, I left the Hall and returned to London. But I didn't feel like going back to my old place in Knightsbridge. Too many bad memories, from the time when I'd been falsely declared rogue, and the whole family turned on me. They'd trashed my flat, looking for secrets or stolen goods or any evidence they could use against me, but really just as an excuse to take their anger out on me. Someone spray painted the word *Traitor!* all across one wall. So I didn't go back.

My nice new flat in Kensington was big, open and very comfortable. The family coughed up for all the best fittings and furnishings, as a way of saying sorry. My new place is not easy to get to, at the end of a cul-de-sac, and I have seen to it that it is very well defended. Against everyone and everything; very definitely including members of my family. Though I hadn't actually got around to telling them that. I thought I'd just let it come as a nice surprise. Besides, they definitely wouldn't approve of some of the nasty, vile and downright unpleasant things I'd put in place to make my new home safe and secure. Right down to the smallest detail. It's not everyone who's got a banshee for an alarm bell.

I also have a preprogrammed poltergeist in residence; it clears things up while I'm out, does the dirty dishes, deals with the laundry and even disposes of the garbage for me. My girlfriend Molly Metcalf gave it to me as a moving-in present. She's very thoughtful about things like that. Though I did have to have words with her later, after I discovered she'd set the poltergeist to remove from my collection all the CDs that she didn't approve of.

How can anyone not like Abba?

Once home, I took a while to just walk around the flat, checking all the defences were in place, and none of the booby traps had been triggered. I sorted through the post and checked my e-mails, opened some windows to let the fresh air in, and retrieved the Merlin Glass from its hiding place. These days, I keep my very special hand mirror in a subspace pocket dimension, tied to my torc. Only I can reach in and retrieve the Glass; even if you could detect the subspace pocket, which you can't. I called to the Glass, and immediately it appeared in my right hand, looking innocently normal and ordinary. Just a standard old-fashioned hand mirror with a silver backing. But Merlin Satanspawn never made an ordinary or an innocent thing in his life. I said the proper activating Words, and the Glass shook itself back and forth, growing quickly in size, until finally it jumped out of my hand and made itself into a Door, right in front of me. Through this new opening I could see Molly's wildwoods, the hidden place she lived in when she couldn't be with me.

Through the Merlin Glass I could see rank upon rank of huge trees, falling away before me, heavy with foliage of so bright a green it practically glowed, interspersed with shady glens and tumbling waterfalls. Dust motes danced in long golden shafts of light. Fresh air gusted through the doorway, carrying with it rich scents of grass and greenery and living things. I stepped through the Glass into the forest, and the doorway closed behind me.

The wildwoods stretched off into the distance in every direction I looked. Massive trees with huge trunks, so tall you could crane your neck right back and still not see the tops of them. Bustling untamed vegetation, that had never known the touch of axe or saw, sprang up everywhere. These were old woods, ancient woods, from primordial times when we all lived in the forest, because the forest was all there was. The air was full of sound; of birds and beasts and insects. These were the woods of Olde Englande, when forests stretched unbroken from coast to coast, and bears and boars and wolves roamed freely, along with other rarer creatures that have long since dropped out of history and into legend. I have seen kelpies and bogles and fenendrees in this place; and they have seen me. Other shapes moved warily among the trees, maintaining a safe distance; large dark shapes that studied me with bright unblinking eyes from the deepest of the shadows. I can come to this place only because Molly loves me; the wild things of the woods are still a long way from trusting me. They were only ever comfortable around me when Molly was there too.

There was no sign of her now, which was odd. The Merlin Glass always sends a warning ahead of itself, just for her, so she knows I'm coming. Most of the time she's already there, waiting for me. But not now. I called out her name, and it was as though the whole forest was suddenly struck dumb. Every living sound shut off, even the breeze among the branches, as though the whole wood was still, and listening. I called again, my voice echoing on and on through the trees, but there was no reply. A cold chill ran down my neck. The woods didn't feel in any way welcoming, or inviting. And then a squirrel dropped down onto a branch right next to me, and I gave an entirely undignified jump of surprise. The squirrel sniggered loudly, its long russet tail snapping back and forth. It sat up on its haunches and studied me disdainfully.

"Hey, rube," it said. "Keep the noise down; some of us have important nuts to be gathering. Molly's not here. Why are you here? You're disturbing the wildlife with your presence, and that aftershave of yours is doing absolutely nothing for the local ambience. I mean, yes, we're all happy she's finally found a boyfriend she can bring back to meet the extended family, and all that, but did it have to be a human? She could have done so much better for herself. Still, she's not getting any younger. Her biological clock is getting pretty damned deafening. Have you got her pregnant yet? Well, why not? You humans are too damned complicated for your own good. I could have been born human if I wanted, but I passed the intelligence test. Little squirrel humour there. Have you met her sisters yet?"

"Not as such," I said, jamming a word in edgeways in self-defence. You might think a talking squirrel is cute, but trust me, they really get on your nerves after a while. "I've heard about Isabella, of course. Who hasn't? Supernatural terrorist, twilight avenger, and so hardcore in her convictions she could scare the wings off an angel. Practically every secret organisation in the world has her on its kill list, and vice versa."

"What about Louisa?" said the squirrel, knowingly. "She's the one you have to watch out for. She's really scary."

"Well," I said. "Something to look forward to."

The squirrel cocked its head on one side, and considered me thoughtfully with a dark beady eye. "You do know this isn't going to work?" it said, almost kindly. "You and Molly? Love doesn't conquer all, and happy endings are just something you humans made up, to help you get through the nights. Molly is at war with the Droods, and always will be."

"You see?" I said. "We have so much in common."

The squirrel shrugged. "None so blind as those who've shoved two fingers in their eyes. Look, Molly's gone off gallivanting with Isabella, and no I don't know where, or when she might be back. She didn't leave any messages, and she didn't talk to anyone before she left. Our Molly's been playing her cards very close to her chest, ever since she met you. You're a bad influence on her, which is strange, because it's usually the other way round. You can hang around here and wait, if you want, but frankly I wouldn't. You make the wildlife uneasy, and there'll probably be an incident."

I had to smile. "I'm a Drood, remember? Untouchable comes as standard."

"Like that means anything, in a place like this. Don't push your luck, Drood. You're only here on sufferance."

The squirrel leapt up into the higher branches, and was gone. I sat down on a nearby grassy bank in an ostentatiously casual manner, just to show I wasn't going to be pushed around. The air seemed to blow distinctly colder, and there were ominous noises and movements in the darker shadows between the trees. I studiously ignored it all, and did some hard thinking. Molly kept saying she was going to introduce me to her older sister, Isabella, but something always came up. I knew Isabella's legend. Everybody did. Molly was a wild free spirit, as dedicated to having fun as fighting all forces of authority. Isabella was more cold, focused, unyielding in her determination to search out all the dark secrets in the world, and then Do Something about them. Molly was cheerful, capricious, and at war with the world in general. Isabella wanted to know everything other people didn't want her to know, and was quite ready to do terrible things to anyone who got in her way.

They know Isabella in the Nightside, and in Shadows Fall. She'd worked both with and against the Droods, and gone head to head with the London Knights on more than one occasion. But then, they've always been a bit stuffy.

Louisa, the youngest of the Metcalf sisters, was a mystery. You heard lots of stories, but never anything definite. But the stories were always scary, and so was she. There were those who said she'd been dead seven years now, and it hadn't slowed her down one bit.

Molly's dark opinion of the Droods was no secret to me. She loathed and disapproved of my family, and all it stood for. She was a free spirit, and the Droods have always been about control. She'd only agreed to fight alongside us in the past because the alternatives were so much worse. She put up with them for my sake, but we both knew that wouldn't last. I might have problems with how my family did things, but I still believed we were necessary. We fought the good fight because someone has to. Molly and I would have to find some common ground we could agree on, or our beliefs and our consciences would drive us apart.

Would I place my love for Molly before my duties, my

responsibilities—my family? I hoped so. But you can never be sure about things like that. I could not love thee half so much, my dear, loved I not honour more . . .

I got up and activated the door again. The Merlin Glass hung before me on the air, my flat in Kensington clear and distinct beyond it. I sighed quietly, took up my burden again, and went home. Behind me, I could hear the woods slowly coming alive again, as the threat to their peace disappeared.

I shut down the Merlin Glass, thrust it back into its subspace pocket, and took a quick shower. Normally I like to soak and relax in a hot steaming bath; but needs must when the Devil pisses on your shoes. I pulled on some fresh clothes, started for my front door, and then hesitated. I slumped into my favourite chair, and looked at nothing in particular. The poltergeist sensed my mood, and thoughtfully faded the lights down. Brooding is always best accompanied by lengthening shadows.

More and more of late I'd been considering who I was, and who I'd turned out to be . . . as opposed to the kind of man I'd always wanted, or intended, to be. This wasn't how I thought I'd end up. How I expected my life to turn out. I'd never been happy running the family. I did it only because it was thrust upon me. The first chance I got to return to my old life as a field agent, I grabbed it with both hands and never looked back. But now . . . having once embraced responsibility for my family, I found it hard to let go.

I never wanted to be important, or significant. Never wanted to be responsible for anyone but myself. That was why I'd run away from the Hall to be a field agent in the first place. But now I worried about the Matriarch, and the family, because I wasn't there to keep an eye on them. It would be so easy for them to slip back into the bad old ways, one very reasonable step at a time. The terrible Heart with its awful bargain was gone, destroyed, but the Matriarch, dear Grandmother, was born with iron in her soul. If she decided that it was in the world's best interests that the Droods should rule the world again, could I stop her? Did I have the right to overrule a freely elected leader?

I needed my freedom and my privacy, and I loved my Molly, but how could I be my family's conscience at a distance?

And, could I really take the family away from the Matriarch a second time? I'd had surprise and all kinds of good luck on my side the first time. She'd have all kinds of new defences in place now, just for me. But if the Matriarch did try to return to the old ways, would Ethel allow it? I liked to think she was my friend, but who knows what an other-dimensional entity will do, or think, or decide?

I forced myself up and out of my chair, and headed for the front door. I can take only so much brooding and existential angst before I have to get up and do *something*. When in doubt, face your problems head on. And head butt them in the face. I called the Merlin Glass back to my hand, and had it open a particular door to Drood Hall. Bright light flared through the opening, and I stepped through. Onto the roof of Drood Hall.

I arrived a safe distance away from the various landing pads, surrounded by a wide sea of tiles, shingles, gables and antennae. We've always been ones for just adding things on, as necessary. And pulling them down again when they weren't. We're not sentimental. I was very high up, below a sky so solidly blue I felt like I could reach up and touch it. I should have made my arrival through the main door, as tradition demanded when summoned by the Matriarch, but I was in no mood to cross swords with the Sarjeant-at-Arms. He represented authority and discipline within and over the family, and I've always had problems with authority figures. Even when I was one.

Up on the Hall roof, all kinds of unusual flying objects were coming and going, heading in for textbook landings and not always making it. Half a dozen autogyros buzzed around like oversized insects, marvellous baroque creations of brass and copper, pumping black smoke and drifting cinders behind them. They'd first appeared in the 1920s, been superseded by the '40s, and then brought back again just recently by steampunk enthusiasts in the family. Beautifully intricate and scientifically suspect, the splendid art deco machines seemed to force their way through the air by sheer brute effort.

Then there were those really brave individuals who were still trying to make jetpacks work. They flew well enough, except for when they abruptly didn't. They didn't care for sudden changes in direction, and they didn't have much of a range. But there are always a few bright young things in the family with more optimism than sense, who never got over the urge to just strap on a jetpack and go rocketing up into the wild blue yonder. Just for the thrill of it. Even though the only thing jetpacks do really well is plummet.

The Armourer keeps promising to provide us with antigravity, but he's always got some excuse.

The usual cloud of hang gliders swept by overhead, circling majestically round the roof, taking their time and showing off, held up by magic feathers. And, of course, there were a few young women riding winged unicorns. (Because some girls just never get over ponies.) A few moments after I arrived, a flying saucer came slamming into the landing pads with its arse on fire, and went skidding towards the far edge, throwing multicoloured sparks in all directions. Proof, if proof were needed, that the Armourer's lab assistants will try absolutely anything once. They know no fear. They also have trouble with fairly simple concepts like common sense, knowledge of their own limitations, and anything approaching self-preservation instincts.

I also couldn't help noticing that some members of the family were still trying to get their armour to grow big enough wings so that they could fly. I could tell this because of the great dents and holes in the lawns surrounding the Hall.

I looked out over the wide-open lawns, enjoying the view. Beyond the neatly cropped grassy extents lay the lake, with swans gliding unhurriedly back and forth on its still waters. There's an undine in there somewhere, but she keeps herself to herself. What looked like a collection of dull grey statues, of people standing in strange awkward poses at the far end of the lake, were actually Droods from the nineteenth century, who'd got caught up in a Time War. Their life signs had been slowed down to a glacial scale, far beyond our ability to help or restore. They were still alive, technically speaking, so we set them out in the open air, with a view that didn't change much. Photographs of the statues, taken over a period of decades, show they are still moving, very, very slowly.

Beyond the lake lies the woods and copses that make up the far boundaries of our estates. Nice places for a walk or a picnic, provided you're one of us. Anyone else walks those woods at their own peril. Not all of the trees are sleeping. Peacocks and griffins stalked across the lawns, dodging in and out of the sprinklers and the misty haze they spread on the air. For such a beautiful bird, peacocks have a really ugly cry. Griffins start out ugly, and their behaviour borders on the disgusting, but since they can see a short distance into the future they make marvellous watchdogs. Just give them enough raw meat, and something nasty to roll about in, and they're perfectly happy.

I frowned as I considered the great hedge maze. It was constructed some time back, to contain Someone or Something that desperately needed containing, but it was all so long ago that no one now remembers who or why. When your family is as constantly busy as ours, it's only to be expected a few things are going to fall through the cracks. Looking down from above, I could see a strange metallic construct, right in the middle of the maze, but absolutely no sign of life. Or movement. If you just stick your head into the opening of the maze, nothing happens. But it doesn't happen in a very menacing sort of way. People who actually venture in don't come out again. Now and again the family throws someone in that we don't like very much, just to see what will happen. Sometimes we hear a scream, sometimes we don't. So mostly we leave the maze alone.

The Armourer wants to set fire to it, just to see what would happen. But that's the Armourer for you.

I enjoyed the view for as long as I could justify it, but I knew I was only putting off reporting in . . . so eventually I sighed heavily, and went down into the Hall via the winding back stairs. The Matriarch was waiting for me, and the Advisory Council. Of which I was a member, and a fat lot of good it had ever done me.

Walking through Drood Hall is like walking through History, with all the centuries jumbled together. The long corridors are packed with tribute (and/or loot)

from all the ages of Man. We've accumulated important and valuable prizes from every period of human
civilisation you can think of, including several that
never officially happened. We've got Sir Gawaine's suit
of armour from the Court of King Arthur; a section of
the Beayue Tapestry that had to be confiscated because
it showed a Drood in action (Harald would have won
that war if so many of the family hadn't been busy with
an extra-dimensional incursion); and a whole bunch of
family portraits daubed by important masters. Nothing
but the best for the Droods. We also have the Koh-i-
noor diamond, the original Mountain of Light from
India. And very definitely not the one Prince Albert
ruined with constant recutting. That was just a duplicate. The real thing was far too important to be trusted
to royalty. The last few Matriarchs have used the diamond as a paperweight, and for throwing at people. I've
ducked it several times.

I sent my thoughts up and out through my torc, and
made contact with Ethel. Joining my mind with hers is
like plunging into a great clear crystal lake—comforting
and intimidating at the same time. Ethel doesn't operate on the same scale as humanity, though she likes to
pretend. She's your best friend, who will always know
better than you, or a somewhat absentminded god. I
guess that's other-dimensional entities for you . . .

*Hi! Hi hi hi! Welcome back, Eddie! Shame about the
hotel. How are you? Did you bring me back a present?*

"I never know what to get you," I said. "What do you
get the invisible and immaterial strange matter entity
who has everything?"

She sniffed loudly, which is an odd sensation to have
inside your mind. *It's the thought that counts.*

"How is Grandmother? And the Council?"

Still arguing.

"Ah," I said. "Situation entirely normal, then."

People passed on by as I strolled unhurriedly down the long corridors and passageways, wandering through huge open rooms and tall galleries. Most people were never quite sure how to react to me. I mean, yes, I used to run the family, but now I don't. I've been declared a traitor, hailed as a saviour, known as a failure and the man who saved the whole of Humanity from the Hungry Gods. The family owes me everything, and a lot of them still resent me for hauling them out of their old complacency. Some nod and smile when they see me coming, while others make a point of stalking by with their noses in the air. But, since Droods are notoriously hard to impress, either way, most just nod briskly and keep going. Which suits me fine.

Two large and ostentatiously muscular fellows were standing guard outside the doors to the Sanctity, where all important meetings are held, and all the decisions that matter are made. These guards had clearly been chosen for their brutal menace rather than their intelligence, because they actually tried to block my way. I gave them my best hard look, and they stepped reluctantly to one side, scowling like I'd just stuck a thorn in their paw. I had to open the doors myself. So I kicked them wide open, stalked into the Sanctity like I was thinking of renting it out as a Roller Derby rink, and nodded briskly to the small group of people sitting round the table in the middle of the great hall.

The Sanctity was suffused with a rich warm, rose-red glow that filled every corner of the massive room. That was Ethel, manifesting herself in the material world. The light was calming and bracing at once, like a spiritual massage; it encouraged calm and composure and clear thinking, but since only Droods ever came here, it had a lot of work to do. The Matriarch sat at the head of the table, stiff and straight backed as always. Martha Drood was a tall, slender and entirely formal personage in her late sixties. She wore smart grey tweeds, elegant pearls, and her long blond hair was piled elegantly up on top of her head. She'd been a famous beauty once, and it still showed in her poise and her fabulous bone structure. We've had Queens that looked less royal. I have actually seen photos of Martha smiling, in her younger days, or I'd never have believed it possible. She glared at me steadily as I approached, for having dared enter the Sanctity without waiting to be invited in.

The Advisory Council sat on both sides of the table. The family Armourer, my Uncle Jack, nodded cheerfully to me. He was tall but heavily stooped, from years of bending over workbenches in the Armoury, devising really horrible surprises to throw at our enemies. He was still wearing his stained and scorched white lab coat, suggesting that he'd been dragged away from his beloved Armoury against his will, just when things were getting seriously interesting and/or dangerous. He was middle-aged now, and looking like he'd worked hard for every year of it. He had a gleaming bald pate, with grey tufts sticking out over his ears, bushy white eyebrows, and steel grey eyes. Under his lab coat he wore a grubby T-shirt bearing the legend WHICH PART OF FUCK OFF AND DIE DON'T YOU UNDERSTAND? Uncle Jack smiled easily at me as I approached the table. He'd always had time for me.

"Eddie, lad! About time you turned up! Come and see me afterwards; I've got some great new gadgets for you to try out."

That was always going to be a mixed blessing, given

that so many of his new gadgets had a tendency to go *boom!* when least expected, but I smiled gamely.

"Thank you, Uncle Jack. You always have the best toys."

Harry Drood, cousin Harry, looked at me thoughtfully from his chair set at the Matriarch's left hand. Harry always liked to be as close as possible to power. He'd actually run the family for a time, while I was away, and a right dog's breakfast he'd made of it. He was a pretty good field agent in his own right, but he'd only ever seen that as a means to an end. Harry believed in Harry much more than he ever believed in the Droods. Still, put him with his back to the wall and no way out, and he could be as brave and heroic as needed. His father was, after all, Uncle James, the legendary Grey Fox. Perhaps the greatest Drood ever. Harry leaned back in his chair and rocked easily back and forth on the rear legs as he studied me silently through his owlish wire-rimmed glasses. He'd already heard about the debacle at the Magnificat, and the loss of the Apocalypse Door, and he couldn't wait to hit me with every unfortunate detail, while he figured out how to turn it to his best advantage. Because that was what he did.

"Just once," Harry said calmly, "it would be nice if you could bring us back some good news after a mission, Edwin."

"You're allowed to lose the occasional battle, as long as you win the war," I said, meeting his gaze squarely.

"Lose enough battles and you run out of war," said Harry.

"You want a slap?" I said. "Only I've got one handy . . ."

"Edwin!" the Matriarch said sharply.

"There will be no violence in this chamber unless I

start it," said the final member of the Advisory Council: the Sarjeant-at-Arms. He sat to attention on his chair, a big ugly brute of a man with a face like a fist and muscles on his muscles. "Sudden and unexpected punishment is my domain. So take your seat at the table, Edwin, before I find it necessary to discipline you."

"Like to see you try, Cedric," I said, as I seated myself at the end of the table, facing the Matriarch. "Really would like to see you try. I kicked the crap out of the last Sarjeant-at-Arms, and he had years' more viciousness under his belt than you."

"Yes," said the Sarjeant. "But I'm sneakier."

I figured honours were about even, but I changed the subject anyway, just in case. "Where's William? He's still part of the Council, isn't he? Surely we need the Librarian here, if we're to discuss the significance of the Apocalypse Door?"

"William is still away with the faeries, as often as not," said the Matriarch, regretfully. "I had hoped letting him live in the Old Library, away from the pressures of family life, might help to settle and stabilise him, but I can't honestly say I've seen any signs of improvement."

"The Librarian is a looney tune," said Harry. "Crazier than ever, if anything. He only appears at Council meetings through spiritual projections, insists his assistant Rafe acts as his food taster, and keeps wittering on about Something unseen that lives in the Old Library with him and steals his socks. It's well past time we retired him, and let Rafe take over as Librarian."

"William is a better Librarian crazy than most other men sane," the Armourer said stubbornly. "It's amazing how much that man knows, when he can remember it. No one knows the Old Library like he does. But he is only a part-time member of the Council now, Eddie. We've been forced to consider bringing in new members."

"Fresh blood," said Harry, with entirely too much relish in his voice.

"Howard has been in charge of Operations for some time now," said the Matriarch. "And done an excellent job. All right, he is overbearingly arrogant, and his company is best enjoyed in very small portions, but he's very good at thinking outside the box. We can always insist he sits next to the Sarjeant, and issue the Sarjeant with a Taser. Being part of the Council might actually help teach him how to play nicely with others. Then there's Callan, who's been a real success as Head of the War Room. And yes, I'll admit that some days it does seem like he fell out of the sarcasm tree and hit every branch on the way down, but we can live with that. We've lived with worse." She glared at me. "I've allowed you to distract us long enough, Edwin. It is time to talk about what happened in Los Angeles. Why didn't you report here directly?"

"I needed some downtime," I said.

"So you could think up some excuses for your many failures on this mission?" said Harry.

"You always expect everyone to think like you, Harry," I said. "I was only supposed to infiltrate an auction before it started, and liberate a single item. No one said anything about having to take on two heavily armed armies, and the Lampton Wyrm! I had to improvise. All right, the Apocalypse Door has disappeared, but this is Doctor Delirium we're talking about! A mad scientist going through a midlife crisis. Anyone else would have bought a Porsche. How serious can this be?"

"The total destruction of the Magnificat Hotel is

extremely serious!" said the Matriarch. "If only because so many people outside the family will have to be involved in explaining it away and cleaning up the mess! You and Luther not only failed to stop the two armed forces from reaching the Apocalypse Door, you couldn't even identify one of them! And the Door has to be important, Edwin, and dangerous, or so many people wouldn't be ready to risk so much just to get their hands on it. There aren't many important and dangerous devices in this world that the family doesn't know about, and that is in itself disturbing. Armourer!"

"Just resting my eyes, Matriarch!" He grinned at me. "Did you really turn the Lampton Wyrm inside out?"

"Yes, Uncle Jack."

"Good boy. Love to have seen it. Yes, Matriarch, I'm getting to it . . . Ah. Yes. There's no information at all about the Apocalypse Door in either of the family libraries. Of course, William and Rafe are still busy cataloguing and indexing the contents of the Old Library, so there's still a good chance something will turn up . . . But given the sheer scale of the Old Library, that could take some time. And time is what we don't have; yes, Matriarch, I am aware of that. Where was I? Oh yes. The two of them are making important new finds all the time, but we need to know what this bloody Door is now, or at least before Doctor Delirium makes use of it."

"We have some time," I said. "Doctor Delirium always makes threats first, just to show he has the power. And so he can demand his payoff in postage stamps. Not a bad investment, given the current economic conditions. Unless his midlife crisis is really kicking in, and he wants respect more than he wants payment. He might make use of the Door briefly, just to show he can."

"We need to have an answer in place before he tries anything," the Matriarch said heavily.

"Normally we'd just grab someone low down in his organisation, and squeeze the information out of them," said Harry. "But he's called all of his people back to his main base in the Amazon rain forest, nailed all his doors shut and set fire to the moat. Full security measures and state-of-the-art defences. We took over a CIA surveillance satellite, and tasked it to give us coverage of the area for forty minutes. Got some really good images. No one can get anywhere near his base now without setting off all kinds of alarms and booby traps. No one's allowed in or out, until this business is over. We could try bombing him again . . ."

"No, we couldn't," the Armourer said firmly. "If you'd studied the satellite images properly, you'd have seen the brand-new force field generators. I don't know who sold him the offworld tech, but it's prime stuff. Very powerful. Doctor Delirium may be delusional, but he isn't stupid. He knew we'd be coming after him, and he's clearly learned from past mistakes."

"I want to know where and how Doctor Delirium learned of the Apocalypse Door," said the Matriarch. "Who could have told him of a device so obscure even we've never heard of it? The Doctor rarely leaves his base in the Amazon, and the only research he's ever shown any interest in concerned his own field of expertise . . . So someone from outside must have contacted him, told him about the Door, and where he could find it."

"Take it a step further," said the Armourer, scowling fiercely. "Why didn't these people make use of the Door themselves? Did they intend for the Doctor to do all the dirty work of grabbing the Door from the auction, with the intention of taking it away from him later? Did they know the other army was going to show up?"

"Maybe the auction people set it up themselves, for the insurance?" I said.

The Matriarch looked at me. "If you don't have anything *useful* to contribute, Edwin . . ."

"Who is there out there," said the Armourer, "who knows more than we do?"

"Even though the family doesn't like to admit it," said Harry, "there are a number of well-informed people and organisations, some almost as experienced as us. Do I really need to mention the Carnacki Institute, the London Knights, or the Deep School, the Dark Academy? And there's always the Regent of Shadows . . ."

"We don't talk about him," said the Matriarch, very sternly.

There was a short pause, as we all avoided each other's eyes.

"These people are all long shots and you know it," I said finally. "I say we need to look closer to home. Inside the family."

"Paranoia doesn't suit you, Edwin," the Matriarch said patiently. "The days of Zero Tolerance and Manifest Destiny are over. Those traitors have been executed, expelled from the family, or very forcibly shown the error of their ways. The family is united again. I have seen to that. If the Droods are to thrive and prosper again, and take their place on the world stage, it is vital we are all singing from the same hymn sheet."

"I do like a good male voice choir," said the Armourer wistfully.

"I'm not talking about traitors within the family," I said doggedly. "I'm more concerned with *infiltration*. A dying mercenary in the ruins of the Magnificat claimed to be part of an organisation that's always been our greatest bogeyman: the Anti-Droods. Another family, dedicated to everything we oppose. He used the phrases *wolf in the fold* and *serpents at our bosom*. That implies an enemy who is someone we trust, someone who's worked their way inside this family, just to work against us. It has happened before. Remember Sebastian? He was one of us, until he was possessed by a Loathly One. We never did find out who killed him, presumably to keep him from talking. We have to face up to the possibility that someone inside the family is not what they appear to be."

"But maybe . . . that's what he wanted you to think," said Harry. "A dying man's last chance to mess with your head, and spread distrust inside the Droods. There can't be an Anti-Droods. There just can't. We'd know."

"We didn't know about the Apocalypse Door," said the Sarjeant. He was frowning thoughtfully, clearly considering certain names. And I didn't like the way he looked at me.

"If these Anti-Droods really are as good as us," said the Armourer, "as old and as experienced and as practiced as us . . . We wouldn't know. That's always been our greatest fear; that somewhere out there were people just like us, but opposed to everything we believe in."

We all sat and looked at each other for a while, and there was no telling where the conversation might have gone if we hadn't all been distracted by the sounds of sudden violence outside the Sanctity doors. Violence, heavy thuds and screams, followed by muffled moans of pain and the sounds of heavy bodies slumping to the floor. The doors burst open, and Molly Metcalf came storming into the Sanctity.

My sweet Molly, a precious china shepherdess with

bobbed black hair, dark eyes, and really big bosoms. She was wearing a glorious white silk creation that clung to her like a second skin in places, emphasising her curves—like they needed any help—spotted here and there with fresh blood. She was wearing . . . shoes. Don't ask me what kind; expensive, probably. Men don't understand shoes.

I stood up to greet Molly, and she flashed me a wide grin. The wild witch, the laughter in the woods, the eternal rebel. Molly fought for a better world, on her terms, and often in disturbingly violent ways. My love, my everything. She threw herself into my arms, slamming me back against the end of the table, and kissed me like we'd been apart for years, instead of a few weeks. I lifted her off the ground and held her above me, and she shrieked delightedly, kicking her legs. I laughed along with her. Sometimes it seems to me the only times I get to laugh are with my Molly.

I put her down, and she punched me lightly on the chest and gave me her special low growl, that means later . . . And then she pushed me away, and glared at the Matriarch.

"I know now why my parents were killed! And Eddie's! And it's all down to the Droods!"

And it had all been going so well . . . I moved in beside her. "You have proof?" I said. "Evidence, and I mean hard evidence?"

"Not yet," said Molly, still scowling at the Matriarch. "But I'm getting close. Isabella and I are right on top of it. I came straight here to tell you, Eddie. There's a definite link between the murder of my parents and yours! Don't trust any of these people."

"You're wrong," said the Matriarch, her cold composure utterly unmoved. "No one in this family would have ordered the execution of Eddie's parents. Certainly not without my knowing."

"Well, you would say that, wouldn't you?" said Molly.

"Do you really think I'd order the death of my own daughter? Do you really think me capable of such a thing?"

"You had no problem ordering the death of your grandson," I murmured. "Sending me to my death didn't seem to bother you at all, Grandmother."

Her face didn't give an inch, but when she spoke she chose her words carefully. "That was different, Edwin. I thought it was necessary, for the good of the family. It has been made clear to me that I was wrong about that . . . and other things. Emily was my dearest daughter. And I approved of Charles, your father. A bit of a rogue, but a good man with a good heart. Did you think I'd let just anyone marry my daughter? I liked Charles, and trusted him implicitly. He and Emily made a formidable team as field agents. Until that unfortunate business in the Basque area . . . I investigated their deaths thoroughly, Edwin. If there'd been even a hint that anyone had intended their deaths, I would have torn the family apart to find the culprits, and executed them myself. But it was just a stupid, regrettable accident. The result of bad intelligence and worse planning. These things happen, even in the best-regulated families."

"Nothing just happens, where the Droods are concerned," said Molly.

"Your parents died in the middle of a firefight," the Matriarch said calmly. "They should never have sided with the White Horse Faction. Those people were extremists, terrorists, and always far too ready to shoot first. They were a bloodbath waiting to happen."

"They were freedom fighters," said Molly. "Idealists.

And you had them all killed, including my mother and father."

"We offered them every chance to surrender. Causes like that are always half in love with Death, one way or another."

"You killed my mum and dad," said Molly.

"You could have found another way," I said to the Matriarch.

"You know that isn't always possible," she said flatly. "Did you take the time to consider all the possibilities, when you murdered your Uncle James? My son? The legendary Grey Fox?"

"That wasn't Eddie's fault!" Molly said immediately. "You sent James to kill Eddie! And you're still trying to manipulate him, even now, working on his emotions, and the sense of blind duty you pounded into him! It's all you know how to do. *Anything, for the family.* You're already responsible for the deaths of so many; what are a few more, even if they have familiar faces? I'll see you dead for what you've done, you coldhearted bitch!"

The Sarjeant-at-Arms was already on his feet and armoured up, two oversized guns appearing out of nowhere in his hands. The Armourer was up and on his feet only a second later, moving to put himself in front of the Matriarch, protecting her from all harm with his own body. But he hadn't armoured up. Uncle Jack liked Molly. He didn't really believe she would hurt the Matriarch, but he knew his duty. Harry hadn't budged at all. He just sat there, entirely at his ease, watching the drama before him with cheerful detached interest.

I could see this situation going to hell in any number of unfortunate ways, so I grabbed Molly from behind, heaved her over my shoulder, and strode quickly out of the Sanctity. She stiffened ominously for a moment, but didn't struggle, and allowed me to remove her from the scene. Though I was pretty sure I'd be made to pay for the indignity later. Behind us, I could hear the Armourer laughing, and applauding. My back crawled, in anticipation of a bullet from the Sarjeant, but I'd been careful not to provoke him by armouring up. And besides, I didn't think my grandmother would allow the Sarjeant to shoot me in the back. If she ever decided to order my death again, she'd want me to see it coming.

I left the Sanctity behind, and strode nonchalantly through the Hall, Molly still slung over my shoulder.

"Anyone else I'd have turned into a toad," she said casually. "Or something small and squelchy with its testicles floating on the surface."

"Yes," I said. "But I have boyfriend privileges."

"You are pushing it, big time."

"I know," I said. "Next time, you can carry me off."

"I love it when you talk dirty."

After a while I put her down, and we went back to my room at the top of the Hall, and made up. Afterwards, we lay cuddled together on my bed, our clothes scattered everywhere, sweat drying slowly on our naked bodies. I could feel scratches from her fingernails smarting on my back. Molly rested her head on my chest, and made quiet noises of contentment. I let my gaze drift slowly around my room. It wasn't very big, as rooms went, but it was bigger than most in Drood Hall. Even with four extra Wings added on down the years, space was always at a premium. The family gets bigger every year, and every year it gets harder to find somewhere to put us all. In the not too distant future, we're either going to have to expand the Hall again, or move. But no one wants to talk about that, just yet.

The room had all the usual comforts, but little in the

way of character. I was never around long enough to stamp my personality on it. Still, it seemed very peaceful, and quiet, just then, so far away from the rest of the family and all their many troubles.

"So," I said finally. "What have you and Isabella been up to?"

"We went to see the Mole," she said, not raising her head. Her lips brushed against my skin. "He's still a rogue; prefers it that way. If he were to rejoin the family, they'd try and make him come home, and he just couldn't. He's been alone too long. He couldn't stand being forced to mix with people again. It would kill him. Anyway, he wasn't comfortable with anyone knowing where his hole was, so he moved. And this time he pulled the hole in after him. Even I don't know where he is now. I can only talk to him via e-mail, bounced back and forth so many times it can never be traced. I figured if anyone knew the truth about what happened to our parents, it would be him. He didn't know, but he thought he knew someone who might. He sent Isabella and me to this small town in the southwest of England, a place called Bradford-on-Avon. To talk to the oldest living human in the world: Carys Galloway, the Waking Beauty."

Molly's story:

Bradford-on-Avon is a really old town. It was the last Celtic town to fall to the invading Saxons in 504 A.D., and there are remains of an Iron Age settlement in the hills above the town. Strange creatures and stranger people live in this small country town, and marvels and wonders can be found there. Along with dark powers and darker secrets. Some of the people who live there have lived there so long they're not even people anymore. And they know things no one else does.

It's a pleasant place. Isabella and I left the train station and just walked around for a while, enjoying the many styles of architecture, from old thatched cottages to seventeenth-century weavers' tenements, from manor houses to futuristic apartments. All of time, crammed together in one place. Reminded me of Drood Hall, a bit. Except the people were a lot friendlier.

The town looks perfectly normal at first, but once we raised our Sight, everything changed. It was as though just the act was enough to push us sideways, into a subtly different realm. We strolled across the thirteenth-century town bridge, over the river Avon, and passed an old stone chapel built into the bridge wall; just big enough to hold one or two people. Something inside threw itself against the confining walls, and a terrible scream filled my head, an inhuman howl of suffering and despair, rising and falling but never ending. Isabella grabbed my arm and hurried us on. I found out later it's called the Howling Thing; one of the really old monsters. Imprisoned there centuries ago, and still doing penance. It's doing Time, every damned bit of it.

Wispy, multicoloured sylphs danced across the surface of the river, darting and speeding and leaping high into the air, leaving shimmering sparkling trails behind them. A dozen of them leapt right over the bridge, and when the shimmering trail fell across me, I was briefly touched by pure unadulterated joy. Other things moved on and in the slowly moving dark waters—creatures old and new, and some I would have taken an oath on a pile of grimoires didn't even exist in the material world anymore. There were swans too, proud and majestic, moving unaffected among all the other magical creatures.

In the centre of town we found the memory of old gibbets, from when so many men had been hanged during the old Wool Riots. Ghosts could still be seen, hanging from their gibbets, chatting amiably with each other. They were more than half transparent, colours moving slowly over them like so many soap bubbles, but their presence felt harsh and almost brutal in the clear sunlight. I did offer to release them from the place of their death, and help them move on, but they declined. They weren't trapped in the town; they had chosen to remain, to protect the town and their descendants. A few of them laughed nastily. *The town has enemies,* they said, laughing nastily. *Let them come. Let them all come.* Apparently if you stay a ghost long enough, in a place like this, it's amazing how much power you can accumulate. They did offer to demonstrate, but there was something in their voices, and in their laughter . . . so I declined. I did ask where Isabella and I might find the Waking Beauty, and one of them directed us to an old pub called the Dandy Lion.

We found the place easily enough, right in the middle of town. It had clearly been around for some time. The painted sign above the door featured a lion walking upright, dressed in Restoration finery. It turned its head and winked at us as we passed under it. The oak-panelled doors swung open before us, revealing a carefully maintained old-fashioned ambience, with pleasantly gloomy old-time lighting, and a long bar stocked with every drink under the sun. It wasn't until my eyes adjusted to the gloom that I realised there were flowers growing right out of the wood-panelled walls, their delicate petals pulsing like heartbeats. The music box was playing a Beatles song, but one I'd never heard before. The chairs at the traditional wooden tables politely pulled themselves out so people could sit down. A pack of cards was playing solitaire by itself, and cheating. And behind the long bar, a young woman in authentic sixties hippie gear was just cutting off a Yeti, on the grounds that he got mean when he was drunk. The big hairy creature slouched out of the pub, sulking, shedding hairs all the way.

We found Carys Galloway sitting tucked away in a corner, on her own, next to the window, so she could see anybody coming. She looked us over coolly before gesturing for us to sit down facing her. The chairs were very helpful. The Waking Beauty was a small delicate creature with a personality so powerful it almost pushed me back in my chair. She had a pointed chin, prominent cheekbones, a wide mouth and more than a hint of ethnic gypsy in her. Dark russet hair fell to her shoulders in thick ringlets, and her eyes were so huge and deep you felt like you could fall into them forever. And she smiled like she already knew everything you had on your mind. She had long bony hands, with heavily knuckled fingers, weighed down with gold and silver rings set with unfamiliar polished stones. Bangles on her wrists made soft chiming sounds with her every movement. She wore traditional Romany clothes, and wore them well. She could have been any age from her twenties to her forties, but even sitting there at her ease, her gaze hit me like a blow. She burned, she blazed, with a fierce unwavering intensity, like nothing human.

I let Isabella do all the talking. I know when I'm outclassed.

"Word is, you're connected," Isabella said bluntly. She waited for a moment, to give the Waking Beauty an opportunity to confirm or deny, but there was no reaction, so Isabella pressed on. "You're supposed to be the oldest person in this town. In fact, there are those who say you're older than the town. You draw your power from the many ley lines that cross here, and from never sleeping. Are you the oldest living person in this town, Carys Galloway?"

"Well," she said, "There's Tommy Squarefoot. But he's a Neanderthal."

"Are you immortal?" insisted Isabella.

"Who knows?" said the Waking Beauty. "I just haven't died yet, that's all. There are those who call themselves the Immortals, but I'm not one of that family."

"Some say you made a deal, for long life and power," said Isabella. "A deal you would like to break, if you dared. How am I doing so far, Carys Galloway?"

"I've killed people for knowing less than that about me," the Waking Beauty said calmly. "Fortunately for you, I've mellowed these last few years. And I always did have a soft spot for Hecate's children. Witches know how to have fun. So, Isabella and Molly Metcalf. Where's Louisa?"

"Walking in the Martian Tombs, last I heard," said Isabella, which came as something of a surprise to me.

"Why have you come to talk with me, my sisters?" said the Waking Beauty. There was a trace of warning in her voice, that made it clear we'd better have a really good reason.

"Our parents were murdered by the Droods," said Isabella. "We were always told they were just in the wrong place at the wrong time, but there have been . . . suggestions, that there may have been more to it than that."

"We think they were killed deliberately," I said, unable to keep quiet any longer. "Someone in the Droods ordered their deaths. We want to know who, and why. And, whether there's any connection with the death of Eddie's parents."

"Ah," said the Waking Beauty. "I always knew that would come back to bite the Droods on the arse. Droods killing Droods . . . secrets within secrets, lies within lies to hide a terrible truth . . . But first, you need to know about the Apocalypse Door."

Isabella and I looked at each other.

"We do?" I said.

"Unfortunately, yes, you do. Follow the trail, oh my sisters, from the Door to Doctor Delirium to the Immortals. And if you're still alive at the end of it, you'll get your answers. Quite possibly more answers than you can comfortably deal with. The Apocalypse Door is one of the thirteen true entries to Hell in the material world. Open this Door, and you can let loose all the inhabitants of Hell, to run loose on the Earth. Set the damned free, to do as they will, to trample the cities of men and slaughter their inhabitants. Hell on Earth, forever and ever, and the Triumph of Evil."

"Has anyone . . . ever tried to open this Door?" said Isabella, leaning forward, fascinated.

"Usually, the owner of the Door only has to threaten to open it, and the world will give them whatever they want," said the Waking Beauty. "They want to be persuaded, to be paid off. But there have always been a few, who for their own various reasons wanted to unleash Hell on Mankind. Famous names like Faustus, and a certain Doctor Ware, back in the 1960s . . . These people always come to bad ends. You can't play with Hell and not get your fingers burned. The Droods, or someone else in the same line of work, always turns up just in time to stop these people, and stamp on their heads." The Waking Beauty stopped, and frowned thoughtfully. "Theoretically, or theologically, speaking . . . should the Door be opened, and the contents of Hell let loose on an unsuspecting populace; then the forces of Heaven would be obliged to turn out to stop them. Though the conflict would almost certainly lay waste to the Earth and everything on it. So Apocalypse would seem to be the appropriate name, for this particular Door."

"What has all this got to do with us?" I said.

The Waking Beauty smiled upon me, like a mother with a really dim child. "Follow the connections. All the way to the end."

"You mentioned a name I didn't recognise," Isabella said suddenly. "A family called the Immortals."

"Who are they?" I said.

The Waking Beauty sat back in her chair, her face slipping into shadow. Her bangles clattered softly. "A great many people would like to know the answer to that question. Well, here is wisdom, for those wise enough to receive it. If the Apocalypse Door has re-appeared in the world of men, it can only mean the Immortals are close to revealing themselves, at last. They've been trying to get their hands on the Door for centuries, for their own inscrutable reasons, but some-how it's always eluded them. However; just before the legendary Independent Agent died, he sold off many of his accumulated treasures, and one of them, to the sur-prise of many, turned out to be the Apocalypse Door. Apparently he needed a great deal of money at the end, for some last scheme . . . I have heard that a battle has just been fought over the Door in Los Angeles, involv-ing Doctor Delirium, the Immortals, and one Eddie Drood."

"Is he all right?" I said.

"Oh, he's fine. But the hotel will never be the same again."

"Yeah," I said. "That sounds like Eddie."

"What about the Immortals?" said Isabella.

"It's not easy to talk about them," said the Waking Beauty. "They're powerful, they're vicious, and they're everywhere . . . and no one knows who they really are. They can be anyone, anywhere, hiding behind faces you've trusted all your life. But if you want to know what I know, you're going to have to pay my price."

Isabella nodded slowly. "I know. You want an end to your bargain, to your curse. You want to be able to sleep again."

"Okay, you've left me behind now," I said. "Bring me up to speed. How do you know what she needs, Is?"

"Because I did my homework before we came here," she said. "I don't just go rushing into things. Like you."

I ignored her, giving all my attention to the Waking Beauty. "If you break your bargain, you'll die. Won't you?"

"Perhaps. I don't know. But I'm ready to find out."

"So, who did you make your deal with?" I said. "The Devil?"

Carys Galloway snorted loudly. "Please, I'm older than Christianity, and your limited concept of the Enemy. I made my deal with Queen Mab, original leader of the Faerie. Humanity, as such, hadn't been around long then, and Mab saw us as no threat to her people. But still, we had something they didn't have, something Mab wanted for herself. The Fae don't sleep, don't dream, and that limits their imagination, their creativity. Faeries are always curious, always wanting what they don't have . . . So Mab chose me. I don't know why. And we made a deal; my ability to sleep and dream, in return for immortality. I had no idea what I was giving up, and she had no idea what she was getting. Mab slept, and dreamed, and was never the same afterwards. She dreamed marvellous new cities, and weapons, and customs, and woke to make them real. She made the elves mighty. But she also became a little less Fae, and a little more human. Perhaps that's why Oberon and Titania were able to end her reign, replace her, and throw her down into Hell. I like to think so."

"Mab is back," I said. "She rules the Fae again, in the Sundered Lands."

"I know," said Isabella. "I met with her, some time back."

Again, this was all news to me, but Isabella silenced me with a hard glare before I could ask any more questions. She'd tell me what she thought I needed to know, on her own time. She always was the bossy one.

"I also made a deal with Mab," said Isabella. "I took her humanity from her, so that she could be pure elf again, and retake the Ivory Throne. I took back her ability to sleep and dream. And I have it right here, with me."

She placed a small plastic snow globe on the table, between us and the Waking Beauty. It looked like a cheap toy, until you looked at it closely, and then wished you hadn't. Behind the continually falling snow, something looked back . . .

"All you have to do is break this, and sleep and dreams will be yours again," said Isabella. "Whether you'll still be immortal or not . . . is probably up you. You're not losing anything, after all, just getting something back."

The Waking Beauty cupped her large hands around the snow globe, staring unblinkingly into its unknown depths. "You have no idea how tired you can get, when you haven't been able to sleep for thousands of years. Never any rest, never any ease, never any break from the sheer effort of living, and thinking . . . You can have too much of a good thing."

"You've got what you wanted," said Isabella. "Now tell me about the Immortals."

"I'm the only one who can tell you about them, because I was there before them," said Carys Galloway. "I am the only living human being older than both the Droods and the Immortals. I was already centuries old when the other-dimensional entity known as the Heart crash-landed in ancient Britain. When the Heart materialised, its emanations affected the genetic material of every living thing for miles around. Most died, some mutated, and a few survived by making deals with the Heart. The Druid ancestors of the Droods were granted the armour they requested, so they could be shamans for the human tribe.

"But one man got to the Heart before them, and he asked to be made immortal. Him, and his wife and children. Apparently this amused the Heart, and it agreed. The first Immortal went back to his family, and passed his blessing on to them, and so were born the Immortals. They can be killed, if you try really hard, but otherwise they just go on, and on and on and on. Fortunately they breed only rarely, and never with each other. Their children are half-breeds, incredibly long-lived but not immortal. They serve the Elders in the family. Down the centuries, the Immortals have learned the art of flesh dancing, of shape-changing. They can take on the appearance of anyone, be anyone, infiltrate any organisation, or family, so that they can shape the world as they wish, for their benefit. They are always on both sides of every conflict, whipping up the flames, growing rich and powerful on the proceeds of war. We're just mayflies, to them. We don't matter. Only family matters, to the Immortals. Remind you of anyone?

"And like the Droods, the Immortals take the long

view. They deal in small, subtle changes, designed to bear useful fruit in three or even four generations time. No wonder no one ever detects the truth, of their slow and remorseless influence; not even the shadowy agencies who like to think they guard the world. The Immortals have been shaping and manipulating history for fifteen hundred years, right under the Droods' noses.

"Anyone can be an Immortal. Even a Drood. They've all had many names and identities, down the years. Some of them you'd know. Some of them Eddie would recognise. How can you fight an enemy who can be anyone?"

"How does all of this tie in with the death of our parents?" I said, unable to hold back any longer.

"I have had dealings with the Droods, down the centuries," said the Waking Beauty. "Perhaps mostly because they're almost as old as I am. It's good to have someone to talk to . . . But I never worked for the Immortals. At least, not knowingly. They use people, that's all. But you can't live as long as I have, and not hear things . . . And one of the things I've heard is that your parents and Eddie's parents knew each other. They met in battle, and ended up as allies. Very secret allies. They found out something, you see, discovered something they couldn't be allowed to tell anyone else. So a decision was made, to kill them and make it look like unfortunate accidents. The Immortals decided this, but the orders came from inside the Droods.

"The Immortals infiltrated the Droods long ago, and they've been steering policy, sabotaging missions, and leading them around by the nose for their own purposes, for centuries. So, go back to the Droods. Find the hidden traitors, and make them tell you what you need to know. And tell Eddie . . . to watch his back. Now go. I'm tired . . ."

We left her, sitting alone, staring into the depths of the snow globe.

I held Molly close to me, trying to make sense of everything she'd told me. Traitors, inside the Droods? Inside the Hall? People in my family, who weren't family? Malevolent eyes watching me from behind trusted faces? And . . . if the Apocalypse Door was everything Molly said it was, then Doctor Delirium really was a Major Player at last, and a clear and present danger to the whole world.

"I shouldn't have blown up at the Matriarch like that," said Molly, cuddling up against me. "It's hard being angry all the time. Sometimes, I just want to hold and be held. I'm glad you're here, Eddie."

"Hush," I said. "Sleep. Everything will seem clearer, in the morning."

It seemed only moments later when we were both awakened by a thunderous knocking on my bedroom door. The room was dark. I looked at the glowing face of the clock beside the bed; it was a little short of four in the morning. Someone was still pounding on my door, and yelling my name. I turned on the light, pulled a dressing gown around me, and went to the door. It wasn't locked, but even in an emergency a Drood's room and privacy were sacrosanct. I pulled the door open, and there was Howard, Head of Operations. His face was grey with shock, and his eyes were wide. He looked like he'd been hit.

"What is it?" I said.

"You have to come with me, Eddie, you have to come now!" he said. "The Matriarch's been murdered."

CHAPTER THREE

Sudden Death at Drood Hall

Molly and I threw on some clothes while Howard waited impatiently outside in the corridor. I could hear him shuffling heavily from foot to foot. And all the time I was thinking, *He has to be wrong. It has to be some kind of mistake. She can't be dead. Not her.* I reached out to Ethel with my mind.

"Ethel, what the hell is going on? Is the Matriarch really dead? Has she been murdered?"

I don't know! said Ethel. *I can't tell! I can't tell anything! The entire Hall is awake, thousands of minds, all of them yelling at once!*

"Are we under attack? Has someone broken into the Hall?"

No, Ethel said immediately. *All defences are in place, all protections are in order. We're the only ones here.*

By now, Molly and I were dressed and out the door, following Howard down the corridor to the Matriarch's suite. The corridor looked dim and unfamiliar in this early hour of the morning, and my head was still half full of sleep. I kept throwing questions at Howard, and he kept trying to answer, but couldn't, because he was fighting back tears. All I could get out of him was that the Sarjeant-at-Arms had told him the Matriarch was dead, murdered, and that he should come and get me. I was still having trouble believing it. My grandmother couldn't be dead. How could someone as important, as powerful as her, be dead? Martha was the longest serving and surviving Matriarch the family had ever known. Most living Droods had never known another. To so many of us, she was the family.

I was still too numb, too confused, to feel anything. She tried to have me killed, and then supported me when I led the family against the Hungry Gods. She was always the authority figure I hated, with good reason, and the grandmother I loved, for no good reason. She'd always been there, my whole life, for good and bad. I could always depend on her . . . to be her. I couldn't imagine life without her. Molly moved silently along beside me, clinging tightly to my arm, trying to support and comfort me with her presence.

When we finally got to the Matriarch's suite, the door was standing open. That was enough to make me stumble to a halt. The Matriarch's door was never open. You always had to knock, politely, and then wait to be summoned in. The open door was a slap in the face—a sign that things would never be the same again. Howard stopped in the doorway, looking back at me inquiringly. So I took a deep breath and went in, Molly pressed close at my side. We passed through the antechamber into her bedroom, and there was the Sarjeant-at-Arms, standing at the foot of the bed, scowling fiercely, looking at nothing, his arms folded tightly across his chest as though to keep him from flying apart. The Armourer was sitting on a chair pulled up to the side of the bed, holding one of the Matriarch's hands in his. He looked old and tired, and broken.

Martha Drood lay in bed, on her back, her nightdress and the sheets around her soaked in blood. She was utterly still. Her eyes stared sightlessly up at the ceiling. Her long blond hair, of which she was always secretly proud, stretched shapelessly across the pillows, in a state she would never have allowed herself to be seen, in life. And then, finally, I believed it.

"About time, Edwin," said the Sarjeant. His voice was unusually harsh, even for him, but somehow unfocused. "Our Matriarch has been murdered." He looked at Molly. "What is the witch doing here? She's not family."

"Not now, Sarjeant," I said. I made myself walk past him, to the side of the bed. Made myself look closely at the body. "What happened here? How was she . . . murdered?"

"Stabbed," said the Sarjeant. "A single thrust, from the front, through the heart. I knew it, the moment it happened. One of the little secrets of my position—I'm linked to the Hall, and everyone in it. It is necessary for me to know exactly where everyone in the family is, so that they can always be found, and disciplined. So I always know, when one of us dies. The Matriarch's sudden death brought me right up out of a deep sleep. For a moment, I tried to tell myself it was just a bad dream, but I knew it wasn't. So I came straight here, found the door open . . . and found her dead in her bed."

"Ethel's quite positive the Hall is still secure," I said. "No one's broken in, or out. No intruders means . . . this wasn't the work of any of our enemies. This was an inside job. The killer is one of us."

"One of the family?" said Howard, still just inside the doorway. He couldn't look at the body. "How could one of us do something like this? It's not possible! She's . . . she's the Matriarch!"

But I was looking at Molly, and we were remembering what she had said to me earlier about Immortals infiltrating the family. Our deadliest enemies, hidden behind familiar faces. And I suddenly had to wonder about the timing of the Matriarch's death. Could we have been overheard? Had the Matriarch been killed just to send me a message? Was this my fault? Molly started to say something, and I stopped her with a quick gesture. We couldn't talk here. Not when there was no telling who might be listening.

The Sarjeant-at-Arms saw the look, and the gesture. He started to say something, so I cut quickly across him.

"Stabbed right through the heart," I said, bending over the body and examining the wound closely. "A practised, professional blow. And no defensive wounds on the arms . . . No signs of any struggle, the bedclothes are hardly disturbed. All of which suggests the attacker was someone she knew, and trusted, right up to the last moment. He must have just knocked on the door, and been invited in. She sat up in bed, he walked up to her, and . . . He must have been quick. She was a teacher of unarmed combat for thirty years. No one could have overpowered her, if she felt threatened. She could have held off even the most determined assassin long enough to summon up her armour. But a face she trusted, with a knife she never saw until it was far too late . . ."

"But how could the killer just walk in here?" said Molly. "Didn't she have any guards outside her door?"

"Inside the Hall?" said Howard, shocked. "We don't have guards here. We're safe, here. Danger always comes from outside."

"There are . . . protections in place, to prevent any outsider from doing harm inside the Hall," said the Sarjeant. "But they wouldn't affect any member of the family, or a really powerful magic-user . . ."

I didn't like the way he was looking at Molly. "Now wait just a minute . . ." I said.

"You threatened to kill the Matriarch," the Sarjeant said to Molly. "To her face, in front of the Advisory Council."

"I was angry!" said Molly. "But I'm not stupid enough to kill her here, surrounded by her family. And I'm certainly not stupid enough to stick around afterwards. Besides, I wouldn't just stab someone! I'm the wild witch of the woods! I'd use some really subtle magic, make it look like natural causes. Or, if I wanted you to know it was me, I'd do something really vile and horrible, and then disappear while you were all still throwing up. I don't do stabbings."

"What better way to disguise your involvement, than a crude attack with an anonymous blade?" said the Sarjeant.

"Stop this," I said. "Stop it right now. Molly had nothing to do with this. She's been with me ever since we left the Sanctity. It couldn't be her."

"Well, you would say that, wouldn't you?" said the Sarjeant. "But even if it were true, you had to sleep sometime. She could have left your side, done the deed and returned while you were still sleeping. Couldn't she?"

"No," I said. "No." I looked at the Armourer. He was still holding the Matriarch's dead hand, his head bowed over it. "Uncle Jack? You don't believe it was Molly, do you?"

"Hush, Eddie," he said, not looking round. "My mother is dead."

A thought struck me, and I looked back at the Sarjeant. "Does Alistair know? Has anyone told him?"

"The Matriarch's consort doesn't know anything anymore," said Howard. "It's a miracle he's still alive. After what you did to him."

"He threatened to kill Molly, and me," I said.

"He's still in a coma," said Howard. "Hooked up to a whole bunch of life support, down in the hospital ward. He hasn't said anything in months. Why disturb him now?"

I leaned forward over the bed, and studied the Matriarch's face. Dead bodies were nothing new to me, but it's always different when it's someone you know. There was nothing in her face—no shock, no outrage, no fear or pain. It was just . . . empty. She seemed smaller, as though the most important part of her was gone, and this was just something she had left behind. I took her free hand in mine, and then dropped it again because just like that she was standing beside the bed, staring at me. A tall regal figure in her best tweeds and pearls, looking very much alive. I looked back at the bed, but the body was still there. I looked at the others, and it was clear they could see the vision of my grandmother as well. It couldn't be her ghost; Martha had always been very firm that ghosts had no place in the Hall. The family always looks forward, never back. So this must be a vision; a recording made earlier, and activated by the touch of my hand. I felt obscurely affected, that she had chosen me as the trigger for her message. The Matriarch started speaking, and I gave her my full attention. Her face was calm and unmoved, as though this message from beyond was just another necessary task.

"If you're seeing this, then I'm dead," she said flatly. "I suppose it could have happened in any number of ways, but I'm betting on violence. Droods live well, but we don't live long. Comes with the job. It doesn't really matter how; what matters is the family. Do not let my death divide or weaken the family. The Council must take over the running of things, until a new leader can be decided on. Work together; this is my last instruction to all of you. Edwin, we never agreed on anything much, except that the good of the family must always come first. *Anything, for the family. Anything, for England. Anything, for Humanity.* Remember that, and you won't go far wrong. I was always proud of you, Edwin, hard though you may find that to believe. Even when you outraged and defied me. Perhaps especially then. It's good to know the family can still produce lions as well as drones.

"Jack . . . Good-bye, my dear. My only living child. I wish . . . we'd found the time to talk more. But you were always so busy in your Armoury, and I had the family to run, and the world . . . just kept getting in the way. You always think there'll be more time, to say the things you want to say. Until suddenly there isn't.

"Sarjeant-at-Arms, do your duty. Protect the family. And if I have died at some assassin's hand, let nothing stand between you and getting to the truth. I think that's it. I can't think of anything more to say. I have no regrets. No apologies. Everything I did, I did for the family. Nothing else matters."

She stood there for a moment, seeming to see us all clearly with her fierce cold gaze, and then she was gone.

I looked back at the body on the bed. It was hard to think of them as the same person.

"So," said the Sarjeant. "An unliving will. How very . . . practical. A pity she didn't name a successor. We can't take time out for elections; it would leave the family vulnerable."

"Who would have been the next Matriarch?" said Molly.

"Irrelevant," said the Armourer. He held his mother's dead hand in both of his, squeezed it briefly, and then let it go. He stood up and looked severely at the rest of us. "The old ways are gone. No one can inherit leadership; we have seen where that leads. We are a democracy now, for the good of our souls."

"The family chose to put Martha in charge again," said the Sarjeant-at-Arms.

"As leader," the Armourer said firmly. "The title Matriarch was purely honorary. The family just felt . . . more secure, that way. No, the Advisory Council will run things, for now."

"The line of inheritance is broken anyway," said Howard. He was still by the doorway, still unable to bring himself any farther into the room. "The Matriarch's only daughter, Emily, is . . ."

"Dead," I said. "My mother is dead."

The Armourer came forward, and we looked into each other's faces. Then he opened his arms, and we hugged each other. Two sons who had lost their mothers. We let go, and the Armourer stepped back and nodded to me brusquely.

"I'll make all the arrangements. I know what she would have wanted."

"Any funeral will have to wait," said the Sarjeant. "The body must be examined, and the room, and the whole Hall must be searched, thoroughly." He looked at Molly again. "But the witch . . . must be excluded from all our discussions. She is not family. Edwin must also be excluded, because of his relationship to the witch. Both of them must be securely confined, until their guilt or innocence can be established."

"Not going to happen, Cedric," I said.

"You heard your grandmother's last orders," the Sarjeant said, unmoved by the clear threat in my voice. "Let nothing stand between me and the truth. Certainly not an ungrateful grandson and a notorious witch."

The Armourer made a sudden shocked sound, and we all looked round sharply. He was leant right over his mother's body, pointing at her bare neck.

"Her torc is gone! How did we miss that? How is it even possible? Every torc is bound to its wearer on the genetic level!"

We all crowded round the bed. There was no torc. Martha's neck looked almost obscenely naked without it.

"Is that what this was all about?" said Molly. "Was she killed so someone could take her torc?"

"No," the Sarjeant said immediately. "Far easier to kill a field agent, outside the protections of the Hall, and take their torc. But . . . there is a very old and awful weapon, right here in the Hall, that could have been used. Armourer, where is Torc Cutter?"

"Still safely locked away in the Armageddon Codex, along with all the other forbidden weapons," said the Armourer. "And no, the Codex hasn't been opened. I'd know. Whatever did this, it wasn't Torc Cutter."

"Could anyone have got the torc outside the Hall without setting off all the alarms?" said Molly.

"No," said the Sarjeant. "Which means it must still be here. Somewhere in the Hall."

A sudden thought struck me, and I contacted Ethel again. "Did you see what happened here?"

You know I don't watch individuals anymore, she said reproachfully. *Not after we had that little talk about personal privacy. Still not sure I entirely grasp the concept, but whatever keeps you happy . . .*

"Can you locate the Matriarch's missing torc?" I said.

Hmmm . . . That's odd. No, I can't. I should be able to, I should be able to isolate and identify every individual torc; but not this one. How very intriguing. Either someone of great power is blocking my probes, which I would have said was impossible, or . . . Actually, I don't have an or. The Sarjeant is quite correct, however, it must still be in the Hall somewhere.

"You've been listening!"

Of course I've been listening! This is an emergency, and I am part of the Hall's protections, after all.

I passed Ethel's comments on to the others, and they all considered them, in their various ways. The Sarjeant wouldn't stop staring at Molly.

"Inside job," she said. "Has to be."

"But not by one of us," said the Sarjeant. "It would take a witch of your power to block Ethel's probes."

"You really are pushing your luck, Cedric," I said.

"You keep using my name as though it is an insult, or a weakness," said the Sarjeant-at-Arms. "It's just my name. And all of your sentimental attraction to the witch, and all your usual arrogance, will not stop me from carrying out my duty."

I sneered at him, but I was already preoccupied with another thought. When the Blue Fairy died, I took back his stolen torc by absorbing it into my own armour. I didn't know my new armour could do that, until it did. I hadn't told anyone about that. Could another member of the family have discovered this trick, and be hiding the Matriarch's torc inside their own armour? It would explain why Ethel couldn't find it . . .

"Who investigates murders, inside the family?" said Molly, still doing her best to seem reasonable and cooperative. "I assume such things do happen, even in this best-regulated of families?"

"Rarely," said the Sarjeant. "And then it falls to my office to investigate. With the help of my CSI people. They're on their way."

"CSI?" I said. "You've been watching far too much television."

He sniffed loudly. "We have tech those people never even dreamed of. And all kinds of forensic magic. I will discover the truth, Edwin, no matter how hard you try to muddy the waters."

"There's a lot of blood, on the body and on the sheets," Molly said doggedly. "Whoever stabbed the Matriarch must have got in close, and been covered in blood themselves. Surely your special CSI people can track down a set of bloodstained clothes?"

"Of course," said the Sarjeant. "Unless someone has already removed the bloodstains magically."

I moved in close beside Molly, glaring at the Sarjeant, and he glared right back at me. The threat of violence hung in the air. And then we all looked round sharply, distracted by the approaching sound of urgent running feet. The Sarjeant suddenly had a gun in his hand, trained on the open door. Perhaps coincidentally, it was also covering Molly. I moved forward a little, to put myself between Molly and the Sarjeant. We were both just a moment away from armouring up, when Harry burst in through the door, and then stopped dead at the sight of the gun in the Sarjeant's hand. He was breathing hard, sweat on his face. He looked past us at the Matriarch, dead in her bed. He swallowed hard, and then turned his gaze back to Molly, and me.

"You've got to get her out of here, Eddie," he said harshly. "There's an angry mob headed this way, dozens of them, and not that far behind me. News of the Matriarch's murder has spread all over the Hall. Most of the family are shocked, or mourning, but a hell of a lot of them are out of their minds with shock and fury, and the need to take it out on someone. They've decided Molly is guilty, and they want blood. Someone's been whipping them up against the two of you, and for once it wasn't me."

"Really, Harry," I said. "Couldn't wait to bring me the bad news, though, could you?"

"Will you forget that shit!" he said loudly. "They're coming, and they want Molly dead! They'll tear her apart with their armoured hands!"

For once, I believed him. "How much time have we got, before they get here?"

"You need to get moving now," he said. "I don't know where all this rage is coming from, but there's no way you can talk or bluff them out of this." He looked at Molly. "You did threaten to kill the Matriarch. In the Sanctity. News like that gets around fast."

"And someone's taken advantage of it," I said.

Surprisingly, the Sarjeant didn't pick up his cue. He was already mad as hell at the thought of Droods rioting in the Hall.

"A mob?" he said. "On my watch? Droods running wild? I will not have such a lapse in family discipline! I decide who is guilty here; no one else!"

I looked at Molly. "Time we were leaving."

"Got that right," she said tightly. "I think we've overstayed our welcome."

"Get her down to the Armoury," said the Armourer. "Shut all the doors and instigate full lockdown. No one can get through that. And don't open up again until I tell you it's safe."

"You don't understand," said Harry. "You've got to go now! They were right on my heels! Just . . . run! While you still can. They'll kill her!"

"The Merlin Glass is back in my room," I said to Molly. "I didn't put it back in its subspace pocket because I thought I'd be using it to send you back to your woods. If we can get back to my room, that's our way out."

"Go," said the Sarjeant. "I'll stand between you and the rabble."

"You're not worried about losing your chief suspect?" I said.

"Go," he said. "When I want you I'll come and get you."

I grabbed Molly's hand and we ran out of the Matriarch's suite. And there was the mob, just spilling onto the top floor from the end stairs. They saw Molly, and a great shout went up, of almost hysterical rage and bloodlust. Harry was right. Someone had put a lot of hard work into driving them completely out of their minds. At least they hadn't thought to armour up yet. They were still moving at human speeds, with human limitations. So I couldn't armour up to protect Molly, in case it gave them ideas. They came charging down the corridor, screaming and howling like animals, with out-stretched clutching hands, fighting one another in their eagerness to get to Molly.

The Sarjeant-at-Arms stepped out of the Matriarch's suite, and took up a stand in the middle of the corridor, between Molly and me and the mob. The Armourer came out and stood by his side. The Sarjeant had two big guns in his hands. He fired a series of warning shots over the heads of the mob, and it didn't even slow them down. So the Sarjeant and the Armourer armoured up, and the moment they did, a great roar went up from the mob, as though they'd just been given permission to do what they wanted all along. They armoured up, every one of them. The Sarjeant shouted a powerful Word, and swore briefly when nothing happened. Under normal circumstances, the Sarjeant had the ability to take control of torcs and force Droods to armour down, that he might discipline them. But for whatever reason, the Word wasn't working. He opened fire again, but his bullets had no effect. His weapons had only ever been intended for use against enemies of the Droods. The Armourer produced his latest toy, something he'd still been testing the last time I was home: a tanglefield grenade. He lobbed it along the floor towards the mob, and it exploded in a shower of shimmering energy fila-ments that wrapped themselves around the first row of the mob, and brought them crashing to the ground. But the maddened rows behind just vaulted over the strug-gling bodies and kept coming. I hadn't realised just how many of them there were—dozens of Droods in full ar-mour, coming to murder my Molly.

They hit the Sarjeant and the Armourer like a vi-cious tidal wave, and the sheer weight of so many bod-ies slammed the two men aside, throwing them back against the corridor walls. They struck out fiercely with their golden fists, felling man after man, but they could do nothing to stop the horde that rushed past them.

It all happened in a few moments, while Molly and I stood frozen in place, watching. I never really thought they'd get past the Sarjeant and the Armourer so easily. I'd never seen so many armoured figures coming at me, with murder on their minds. I'd never understood before how scary a blank golden face can be. Time . . . seemed to slow right down, giving me all the time I needed to study them.

Their golden armour was changing shape and form even as they advanced, becoming strange and awful, taking on the individual characteristics of their maddened owners. Changes that were usually only achieved after much thought and with great concentration were now thrown up in moments, imprinted on the armour by the sheer intensity of so many enraged minds. Their helms took on the shapes of strange beasts and unnatural insects, of horrid forms born out of nightmares. They weren't in control of their armour anymore; it was responding to their emotions, their instincts, and all their darker impulses. Monsters from the id.

New arms sprouted from golden sides, ending in jagged claws and pincers. Some of the mob dropped forward, and ran on all fours, while others became utterly inhuman, horrid creatures from the worst parts of the imagination; nightmares forged in gold and let loose in the waking world. All the things Droods are never supposed to be. The Armourer cried out in shock, to see such violation of the armour, and the Sarjeant swore fiercely as he fought against the rushing mob, but even as his fists rose and fell, striking men down left and right . . . he was just one man, and they were many.

The Armourer crashed to the floor, buried under a pile of flailing armoured figures. The rest of the mob vaulted right over them, intent only on Molly. The sounds they made . . . were not human sounds.

By this time Molly and I were running full pelt down the corridor, heading for my room, the mob ravening at our backs. It felt like we were running in slow motion. I could have armoured up, just grabbed Molly up and ran with her. But she needed to be free to use her magics, if it came to that. When we rounded the corner that led to my room, more of the mob were already there, waiting for us. Some were already inside my room, between me and the Merlin Glass. It sounded like they were smashing the place up. And even in the midst of all that was happening, I thought, *Why do they always break my things?* I reluctantly armoured up, ready to make a stand. I concentrated, and long golden blades protruded from my hands. I yelled to Molly to run, to run anywhere, just get away, already knowing there was nowhere she could run. And the Hall's protections wouldn't let her teleport out.

"Hell with that," she said crisply. "You think I'd leave you here, to face these crazy bastards alone? They'd kill you too, just for loving me. And I won't have that."

She gestured sharply, and a great storm wind hit the advancing mobs like a hammer. The raging winds blew in both directions at once, hitting both mobs head on. The smaller mob was completely blown away, tumbling head over heels back down the corridor. The main mob was stopped in its tracks, as winds of hurricane strength picked them up and threw them this way and that, golden bodies slamming against the walls and ceiling. Wood panelling cracked and fell apart. But some in the mob just bowed their misshapen golden heads and refused to be moved, trudging slowly forward into the face of the hurricane, driven on by the amazing strength of their armour. And soon enough, the storm blew itself out. There wasn't enough air on the top floor to support it. The mob started forward again, and Molly considered them thoughtfully.

"Please," I said. "Don't kill them. I don't think they're in their right minds. Droods aren't like this!"

"Oh Eddie," she said. "Always so charitable. Always so forgiving."

"Please, Molly! They don't know what they're doing!"

"I do."

She thrust out both her hands, and blasted them with hellfire, with a heat so vicious I actually flinched back from it, even inside my armour. The floor and the walls and the ceiling burst into flames, as great waves of searing liquid fire rolled over the advancing mob. It splashed across their golden forms, seemed to hesitate, and then dropped thickly away. The armour held, and the Droods walked through hellfire to get to us.

Molly cut off the flames with a gesture, though the rest of the corridor still burned fiercely. Priceless paintings and tapestries were reduced to ashes, and ancient marble statues blackened and cracked. The air shimmered with heat haze. Molly's hands closed into small determined fists, and she said a Word that sickened me just to hear it. Crackling energy beams shot from her eyes, and every Drood she hit was blasted right off his feet. But they always got up again, and the mob just kept coming. They weren't howling anymore. They moved slowly, in a terrible silence, as though they meant to enjoy their triumph.

"Ethel!" I cried out desperately. "You gave the Droods their torcs! Take them back! They were never meant to be used like this! Take them back!"

I can't, Eddie, she said sadly, compassionately. *You know I can't. The torcs were freely given and freely accepted, joined to every one of you at the genetic level. To take the torcs back now would kill them. Do you want me to kill them all, to save Molly?*

Tears were streaming down my face, inside my golden mask.

"Get into my room!" I yelled to Molly, as the last of her energy bolts crackled and died. "Take out the Droods there, find the Merlin Glass, and use it!"

"I don't know how! Only you know the Words to make it work!"

"You're a witch! Make it work! I'll hold them off!"

And I ran forward, right into the awful faces of the mob. I hit them hard, my hands rising and falling like hammers, beating them down and throwing them aside with savage force and all the terrible skills of an experienced field agent. Anywhen else, I would have littered the floor with bodies, but these were Droods, in their armour. I stopped them for a moment, because they'd never faced anyone like me before, but only for a moment. There were just too many of them. They swarmed all over me, grabbing on to my arms and hanging off me, dragging me down by sheer weight of numbers. I hit the floor hard, still struggling with all my strength. I forced myself back up on one knee, and that was as far as I got.

I saw the rest of the mob rush past me, just as Molly came racing back to help. She was screaming at the Droods to leave me alone, threatening them in an almost incoherent voice, energy trails flaring around her hands. The mobs hit her from both sides at once, yelling her name, baying for her blood. Golden hands formed into spikes, swords, and axes.

They slammed her back against the wall, even as she spat defiance at them. And I cried out as the first golden spike slammed into her stomach. Blood flew, but she wouldn't cry out. She gritted her teeth, while blood spurted between them. The spike pinned her to the wall, holding her in place as more blades cut and hacked at her. Blood sprayed on the air. Golden blades pierced her flailing arms, forcing them aside so more blades could slam into her chest, again and again and again. An axe sheared clean through her shoulder blade, and Molly finally screamed. She sounded like an animal, driven beyond all endurance. I was screaming too.

And then she stopped screaming. Her head lolled forward, blood spilling from her slack mouth. The mob fought each other to get at her. She still moved a little, as golden blades thrust in and out of her, but that was all. I couldn't scream anymore. I was sobbing too hard. I couldn't even get to her. They were still holding me down.

Thunder roared and lightning blasted, and everything stopped. Golden masks turned, uncertainly, as Isabella Metcalf appeared in the corridor out of nowhere. Her face held a cold, cold fury. She raised one hand, and vivid energies seized the Droods and pulled them away from Molly. They went flying down the corridor, flailing helplessly. Isabella didn't even look at them. All her attention was on Molly, sliding slowly down the wall to the bloody floor. The rest of the mob were frozen in place, stunned.

Outsiders couldn't teleport into the Hall. It just didn't happen. Drood Hall has defences that would keep out gods and demons. The sheer amount of power she must have used was staggering . . . Whispers began, in the fragile silence.

It's her. It's Isabella . . .

She looked just like the photo in her file. A tall, muscular woman in crimson biker leathers, with black short-cropped hair and a sharp intense face. She walked over to her sister Molly, and I swear the floor shook with every step. The Droods just watched her. They weren't a mob anymore. Many of them were already armouring down. Their faces were dazed, confused, as though awakening from a nightmare. We all looked on in silence as Isabella picked up Molly's still body effortlessly, ignoring the blood that welled from so many wounds. She looked at me, and I almost flinched back from what I saw in her face.

"I should never have trusted you with my sister," said Isabella.

And then she disappeared, taking Molly with her.

CHAPTER FOUR

Life Goes On, Whether You Want It to or Not

With Molly gone, the madness of the mob quickly subsided. Men and women stood around the length of the corridor, looking dazedly at one another, armouring down. Most couldn't remember what they'd just done, or even how they got there. A low murmur of confused voices rose and fell, as they asked each other the same questions, over and over again. Some vaguely remembered their armour taking on awful shapes, but flinched away from knowing what they did with them. A few did remember, so traumatised they ended up sitting on the floor with their heads in their hands, shaking and sobbing as tears ran down their cheeks. One kept saying *But I liked Molly, I did!* And another knelt before the splintered and bloodstained wall where Molly died, and smashed his face against it, over and over again, reducing his features to a bloody pulp, until someone came and gently led him away.

I didn't give a damn what they felt. It was nothing, compared to what I felt.

None of them could remember what it was that had got them so worked up, or what it was that had persuaded and encouraged them into such an extreme state of mind. They all had a vague belief it was one particular person, but no one could remember a name, or even a face. But they were all very sure it was someone they trusted, someone they had reason to trust. One of the family? Oh yes, they all said, in their shaken broken voices, quite definitely a Drood. The Sarjeant-at-Arms moved among them, slamming people up against walls and shouting his questions right into their faces, almost incandescent with rage; but no one had any answers for him.

And I sat on the floor, armoured down, hands lying helplessly in my lap, staring at nothing. Men and women who'd been parts of the mob only minutes before came listlessly forward and tried to talk to me, to explain themselves and apologise, or just to try and comfort me. I didn't hear them. The world was just a blur. A small part of me wanted to kill every one of them, just rise up and strike them all down for what they'd done, but I didn't have the energy. All I wanted to do was just sit there, and not think or feel anything.

After a while, the Armourer came over and crouched down before me. His knees made loud cracking noises. He was asking me things, in a quiet concerned voice, but I didn't care. I couldn't have answered anyway; my throat pulsed with a raw, vicious pain. I'd damaged it from screaming so hard. I could feel tears drying on my face. I couldn't remembered when I'd stopped crying. I finally realised the Armourer was asking me if I had any idea where Isabella might have taken Molly. I wondered about that, in a vague drifting way. Would Isabella have taken Molly back to the wildwoods, to bring her home, so she could be buried there among her beloved trees and animals? And if so, might I be allowed to visit her there? Or would the beasts of that ancient forest rise up and kill me on sight, for taking her away from them to the place where she was killed? And if so . . . would I just stand there and let them do it?

I struggled to my feet, with the Armourer's help, and looked desperately around me. I needed to be doing something, anything. I said something about going after Isabella, forcing the words past my ruined throat. The Armourer talked me out of it, with slow, kind, soothing words. Molly was beyond my help now, but I could still track down the bastard who'd created the mob that killed her. Molly wasn't the only victim here; many people in that mob would be seriously traumatised for years to come. My responsibility to Molly was over, said the Armourer, but I still had duties and responsibilities to the family. To find Molly's killer, and the Matriarch's. And make them pay in blood and suffering.

Just like Grandmother always said, *Anything, for the family.*

I looked around at the remains of the mob, already dispersing, or being led away, stumbling and crying, shaking their heads violently as though they could deny what had just happened. The Armourer followed my gaze, but misinterpreted my feelings.

"It wasn't their fault, Eddie. They weren't responsible for what they did. Someone deliberately drove them out of their minds, and aimed them at you like a bullet."

"Not me," I said. "They could have killed me, if they'd wanted. Someone wanted my Molly dead, at the hands of Droods."

The Armourer winced at the sound of my voice. Perhaps because it sounded so painful, or perhaps because of the cold harsh emotions he heard in it.

"Do you have any ideas who might be behind this, Eddie?" he said finally.

I shook my head. I wasn't ready to talk to him about the Immortals, not just yet. Not when I couldn't be sure who was who, or who might be listening. I felt cold, so cold, like I'd never feel warm or alive again. All the horror and loss and heartbreak had sunk right down, buried deep within me, so I could be focused and determined on what I had to do. I would find out who was responsible for this atrocity, and I would make them pay. Every damned one of them. I would make the Immortals die slow and hard, wade in blood up to my knees, and do terrible, unforgivable things, if that was what it took to avenge Molly Metcalf. Grieving could come later.

It was what Molly would have wanted.

The Armourer winced at what he saw in my face, and patted me gently, awkwardly, on the shoulder with his large engineer's hand.

"Come with me, Eddie," he said. "We'll go down to the Armoury. We can talk properly there. I put in my own wards and protections, after that Zero Tolerance business."

"All right," I said. "But I have to stop off somewhere first."

It still hurt to talk. My voice sounded to me like a dead man's. God alone knew what it sounded like to the Armourer. But he just nodded, and let me lead him into my room. The door was hanging open, half wrenched off its hinges. The mob had overturned and smashed my furniture, and broken everything else. It didn't matter to me. Not now. There was only room for one hatred in my head. I found the Merlin Glass, just lying on the floor, unnoticed and unbroken. It had its own inbuilt protections, like everything Merlin created. I picked it up and said the activating Words, and the Glass jumped out of my hand, growing in size to become a doorway. The Armourer and I stepped through into the Armoury.

The Armoury never changes much. A long series of interconnected stone chambers, with high arching ceilings, packed with scientific equipment, magical apparatus, and more weird shit than you could shake a Hand of Glory at. The air-conditioning system gurgles loudly to itself, when it feels like working. Multicoloured wiring, following a colour code nobody really understands, lies tacked haphazardly across the walls, you have to be really careful where you step, and there's always something seriously dangerous, unpleasant or suddenly explosive going on in the testing area.

But this was four o'clock in the morning, and the place was practically deserted. The Armourer sat me down in his favourite chair, and bustled around making us both a nice cup of tea. *Always good for what ails you,* he said briskly. He always felt better when he was doing something practical. He used proper tea leaves, from an old tea caddy with the willow pattern on the sides, and got out the good china, and a silver tea strainer presented to us by Queen Victoria. Because this wasn't an occasion for a tea bag in a plastic mug, and find your own milk and sugar. I just sat in the chair and let him get on with it. The moment I sat down, all my strength seemed to run right out of me.

I looked vaguely round the Armoury. Most of the lights had been turned off, giving the deserted labs a calm, reflective ambience. A few lab assistants were still working quietly, here and there. They should have been tucked up in bed at this ungodly early hour of the morning, but there are always a few night owls. They tapped away at computer keyboards, or scribbled frantically on oversized writing pads, lost in their own little worlds. One of them appeared to have a halo, but I decided not to mention it.

They probably didn't even know what had just happened in the Hall. They didn't know what had happened to the Matriarch, and my Molly.

The Armourer served me tea, with honey and lemon. I sipped at the tea automatically. It tasted good, soothing.

"No jaffa cakes, I'm afraid," said the Armourer, pulling up a chair and sitting down opposite me. "Damn lab assistants go through them like locusts. I've got half a packet of chocolate hobnobs around here somewhere, if you'd like . . . Ah. Well. Maybe later, eh?"

We sat quietly together for a while, drinking our tea, thinking . . . doing our best to come to terms with so much having happened so quickly, in such a short time. Both our worlds, overturned and destroyed, in just a few hours. Uncle Jack had lost his mother, I had lost my Molly, and just maybe the Droods had lost their innocence. Trained all their life to serve the good, they had been made to do an evil thing, and some of them might never get over it. We all have monsters within us, but most of us never have to see what happens when they get loose. Droods are taught from an early age to roll with the punches, to take what punishment you have to, to get things done, to carry on the family business and mourn your losses later. But this . . . was hard.

"You never knew your Aunt Clara, did you, Eddie?" Uncle Jack said finally. His voice was calm, quiet, reflective. "My wife. She died when you were still a baby. Blood vessel just popped, in her brain. Dead before she hit the floor. It happens like that, sometimes. We're Droods, with every advantage, but we still get sick and die sometimes, just like everyone else. She was always so full of life . . . my Clara. I left the field to come back here. There was nothing I could do for her, but I still had a young son to raise. I never left the Hall again."

"You never talk about your son, Uncle Jack," I said.

"He let himself down," the Armourer said flatly. "He let all of us down. Not all sons turn out as well as you, Eddie. If his mother hadn't died . . . if I'd been around more when he was younger, instead of running around half of Eastern Europe stamping out political bushfires . . . Kipling was right. *If* is the cruellest word. The point is, don't bury yourself in work, like I did. You're still young. You can still find someone else."

"Not like Molly," I said.

"Well, no," said the Armourer.

We sat, and drank our tea, and thought some more. The tea soothed my throat, if not my heart.

"So," the Armourer said. "That . . . was the notorious Isabella Metcalf. Impressive."

"You know her?" I said.

"Well, of her. The female Indiana Jones of the supernatural world. Always looking for answers in strange places, digging up things any sane person would let lie. She always has to *know*, and to hell with the consequences. Not for any particular end, or purpose; knowledge has always been its own reward, with Isabella. She's petitioned me a dozen times for access to the Old Library. Had to turn her down, of course. She's not family."

There was another long pause, the Armourer making it clear with long looks from under his bushy white eyebrows that he was waiting for me to contribute something to the conversation. So I told him what I'd discovered about the Immortals, and their possible infiltration of our family. He took it surprisingly well; no furious outbursts, no insistence that such a thing couldn't be possible. He just leant back in his chair, sipping slowly from his cup, while his expression grew colder and colder, and his eyes became positively arctic. I'd never seen him look so dangerous. When I'd finished, draining my cup of tea to sooth my raw throat, he nodded slowly several times.

"Zero Tolerance and Manifest Destiny was bad enough," he said finally. "They might have been traitors, but at least they were family. These are outsiders! I feel like I've been violated. How long has this been going on?"

"Who knows?" I said. "Given who and what they are, it could be decades or even centuries."

"That maddened mob didn't just happen," said the Armourer. "Someone messed with their heads, used them to do the dirty work, to hurt them as well as you. Makes me sick."

"Have you ever heard of the Immortals before, Uncle Jack?"

"Vague rumours, down the years. Stories . . . of the men who live forever. Always kingmakers rather than kings, always the power behind the throne; because kings and thrones come and go, but the Immortals go on forever. If there's never any obvious villain to blame, blame the Immortals. I never paid much attention to the stories. There are always stories, in our line of work. The Immortals are . . . the urban legends of the supernatural field."

He scowled into his cup, brooding, and I left him alone to think through the implications. It's not every day your whole worldview gets overturned. I looked around the Armoury. The handful of lab assistants were still working quietly, or sitting staring off into space, contemplating the creation of awful and appalling things to throw at the family's enemies. Our lab assistants are always at their most dangerous when they're thinking. Word of the Matriarch's death hadn't got down here yet. Or Molly's. We keep the Armoury isolated from the rest of the Hall for many good reasons. But eventually word would get down here, and I wanted to be long gone before that happened.

The Armourer started talking again, but not about the Immortals.

"I never really thought my mother would ever die. She'd always been there, so I thought she always would. I thought she'd go on forever, too stubborn to give in to anything as small as death. I'm all that's left of the main line now. Father, mother, brother, sister . . . all gone."

"Do you think it's possible the family is responsible for the murder of my parents?" I said bluntly.

"James and I looked into their deaths, the moment we heard what had happened," said the Armourer. "We questioned everyone we could get our hands on, and we weren't polite about it, either. If anyone had known anything, they would have told us, after what we did, and threatened to do. We were both a little crazy, after losing Emily. And Charles too, of course. We both liked Charles. But Emily . . . was always special to us. She was the best of us. She could have been a greater field agent than me, or James. But she met your father, and then she had you, and after that she semiretired from the field, only working on information-gathering missions, with your father. Do you remember much about your parents, Eddie?"

I thought about it for a moment, before answering. "I was very young when they were killed. I'm not sure how much of what I remember of them is actual memory, and how much is what I want to remember. When I think of them, I see their official family portrait, rather than any real image, because I've seen the portrait far more often than I ever saw them."

"We never turned up any evidence it was anything other than a series of stupid mistakes. Bad advance information, insufficient preparation, a mission that went wrong every way it could from the moment they hit the ground. It does happen. Do you really think I'd still be working for the family if I thought they were responsible for the death of my sister? We all loved Emily. She would have been the next Matriarch, if she'd lived."

"Could that have been a motive?" I said. "Could she have been murdered because someone didn't want her taking control of the most powerful family in the world?"

"We looked," said the Armourer. "We never found anything. Not even a suggestion of anything out of place. But now, I wonder; if there really are enemy agents hidden inside the family, posing as Droods . . . I really hoped we'd put this paranoia behind us, with the destruction of Zero Tolerance. Now we have to worry about the Immortals? The men who could be anyone? If it's true . . . then we can't trust anyone anymore."

"It could give us an answer to an old mystery," I said. "Who was responsible for bringing the Loathly Ones into this world? Maybe it wasn't our fault after all; it was theirs."

"And they could have killed Sebastian," said the Armourer. "I always said only one of the family could have got to him, locked securely away in the isolation wards."

"That would simplify things," I said. "God forbid there should be two sets of traitors within the family."

"I'll drink to that," said the Armourer, producing a hip flask of brandy and liberally lacing what was left of his tea.

My throat was feeling a lot better. The Armourer must have put something in my tea too.

"There is something else I wanted to talk to you about," I said carefully. "Something I was wondering about even before all that's happened. Uncle James once had a gun he said could fire bullets made of strange matter, that could pierce Drood armour."

"Yes . . ." said the Armourer. "I remember that. James asked me to make it for him. A very difficult project . . . quite a challenge, actually. I had it destroyed, after he died. It was just too dangerous to have around. I wanted it gone, and no threat to the family."

"But why did you make it in the first place?" I said. "Why create a gun specifically designed to kill Droods?"

"Because he asked me to," said the Armourer. "He was the legendary Grey Fox, after all, and if he said it was necessary, who was I to doubt him? I just assumed he had a good reason. Now, I have to wonder . . . did he suspect there were enemies hidden among us, even back then? He never said anything. He always kept things close to his chest. Even from me . . ."

The Armourer sighed heavily, and made a clear effort to pull himself together. "Come along, boy. If you've been declared a target by the Immortals, it's my responsibility to see you properly armed and prepared. Look at this: a new Colt Repeater, because you wore out the last one. The new and improved version holds every kind of ammunition mortal mind could conceive of: hollow points, dumdums, silver, wood, blessed and cursed. Just say aloud what kind of ammo you need, and the Colt will have it. Even you couldn't miss the target with this version, and you'll never run out of ammo. Just try not to get it wet. Ruins the finish."

"Where does all the ammunition come from?" I said, accepting the new Colt from him. "Is it held in a subspace locker, of some kind?"

"Oh please," said the Armourer, choosing not to watch as I struggled to fit the Colt into my battered old shoulder holster. "Subspace is so last season. And don't pretend you'd understand the physics, even if I did try to explain it to you. You never were any good at maths, Eddie. Now, what new gadgets have I got for you . . . Oh! Yes!" He glared at me. "I remember now. You're on my special list. No more new toys for you, because you didn't use the last lot I gave you."

"Oh, come on!" I said. "You're not still sulking over that, are you? I was busy! There was a lot going on! I just . . . never got around to using them."

"You aren't getting anything new until you've proved to me you can handle the last batch properly," the Armourer said firmly.

I sighed quietly. Some arguments you just know you're never going to win. "All right, talk me through how to use them again. You know that always cheers you up. And it's been so long I've probably forgotten something important anyway."

"Wouldn't surprise me in the least," the Armourer said darkly. "Here we are. I had them put out specially, when I heard you were coming home. This . . . is the Gemini Duplicator. Looks like a simple gold signet ring. You activate it by pressing hard against it with the adjoining fingers. Put it on, put it on . . . Yes. You now have the option of bilocation. And please, I have already heard every possible variation of every joke involving the word *bi*, and not one of them was worth the breath it took to tell them. Your generation thinks it invented sex. In this case, bilocation means the ability to be in more than one place at the same time. Means you can get twice as much work done, whilst at the same time providing an unbreakable alibi. Sort of like multitasking, only more so. And yes, I am way ahead of you as always, you can make more than two of yourself at the same time, but the more duplicates you call up, the harder it will become to concentrate, to control you all. Make too many of yourself, and you could end up lost in the crowd, and unable to find your way back."

He handed me a small black box, containing a pair of silver cuff links.

"Ah," I said. "I remember those. The Chameleon Codex. They pick up trace DNA from people I come into contact with, so I can make myself into an exact duplicate of them. Oh, I can see endless possibilities for fun here. I can do women as well as men, can't I?"

"You have no shame," said the Armourer. "Now, this is a skeleton key, made from real human bone. Don't ask who it came from; you really don't want to know. Opens any lock, physical or electronic, and in an emergency, will even open a bottle of wine. Right. That's it. I expect a full report on all of them as soon as this is over, detailing every way you made use of them, complete with problems and recommendations. And then I'll let you see some of the really fun stuff I've been working on."

I slipped the cuff links into place, popped the skeleton key in my pocket, and then looked thoughtfully at the Armourer.

"Uncle Jack . . . There's something I never told you. When the Blue Fairy was killed last year, during the great spy game, I went to take the stolen torc off his body. But when I touched it with my armoured finger-tip, the armour . . . absorbed the Blue Fairy's torc. Just sucked it right in. I kept quiet about it, because the implications worried me. There's still a lot we don't understand about this new armour Ethel's given us. But now I have to wonder . . . Could the Matriarch's killer have taken her torc in the same way? And if he did, would that make his armour twice as strong? You read my report on what happened when I encountered the old monster, Grendel Rex, the Unforgiven God, in Tunguska last year. He absorbed the torcs of others, to make himself a living god. Until the family took him down, and imprisoned him under the permafrost. Could something like that happen again?"

"You do enjoy giving me things to worry about, don't you?" said the Armourer. He scowled thoughtfully. "We still don't know enough about the properties and limitations of the new armour. We treat it like the old armour because that's what we're used to, but it's potentially very different. It is strange matter, after all. Not of this earth . . . Ethel? Are you listening?"

Oh sure! Ethel said cheerfully. *I'm always listening, except when I'm not. But there isn't much I can tell you about the armour I provide. It's as close to the old armour as I could make it, only more so. I'm constantly amazed at all the wonderful things you've learned to do with it. But I can't help you with its limitations; this world and its physical restrictions are still something of a mystery to me.*

"Are we going to have to go through the privacy thing again, Ethel?" I said.

But you weren't alone! There were two of you!

"Sometimes two people need their privacy even more," I said pointedly.

Oh pooh! You're talking about that sex thing, aren't you. Like I care . . .

"Let us talk about the armour," the Armourer said doggedly. "Eddie, did you feel any stronger, after you'd absorbed the Blue Fairy's torc?"

"Not that I noticed," I said. "But given how strong the armour is normally . . . I have just survived being inside a hotel when it collapsed, but so did Luther, and he only had the standard armour."

"I can see I'll have to run a whole series of tests," said the Armourer, brightening up a bit. "The whole family depends on the armour. We need to know everything there is to know about it."

Good luck with that, Ethel said cheerfully.

"Go away, Ethel," I said firmly.

I've been talking to your poltergeist, said Ethel. *Oh, the things I could tell . . .*

I waited, but her vague sense of presence was gone. It's never easy talking to Ethel. She does her best to be human, but it's only ever an act. So much more than human, but hopefully less than a god. I couldn't help noticing she hadn't said anything about Molly's death. I hadn't raised the subject for fear she'd start wittering on again about how life and death are just different states of being. I really wasn't in the mood. I took the Merlin Glass out of the subspace pocket it had disappeared into on arriving in the Armoury, and every alarm in the world went off at once. The Armoury was full of bells, sirens, flashing lights, the works. All the lab assistants galvanised into action and dived for cover. Uncle Jack ran madly around the Armoury, shutting down one system after another, swearing at the top of his voice. After a while, peace and quiet grudgingly returned. Lab assistants reappeared here and there, peering cautiously out of their hiding places with eyes like owls, brandishing various nasty-looking weapons. The Armourer looked them over, with cold calculation.

"Very good, boys and girls, excellent reflexes. Claudia, put that portable disintegrator back where you found it. Kenneth, has Matron seen those gills? And Gregory, where did that trapdoor come from? I've told you all before—you're not to add modifications to the Armoury without submitting plans in advance. All right, everyone, back to work. Make me proud. Come up with something really upsetting, and there'll be ice cream for everyone."

He turned his back on them and looked at me.

"Sorry about that," I said.

"Doesn't matter," he said. "The occasional emergency and threat to life helps keep them on their toes."

"Why didn't the Glass set off the alarms when it brought us here?"

"Because I've programmed the Armoury to ignore that. Just hadn't got round to telling it to ignore the Glass' presence. It really is a very dangerous item." He looked at the Merlin Glass thoughtfully. "In fact, the more I discover about it, the more disturbed I become. The Librarian sent me a book he found in the Old Library the other day. It had a lot to say about the Merlin Glass, mostly operating instructions, all the practical stuff; but not a lot about why it was created in the first place. Officially, it was a gift to the Droods, from Merlin himself, for *services rendered*. Back then, that could cover a whole lot of ground. Hardly anything in the book about the Glass' history, who used to own it, and what happened to them. Though I did come across a rather interesting footnote, suggesting that there might be Someone or Something imprisoned inside the Glass. Apparently you can sometimes catch glimpses of it in the Glass' reflection. It might be what powers the Glass."

"As long as it doesn't turn out to be a small Victorian girl with long blond hair," I said solemnly.

"Never liked those books," said the Armourer. "Creeped the hell out of me when I was a boy. Entirely unsuitable for children, I've always said."

"How is William?" I said, carefully changing the subject. "Has he settled into his position as head Librarian?"

"Not really," said the Armourer. "He's still crazy, and not in a good way. But if anyone in this family knows anything that matters about the Immortals, it will be William. He knows everything. When he can remember it."

"He didn't know much about the Apocalypse Door," I pointed out.

"You need to pop into the Old Library and have a good talk with him," said the Armourer. "I'll stay here, where it's safe and sane."

"What if the Sarjeant-at-Arms turns up here looking for me, and starts putting the pressure on you?"

"Like to see him try," said the Armourer. "I think sometimes people forget I used to be a field agent. I'm just in the mood to get unpleasant and unreasonable with someone. I've got a set of depleted uranium knuckle-dusters around here somewhere."

I never know when he's joking.

CHAPTER FIVE

Secret Discussions, with Unexpected References to Heaven and Hell

I stepped through the Merlin Glass into the Old Library, and the Glass shrank down and disappeared back into its subspace pocket with even more haste than usual. As though it was actually disturbed by the place I'd brought it to. Which was fair enough. The Old Library contains far more than just shelves and shelves of old books. It is a place of secrets, a depository of knowledge too terrible for the everyday world. I was standing somewhere among the rows and rows of stacks, stretching away in every direction I looked. Not that far away, the Librarian, William, and his young assistant, Rafe, were talking quietly together, so intent on the book before them they hadn't even noticed my arrival.

I took a moment to look around me. Simple, functional, standing shelves packed with books rose all the way to the gloomy ceiling. The floor was just bare wooden boards, that clearly hadn't known wax or polish in a very long time. There were no windows, the only illumination a sourceless golden glow that seemed to come from everywhere and nowhere. Presumably real lights would be too much of a fire risk. I had to wonder about central heating, since the air was toasty warm—again, presumably to help preserve the books. There wasn't a touch of dust anywhere, and not a single cobweb, despite the Old Library having been lost and abandoned for centuries before I rediscovered it.

The golden glow reminded me of the last days of summer, and the place felt more like a chapel than a library. A repository of wisdom, of worship. And yet, not a comfortable setting. Although the many rows of standing shelves limited my view of the Old Library, it still felt unnaturally large, as though the stacks stretched away farther in every direction than the human mind could comfortably accept. There were rumours that the Old Library was actually growing, quietly, to make room for all the books and papers entrusted to it, and I was quite prepared to believe it. Just looking around I had no idea how to find an exit, without the help of a map, a compass, and a ball of thread to follow. And I also had to wonder: if this was a labyrinth, might there be a monster somewhere, lurking at the heart of the maze?

Rafe was patiently trying to persuade William to put aside his work for a while, and get some rest. William ignored him, standing stooped before a great oversized volume set out on a podium. The Librarian was a frail old man, with a sad lost face, wearing a bright cheerful dressing gown and a pair of fluffy bunny slippers. His bushy grey hair seemed to stick out in every direction at once, but his mouth was firm and his gaze was sharp and keen. William had a great mind, but a lot had happened to it, little of it good.

The assistant Librarian, Rafe (*never call me Raphael, I am not a turtle*) was a pleasant young man with a bright beaming face. He always looked like he'd got dressed in a hurry and didn't give a damn. He had a first-class mind, and was devoted to the old Librarian. He was currently trying to persuade William to be sensible, and getting nowhere.

"You need to go to bed, William; get some proper rest."

"Haven't got a bed," William said craftily. "I've got a nice little cot, and my very own blanket. All I need."

"When was the last time you got a good sleep?" said Rafe.

The old man shrugged. "My memory doesn't go back that far. Besides, I don't like to sleep. I have dreams . . . bad dreams. And anyway, I've far too much work to do. So many books, so little time . . ."

They both looked round sharply as I approached, but William accepted my sudden appearance the way he accepted everything, because everything was equally important, or unimportant, to him. Rafe gave me a hard look.

"Hello, Eddie. I didn't think anyone could just walk into the Old Library these days, without setting off all kinds of alarms."

"I think the Merlin Glass is getting sneaky," I said. "That's what happens when you hang around with Droods. Hello, Rafe. Hello, William."

"Hello, hello, nice to see you, don't bother me now, I'm busy." William turned back to the book on the podium. "If you want to make yourself useful, see if you can find my socks. Someone's been stealing them."

I looked at Rafe. "I thought the whole idea of allow-

ing William to live down here was that it would help to
stabilise him?"

"That was the theory, yes," said Rafe, coming over
to join me. "But it appears that there's stable, and then
there's stable. He knows who he is, and where he is, and
his work is impeccable; everything else tends to vary
from day to day."

"I like it down here," William said loudly. "I'm not
ready to live in the Hall. Too many people. Had enough
of that living in the asylum. No, no, I'm not at all ready
for people . . . I'm fine down here. Fine." He broke off,
and looked carefully left and right. "Though I'm not entirely alone, down here. Not strictly speaking. There's
Someone in here with me. Someone, or Something. It
watches me. Or watches over me . . . hard to tell."

I raised an eyebrow to Rafe, who shook his head
firmly. "I heard about what happened to the Matriarch,
Eddie, and to Molly. I'm so sorry. I can't believe it. It's
been years since there was a murder in the Hall, let
alone two in one night."

"Eighteen fifty-two," said William, unexpectedly.
"And that was a murder/suicide. We were a lot tougher
about cousins marrying, in those days."

"I popped up for a quick look," said Rafe. "Everyone was running around, shouting and screaming like
mad things. Couldn't get a straight answer out of anyone. Everyone's looking for you, Eddie. Either because
they think you're guilty, or because they want you to tell
them what to do. You did lead the family once, after all."

"Once was enough," I said. "Let the Sarjeant-at-
Arms run his investigation. He knows what he's doing."

"Never thought I'd hear you saying good things about
the Sarjeant," said Rafe. "What have things come to?"

"In a situation like this, a merciless thug and bully

is just what we need," I said. "If there are answers to be got, he'll get them. But I can't help feeling . . . there won't be anything left behind for him to find. This was a professional hit. Someone put a lot of time and effort into planning it . . ."

William slammed his book shut, and spun round to smile cheerfully at me. "It's really quite fun, having everyone as paranoid as me, for as change."

"William," said Rafe. "The Matriarch is dead. Murdered."

"Never liked her," William said briskly. "She never liked me. She was a real cow when she was younger, and age did not mellow her. Oh, I'll stand up to see her avenged; she's family. But I'm too old, too talented, and too crazy to bother with crocodile tears."

"Molly's dead too," I said.

William looked at me. "Who?"

"Molly! Molly Metcalf! She used to come and visit you, while you were in the madhouse! You met her dozens of times; you must remember her!"

The Librarian's lower lip trembled, and he looked down at his hands, crestfallen. "I'm sorry, Eddie. I try not to remember anything about that place."

"Did they treat you badly?" said Rafe.

"It's more like . . . it worried me, how much at home I felt. Like I belonged there . . . Far more than I ever did here. I'll think about Molly, Eddie. I'm sure she'll come back to me . . . What did you come here looking for? No one ever comes down here just to see me, for which I am inordinately grateful. So, what do you want? All the knowledge in the world is on these shelves, somewhere. Try me. My thoughts are clear, even if my memory isn't what it was. If it ever was . . . Who can tell? I like butterscotch."

"I need to know about the Immortals," I said. "And the Apocalypse Door."

"The Immortals are just a legend!" said Rafe. "Everyone knows that. There are a number of technically immortal individuals out there, or at least, very long-lived . . . but you're probably already familiar with most of those. Mr. Stab, of course. The Djinn Jeanie. The Griffin . . ."

"No, he died just recently, in the Nightside," said William. "And his appalling wife. I got a letter from the chap who runs the Nightside . . . Walker! That's the fellow! Yes. Apparently Satan turned up personally, just to drag the Griffins down into the Pit. Well, that's the Nightside for you. Terrible place. I don't know why we don't just go in there in force, and Do Something about it."

"I said that," I said. "It seems there's an old and very binding pact: no Droods allowed in the Nightside."

"Really?" said Rafe. "And what do we get out of it?"

"I did ask the Matriarch," I said. "And she made a point of changing the subject." I looked at William. "Why would Walker be writing letters to you? Do you and he know each other?"

"Who can say?" said William. "Immortals . . . There's the Lord of Thorns, Old Father Time, Jimmy Thunder God for Hire, the Regent of Shadows . . ."

"We don't talk about him!" Rafe said immediately.

"Well, pardon me for breathing," William said testily. "Even when my mind was working perfectly, I never could be bothered remembering who was In and who was Out. The important thing is, there are any number of individual immortals running around, making nuisances of themselves, and always have been. Not all of them human, of course. I once met a Lamia in Liverpool . . ." William grinned nastily. "Big teeth . . ."

"But never a family of Immortals," said Rafe. "Not organised, like us . . ."

William frowned suddenly. "There are at present two hundred and seventeen books missing from the Old Library, not including folios, bound manuscripts and collected letters. No doubt more absences will make themselves known. With no Index to consult, we can only deduce what these titles might have been from gaps on the shelves, and references in other books. It's always possible some of these books were removed because they contained information on the Immortals. Or the Apocalypse Door. Lots of people have been bothering me about that Door, just recently."

"Interesting items have turned up in Alexander King's secret files, removed from Place Gloria," said Rafe. "The Independent Agent hoarded all kinds of secret knowledge and lost information. We've uncovered strange and wonderful stuff, including a whole crate of books from alternate Earths, where history had taken very different turns. One was written in Martian. With very unpleasant illustrations. New material is turning up all the time, in truckloads. They just dump it here, once a week, and leave it for us to sort out. As if we didn't have enough on our plate already. Just identifying, sorting and indexing the Old Library's contents is taking us forever."

"And the Matriarch won't allow us any extra help, because so much of the material is *sensitive*," said William, disparagingly. "Silly cow. If you can't trust a Drood, who can you trust?"

"The Matriarch is dead, William," said Rafe.

"Oh all right, I'll have a word with her later. You know, I'm almost sure I saw something about the Apocalypse Door just recently . . ."

He tottered away and started rummaging through an old tea chest full of papers.

"How is he?" I said quietly to Rafe. "Really?"

"Not good," Rafe admitted. "Better some days than others. He still has a brilliant mind, when it's working. But there's no doubt all those years in the madhouse put their mark upon him."

"And there's no telling how much damage the Heart did to his mind, before he fled the Hall." I frowned. "I think we need to put up the money and hire a major-league telepath, and have them dig around inside his head."

"I have suggested that, on more than one occasion, but the Matriarch was always very firm," said Rafe. "She wouldn't allow it. Apparently William knows far too much about this family, too many dirty little secrets. Things no outsider can be allowed to know. Even if William can't remember them. We do have a few telepaths in the family . . ."

"You have got to be kidding," I said. "I wouldn't trust that bunch to guess my weight. I certainly wouldn't let them trample around inside a mind that's been messed about with as much as William's has . . . They might never get out again. The Armourer did say he'd come up with some kind of mind-scanning device . . . but his methods aren't exactly subtle, either."

"You just have to give William some time," said Rafe. "He'll recover, eventually."

"What can you tell me about the rogue Drood known as Tiger Tim?" I said, deliberately changing the subject. "His name came up in connection with the LA auction and, surprisingly, with Doctor Delirium."

William looked up suddenly from his tea chest. "Now there's a name from the past! Timothy Drood . . . Yes.

Nasty little man. Nice enough when you had something he wanted, but it was always him first and everyone else second. What we used to call a bad seed, in my young days. I can't believe someone hasn't killed him yet, if only on general principles . . . He was hiding out somewhere in South America, last I heard. Peru?"

"He's moved, since then," said Rafe. "Just ahead of being kicked out, as usual. He's holed up deep in the Amazon rain forest these days."

"The same area as Doctor Delirium," I said.

"Well yes, technically," said Rafe. "But the Amazon rain forest does cover a hell of a lot of ground. They're not exactly neighbours."

"Doctor Delirium and Tiger Tim," said William. "The team-up you never expected! The horror, the horror . . ." He got the giggles, waved a careless hand and turned back to his tea chest. He grabbed something, studied it closely, and then straightened up waving a dusty file triumphantly. "Here it is! Knew it was somewhere near the top . . . *The Shudder File.* Carefully annotated in the Independent Agent's own handwriting. And according to this Post-it note on the cover, from the Drood cleanup team, Alexander King kept this particular file inside a locked box, inside a wall safe. So it must be worth looking at . . ." He opened the file and leafed quickly through it. "Yes . . . Oh, this is bad and nasty stuff, all right. A lot of supernatural and super-science weapons and devices, all of them banned by any number of international treaties. The Speaking Gun, the Ubershreck Device, Mephisto's Minuet . . . All the kind of thing no one in their right mind would want to mess with."

"Did Alexander King actually possess these things?" I said, reaching for the file. Walker pulled it away, glaring at me as I held my hands up in surrender. "I just meant," I said, "that if some of these things are still lying around Place Gloria, we need to warn the people working there."

"Oh no," said William. "This is more of a wants list—items he was interested in acquiring. If only so other people couldn't use them against him. Ah! Yes, here we are! The Apocalypse Door!"

"What does it say?" I said, trying to peer over his shoulder. He hurried around the other side of the chest, so I couldn't.

"Wait a minute, wait a minute, I'm reading!" he said testily. "Hmmm. Not a lot, actually. It's not just another hell gate, however. A hell gate is just a rather dramatic name for a dimensional door that allows limited travel between the various planes of existence. The Apocalypse Door . . . is far more than that. Oh yes. It opens the Gates of Hell, and lets out all that may be found there. The Dukes of Hell, all the major and minor demons, all of the fallen and all of the damned, from the very beginnings of Time. To do what they will upon the Earth. Even Satan himself will come forth, the ancient Enemy, to trample the cities of man beneath his cloven hooves . . ."

"Hell on Earth," I said. "Forever, and ever, and ever . . ."

"How is that even possible?" said Rafe, snatching the file out of William's hands, and studying it himself. "How could any material being release those imprisoned by God?"

"A disturbing thought, I'll grant you," said William, sneaking up on Rafe and grabbing the file back again. He pulled a face at Rafe. "No one knows how old the Apocalypse Door is, but it says here . . . that the

Door was possibly created by one Nicholas Hobb, the Serpent's Son. Oh, we are definitely into legend here, rather than history. According to these handwritten notes . . . the Door has been passed back and forth for centuries, from one careful owner to another, its true nature largely forgotten. Most of its owners thought of it as little more than a curiosity, a charming fake, or just a conversation piece. The last known owner was . . . the Collector! I did hear he was dead; maybe that's how the Door came up for auction in Los Angeles."

"I don't think the Really Old Curiosity Shoppe people realised just how important the Door was," I said, just to show I was keeping up. "If they had, they'd have held a separate auction just for the Door, under much heavier security."

"Now this really is interesting!" said William, sitting precariously on the edge of the tea chest. "It's not just enough to own the Door, you see. Oh no! You need very specific and powerful magics to open it. Or it's just a door. There's nothing here, unfortunately, as to what those items might be . . . but I'm guessing they'd be very hard to come by. Don't look at me like that! I'm just curious!"

"Magic isn't really Doctor Delirium's area of expertise," I said.

"No," said Rafe. "But I did hear something about Tiger Tim breaking into the Infernal Museum in Vienna last year, and making off with a whole bunch of rare and restricted grimoires . . ."

"It's all coming together, isn't it?" I said. "And not in a good way. Presumably, Doctor Delirium will threaten to open the Door, unless all the governments of the world give him . . . well, everything he asks for. And he could ask for *anything*, because who would dare say no?"

"What if the world calls his bluff?" said Rafe. "How can it profit the Doctor, or Tiger Tim, to actually open the Apocalypse Door?"

"Indeed," said William, dropping the file carelessly back into the tea chest. "There's absolutely nothing in there about closing the Door again, or compelling the damned to go back through it into Hell again." He sniffed loudly. "Bit of a design fault there, if you ask me. Unless the Door's designer was having a bit of a down day. I get those."

"And if Doctor Delirium is pissed off enough at being laughed at and not taken seriously all these years . . ." I said. "Oh, we have got to get the Door back from him, before he does something silly that we'll all regret."

"Would Tiger Tim really let Doctor Delirium open the Door?" said Rafe. "I mean, he may be rogue, but he's still a Drood. Would he really allow the end of the world?"

"Probably," I said. "When we go bad, we go all the way."

"And Timothy was always so much more than just a rogue," said William. "I remember him, though I really wish I didn't. Not actually a sociopath, as such, but a long way down that road. When he set his mind to something, he wouldn't let anyone or anything get in his way. He tried to force the Armourer to open the Armageddon Codex for him once, so he could make off with the forbidden weapons. Half killed the old boy in the process. If Timothy hadn't been interrupted and driven out . . . He has no reason to love this family, or the world, or anything but himself."

"Janissary Jane once told me about a dimension where demons ran loose in the material plane," I said. "Hell got out, and slaughtered everything in its path, destroying civilisation after civilisation. Jumping from planet to planet, leaving worlds burning like cinders in the dark, and suns screaming as they died. Jane and the people she was with ended up having to destroy everything, to stop the demons. They used the Deplorable End, and wiped out a whole universe."

"Isn't that what you used?" Rafe said carefully. "To destroy the Hungry Gods?"

"Yes," I said. "And I don't have another one."

"I'm not sure whether I feel relieved or not," said Rafe.

William looked around abruptly, his eyes darting, listening to something only he could hear. The tension in his face and body was written so clearly it raised all the hackles on my neck. I glared around me into the golden glow, but nothing moved among the stacks, and the shadows seemed entirely still and empty.

"It's here," whispered William, standing very still. "I just catch glimpses of it, sometimes, out of the corner of my eyes. I can feel its presence, like a pressure on my soul. Feel it watching me . . . I think it wants to tell me something. Something I don't want to know . . ."

I looked at Rafe, but he just shook his head helplessly.

And then we all looked round, at the sound of approaching footsteps. Perfectly normal, human footsteps, making no attempt to hide themselves. We all relaxed, though not entirely, when Harry Drood appeared at the end of the stacks, accompanied by his partner, the half human, half demon hellspawn, Roger Morningstar. Harry smiled smugly at us, as though he'd done something clever. Roger's smile was rather more disturbing.

The hellspawn was tall, slender, but powerfully built, looking entirely at home in an expensive Armani suit. He had an unnaturally pale face, dark hair, thin lips, and a gaze you didn't like to meet for more than a few seconds. Roger was an infernal creature, and it showed. He strolled towards us, following Harry, moving with almost inhuman grace, like a predator that had escaped from the zoo, and had absolutely no intention of ever going back.

I knew up close he would smell of sulphur and blood and sour milk, like all hellspawn. And as he sauntered along between the stacks to join us, he left dark scorch marks behind him on the wooden floor. (Though I couldn't help noticing that the burn marks quickly disappeared, as though the floor was healing itself. There's a lot about the Old Library we don't understand yet.) Rafe scowled at Roger and Harry with equal disapproval.

"We really are going to have to install some better security. And just possibly some flashing lights, warning sirens, and a whole bunch of concealed mantraps. It's getting so just anyone can walk in here these days."

Harry ignored him, and nodded briefly to me. "Thought I'd find you hiding out down here, Eddie."

I ignored him, to glare at Roger. "What are you doing here, Morningstar? I thought you were safely abroad, on some terribly important mission that kept you well away from the rest of us?"

"Harry contacted me," said Roger, in a voice that chilled the blood without even trying. "He told me about the Matriarch, and the witch. So I made a swift return, via the infernal underground. To support my dear Harry, in the hour of his family's need."

He didn't say anything about being sorry for my loss, for Molly, and the Matriarch. He knew no one would have believed him.

"I am down here because I don't want to be found,"

I said. "There's important work to be done and I don't wish to be . . . distracted."

"I know. Roger and I have been listening," murmured Harry.

"Fascinating stuff," said Roger.

I met his gaze squarely, just to show I could. "You're one of Hell's creatures, Roger. What do you know about the Apocalypse Door?"

"Not a thing," said Roger. "Can't help you, Eddie."

"Are you, by any chance, getting ready to run out on the family again, Eddie?" said Harry.

"And leave you in charge again?" I said. "I don't think so. Not after the balls-up you made of things the last time I stepped out for a moment. I'm not abandoning my family; I'm just preparing to do my duty as a field agent. I have a history with Doctor Delirium, and that makes me the most suited agent to track him down and step on him hard, before he does something silly with the Apocalypse Door. How do you feel about the Door, Roger? Looking forward to seeing old friends again?"

"Now who's being silly?" said Roger. "I like the world just as it is. So many opportunities for pleasure . . . people are such easy prey. And I do so enjoy being better than everyone else. I don't see the need for any competition."

"Droods have had dealings with the Inferno before," said William, quite offhandedly. "And the Courts of the Holy, of course."

We all looked at him, struck silent. He blinked a few times, and smiled uncertainly.

"We have pacts, with Heaven and Hell?" I said, trying to keep the shock out of my voice.

"Of course," said William. "You have to work with all sorts, in this job. And be prepared to talk to absolutely anybody. Goes with the territory. This family has long-standing pacts with the Nightside, Shadows Fall . . . aliens, elves, etc. . . ."

"Etc.?" I said.

"Oh yes," said William, chuckling in a quiet, unnerving way. "Very definitely etc. This family is responsible for a lot more than most people realise, and contains secret departments within secret departments. Like those Russian dolls, you know . . . All to deal with the things that no one else wants to admit exist."

"First I've heard of this," said Rafe. "You mean . . . there are special agents out there, apart from the regular field agents?"

William sat down suddenly, as though all the strength had gone out of his legs. He looked older, and very tired. "The more I remember about this family, the less I like it. Discovering the true nature of the Heart, and the price we paid for our original armour, weren't the only things that broke me. Yes, there are undercover agents, out there in the world . . . doing secret, necessary, unpleasant things, in the name of the family."

"Hold on," I said. "I actually ran this family for a while, and no one ever told me about this!"

"There was a war on," said William. "You didn't need to know. Only the Matriarch knows everything. The keeper of secrets. She carries the burden of knowledge, so the rest of us don't have to, for the good of the family."

"And perhaps," said Harry, "for plausible deniability, should any of this ever blow up in our faces."

"Who are these other agents?" said Rafe.

"If I ever knew, I've forgotten," said William. "Perhaps . . . I made myself forget."

I looked at Harry. "I have to go after the Apocalypse

Door. The whole world, all of Humanity, is in danger. I need you to do something while I'm gone."

"Do tell," murmured Harry. "I live to serve."

I looked from him to Roger, and then back again. "The family needs to send someone down into the Pit, as an emissary, to negotiate on our behalf. So that if Doctor Delirium should try to open the Door, Hell will keep it shut from the other side. And there's only one person here suited to that task."

"You want to send Roger down into the Inferno?" said Harry. "Are you crazy?"

"Why would the fallen and the damned choose to remain in Hell?" said Roger.

"Find something else they want, and offer them that," I said. "Bargain. Hell does so love to make a deal."

"And the Enemy might not want to start an Apocalypse he isn't sure he's ready to win," said Rafe. "If Hell rises up, Heaven will come down. In a full-out war, timing can be everything."

"Good point," said Roger. "Very well, I'll go. It's been a while . . . but I do know a few people I can talk to."

"People?" said Rafe.

Roger smiled unpleasantly. "You know I don't like to name-drop."

"Hold it, hold it!" said Harry. "I don't like the sound of any of this. What if they don't let you out again? This is Hell we're talking about, the afterlife, not some road trip to a holiday dimension!"

"My body won't be going anywhere, Harry," Roger said patiently. "Just my spirit. My body will remain here, in the Hall, properly guarded. I have done this before, you know. In fact, I'm quite in the mood to pay a visit to the old homestead. I've done far too many . . . good things, since I joined up with this family. I feel the need to . . . rededicate myself. It's not easy being a half-breed; you get drawn in so many directions . . ."

"If you're going, I'm going with you," said Harry.

"No, you're not," Roger said immediately. He took both of Harry's hands in his, and looked at his partner firmly. "You can't go where I must go. You're only human. You wouldn't get out again. I need you here, to stand guard over my body while I'm gone. Protect me, from my enemies." He didn't look at me. He didn't have to. "Listen to me, Harry. The Hall is a dangerous place, these days. Who else can I trust, but you?"

Harry glared at me. "This is just your way of keeping me out of circulation, while you're gone!"

"No," I said. "Just a useful side effect." I paused, as a thought struck me. "Should we send an emissary Above, as well? To the Court of the Holy, on the shimmering plains? Just to let them know what's going on?"

"I think we can be pretty sure they already know," said Rafe. "Comes with the territory . . ."

"The last thing we need is for this to escalate," said William. "Or we'll be hip deep in angels and smiting. You know what they did in the Nightside; the poor bastards are still rebuilding. Angels are even more hardcore than Droods."

CHAPTER SIX

Lord of the Flies

I f there's one thing in life I can rely on, it's that every time I go home to Drood Hall, just when I think things can't get any worse, they do. We all looked around, as yet again there came the sound of approaching footsteps. They were slow and unhurried, not even trying to hide themselves. Rafe threw up his hands, and looked like he might actually stamp his foot. I'd never seen him this angry before. It was quite entertaining.

"I don't believe it! Who the hell is it this time? Am I going to have to put up barbed wire and lay down some land mines, just to get a little privacy around here? This is not a lending library!"

"I came down here to get away from the family," said William, wistfully. "Now it seems they're following me down here. Maybe we should lay in some more cots. And another chemical toilet. I'm not sharing."

"I don't think they're here for you," I said.

"How very typical," murmured Harry. "You always assume it's all about you, Edwin."

"To my continuing displeasure, mostly it is," I said. "I think I recognise those arrogant, overbearing footsteps. Over here, Cedric."

The Sarjeant-at-Arms appeared at the end of the stacks, paused briefly to fix us all with a fierce glare, so we could all get a good look at him, and then he strode officiously forward, heading straight for me. I struck a casual pose, just to annoy him. He crashed to a halt before me, sniffed loudly, and glared right into my face.

"Edwin Drood," he said, in his best formal voice, "I am here to arrest you, on behalf of the family."

"You see?" I said to Harry. "It is all about me. Aren't you jealous? Don't you wish he was here to arrest you?"

"I told you I always know where everyone is," said the Sarjeant-at-Arms, as if I hadn't spoken. "There's nowhere you can run, nowhere you can hide in the Hall, that I can't find you."

"Hide from you?" I said. "Perish the thought. We always have such fun together. Are you here on your own, Sarjeant? No backup? You really think you can take me, without an army to drag me down?"

"I don't need an army. I'm the Sarjeant-at-Arms. You will come with me, Edwin, because to do otherwise would be to defy the will of the family. Are you really ready to be declared rogue again?"

"Arrested," I said thoughtfully. "For what, exactly?"

"As a material witness," the Sarjeant said calmly. "For suspected involvement in the murder of Martha Drood. As a suspected accomplice of the suspected murderer, the witch Molly Metcalf. I am sorry about what happened to her. You have my word that I will track down whoever it was that drove the mob to a killing madness, and I will see them punished. But it doesn't change anything."

"No," I said. "Nothing ever really changes, when it comes to me and the family. How many times do I have to prove myself?"

"No one is bigger than the family," said the Sarjeant. "Now come along with me. You'll be kept safe and secure, until your trial."

"Like Sebastian was kept safe, inside the isolation ward?" I said. "No one even saw his killer come and go. Lock me up, and I won't live long enough to stand trial."

"That will not be allowed to happen to you," said the Sarjeant, his face and voice entirely unmoved. "You will be kept under twenty-four-hour watch, for your own protection."

"This must feel like all your birthdays come at once, Sarjeant," I said. "But what about the Apocalypse Door, and Doctor Delirium?"

"The family does have other field agents, Edwin. Really quite competent ones. They will deal with the problem. You are not irreplaceable. Now come with me. The needs of the family must always come first."

"No," I said. "Not always. Because the family doesn't always know what's best for it."

"And you do?"

"Sometimes, yes."

"And you say I'm the arrogant one," said the Sarjeant-at-Arms.

We were staring right into each other's faces when William suddenly pushed himself between us.

"You can't fight here!" he said sharply. "What are you thinking of? This is the Old Library, repository of Drood knowledge! I will not risk these books being destroyed, and precious knowledge lost! You can't fight here; I forbid it!"

"Step aside please, Librarian," said the Sarjeant. "I must do my duty. Some things are more important than books."

William suddenly threw his arms around the Sarjeant, pinning his arms to his sides and holding him in place. Since he was only half the Sarjeant's size, this was impressive.

"Go, Edwin!" William said loudly. "Do what you have to do! I'll hold him!"

The Sarjeant stood very still, though he could have thrown the Librarian off just by flexing his chest muscles. He looked rather embarrassed.

"Please, Uncle William. Let me go. I have no intention of taking Edwin anywhere."

We all looked at him. William let go, just a bit shamefacedly, and stepped back. The Sarjeant cleared his throat, and looked at me.

"As you said, Edwin, if I was going to take you away by force, I'd have brought reinforcements with me. A lot of them. But from what my CSI people have already told me, it's clear neither you nor Molly were involved in Martha's murder. However, there is still a large faction in the family who want you arrested, on general principles, and it will make my investigation easier if people don't know I've already cleared you. Since I know where every member of the family is, at any given time, it wouldn't be plausible for me to say I couldn't find you. So I have tracked you down here, and arrested you, in front of these impeccable family witnesses. Not my fault that you got away afterwards, is it? I told you, Edwin. I'm the sneaky one."

"So you are," I said. "But why are you letting me go?"

"It is clear to me that Molly Metcalf was murdered because you were getting too close to the truth, over whatever is going on with Doctor Delirium and the Apocalypse Door," said the Sarjeant. "So it is clearly in the best interests of the family to let you continue your investigations."

I looked at Harry, who shrugged. "Far be it for me to stand in the way of greatness. Off you go, and save the world again. I'll do my best to hold the family together in your absence."

Roger Morningstar just smiled briefly. "Bye, Eddie. See you in Hell."

I nodded briefly to them all, and strode quickly away. And the moment I was out of sight behind the next stack, I called up the Merlin Glass and went travelling again.

I stepped through the glass into the War Room. I wasn't done with the Hall yet. There were things I needed to know, and the War Room always had the most up-to-date information. No alarms sounded when I appeared out of nowhere right in the middle of the most closely guarded part of the Hall, though they very definitely should have. The Merlin Glass was learning, and I had to wonder what its limits might be. Still, that was a problem for another day. I had enough on my plate as it was. The Glass took its time about disappearing, in a smug sort of way.

The War Room is a vast auditorium carved out of the solid rock beneath Drood Hall. From here, we see everything—or at least, everything that matters. The whole world is our playing field, and we don't miss a trick. The stone walls are covered in row upon row of state-of-the-art display screens, showing every country, place and individual of interest in the whole world. And not just the parts the official maps show. Lights blazed on all the screens, showing developing situations and all the places where the family was at work. A green light for every successfully completed mission; blue for persons of immediate interest, or those on our current hit list; amber for potential trouble sites; and red for a current threat. There was a hell of a lot of red on the screens, but that was just business as usual in the War Room.

This is where the family makes the decisions that keep the world turning.

Men and women sat in long rows, concentrating on their workstations. Farcasters peered into their crystal balls, while technicians worked their computers, and a whole crowd of people murmured constantly in the communications centre. Runners hurried quickly back and forth with urgent information. Chatter was kept to a minimum, and no one hung around the watercooler. The new head of the War Room ran a tight ship. The only one allowed to have hissy fits and throw things was him.

Callan Drood hadn't been in charge long, but he applied himself to his new position with all his usual vim and vigour. He looked a lot thinner than the last time I'd seen him, and a hell of a lot more intense. If that was possible. He was dressed smartly, as befitted his new authority, but wore it awkwardly, as though he was wearing it only because he'd been told to. His thin blond hair had been cut raggedly, and was plastered to his head with sweat. He stood right in the middle of it all, glaring about him, his eyes darting back and forth as he tried to see everything at once. His mouth was a flat compressed line, when he wasn't shouting at someone.

He just nodded distractedly when I made myself

known to him, and gestured abruptly for me to wait until he was ready to talk to me. Everyone made a lot of allowances for Callan. Word was, he was still adjusting to the new torc he'd been given, after the Blue Fairy had ripped the last one from around his throat, during the Hungry Gods War. Mind you, a lot of us thought he was just putting it on, to let him get away with things. Callan was like that. When he finally deigned to give me some of his attention, all the time he was talking one or other of his hands would sneak up to touch or play with the torc at his throat, as though to reassure himself it was still there.

"Eddie. As if I didn't have enough problems. Why aren't you under arrest, and safely locked up, rather than coming here and bothering me? I have work to do. Important work. I'm in charge here, you know! It's a mistake, but I'm not going to tell them. I have a room on the second floor now. With a view! Not much of a view, admittedly, but . . . Look, I could say I'm glad to see you, but we both know I don't meant it, so what's the point? Tell me what it is you need me to do, so I can do it and get you the hell out of my War Room."

"Hello, Callan," I said. "I think we need to review your medication again."

"Oh, would you? I'd be ever so grateful. Look at the situation screens. Look at them! I haven't seen this many flashing lights in one place since I was at a San Francisco disco. Everyone out there's talking about the Apocalypse Door, even if most of them aren't entirely sure what it is, yet. Some of the rumours are getting really extreme. Everyone's going on a war footing, just in case, and a lot of them are already planning to get their retaliation in first. It's a mess . . . I've got field agents reporting subterranean action and intrigue all over the world. Tell me you've got a plan to deal with all this, Eddie. Lie to me if you must. I won't mind."

"Can you show me where Doctor Delirium's secret base is located these days?" I said.

"Oh sure! No problem. There's not many people can hide from us for long, and Doctor Delirium wouldn't even make the short list. He's very predictable, and he never learns."

He had one of his people task an orbiting surveillance satellite to show us where Doctor Delirium had gone to ground, this time. We could launch our own satellites, but it's always been more cost efficient to hitch a ride on the existing ones. Never any shortage of spy satellites.

"It's a Russian eye in the sky, but they won't notice we're piggybacking the signal," said Callan. "We like to keep an eye on Doctor Delirium's movements, but after that business at LA we've upgraded the Doctor from nuisance to actual threat. Don't suppose you know what the Apocalypse Door is, do you, Eddie?"

"Trust me," I said. "You really don't want to know."

"Oh . . ." said Callan. "One of those . . . Batten down the hatches, people! It's going to be a long night! Extra tea and jaffa cakes for everyone, and someone get me a refill of those nice little blue pills." He looked at me, suddenly very sober. "Is it true? Is the Matriarch really dead?"

"Yes," I said. "She's gone."

"I still can't believe it. Not her, of all people. I thought she'd go on forever. I'll miss her. I don't think she ever approved of me much, but she never let me forget what it meant to be a Drood. I've had all my people on full alert, ever since I heard. This would be a really good time for an enemy attack, while we're all so disorganised. Maybe that's why they killed her? Cut off our head, and we'd all run around in circles? They don't know us. They don't know Droods."

"The Sarjeant-at-Arms is on the case," I said. "Now, Doctor Delirium . . ."

"Can't show you the base itself," said Callan, immediately all business again. "It's hidden from view, under the jungle canopy. The Amazon rain forest is bigger than some countries, and most of it has never been mapped. But we can give you a pretty specific location." He pointed to one particular display screen, now showing an aerial view of the jungle. From really quite high up. The tightly packed greenery stretched away for miles, dark and unbroken, like the surface of an unknown planet. One of Callan's people obligingly put a large red cross over one area.

"And you're sure he's there, because?" I said.

Callan smiled smugly. "Abnormal energy spikes, unique electromagnetic fields, and far too many human life signs coming and going in what should be nothing more than miles and miles of jungle. And because we've got a low-level spy tucked away inside his organisation, who keeps us up to date on his every move. Technology is all very well and good, but you can't beat cheating and a good-sized bribe to get you results."

"I think it's time I dropped in on Doctor Delirium, for a little head to head," I said. "And maybe a slap or two, to put him in his place. Contact the local field agent, and tell him I'm going in. Do we know how far he is from Doctor Delirium's new base?"

"Conrad's already heading in the right direction, but given how far off the map the Doctor is now, even at best speed . . . forty-eight hours. Minimum. It's a big area, Eddie. It's not like there's a local bus. What are you going to do, grab a ride on one of the Blackhawkes, and then parachute in?"

"I think I can do better than that," I said. "Tell Conrad to make his best speed, and join up with me at the base."

I called the Merlin Glass into my hand, and shook it out into a door. Through the gap, I could immediately see the same aerial view of the jungle as on the display screen. The Merlin Glass was on the job. Callan looked at me sulkily.

"It's not fair. You always get the best toys! When I was in the field, I couldn't even get a short-range teleport bracelet without filling out a dozen forms in triplicate. Did you know the Armourer once used one to take care of a kidney stone? Just programmed the bracelet and then teleported across the Armoury, leaving the kidney stone behind?"

"Certainly sounds like the Armourer," I said.

"Wonder whether it would work with haemorrhoids . . ."

"You know very well you weren't allowed gadgets in the field because you kept losing them," I said, quickly changing the subject. "You were legendary for not knowing where you'd put things. The Armourer still keeps a list of all the things you've lost on his wall, and when I say lost, I also include broken and exploded. How can anyone misplace an enchanted motorbike?"

Callan shrugged. "It's a gift. Not everyone could do it."

I looked through the open door standing before me. The jungle canopy didn't have a red cross superimposed over it, but I was sure the Glass could take me to the exact spot. It had never let me down yet. So I gave Callan a cheery wave good-bye, stepped through the Merlin

Glass, and found myself high up in the sky, falling more and more rapidly towards the jungle canopy below.

"Stupid bloody literal Glass!"

The Merlin Glass had already disappeared back into its subspace pocket, leaving me plummeting towards the jungle, grabbing handfuls of fresh air along the way. I turned myself over so that I could look straight down. I really was a hell of a long way up. The cold air slammed against me, buffeting me this way and that and tugging at my clothes, but not slowing me down in the least. My first thought was to summon the Glass back, and go somewhere else through it, but I was already travelling at such a speed that my arrival at another destination would prove just as tricky. Besides, I'd come here to get my hands on Doctor Delirium, and I wasn't giving up yet.

So I subvocalised my activating Words, and armoured up. The golden strange matter flowed swiftly from my torc, and engulfed me in a moment from head to toe. The air that had been slamming me about with increasing force was immediately cut off, and I could breathe more easily. I hadn't realised how cold I was, until the armour warmed me up again. I was still falling hard, but the jungle canopy didn't look that much closer. I had time to think about this.

I concentrated hard, and huge golden glider wings spread out from my armoured back. They cupped the air, and slowed me down some. I was still falling, but at least now I had some control. The armour couldn't fly, but by gliding in a series of tight circles, I was at least slowing my descent. I spiralled down and down, the huge green jungle rotating swiftly beneath me. I fell and fell, and I made a point of enjoying as much of it as I could. On the grounds I'd probably never have such an experience again. The jungle canopy suddenly leapt up towards me, becoming clearer and more detailed with every moment. I waited as long as I dared, and then pulled the glider wings back in, curled up into a foetal ball, and braced myself as best I could.

I hit the canopy hard, like being thrown naked through a brick wall. I punched through the outer layers in a moment, my armour protecting me from the worst of the impact. It still knocked the stuffing out of me. I smashed through layer after layer of the canopy, slamming through one thick branch after another, shearing them off their trunks. Each breaking branch threw me back and forth, knocking me out of my curled-up ball. My arms and legs flailed helplessly. All I could see was a green blur, with dark shapes rising swiftly up to hit me again and again.

I was still falling at a dangerous speed, trees and greenery whipping past me so fast I lost all track of which way was up. We Droods trust our armour to protect us from everything, but that's only because we haven't tested it against absolutely everything yet. It was entirely possible that the golden armour might survive the fall intact, but I'd be crushed to jelly inside it. The continuous impact of branch after branch was slowing my fall, and I grabbed at every passing branch as I fell, but they all broke off in my hands. I fought to turn myself over, so I was facing down, and the ground shot suddenly up and hit me in the face.

I don't think I've ever hit anything that hard in my life. Riding a collapsing hotel from the penthouse floor down to the lobby, from the inside, was nothing compared to this. The ground hit me like a flyswatter, the impact jarred every bone in my body, and the world went away for a while. When I slowly came back to myself, I ached all over but . . . I was alive. I just lay there for a while, enjoying the idea of not being suddenly dead after all, my golden mask buried deep in the dirt of the jungle floor. I slowly got my breathing back under control, wriggled my toes and fingers to make sure everything was connected, and grinned stupidly. The armour had got me through again.

I pushed down hard with my golden arms, and slowly forced myself up and out of the hard compressed earth. Light returned as dirt fell away from my golden mask, and when I finally rose to my feet I found I was at the bottom of a deep crater. I'd hit the jungle floor like a meteor, and blown out enough earth to make a hole a good twenty feet in diameter. Steam was still rising from the smooth sides. I punched holes in the compacted dirt of the crater walls, and used them to climb up out of the hole.

The jungle pressed in close all around me, crowding right up to the rim of the crater. The trees were packed tightly together, stretching away in all directions, the space between them filled with hanging lianas from above, and thick bushy undergrowth. The only open space was the one I'd made, by falling through it. Broken branches and splintered stumps showed down the stripped sides of trees, and bits of broken vegetation were still floating slowly down. The thick overhead canopy blocked out most of the light, lending the jungle floor a gloomy, twilight ambience. Bright light streamed down through the hole I'd made, so that I seemed to be standing in a golden spotlight. Dust motes danced and swooped in the illuminated air.

I moved out of the spotlight. It made me feel like a target. I amped up the mask's sensory input, and the stench of the jungle hit me like a fist in the face; all rot and decay and thick unfamiliar smells. Out of the spotlight, I could see a long way into the twilight, but everything was packed so closely together it was hard to make out any details. There were large animals out there, watching me silently from a cautious distance, but none of them seemed interested in bothering me. Inside my armour, I gave off no scent to mark me as prey.

The jungle was full of sound: growls and howls, cries and screams, coming from every direction at once as the jungle got on with life as usual. It was all eat or be eaten, with a hell of a lot of running in between. Higher up, there was a constant squalling of disturbed birds. I caught brief flashes of gorgeous colours, and the occasional rush of disturbed air, but the birds kept their distance. The loudest, closest sounds were the buzzings, clickings and rustlings of the millions of insects that swarmed all over the jungle floor. Any number of little darting things flicked through the air, while a great sea of motion swirled around my feet. There were ants and beetles and things I couldn't even put a name to, boiling all around me. I saw centipedes as long as my arm, rippling slowly as they moved, and tiptoeing spiders as big as my fist. Some tried to climb up onto my feet, but just slid back down again, unable to gain any purchase on the armour. The bigger ones kept well away; I think the armour upset them.

I turned the sensory levels back down again; it was all just too much to bear. And I'd already spotted what I was looking for. The Merlin Glass, for all its bloody-minded literalness, had delivered me to the right spot. I could see Doctor Delirium's secret base, not half a mile away, glowing brightly in the sun beyond the trees.

There was no track or trail, or anything like a path, so I just moved forward in a straight line, forcing my way through the thick masses of vegetation by sheer brute strength. I kicked through the undergrowth, broke protruding tree branches with my hands, and elbowed aside the smaller trees. Nothing in the jungle could stand against me. Sometimes, when I'm in the armour, it feels like I'm moving through a paper world. Through something less real than me. I try not to let it affect me. It's a dangerous thing to believe. The armour can make you feel like a god, but it's important to remember that it's only as good as the idiot inside it.

Hanging lianas slapped against my shoulders and tried to curl around my arms, but I just tore them away and continued on. The bushy undergrowth didn't even slow me down. Thorns three or four inches long, thick as spikes, clattered harmlessly against my armour. I could hear small things hissing and squealing under my feet, and made a point not to look down. The larger local wildlife continued to observe me, from a respectful distance.

A huge millipede, nine or ten feet long, fell on me from above, and I made a high-pitched startled sound despite myself. The millipede tried to coil around my head and shoulders, failed to find any footing, and dropped away. I cringed, even inside my armour. I've never liked insects. Especially ones big enough to have forgotten their proper place in the scheme of things.

A large spatter of bird poo hit my right arm, white against the gold. I flexed the muscle, and the poo flew away as though shot from a gun, leaving nothing of itself behind. It was such a familiar reaction, I didn't even have to think about it. (London is, after all, a city full of pigeons.)

The tree line came to a sudden halt, looking out across a vast earth clearing. I stopped in the shadow of the last trees, to take a good look at Doctor Delirium's base. The first thing that struck me was that there was no sign of movement anywhere. No guards, no people, nothing. And all the jungle sounds had died away. No living thing had followed me to the edge of the clearing. No birds sang, no wildlife stirred. Even the insects at my feet seemed strangely subdued. As though something about the base frightened them . . . I held my position, studying the characterless buildings carefully, looking as far down the empty dirt streets as I could. There was something unnatural about such stillness, such silence . . .

I stepped forward, leaving the jungle behind me, and moved out into the earth clearing. Immediately a powerful force field seized me and held me in place, brought into being by my presence. It pinned me to the spot, great waves of energy coruscating around my armoured form, while small stabbing lightnings crawled all over it, searching for a weak spot and a way in. The air shimmered like heat haze, and the dirt at my feet was scorched black by discharging energies. But powerful as the field was, it was no match for my armour. It couldn't touch me.

I flexed my golden arms slowly, testing the strength of the field holding me in place. There was a definite tension, a solid resistance, like pulling against chains, but nothing the armour couldn't handle. I leaned forward, into the field, and set my strength against it. The lightnings jumped furiously, and great sparks detonated on the air, but I moved forward, step by step, chest stuck out as though breasting a tide, and the field could not stop me. I walked right through it, and suddenly it fell away, defeated. The crawling energies were gone, the air was clear again, and there was nothing left to stop my walking into Doctor Delirium's secret base.

I looked around me, braced for an attack from any direction, ready for shouting guards with big guns, or mercenaries with super-science weapons . . . but there was nothing. Just the silence and the stillness and the empty dirt streets. Except, when I looked carefully, there was something. The slow buzzing of flies, not far away.

Inside the huge earth clearing, the sun shone harshly on blunt and ugly steel and glass structures, presumably the science labs, surrounded by blocks of simple wooden terraces, low-ceiling huts mostly, the size of a village. It had clearly all been built for function, not style; thrown up quickly by people who had been on the move before, and were prepared to move again at a moment's notice. Doctor Delirium's little kingdom was a shabby state of affairs. The main building dominated the centre of the village, a steel and glass monument to the Doctor's ego. His main science lab, where he let his genius run riot.

I started down the narrow street, heading for the main lab. I was still tense, my skin crawling in anticipation of the attack I'd never see coming. From some hidden gun position, or some automated defence system like the perimeter force field. The sound of my heavy feet crashing on the ground carried clearly in the hush, and my golden armour blazed brightly under the hot sun, but still nothing moved in the streets between the low buildings. Nothing but me.

The sound of buzzing flies was getting louder.

I rounded a corner, and there on the street ahead were a series of vague black shapes. I couldn't work out what they were until I got close enough to disturb the black blanket of flies, and they sprang up into the air, leaving the bodies behind. There were dozens of them, stretching the whole length of the street. I looked back and forth, checking the side streets, and the bodies were everywhere. Dark huddled shapes, buried under flies. The dead men and women lay alone, in twos and threes, and in great piled-up heaps. I made myself walk on, flies buzzing angrily all around me now, harsh and strident. I stepped around and over bodies, some dressed in black and gold, others clearly scientists and workmen. Their ragged clothes were soaked in blood and their wounds were terrible. Flies crawled all over them, jumping up when I came close, and settling again after I'd passed.

The whole place was a Jonestown—everyone was dead. Only here, the people hadn't killed themselves; they'd killed each other. I moved out of one street and onto another, and the dead lay everywhere, broken and butchered. I knelt down to examine some of the bodies, waving the flies away with my golden hand. They hung on the air nearby, buzzing angrily but unwilling to approach my armour. I checked out the extent and origins of the wounds with my golden fingers. I didn't have to bother about infection, as long as I didn't armour down. The stench, of spilled blood and exposed guts, of so many dead people, suddenly became too much for me and I shut down the mask's scent detectors. I daren't armour down long enough to throw up. I straightened up, and stepped back from the bodies.

I felt sick, in my stomach and in my soul. I had no place here, in this village of the dead. I wanted to turn and run and get the hell away, leave this madness behind. People aren't supposed to see things like this, do things like this. But I was a field agent, and I had work to do. I'd be weak later, when I had time. And if I had nightmares later, well, that came with the job, sometimes. Something terrible had happened here, and I had to find out how and why, to make sure it could never happen again. Duty and responsibility have their uses—they keep us going when courage might not be enough.

I made myself let the stench back in. It wasn't so bad, knowing it was coming. And bad as it undoubtedly was, there wasn't much actual decomp. Blood and guts, yes, but not much rot or decay. Given the blazing heat of the overhead sun, this wholesale slaughter couldn't have happened that long ago. This . . . was a recent massacre. Whoever or whatever had done this, I hadn't missed it by much.

So many dead. Dozens, maybe hundreds. I hardened my heart, and concentrated on the evidence. It was the only way to stay sane. I moved slowly, steadily forward, and the flies leapt on the air around me, buzzing hungrily. From the nature of the wounds, these people had shot each other until they'd run out of bullets, used the guns as clubs until they broke, and then they went at each other with machetes and axes, all kinds of improvised weapons, and finally, their bare hands. Empty guns with shattered butts lay discarded to every side, and bullet casings glistened in the bright sunlight. There was bullet damage all around, riddling the wooden walls of the surrounding huts. The sheer savagery of the wounds suggested . . . an overwhelming rage, a desperate vicious need to kill.

For a moment I was back in the Hall, as the mob killed my Molly, stabbing her over and over again.

These people had shot and stabbed and hacked at each other, gouging great wounds in unprotected flesh. Hands cut off, bodies decapitated. Some had died with their hands locked around each other's throats, a grip so fierce it had not relaxed even in death. Others had died with their arms buried deep in opened-up guts. One man had yanked out his opponent's intestines, while his enemy had thrust his thumbs into his attacker's eyes. There were never any signs of defensive wounds. These people had been so intent on killing they hadn't even tried to protect themselves. Many of them looked as though they'd been attacked by wild animals, rather than anything human. But the real clue, as to what had happened here, lay in the faces of the dead. They were all the same: withered and ancient, burned out by the terrible forces that had raged within them. I knew what this was. I'd seen it before.

Everyone in Doctor Delirium's secret base had been given the Acceleration Drug. It could make you superhuman, for a while; incredibly fast and strong, inhumanly resistant to pain and punishment. But the Drug burned up all the years of your life, to fuel the superhuman abilities. A lifetime's energies, to make a man superhuman for a few days, or even just a few hours. They started out as Manifest Destiny's shock troops, created to be thrown against the Droods in armour. They fought well, and died quickly, like so many superpowered mayflies.

But they were fanatics; they knew what they were getting into. They paid the price willingly, the fools. This . . . was different.

I straightened up from examining a body that had been torn open from throat to crotch, and flicked the blood from my golden hands. The flies settled happily on the body again as I turned away. On the wall before me was a huge bloody stain, splattered across the whitewashed wood from top to bottom, spattered here and there with bloody bits and pieces. It took me a while to figure out what it was, until I looked down, and saw the deep footprints in the dirt, leading straight to the great stain. An Accelerated Man had run into the wall at superhuman speed, and exploded across it when he hit. Larger pieces had slid slowly down the wall, leaving dark trails behind them. There was nothing left on the ground to identify, even after I'd waved the flies away. It had all just . . . shattered, under the impact.

I wondered if he'd even tried to stop.

I walked on down the street, still heading for the main science lab. Halfway down, a house had collapsed in on itself, as though a bomb had gone off inside. I took a moment to peer through the empty window frame. In the gloom, I could make out several bodies, and bits of bodies. They'd destroyed the house, and brought it down upon themselves, because they couldn't break off from killing each other.

I hurried down the street, and turned into another, feeling like the only living thing in this place of the dead. I'd stopped trying to count the bodies, or even estimate their numbers. There were just too many. The closer I got to the main lab, the more there were. Hundreds, maybe thousands, of once rational men and women, driven to slaughter every living thing they saw by some insane rage. I wondered if they laughed, or cried. Or whether they'd been driven beyond such limited emotions.

Someone would pay for this. I would not stand for this. I would see someone paid, in blood and suffering.

I stopped abruptly, and looked quickly back and forth. I'd heard something. The first real sounds I'd heard in this place, apart from the constant maddening buzzing of the flies. I turned around and around, trying to pin down the sound. A rapid, repetitive noise, moving incredibly fast. My head snapped from left to right, following the sound. And then it suddenly changed direction, growing louder and more urgent as it headed right for me. I looked down a side street, and there was an Accelerated Man, sprinting towards me so quickly he was little more than a blur. My armoured mask slowed the image down for me, so I could get a better look. He was running horribly quickly, much faster than a man was meant to move. His arms flailed wildly, his ribs rising and falling so quickly I could actually hear them cracking and splintering under the strain. His feet dug deep ragged holes in the earth path, throwing puffs of dust and dirt up behind him. His clothes were ragged, and soaked in blood. More blood was spattered across his wild face, with its feral smile.

He covered the whole length of the street in just a few moments. Even with my armour speeding up my perceptions, I still had no time to react. I couldn't evade or stop him. All I could do was stand my ground, and brace myself. The Accelerated Man slammed right into me at incredible speed, but the impact didn't budge me back one inch. I felt nothing, even as I heard his bones crack and break and shatter as he slammed into me. He was thrown back, blood flying on the air, but somehow he still kept his feet. He regained his balance, and then bent forward sharply and threw up. There was blood in the vomit, and other things. He'd damaged himself seriously, inside. But still he wouldn't fall. The Acceleration Drug kept him on his feet, and the rage in his face kept him going.

He snatched up something from the ground. At first I thought it was a club, but as he waved it before me I realised it was a human thighbone, with blood and meat still on it. He flailed at me with the long bone, attacking me with superhuman strength and speed. But the bone just shattered against my armour, reducing itself to splinters in his hand. He finally made a sound—a high wailing scream of frustration, because he couldn't hurt me. I speeded up my armour's reflexes to match his Accelerated speed, slapped what was left of the bone out of his hand, and grabbed his forearms with my hands. He tried to break free, using all his strength, and his arm bones snapped.

And then suddenly his face grew older, sprouting thousands of wrinkles, years piling on in a moment. His eyes sank back into his skull, and the fierce light went out of his gaze. His strength and speed all ran out, and I was holding a man so ancient it was a wonder he was still alive. I let go of him, and he fell to his knees. I knelt down beside him. His breathing was shallow and ragged, and blood drooled from his slack mouth. His skin was still aging. He looked desiccated, almost mummified. He forced his head up, just enough to look at me.

"A Drood," he said, his voice just a dry whisper. "Should have got here sooner, Drood."

"What happened here?" I said. I would have liked to lower my golden mask, so he could see a human face, but I couldn't do that. Too risky. "Where is Doctor Delirium? Did he do this? Can you . . . tell me your name?"

"The Drug," he said, and I had to lean forward to make out what he was saying. He was little more than skin and bone now, held together by a last few sputters of energy. "They gave us the Drug. It was our reward, for good service. Said it would make us stronger, faster. Superhuman. We'd feel like gods, they said . . . And we did, for a while. But we couldn't control it. I think . . . they added something to it. It drove us mad. Drove us all mad. They ran away and left us to each other. It's not fair. Not fair. I didn't come here to drink the Kool-Aid."

He died. I left him lying on the ground, as the flies descended. There was nothing I could do for him. My armour can do many wonderful things, but it can't heal.

I stood up and glared at the main science lab, my hands clenched into impotent fists at my sides. I could understand Doctor Delirium dosing his own people with the Acceleration Drug as a last line of defence, if he thought he was under attack . . . but no one knew I was coming. I hadn't known I'd be coming here, only a few hours earlier. And why add something to the Drug, to make them kill each other? Was this a Jonestown after all—had the Doctor killed his own people, and then killed himself? Unlikely. It wasn't in character for the Doctor, he was never that ruthless. He looked after his people, paid better than most, and anyway, Doctor Delirium should be on top of the world, right now. He'd finally found a way to blackmail the world and make it stick. He had no reason to give up.

And, the dying man had said *They* handed out the Drug. Doctor Delirium and . . . Tiger Tim? What the hell had happened here, when those two finally got together?

I strode on through the village of the dead, ignoring the bodies, all my attention concentrated on the science lab before me. The impeccably clean steel and glass structure shone brightly in the fierce sunlight, dominating the massive clearing made to hold it. When I finally came to the main entrance, the first thing I noticed was that the sliding doors were standing half open. I forced them all the way open, and the metal crumpled like paper in my grasp. I pulled the doors out of their frames, and threw them aside. I was past caring about the noise. I walked into the lobby, and there were no sirens, no alarms. No people anywhere. But the massive reception desk had been smashed and overturned, and all the furnishings were broken and scattered in pieces. The madness had found its way here.

The overhead lights were flickering fitfully, on the brink of giving up and going out. I couldn't hear any air-conditioning working. Main power had to be going down, on its last legs. The lobby gave onto a series of bland, featureless corridors that led deeper into the building. Gaudy coloured lines had been set down on the floor as a guide, but I had no idea what they stood for, so I just picked a corridor and started walking, threading my way through the maze. As I made my way inwards, the first bloodstains and bullet holes began to appear. And the first flies.

Someone had gone crazy with an axe; I found it embedded in a grey wall, the blade still smeared with dried blood and matted hair. Someone had shot out the windows, leaving broken glass all over the floor. It crunched loudly under my golden feet. Bodies lay here and there, in ones and twos, each one a bloody mess and a feast for the flies. More and more, I saw men and women dead at their desks, in offices and cubicles, still at their posts. From the look of them, they never took the Acceleration Drug. Maybe they never got the memo. Maybe . . . the Accelerated Men needed something simple to start on . . .

Blood-spattered white lab coats, cut throats and smashed-in heads, people thrown around like discarded toys. A few had been smashed through glass partitions, some had been battered to death with broken chairs. Half a dozen were still sitting in their chairs, their heads torn off and piled up in the corner. When superhumans go bad, it's bound to be messy.

Scattered papers were everywhere, littering the floor.

Probably important once, crumpled and torn now, all of them soaked in blood. Smashed windows, doors torn off their hinges, holes punched in walls, spattered with blood from broken hands. Fire damage here and there, put out by automatic systems. Smoke and water damage, from putting out the fires. And dead men and women, mostly scientists and office staff, who probably never even understood why they were being butchered.

I strode quickly on through the corridors, increasing my pace till finally I was running, doubling back and forth through twisting corridors whose pattern made no sense. I started to find corpses who had taken the Drug. Two young secretaries, little more than teenagers, had gone at each other with office scissors as their only weapons. They'd cut and slashed and gouged great chunks out of each other, stabbing and hacking with superhuman strength, giving and taking awful damage while the Drug kept them on their feet and fighting, long after they should have lain down and died. I didn't stop to mourn them. I couldn't. I had to find who was responsible. I needed to get my hands on them.

Why would Doctor Delirium have allowed this? To cover his tracks after he left? So no one would be left alive to speak of his future plans? Why kill all the soldiers? The Doctor had always relied on his mercenaries to do the heavy lifting. He was the boss, he never got his hands dirty. I'd been surprised to see him present at the Magnificat. Now this . . . Could it be, that just ownership of the Apocalypse Door was affecting him? Changing him, corrupting him . . . to the point where he would willingly open the Door and let loose all the hordes of Hell?

I made myself stop, and think. I found an office whose computer systems seemed undamaged. One machine was still running; someone had turned it on but hadn't lived to turn it off. I worked quickly, while the power still lasted. I pressed one fingertip against the computer, and willed golden filaments to worm their way into the guts of the machine. Luther was right; all I had to do was concentrate on what I wanted, and the armour did the rest for me. (I was going to have to think about the implications of that, when I had the time.) I persuaded the computer to throw up a map of the main lab, and put it on the screen. Doctor Delirium's private office was only a short distance away. I couldn't believe he'd still be here, after all that had happened, but even if he wasn't I should be able to find some answers. After all I'd seen, I needed some answers.

The office actually had a big brass plaque on the door saying DOCTOR DELIRIUM: STRICTLY PRIVATE. With green and red lights set in place above the door, to inform lesser mortals whether he was In or Out. Both lights were dead, and the door stood ajar. I stopped just short of the door. The Doctor might be gone, but in his present mood he might well have left all kinds of booby traps behind. Hidden guns or energy weapons, explosives triggered by an unwary footstep, deadfalls under the carpet. None of this would have had any effect on my armour, but I didn't want important evidence destroyed by a convenient fire or explosion. The office seemed quiet, and I couldn't see anything suspicious, so in the end I just pushed the door all the way open with a single golden finger. Nothing happened. I looked inside. The office was deserted. No bodies, no blood, no destruction—and no Doctor Delirium.

I strolled into the office and had a good look around. It wasn't much of an office, for a mad super-science villain. No frills or fancies, no super-science executive toys, not even a *Tomorrow The World!* poster on the wall, or a potted plant. Just a plain office desk, with the usual computer equipment, neat piles of paper in the In and Out trays, and two chairs, on either side of the desk. No photos anywhere, of family or friends. He gave all that up, to become Doctor Delirium. I had to wonder . . . if he thought it had all been worth it.

I used my armour again to break into his computer, and ran quickly through his files. And almost the first thing I found was a connection between Doctor Delirium and the rogue Drood, Tiger Tim. It went back almost a year. Tiger Tim brought the Acceleration Drug to Doctor Delirium, as a peace offering and a payment, to ensure a face-to-face meeting. Even Doctor Delirium had enough sense to be wary of a rogue Drood. Tiger Tim had acquired a large batch of the Drug from Truman, back when he was head of Manifest Destiny. And that . . . was a connection I hadn't expected to find.

I dug further, and found a connected video file, from a hidden camera feed in the office. A recording of the first face-to-face meeting between the Doctor and the rogue. I settled myself comfortably in the Doctor's chair, and punched up the recording. I was still worried about the power supply, but the image on the screen was sharp, and the sound only a bit fuzzy.

Doctor Delirium was a middle-aged, overweight man, with jowls and a seriously receding hairline. He wore a spotless starched white lab coat, perhaps because he liked to remind everyone that he was still primarily a scientist. His voice was high and nasal, and he made it clear from the very beginning, with every word and gesture, that he didn't approve of Tiger Tim.

The rogue Drood, on the other hand, gave every indication of being entirely relaxed and at ease. He lounged bonelessly in the visitor's chair, and smiled happily at everything. He was heading into middle age, and fighting it every step of the way. He had the kind of aesthetic musculature you get only from regular workouts with professional equipment, the skin on his face was just that little bit too taut, and he wore his hair in a buzz cut, to hide how much it was receding. His tan was deep and surprisingly natural. He wore a rich cream safari outfit, very much the Great White Hunter, topped off with a white snap-brimmed hat, complete with tiger skin band. He smiled a lot, but it never once touched his cold blue eyes. He seemed entirely at his ease, as though this was his office, and he was favouring Doctor Delirium with his presence.

"Tiger Tim," Doctor Delirium said heavily. "Why hasn't someone killed you yet?"

"Because no one's sent anyone good enough," the rogue said easily.

"You've been off the map and under the radar for quite a while," said the Doctor, lacing his podgy fingers across his generous stomach as he leaned back in his chair. Trying to appear even more relaxed than his visitor, and failing miserably. "And now here you are, sharing the rain forest with me. What do you want, Drood?"

"Please," said Tiger Tim, flashing one of his meaningless smiles. "I prefer the name I've made for myself. I am Tiger Tim now, and not in any way a Drood. You could wipe my whole family off the face of this planet, and I wouldn't give a damn. In fact, I'd probably sell tickets. As to where I've been all this time; why, I've been right here in the heart of darkness with you. Only my heart was considerably darker. I felt the need for a nice little holiday, you see, well away from the cares and tribulations of the civilised world. So after I had to leave, in something of a hurry, I jumped from place to place, and finally ended up here, deep in the jungle. Where no one could hope to find me.

"Imagine my surprise, when I stumbled across an unknown, untouched primitive tribe, who knew nothing of the white man and his civilisation. Amazing how many of them there still are, tucked away in the darkness, even in this day and age. I did the usual shock and awe thing to impress them, and they accepted me as their Great White God. I lorded it over them quite happily for some time. Just for the fun of it. The men were ugly brutes, but the women were pleasant enough, with a refreshingly casual attitude to social nudity. Their language was brutal and basic, and I never bothered to learn it. You can get most things across with pointing, and stern looks. Any time they looked like getting a bit rebellious, I'd show them a match or a compass, or shoot half a dozen of them, and they all went back to worshipping me again quite happily."

"Why didn't you just show them your armour?" said Doctor Delirium.

"Because I didn't have it," said Tiger Tim. "The family took it back."

"I had heard . . . something," said Doctor Delirium. "But you learn not to trust anything, when it comes to Droods."

"My family can be very spiteful, when it chooses," said Tiger Tim. "Anyway, I learned to survive without it. I've always believed in being prepared, for absolutely anything. Down the years, I've acquired a number of really quite remarkable items, of sometimes quite appalling power and destructiveness. More than enough to compensate for the loss of my armour. And, just one of the many reasons why I am so very hard to kill."

"Have you brought any of these appalling items with you?" said the Doctor, quite casually.

"Ah. That's the question, isn't it?" Tiger Tim leant back in his chair, smiling quietly, indicating that this was as far as he was prepared to go . . . for the moment, at least.

"If you were having such an enjoyable time, playing Tarzan, Lord of the Undiscovered, why are you here?" Doctor Delirium said firmly.

"You scientists," Tiger Tim said admiringly. "Always so keen to get to the point. Well, I enjoyed abusing my authority over the tribe, in all kinds of amusing ways, but eventually I just ran out of things to do to them. I got bored. They were a very limited people, and I missed all the little comforts of civilisation—like proper eating utensils, and toilet paper. But, it had been made very clear to me as I left South America, with bullets whistling past my head, that I couldn't hope to return to any civilised part of the world until I'd made myself strong and powerful enough to stare down all my many enemies, very definitely including my own family.

"Imagine my surprise when a white man turned up in my territory, looking for me. I wasn't completely cut off from the outer world, you understand. My people had been supplying drugs to a certain cartel, at my direction. They'd been using this absolutely fascinating psychedelic for centuries, as part of their religious festivals. Just one drop of the stuff, and after you've finished throwing up every meal you've ever eaten, you can have long conversations with the deity of your choice. Of course, I put a stop to all that. Thou shalt have no other god than me, on peril of some serious smiting on my part. And no, Doctor, I never took any of it myself. I'm very old-fashioned, in some respects. My body is a temple."

"Because you worship yourself?" said Doctor De-lirium.

"No one likes a catty supervillain, Doctor. Now, with nothing but time on my hands, I did a little experimenting with various parts of the mixture, and found it could make any man a superman, for a time. So I had my people produce tons of the stuff, and I set up a supply line to the nearest city. My people would do anything for me. If they knew what was good for them. But I'd only just started making serious connections, when this very polite young man came all the way into the jungle to see me. He was a representative of Manifest Destiny and a man called Truman. I see you know the name, Doctor; who doesn't? It appeared he was very interested in what he called the Acceleration Drug.

"We got on famously, and I agreed to supply Manifest Destiny with all the raw materials they needed, to produce the Drug on a large scale, and in return I was promised quite staggering amounts of money, plus a high place in the Manifest Destiny organisation, along with guaranteed protection from all my many enemies, whenever I chose to return to the civilised world. I think Truman particularly enjoyed the irony of obtaining such a weapon from a Drood; even an established rogue like me.

"Time passed. The young man came and went, keeping the connection open. Drugs went out, comforts came in. Until I got bored again. The young man, and I do wish I could remember his name, but he was a particularly bland and characterless specimen . . . Anyway, he made the mistake of trying to convert me to the cause of Manifest Destiny. He was a believer, you see, and thought I should be too. As though I'd ever follow any cause but mine. So I killed him, the tribe prepared him, and we ate him. I'd already introduced the tribe to the joys of cannibalism. Just for a laugh.

"Not long afterwards, word filtered through to me that Truman and his entire organisation had been stamped flat by the Droods. I've always had bad luck with timing. And I really couldn't believe it when I heard the family was now being run by London Eddie; I mean, who would have thought it? But it did mean . . . that I needed a new ally. I looked around, put out some feelers . . . and imagine my surprise when I discovered you'd just moved into a new secret base, practically on my doorstep?

"I decided this was a sign. So I killed all that was left of the tribe, to cover my tracks, ate the best bits of them, and walked through the jungle to join you here. That we might . . . discuss matters of mutual interest."

"Hold it," said Doctor Delirium, sitting abruptly upright in his chair. "You expect me to believe that you walked all the way here, one man on his own, through this godforsaken jungle? Packed full of large carnivorous creatures, and any number of poisonous snakes and insects? I lose at least one man every time I send a patrol out!"

"Ah," said Tiger Tim. "But they're not me. I told you, I'm prepared for absolutely everything. When I walk through the jungle, I'm the most dangerous thing in it. I can kill with a look, or blow things up with a Word. And I do! Often just for the fun of it. And now, here I am. Ready to make you an offer you really can't afford to refuse . . . I hold the secret of the Acceleration Drug, that can turn any soldier into a superhuman killing machine. Think of it, my dear Doctor Delirium; an army of your very own superhumans, to fight your corner for you and enforce your will on the world. Mercenaries are all very well and good, but they're very limited, and they die so easily. Truman used his Accelerated Men against my family, and proved they were a match even for Droods in their armour. Wouldn't you just love to be able to tell the Droods to shove it, after all they've done to you?"

"You're right," said Doctor Delirium, after a moment. "Your offer is very tempting. But your reputation precedes you, Tiger Tim. I'll need a lot of persuading before I will accept you as a partner in crime."

"Indeed," said Tiger Tim. "Tell me, my dear Doctor Delirium; have you ever heard of something called the Apocalypse Door?"

The recording stopped abruptly. I looked for more files, but if there were any, the Doctor had wiped them all.

I searched on through his files, letting the armour do most of the hard work, and discovered, very much to my surprise, that Doctor Delirium really was a scientific genius. The work he'd done in his various labs was nothing short of astonishing. He'd taken entirely minor illnesses, and genetically re-created them as killer plagues that would have ravaged the world, if my family hadn't stopped him, every time. He'd taken inconveniences, and turned them into monsters. If only the Doctor had been as interested in producing cures, he could have been the Great Man of Science he'd always wanted to be.

I always said we underestimated the man.

I was struggling to open a really stubborn file marked *Existential Technology*, when the file disappeared suddenly from the monitor screen, replaced by a face I knew very well. Tiger Tim looked out at me with much amusement.

"Well, now. What on earth is a Drood field agent doing in Doctor Delirium's private office?"

I studied him from behind my anonymous golden mask. "Timothy Drood, rogue and scumbag. How did you know I was here?"

"Call me Tiger Tim. That computer you're using was programmed to sound the alert at my end, if anyone tried to access that particular file. Can't have just anyone learning the true nature and function of the Apocalypse Door, can we?"

"We already know what it is," I said.

"Of course you do. You're a Drood. You know everything. I do like what you've done with the armour . . . very stylish modifications. Medieval, with a definite knightly touch. Things have clearly progressed since I was one of the favoured few."

I was a little surprised, but didn't say anything. I hadn't realised my armour was automatically adapting my favourite modifications, without my having to even think about it anymore. As though the armour was learning . . . Something else to think about, when I had the time.

"Of course," said Tiger Tim, "you took my armour away from me. Quite a shock, at the time. I didn't know the family could do that."

Which meant he hadn't heard about the treachery of the Heart, and its downfall. And how different the new armour was. At least the family was still keeping the details of its disgrace and rebirth secret from the world at large.

"All the field agents who suddenly lost their torcs got them back," said Tiger Tim. "Why didn't I?"

"Because you're not worthy," I said. "Because you're not a part of the family anymore. You'll never wear a torc again. Not after all the things you've done."

"Typical Drood. Always so judgemental. Have I really killed so many more than any Drood field agent? My crimes are really quite small, compared to the family's . . . At least I don't meddle with the world. I just want to play with it."

"I walked through a town full of dead people to get here," I said. "The Acceleration Drug drove them into a killing madness. What the hell did you think you were doing?"

"Well, it wasn't liked we needed them anymore, the good Doctor and I. And I never leave anyone behind to speak ill of me. Two men can keep a secret, if a whole bunch of people are dead. Besides, it was such fun to watch. From a safe distance. Aren't surveillance cameras wonderful?"

"Did Doctor Delirium know you were going to do that, to his people?" I said.

Tiger Tim grinned widely. "The good Doctor has been very . . . distracted, since I introduced him to the Apocalypse Door. He doesn't care about anything else, anymore. He talks to it, and it answers him. Or so he says. I've always been very careful to maintain a safe distance. I could have set his whole base on fire and toasted marshmallows on the burning bodies, and he wouldn't have cared. Not to worry, though; I'm here to keep an eye on him."

"We'll find you," I said. "The whole family will be at your back and at your throat until the day you die. What happened to you, Timothy? You might have been a rogue before, but you never used to be an abomination."

"Lot you know," Tiger Tim said easily. "I like to think of this as the real me finally surfacing, after years of repression. I'm not bad; I just want to have fun. Might I inquire which Drood I have the honour of addressing?

You all look the same to me. And after all, the game is only fun if you're playing against a worthy opponent."

"I'm Edwin Drood."

"London Eddie! My God ... You have come a long way, haven't you, from junior field agent chasing second-class scum around the back streets of unfashionable London? Of course, you only got that cushy posting, and your vaunted freedom from the family, because you had your grandmother's support. I never had anyone's support. I never had anyone in my corner, my whole life. Always telling me what to do, what to think ... They were always afraid of me. Of my potential. And quite rightly. I couldn't wait to find a way out of the Hall, throw off their damned brainwashing and get on with my life, far away from all the suffocating restrictions ... What's the point of being more than human, if you're still going to allow yourself to be bound by human limitations? Humanity is a trap, from which it is our duty to escape.

"So, I came up with my own ideas. You see, it isn't just the armour that makes us so much better than everyone else. Though it does help. Droods have accomplished more in world history than all governments put together. Because we're focused, smarter, more capable of taking the long view. Doing what needs to be done, and to hell whether it's popular or politically expedient. The armour has *evolved* us, as people, as a family, far above the common herd. We shouldn't be hiding in the shadows, we should stride out into the open and operate as the world leaders we really are. We are a natural aristocracy, superior in mind and body and will, and we should be lords and masters of all we survey. With everyone else in their proper place as servants, peasants, slaves. Their only real purpose in life is to serve their betters and worship their masters.

"We could put the world in order. No more wars, because everyone would do what they were told. No more want or hunger, because everyone would be equal, under Drood. Of course, we'd have to cut the numbers back, to a more manageable level. I spent ages putting all this together, but when I finally gathered up my materials and presented my Noble Experiment to the Matriarch . . . She said I was mad. I tried to explain, but she wouldn't even look at the materials! She refused to listen to me! No one would listen!"

"Really," I said. "I wonder why. You do like to talk, don't you?"

"Yes, well, I have been positively starved of good conversation, just recently. Anyway, when it became clear that the family was not going to be rational on this matter, I decided I'd have to start the ball rolling myself. A trial run, so to speak. Would I be right in thinking the powers that be in the family still don't like to talk about how close I came to actually getting away with it?"

"I know you half killed the Armourer, trying to get him to open the Armageddon Codex for you," I said. "Is that why you wanted the forbidden weapons? To declare war on Humanity?"

"Not a war, Eddie. Just a short sharp shock, a little practical culling, of the weak and unworthy. The old man shouldn't have tried to stop me. He should have understood. I would have worn him down eventually, if James hadn't turned up to drive me off. Bloody Grey Fox . . . always so full of himself. He never liked me. Still, I was really quite upset when I heard he'd died. I did so want to kill him myself.

"Anyway, that's how it all started. The secret origin

of Tiger Tim. I am finally where I should have been, all those years ago. I have the Apocalypse Door, the Acceleration Drug, and a fiendish master plan. Doctor Delirium and I will rule the world, and everyone else will bow down to us. Including every single stuck-up, straight-backed . . . *stuffy* member of the Drood family!"

"You *and* Doctor Delirium will rule the world?" I said.

"Yes . . . I'd been wondering when that particular penny was going to drop. He will be my partner for as long as I need him, and not one moment longer. He really does have a remarkable mind, but once the threat of the Door has placed the whole world under my control, I won't need him anymore, will I?"

"If you have the Apocalypse Door, why do you need him at all?"

"Because, my dear Eddie—oh, it is so good to have someone I can speak openly with at last . . . Because direct contact with the Apocalypse Door can be very . . . affecting, to the human mind. The dear Doctor seems quite besotted with it. But he can't open it without my help. So he acts as my cutout, so to speak. Should it prove necessary to open the Door, I will make it possible for him to do so. But I'm certainly not foolish enough to get too near myself."

"You don't really think an army of Accelerated Men will be enough to protect you from the Droods, do you?" I said. I needed to divert him. Before he realised just how much information he'd given away. "You must know the Drug is flawed. Your superhumans burn out."

"They last long enough to do what's necessary," said Tiger Tim. "Especially with my new extra magic ingredient. Courtesy of Doctor Delirium's amazing mind and first-class labs. What you've seen at the base was just the trial run, for a much larger experiment."

"How did you find out about the Apocalypse Door?"

"A little bird told me. Come now, Eddie, you don't really think I'll give up all my little secrets and connections that easily?"

"Worth a try," I said. "More importantly, do you understand what will happen, if you ever open the Door?"

"Of course," said Tiger Tim.

"And you're really prepared to do that, if you don't get your way?"

"Yes. If I can't have the life I want, why should anyone else? To hell with them all."

"What about the Immortals?"

He looked at me. "Who?"

And then Ethel contacted me through my torc, her voice high and urgent. *Eddie! You have to come home! Right now! The Hall is under attack!*

"What? That's . . . impossible! Wait a minute . . ." I turned back to Tiger Tim's face on the monitor screen. "Drood Hall is under attack! Is this your doing?"

He smiled dreamily. "It has always been a dream of mine . . . To see the Hall go up in flames, and everything destroyed . . . And all of you will cry out to me, to save you from the fire . . . And I will lean forward, and smile, and say . . . *Burn.*"

I called up the Merlin Glass, and threw myself through it.

CHAPTER SEVEN

War on a Country Lawn

I burst through the Merlin Glass to see thousands of Accelerated Men running wild on the grassy lawns of Drood Hall. Screaming and howling with rage, they streamed out of a dimensional door hanging in the air, and every single one of them wore the black and gold uniform of Doctor Delirium's private army. They spread rapidly across the neatly mown lawns, running and leaping, baying like maddened animals. They moved at superhuman speed, churning up the ground and sending grass clods flying through the air. Their faces were twisted with an insane rage and hatred, fuelled by the Drug, and the noises they made didn't even sound human anymore. They headed straight for Drood Hall with murder on their faces, and more and more of them were coming through the dimensional door all the time.

For a moment, all I could think was: *Where the hell did Doctor Delirium get so many people, to dose with his augmented Acceleration Drug?* And then I remembered what the dosed people he'd left behind had done, at his secret base, and my stomach clenched hard, sickened at the thought of thousands of homicidal supermen running wild in the rooms and corridors of Drood Hall . . . I armoured up, and went to face the Accelerated Men with cold and brutal determination in my heart.

The grounds at Drood Hall stretched away for miles in every direction, or the Hall would have been overrun by now. As it was, the Accelerated Men had a lot of ground to cover. They charged forward at impossible speed—all strength and no grace, forced on by the Drug's terrible imperatives. They spread out in a massive dark wave, crossing the open lawns . . . but my trained mind had already noticed there was no sense of unity to them, no discipline in their movements or advance. They were a crowd of individuals, not a trained army, and a swift sense of relief ran through me. Suddenly, the family had a chance, because Droods are trained. Every one of us.

No one had launched a full-scale assault on the Hall for centuries; the outer defences see to that. First, you can't find us, and second, even if you could, the outer defences would track you down and kill you in any number of appalling ways. But somehow Doctor Delirium had found a way past all those layers of protection, by opening his dimensional door inside them. Which should have been impossible. The gateway was a large glowing circle, a good thirty feet or more in diameter, shining brighter than the sun, surrounded by crackling energies where one reality butted up against another. This was high-end tech, state-of-the-art, not just a brute rip in Space and Time. Almost Drood-level tech . . . and that was just plain wrong. There was no way Doctor Delirium should have access to anything like this. And even with that kind of tech, he still shouldn't have been able to open a door inside our grounds, within reach of the Hall. Not unless someone inside the family had given him the information necessary to bypass all our defences. Perhaps the same traitor who'd made the attack on the Heart possible . . .

Could it be that Tiger Tim wasn't the Doctor's only partner . . . ?

The Merlin Glass had sent me straight from Amazonian midday to early morning in England. The sun was barely up, the sky still streaked with red, and a delicate ground mist wafted across the grassy lawns. Through the mist came the Accelerated Men, running desperately with flailing arms and maddened eyes. Like nightmares broken out of dreams and into reality, from the deepest part of the night into the breaking day. And the only advantage I had was that the Glass had brought me here only a few moments after the Accelerated Men had arrived. I ran towards them with my hands clenched into golden fists. I was only one man against an overwhelming force, but I was a Drood, and sometimes that's enough.

Sometimes.

Part of me was wondering if the family even knew they were under attack, but almost immediately I was answered when the automatic ground defences started up. Huge robot guns and energy weapons rose smoothly up through the lawns from their underground bunkers, and opened fire on the intruders. The early morning air was full of the roar of guns, and the fierce flares of energy beams, but the Accelerated Men were just too fast for them. They could run and dodge faster than the computerised tracking systems could come to bear, and within moments they were upon the gun positions and overrunning them. The guns swayed back and forth, laying down a murderous range of fire, and superhuman men were shot down and blown apart by the dozen, but they just kept coming, leaping over the bodies of their own dead to get at the guns. They ripped them out of their positions by sheer brute force, and smashed the more delicate energy guns with repeated blows from their bare hands. Hundreds died, running into the barrels of the gun emplacements, but there were thousands of Accelerated Men, and more arriving all the time.

The next level of protection kicked in, as twenty living scarecrows appeared out of nowhere. Old enemies who had died at Drood hands, resurrected as scarecrows, so they could atone for their crimes by defending the family—for as long as they lasted. Neither truly living nor dead, they were impossibly strong and merciless opponents. If you listen in on the right frequencies, you can hear them screaming. Forever. Individually, the Accelerated Men would be no match for them, but there were only twenty scarecrows, and thousands of superhumans.

I recognised some of the scarecrows; I'd fought them myself when I broke into the Hall, back when I was a rogue. Laura Lye, still wearing the tatters of a dark evening dress, complete with holed evening gloves. Mad Frankie Phantasm, in the remains of what had once been an expensive Saville Row suit. Bunches of straw stuck out of open wounds in grey flesh. Molly and I had torn them apart, but the family had put them back together again. Because that's what you do with scarecrows. You make them last. And then my heart lurched as I recognised one particular scarecrow—it was the legendary Independent Agent himself, Alexander King. I could still see the hollow in his chest, from where I'd punched out his heart, in his magnificent secret base at Place Gloria. I hadn't known they'd brought him here, and made a scarecrow out of him, but I should have known. Droods bear grudges.

The scarecrows hit the first row of the Accelerated Men, and made mincemeat out of them, grabbing at the black-clad supermen with their implacable gloved hands, and tearing them apart with brute inhuman strength. They tore arms out of sockets, stove in chests, and ripped the heads right off people. Blood spilled thickly across the lawns. The Accelerated Men struck out at the scarecrows with their own appalling strength, but the scarecrows' spongy bodies absorbed every blow, and they felt no pain. Every superhuman intruder they laid hands on died, but in the end their speed was only human, and the Accelerated Men were just so much faster. Once the intruders realised this, they just speeded up enough to avoid the scarecrows and kept going. The scarecrows speeded up too, with all the inhuman pace of their unhuman nature, but even so, they only caught stragglers. The Accelerated Men suddenly changed tactics and swarmed all over the scarecrows, piling onto them in greater and greater numbers, until they bore the scarecrows down; and once they had them helpless, they ripped the scarecrows to pieces. I saw heads roll across the grass, cloth faces with human eyes, eternally suffering, endlessly hating.

The intruders were almost upon me now, appearing clearly through the thinning mists. I was thinking furiously. Doctor Delirium had cleverly adjusted the dose of the Acceleration Drug. These men were driven by homicidal rage, but they could still think, still plan, still change tactics as necessary. They would not turn on each other.

Some of them ran straight through the old hedge Maze, plunging through the heavy green walls as though they weren't even there, determined to get to the Hall by the quickest route possible. But those who went in didn't come out the other side. There weren't even any screams. The Maze just swallowed them up. Presumably, whatever was still trapped inside that Maze was still hungry.

The Accelerated Men concentrated on me for the first time. They recognised my armour, and a great cry of rage went up. I was the enemy they had been prepared for, and aimed at. For the first time, they produced weapons: all kinds of guns, scientific and magical. Cold blue steel and gleaming crystal. Doctor Delirium had armed them for bear. For all the good that would do. I was smiling behind my featureless golden mask.

The nearest Accelerated Man opened fire on me with incendiary bullets. They exploded harmlessly against my chest and head, thick trails of liquid fire running down my armour to set fire to the ground at my feet. I didn't feel the force of the explosions, or the heat of the flames. I just kept going, leaving a trail of blazing footprints behind me. More incendiaries slammed into me, bathing me in white hot flames, that just ran away, defeated.

Next they tried specially prepared cursed and blessed ammunition, but the torc protected me from physical and spiritual threats. You could damn me with bell, book and candle, or hit me with a bullet that had been exorcised, and neither of them would touch me. The Accelerated Men raked me with all kinds of bullets, and didn't even slow me down.

One man stepped forward and pointed a strange apparatus at me: a weird combination of glowing metals that surrounded and enveloped me in a strange glowing field. I knew what it was, the moment it touched my armour: a stasis field. Inside it, Time could not move. They could hold me here, like an insect in amber, and not one moment would pass for me until it was all over. Except, Droods have a similar weapon, and we've all been trained in how to deal with it. The strange matter of my new armour, being quite literally not of this world, has a resistance to Space and Time; all I had to do was set the strength of my armour against the field, and push steadily forward. For a long moment nothing happened, strain as I might, and then the glowing energy field coruscated wildly around the golden fist I pushed into it, and the field shattered and was gone. I lurched forward, back in Time again.

Some of the Accelerated Men had weapons that were clearly the product of alien technology. Energy weapons, distortion field generators, and other less familiar things. Weird energies hit me from a dozen different directions at once, crackling and crawling all over my armour, searching for a weak spot and a way in, before finally falling away defeated. One Accelerated Man appeared out of nowhere, right in front of me, and fired something at me, at point-blank range. He had a teleport gun, powerful enough to blast an enemy through Time and Space to somewhere else. He really shouldn't have used it against my armour. The energies rebounded straight back at him, and a moment later the air was rushing in to fill the vacuum where he'd been standing.

Another Accelerated Man appeared before me, with a new kind of gun. I stepped forward and punched him in the face before he could use it. The blow ripped the head right off his shoulders, and sent it rolling a dozen feet away. The body crumpled to its knees, blood spurting from the ragged stump of its neck. I kicked it out of the way, and ran on. Some blood had sprayed across my armour, but it quickly fell away.

I like to think of myself as an agent, rather than an assassin, but I have been trained to do what's necessary, when I have to. And no one attacks the Droods where we live, and survives to boast of it.

But all the time I was thinking, *Where the hell did they get all these amazing weapons? Doctor Delirium? Tiger Tim? The Immortals?*

I grabbed up a machine gun that had been torn from its mounting in the ground, and sprayed bullets around me. Accelerated Men were thrown this way and that by the impact of the bullets, but the grounds were wide and open, and the Accelerated Men seemed to be everywhere at once. They were crossing the lawns at superhuman speed, but most of them were still a long way short of the Hall itself. I kept firing till I ran out of bullets, and then tossed the gun aside. There were dead men lying everywhere, blood soaking into the ground, but I hadn't even opened up any holes in the advancing waves of superhumans. They just kept coming, thousands of them, more and more arriving all the time, and they didn't care how many of them died. They were riding the Acceleration Drug, raging with the dark joy of being more than human, focusing only on the enemy they'd been aimed at, and the need in their poisoned minds to hunt and hurt and kill, and glory in it. For as long as it lasted.

They came at me with glowing battle-axes, that shattered against my armour. They hit me with gloves made out of shimmering metals, and the gloves shattered and fell apart. I didn't feel the blows at all. I grew golden blades from my hands, and cut down anyone who came within reach, with vicious brutal blows. Accelerated Men threw themselves upon me bodily, clinging with desperate strength to my armoured arms and legs, struggling to pull me down. They piled up on me, trying to force me to my knees through sheer strength of numbers. But I stood firm, and would not fall.

I threw them off, one by one, grabbing them with hands so strong they cracked and broke the bones of my enemies, throwing the Accelerated Men long distances before they hit the ground hard, and did not rise again. I punched in chests, stove in heads, and broke arms and legs and necks. I stabbed and cut and hacked. I threw them down and trampled them underfoot. I killed and killed until there was no one left to kill, and then I moved forward again. And felt nothing but a cold focused rage. No mercy, no quarter, for the Accelerated Men. This was where Droods lived, and they should not have come here.

I'd been back for only a few minutes, but with everything that had happened, it felt like hours. And I hadn't really achieved anything. For all the Accelerated Men I'd killed, thousands more were streaming past me on all sides now, heading for the Hall with murder in their hearts. I looked back, wondering whether I should fall back and raise the alarm, and to my relief I saw the main entrance doors slam open, and a great force of Droods came out to defend the family home, led by the Armourer and the Sarjeant-at-Arms.

I knew them immediately, even though they were fully armoured, by the awful weapons the Armourer and the Sarjeant were carrying. Hundreds of armoured Droods came pouring out after them, because when an enemy comes, everyone fights. Every man and woman, no matter what they normally do. All Droods are trained to be warriors from an early age, because we all know that the day may come when everyone has to fight. For the family.

Many of the emerging Droods had transformed their armour into strange and terrifying shapes, to scare the intruders, but they couldn't concentrate long enough to sustain them, in the face of such an immediate threat. And besides, the intruders were so lost in the embrace of the Acceleration Drug they didn't care who or what they fought.

The Sarjeant-at-Arms was carrying two really big guns, a Colt automatic repeater in each hand. Massive pistols that could fire endless series of bullets, and never run out, and never miss. Their bullets exploded inside human flesh. Only the Sarjeant was authorised to use them, and only then in direct defence of the family. His bullets blew off arms and legs, punched through guts and chests, and exploded heads. Accelerated Men fell by the dozen, but the others kept coming. I didn't know whether they were brave, or determined, or whether enough of them was left to feel such things. They ran right over the bodies of their own dead to close with us.

The Armourer had chosen a really appalling weapon: the Kirlian gun. I winced when I saw it. The Armourer had never authorised its use in the field, not least because it was almost as dangerous to the user as to the people he aimed it at. Every living thing has its own energy field: the Kirlian aura. The gun explodes that aura. The Armourer aimed the Kirlian gun at the Accelerated Men, and they exploded into messy bloody gobbets as the aura that held their bodies together was suddenly removed. The Armourer trained the Kirlian gun back and forth, and suddenly whole sections of the lawns became bloody butcher's shops, with offal lying steaming in the early morning mists.

The two forces finally came together, as hundreds of armoured Droods slammed into the first ranks of the Accelerated Men, and stopped them dead in their tracks. They crashed into the golden armour and were immediately thrown back. Others were savagely clubbed down, or cut open with golden blades, or just thrown aside with such force that they died of it. Even a Drugged-up superhuman is no match for a Drood in armour. But . . . there were just so many of them, and for every Accelerated Man we struck down, more came racing forward to take their place. They moved so terribly fast, shooting past us, sweeping in and out of our ranks, come and gone before we could even lay hands on them, most of the time. Some Droods used their armour to boost their speed, to meet and match that of the intruders, but the Droods couldn't maintain it for long. Use up too much energy, and the armour automatically reverted to basic, to preserve itself and the Drood within. So for a while there was a stalemate, as blurred figures warred up and down the lawns, dead and dying men appearing out of nowhere to bleed out on the soaking ground. And then one by one the Droods reappeared, falling back to only human speed. They struck out viciously at every enemy who came within reach, but far too many of the Accelerated Men just raced straight past them, too fast to be touched.

And more and more came through the glowing circle, in a dark endless tide.

So the Droods nearest the Hall fell back, and linked arms, and made a golden wall between the main entrance and the approaching enemy. More Droods fell back to reinforce the wall, until it was four ranks deep, of Droods standing firm, ready to take on all comers and not be moved. They shall not pass . . . The first Accelerated Men came howling out of the mists at incredible speed and ran straight into the wall, as though they thought they could crash right through it. The golden line didn't budge an inch, the armour protecting the men and women within from the impact. The Accelerated Men had no such protection and were thrown back, dead or damaged. Bones cracked and splintered, organs were torn loose, or crushed through abrupt compression. Some kept their feet, even as blood flew from their mouths and eyes, and the Droods struck them down.

The enemy coming up behind saw what had happened, and were forced to slow their speed to nearly human levels. They threw themselves at the golden wall, and the Droods stood their ground and killed everyone who came within reach of the deadly golden blades protruding from their hands. They cut and hacked, and the Accelerated Men fell before them, but there were always more, pressing forward.

The Accelerated Men took on a new tactic, and used their superhuman strength to leap right over the Droods in the wall. But the Droods in the rear just jumped up to meet them, and cut them out of midair. The Droods threw the dead bodies aside, so they wouldn't get in the way of the fighting, and took their place at the rear again. And that was the end of that tactic.

I was still fighting alone on the lawns, surrounded on all sides by Accelerated Men. I cut them down with my golden blades, over and over again, my arms and my back aching fiercely; and still they came. I could feel sweat running down me, inside my armour. Fight long enough, and I would collapse from my own human weaknesses, long before the armour would wear out. Because the armour only augments the man inside it; he still has to do the fighting. But I had already decided, quite calmly and rationally, that I would fight till I dropped, would die on my feet, inside my armour, before I would stop fighting, as long as one Accelerated Man remained.

The intruders streaming through the glowing circle suddenly had new weapons in their hands—strange bulky guns they turned on everyone who wasn't them. They strode forward, firing indiscriminately into the Droods before them, and I heard shocked and startled screams, as Droods were thrown to the ground by bullets that could pierce Drood armour. I saw one defender rolling on the ground, clapping an unbelieving hand to the blood flowing down his golden side, from the ragged hole in his armour. I saw blood spurt from a featureless golden mask, as a bullet punched through his forehead. More and more Droods lay screaming and dying on the bloody lawns, brought down by bullets that pierced golden armour as though it was paper. A bullet whined past my head, and I crouched down instinctively, because I thought I knew what those guns were, what they had to be.

I'd only seen one, once before, in the hand of my late Uncle James. He'd had a gun made by his brother, the Armourer, a gun specially designed to fire strange matter bullets. The only kind that could pierce Drood armour. The Armourer swore he'd made only one, and had it destroyed, but I'd been told a lot of things that had turned out not to be true after all.

All around me Droods fell, spurting blood and screaming for help that never came. The rest of us were far too busy just trying to stay alive. I glared about me, not knowing what to do for the best. The Accelerated Men with the new guns were pouring through gaps they'd opened up in our ranks, and it wouldn't be long before they reached the golden wall, and forced entry into the Hall . . .

I reached out to make contact with Ethel. "You have to do something! Those guns are using strange matter!"

I know! said Ethel. *It's my strange matter! Those guns are tearing it from me, by brute force!*

"What? How is that even possible?"

I don't know! It shouldn't be possible! And Eddie— some of those bastards have taken enough to make blades out of strange matter!

The Armourer and the Sarjeant-at-Arms were working together to target the invaders with the strange matter guns, taking them out as fast as they could identify them. Through the dimensional door came the next wave of Accelerated Men, brandishing swords and axes of glowing strange matter. The Droods swiftly reorganised, urged on by the Sarjeant-at-Arms, as the last of the enemy with the new guns crashed to the ground, or exploded messily as their Kirlian aura was ripped away. The Droods moved steadily forward to meet the Accelerated Men, with glowing golden swords protruding from their armoured hands.

Droods and supermen slammed together, and fought fiercely under the early morning sky. Duels broke out, with both parties moving at incredible speed. Golden blades crashed together, and both sides stamped back and forth on the muddy, bloody ground. The Droods quickly took the upper hand, because they were experienced in the use of sword and axe, and the Accelerated Men weren't. Superhuman strength and speed is no match for experience and training. The invaders had skill, and the raging fury of the Drug, but the Droods were fighting to protect their family.

And that made all the difference.

Men with glowing axes came running out of the thinning mists towards me. I had time to remember the strange matter arrow that had pierced my armour, fired by an elven lord, and just how much that had hurt . . . but that just made me angrier. I smiled a death's-head grin inside my mask, and went to meet the enemy with long glowing blades protruded from my hands. I'd seen too many Droods die. First the Matriarch, and then my Molly, and now . . . I wanted to hurt the enemy, and kill them, and make them pay and pay and pay . . .

As I was moving forward, a pair of gryphons appeared out of nowhere, hit an Accelerated Man from both sides at once, and then hauled him down. They tore him to pieces, and then ate the pieces. They could do that, because they could see a short distance into the future, and see where the Accelerated Men were going to be. From the blood that streaked their flanks and dripped from their muzzles, they'd been doing this for some time. The sight disturbed me. I was used to seeing the gryphons as ugly, playful creatures. It had been so long since anyone had dared launch an attack on the Hall itself, I'd forgotten the gryphons were part of our defences.

Drood reinforcements arrived, swooping down from above on all kinds of flying machines. A semitransparent flying saucer swept silently overhead, strafing the approaching intruders with blazing guns, blowing great bloody holes in the ranks of the enemy. Young men on autogyros flew jerkily back and forth above the battle, dropping homemade incendiaries. Fires burst out all over the lawns, and blazing Accelerated Men ran madly back and forth as the flames consumed them. Young women on winged unicorns soared gracefully in the sky, dropping shrapnel grenades. The shrapnel couldn't pierce Drood armour, but it cut through the running enemy like razored winds. One Accelerated Man shot a hang glider out of midair. The Drood pilot cut himself free, aimed carefully, and dropped out of the sky onto the Accelerated Man like a living bomb. He hit the intruder perfectly, and drove him into the ground like a nail into wood. After a moment, the Drood climbed out of the hole and moved away, shaking bloody mush from his golden armour.

Everywhere, Droods were fighting savagely, stopping the advance of the Accelerated men and even driving them back, for all their superhuman strength and speed. The strange matter guns might have made a difference, if the Armourer and Sarjeant-at-Arms hadn't made a point of targeting their owners and blowing them away. And while the strange matter blades could cut through Drood armour, mostly they never got the chance.

I went to meet the Accelerated Men with glowing axes, and cut them down, blood flying on the air as my blades gutted them, sliced throats, and cut off heads. I was tired and I was slowing, but I was still death on two legs, a Drood in his armour, and all the awful pains in my back and arms, all the heaving lungs and bone-deep weariness would not stop me. I killed everyone who stood before me, and felt nothing, nothing at all, save a cold focused determination.

I was glad Molly wasn't there, to see me like that. Reduced, to that.

I stopped, for a moment, to get my breath, and looked around me. The lawns were soaked with blood and gore, and churned up into crimson mud. It squelched under the heavy feet that trod it, and was littered with piled-up bodies for as far as the eye could see. The Accelerated Men had come in their thousands, and they had died in their thousands, and the only compassion I had was for the Droods lying dead alongside them. I looked back and forth, and it seemed to me that the number of Accelerated Men was quite definitely dropping.

There were hundreds of them now, rather than thousands, reduced to small groups surrounded by cold and murderous Droods. None of the Accelerated Men had got past the golden wall. I looked at the dimensional door, and my heart rose as I realised no more of the intruders were coming through. They'd finally run out of warm bodies to dose with the Drug and throw at us. I made contact with the Sarjeant-at-Arms, via Ethel and our torcs.

"Sarjeant; any chance we could get some of our people through that dimensional door, before they shut it down? See who or what is on the other side?"

"Excellent idea, Edwin," said the Sarjeant's calm, unhurried voice. "But I can't spare anyone. The Hall must be defended. The family must come first. Feel free to jump through and take a look for yourself, if you can get close enough."

I strode forward, through the scattering Accelerated Men, cutting down anyone stupid enough to come within reach. One threw himself at me, screaming hysterically, trying to pry open my golden armour with his superhuman strength. His hands scrabbled uselessly against the gold, his finger bones breaking, and in the end I just threw him aside. He hit the ground hard, his back snapping, and just lay there, crying. I should have stopped long enough to give him the coup de grâce, but I had more important things on my mind. Later in the day, that lack of basic mercy would upset me. But not then.

I was only a dozen feet short of the great glowing circle when the enemy decided on one last desperate, despicable tactic. A final wave of Accelerated Men burst through the dimensional door, carrying large reinforced pouches strapped to their chests or backs. They ran at the Hall with the best speed their super-human strength could provide. Something about those pouches bothered me, and I reached out lazily, putting out a straight golden arm in the path of one of the runners. He slammed right into it, and my golden arm did not budge one inch. It whipped the runner off his feet and put him on his back in a moment, his chest caved in. He looked up at me with a shocked, surprised face, fighting for breath, and actually struggled up onto his feet again as I closed in. I punched him in the chest as hard as I could, and blood shot from his mouth as my fist emerged from his back. I pulled my hand out, and he collapsed immediately, as though that was all that had been holding him up.

He took his time dying, but I had eyes only for the reinforced pouch strapped to his chest. I ran my hands over it carefully, checking for trip wires and booby traps, and then gave in to my impatience, and just ripped the thing open. And inside, was a small but perfectly functional nuclear device. Big enough to take out the Hall and a hell of a lot of the grounds around it.

"It's a nuke!" I yelled to the Sarjeant. "It's a bloody nuke! All these new arrivals are suicide bombers!"

"They only need to get one inside the Hall," said the Armourer, his voice cutting in sharply. *"The Hall has protections against an outside nuclear assault, but not inside. . . . Never thought we'd need it. And even if we*

keep the bombs outside the Hall, and they detonate just one in the grounds, think about all the Droods out here fighting . . ."

"Could our armour protect us from an atomic bomb?" I asked Ethel.

I don't know! What's atomic?

"Terrific," I said.

"Even if we should survive the blast, about which I for one have severe doubts," said the Armourer, *"the grounds would still be utterly devastated, a radioactive nuclear nightmare for generations to come!"*

"Well, then," I said. "Let's not let that happen."

"I can't use the Kirlian gun!" said the Armourer. *"In fact, any of our weapons might set the bloody things off!"*

"There is another way," I said. "Something I used once, to stop Archie Leach from using his Kandarian amulet."

"And if it doesn't work?" said the Sarjeant.

"See you in Hell, Cedric," I said.

I placed both my hands on the backpack nuke, and concentrated hard. The strange matter of my golden armour spread out slowly, completely covering and enveloping the nuclear bomb in a casing of golden armour. The bomb was now effectively inside my armour, with me. If it went off, the armour should contain the blast, and the radiation. Of course, I wouldn't be around to see it, but . . . Anything, for the family.

Molly? It's me. See you soon, love.

I could see other Droods getting the idea, dragging runners to the ground and enveloping the nukes within their armour. Inside of a few moments, there wasn't a single suicide bomber left in control of his bomb, just dead runners and Droods who'd taken the bombs inside their armour. Presumably breathing heavily and sweating hard, just like me, as we waited to see what would happen. I was just a bit flattered to see that one of them was the Sarjeant-at-Arms. It was nice to know he had such faith in me. I screwed my eyes shut, half cringing in anticipation of the detonation I'd never even feel . . . but the seconds dragged on, and nothing happened. Slowly, I realised that if the bombs were going to go off, they would have done so by now.

It's all right, Eddie, said Ethel, her voice bright and bouncy again. *The activation signal couldn't get through the armour, and I've already sent strange matter into the bombs, to disrupt the timers. You can come out now; the bomb's perfectly safe. So, that's atomic . . . nasty little weapon.*

And then, finally, one by one the Accelerated Men started to fall over. Aging, withering, dying, as the Drug used up the last of the energies that drove them. None of them had got anywhere near the main entrance to the Hall. The dimensional door slammed shut, before any of us could reach it. And just like that, the assault was over.

One by one, we armoured down. I stood up slowly, leaving the deactivated bomb at my feet. I took a deep, deep breath, and the cool morning air tasted good, so good. The man who'd strapped the nuke to his chest had died, somewhere along the line. I couldn't bring myself to care. All over the lawns, exhausted men and women stumbled back towards the Hall, and family. Dead bodies lay sprawled everywhere, in the crimson mud and churned-up grass. Most of them were Accelerated Men, but not all. We'd lost a lot of good men and women, this morning. They would be avenged.

"Get the nukes down to the Armoury, and I'll take

them apart," said the Armourer. He was standing not far from me, looking tired and a lot older. He glanced down at the Kirlian gun in his hand, as though he couldn't remember what he was doing with such a thing, and then he grimaced, and made the gun disappear. "I want the Accelerated Men, too. We need to know more about this damned Drug. I'll have my people run some autopsies, see what we can find. And then . . . I'll make us a whole new batch of scarecrows, to defend the Hall."

I'd never seen him this mad, this vicious. It was easy to forget that the kindly old Armourer had once been one of the most feared field agents, of that coldest of Cold Wars. And truth be told, I couldn't find it in me to feel any remorse, for what was in store for the fallen enemy. They shouldn't have threatened the Hall, the family, the children.

The Sarjeant-at-Arms came over to join us. He was puffing heavily, but all things considered he looked quite cheerful. The man was in his element.

"No one's tried to nuke us since the Chinese, back in the sixties," he said. "We must be getting close to something really important, if they want to stop us this badly. Whoever's behind this."

"Could be Doctor Delirium, could be Tiger Tim, could be both of them working together," I said. "They're the only ones we know are definitely linked to the Apocalypse Door. But where did they get all those people? Or those incredible weapons?"

They took my strange matter from me! said Ethel. *By force! That's . . . impossible!*

"Nothing's impossible, for the Immortals," said the Armourer.

"Hush!" the Sarjeant said immediately. "Not in public!"

I looked at him thoughtfully. "You still going to try and arrest me, Sarjeant?"

"No," he said. "My investigations have cleared you of all involvement."

"Well," I said. "That's nice. Now all I have to do is clear you as a suspect."

It was worth it all, to see that look on his face.

CHAPTER EIGHT

The Only Good Traitor

The Armoury had come alive again. Blazing bright lights, people running back and forth, lab assistants crowded round every workstation. Everyone was talking at once, when they weren't shouting, and from the look of it every lab assistant from every shift was back on duty. The Armourer and I appeared through the Merlin Glass, and everyone immediately stopped what they were doing to point a whole series of really nasty-looking weapons at us. I stood very still, while the Armourer beamed happily about him.

"Well done, very good, nice reaction times everyone, but we are not the enemy. We have met the enemy, and he is dead. Now, everyone back to work! I want full reports on all exterior and interior defences, and in particular why most of them didn't bloody work."

The weapons disappeared, and the lab assistants went back to shouting at each other and bullying their computers. Some were clearly exhausted from fighting, while others were still yawning from being dragged from their beds. All of them were giving everything they had to the problem of why so many of our defences had failed us in our hour of need. The Armourer moved quickly among them, peering over shoulders and asking pertinent questions, like why had the robot machine guns and the automatic energy weapons been the only systems to kick in? I'd been wondering that myself. There should have been force shields, shaped curses, floating invisible incendiaries, nerve gas clusters and teleport mines . . . The Armourer kept reeling them off, and the answer was always the same. Someone had shut them all down, in advance, inside the Hall. Someone inside the family. No one else had the codes, or access to the security computers. The automatic weaponry had remained online only because they were controlled by the Armourer's personal computer.

I found an empty chair, by stealing it from someone else when they weren't looking, and sank into it. It felt really good to be off my feet. I was aching in all my muscles and some of my bones. My clothes were soaked with sweat, like I'd run a marathon. The armour provides us with strength and speed, but it's still all down to the man inside. Someone thrust a cup of hot tea into my hands, and was gone before I could ask for a splash of whisky in it. I burned my mouth on the hot liquid, and blew on it for a while. After all I'd seen and been through, I felt like I could sit there forever.

The Armourer didn't look tired. He raged back and forth, striding up and down the length of the Armoury, driving on his assistants, constantly coming up with different approaches and new leads of inquiry. He hurried from post to post, encouraging and remonstrating,

his voice flat and harsh, his eyes cold. Just the thought
of a traitor in the family had filled him with a terrible
fury. He finally came back to stand before me, scowling
furiously.

"A traitor! Inside the family, working against us,
leaving us wide open to our enemies! We've had rogues
gone bad in the past, but never anything like this. Even
Zero Tolerance didn't want to put the family at risk!
Once, I would have sworn something like this was impossible, but now, after the Matriarch's death, and Molly's, I don't know what to think. It's like everything's
been turned upside down. You can't trust anyone or
anything."

He found another chair and sat down beside me. His
back was still straight, but his hands moved uncertainly,
unable to settle, and his eyes looked strangely lost.

"This is serious, Eddie. Deadly serious. We could
have lost, out there. We could have fallen, and the family could have been wiped out."

"But we didn't, and we weren't," I said. "Because
we're Droods."

We sat and watched a steady stream of bodies being
carried through the Armoury on stretchers, on their
way to the attached hospital wards. Dead Accelerated
Men on their way for autopsy and examination. Most
of the bodies were in pretty bad shape, withered, desiccated, almost mummified. Others had been struck
down and torn apart by golden armour, and those bodies left bloody trails behind them. Some were in pieces,
roughly assembled on stretchers; others were just bits
and bobs, collected in black plastic garbage bags. A part
of me found that entirely suitable. There was no room
left in me for mercy, or compassion. If we could have
brought the dead men back to life I would have spent

all day killing them again, and gloried in it. I shook my head slowly. That wasn't me. That was the tiredness talking. The stretcher bearers just kept passing before us, more and more of them.

"How many died?" I asked the Armourer. "Do we know yet?"

Somebody immediately thrust a file into the Armourer's hand, and he leafed through it slowly. "Two thousand, seven hundred and eighteen dead Accelerated Men. We're having to open up the extra-dimensional arms of the hospital ward, just to hold them all. I've ordered every single one of them brought down here, under full security. Who knows what kind of chemical or bacterial agents they might have buried inside them, for one last assault on the unwary? We'll have no Trojan horses here. I want those bodies rendered down to their smallest parts, and made to give up every secret they have. We need an answer to the Accelerated Men, before they come again."

I looked up sharply from my tea. "You think there'll be another attack? Another invasion?"

"Why do you think I've been yelling at everyone to get all the defences back online? Until they are, we're vulnerable. The whole family is vulnerable."

"How many did we lose?" I said. "How many Droods died out there?"

"Two hundred and thirty-eight, so far. Over four hundred more critically injured, and as many again seriously. More figures are coming in all the time. They're up in the main hospital wards. The living and the dead. I didn't want our honourable fallen lying beside scum."

"Accelerated Men," I said. "I never thought to see their like again."

"Given the way these new Accelerated Men acted,

with almost insane levels of rage and ferocity, it would seem Doctor Delirium has been experimenting with the formula. Improving it . . . Oh yes, I recognised the black and gold uniforms . . ."

I told him what I'd found and what I'd learned, at Doctor Delirium's last base, and he sat quietly for a while, considering. "Every answer leads to more questions. If Doctor Delirium and Tiger Tim killed off all the people they left behind, presumably as a trial run for the new augmented Drug, where did they find the thousands of new subjects they used to attack us? Doctor Delirium couldn't have raised an army that size without our noticing. Unless the traitor has been interfering with our records . . . I hate this, Eddie. I really hate it. I look around, at all these familiar faces, and I feel like I don't know them at all. Any one of them could be the traitor. In an ever-changing world, the only thing everyone could trust, and count on, was the family. And now even that's been taken away from us."

"I have an answer, as to where this new army might have come from," I said. "But you're really not going to like it. What if Doctor Delirium and Tiger Tim have made an alliance with the Immortals?"

"You're right," said the Armourer. "It is an answer, and I really don't like it. As if things weren't bad enough. I thought you said you saw the Immortals fighting with Doctor Delirium, to get their hands on the Apocalypse Door in Los Angeles?"

"That was then," I said. "They could have teamed up since, to handle something they couldn't control on their own. Doctor Delirium provides the genius, the Immortals provide the warm bodies, and Tiger Tim acts as go-between. Maybe the Door was just . . . too scary?"

We were interrupted before we could follow that

thought any further, by two young lab assistants bearing a limp form on a stretcher. The man in the black and gold uniform was still alive, and carefully strapped down. He looked about a hundred years old, but there was enough fight left in him to glare viciously in all directions. He cursed us all, impartially, in a dry cracked voice. The two lab assistants smiled cheerfully at the Armourer, and dropped the stretcher on the floor before us. The impact shut off the swearing, for a while.

"Maxwell and Victoria," the Armourer said heavily. "It would have to be you. My two most successful and irritating students. All right, where did you find him, and why isn't he dead like all the others?"

"We found him under a gryphon," Maxwell said proudly. "It was sitting on him. Apparently it had already eaten its full of intruders, and was just keeping this one around for when it got hungry again."

"Max got him out from under the gryphon," said Victoria. "He was very brave."

"Oh hush, Vicky."

"You were! You never take enough credit, Max. You're always talking yourself down, and I won't have it. You should have seen him in battle . . ."

They were both young, little more than teenagers, and they looked on each other with wide, loving eyes. The Armourer sighed, and stood up.

"Get back to the gryphon. Explain. How did you . . ."

"Oh, it was really terribly easy," said Maxwell. "We just bribed the gryphon with a good back rub and a few friendly words, and then Vicky distracted him with an awfully sweet dance, while I dragged the Accelerated Man out from under. He wasn't much to look at, and he smelled really bad, from being under the gryphon, but

I could tell he was still alive from the vile things he was saying, so . . ."

"So we knew you'd want to talk to him!" said Victoria. "You're quite right, Max, he does smell. But then, gryphons do love to roll in dead things, and they're positively spoilt for choice at the moment."

"We did think about pushing him into a shower first, before presenting him to you," said Maxwell. "But we weren't actually sure how long he'd last . . ."

"So we just tied him down and brought him here!" said Victoria. "Do we win a prize?"

"You should get the prize, Vicky, it was all your idea . . ."

"Oh hush, Max, you're talking yourself down again! You're as entitled to a prize as I am!"

"Young love among the lab assistants," said the Armourer. "The horror, the horror . . . All right the two of you, very well done. There will be gold stars and extra ticks on your next reports. Now go back out and look under some more gryphons. You never know your luck."

Maxwell and Victoria departed quickly, holding hands. The Armourer glared after them. "I think it's time we started putting that white powder in their tea again."

"Given that they clearly only have eyes for each other, it's a wonder they found anyone," I said solemnly.

"Probably tripped over him," sniffed the Armourer.

I levered myself up out of my chair, found a handy surface to put my cup on, and the Armourer and I glared down at the Accelerated Man on his stretcher.

"So," I said. "Why aren't you dead?"

"Let me up," he said. "I've got cramps. You can't keep me tied up like this. I've got rights."

"No, you bloody haven't," I said briskly. "We are not

the law, we are not the government. We are Droods, and you are in deep shit. A lot of good people died this morning, at the hands of you and your kind, so if you like having your organs on the inside, this would be a really good time to start answering questions."

Give the man his due. In his position, he had to be scared out of his wits, but with the Acceleration Drug already killing him by inches, he must have realised we were his best hope for keeping him going. So he just sniffed loudly, and addressed the air as though we weren't there.

"All right, all right . . . I was one of the last men through the dimensional door. Last wave in, before the suicide bombers. And I just want to say right now, that no one told the rest of us about that particular addition to the plan. We are mercenary soldiers, not martyrs. Anyway, I got sideswiped by a Drood, had the wind knocked out of me, and hit the ground hard. Next thing I know, I'm under a bloody gryphon. Great big smelly beast. And of course, that was when the Drug ran its course, and the side effects kicked in. All the extra strength ran out of me, and I could feel myself aging. Felt my muscles shrivelling up, my heart slowing down, my lungs straining . . . really bad experience."

"Of course," said the Armourer, tapping his chin thoughtfully with one fingertip. "Trapped under the gryphon he couldn't move, so he couldn't use up the last of his energies. Basically, he's just running on borrowed time now."

"Am I going to die?" said the mercenary.

"Of course you're going to die, you appalling creature," said the Armourer. "And quite right too."

"But," I said. "The more helpful you are, the harder we'll try to stave off the results of the Drug. Deal?"

"I hate Droods," said the mercenary. "Always so bloody reasonable."

And that was when the Sarjeant-at-Arms appeared. He stamped over to join us, still full of the fury of battle.

"Heard you had a prisoner! That him! Course it is, course it is. Look at the state of him. I've buried people that looked less dead than he does. Now, why wasn't I informed about this? I demand to be a part of the interrogation!"

And he cracked his knuckles eagerly.

"You don't get to demand anything, Cedric," the Armourer said coldly. "This is not your job. What the hell are you even doing here? Your job is to protect the Hall, and the family. So get your people together and make sure no one slipped past us and sneaked into the Hall during the confusion. And while you're at it, I want every acre of our grounds searched thoroughly, to make sure no one's hiding anywhere."

"You could help Max and Vicky look under the gryphons," I said helpfully. "That's where they found this one. Yes, I know; the gryphons are smelly, disgusting and generally revolting, but someone's got to do it, and I can't think of anyone else I'd rather recommend for the job."

"My people are bringing all the interior defences back online," said the Armourer, not giving the Sarjeant a chance to get a word in. "But you need to check that they're all functioning properly. And determine the state of the outer defences. When you've done that, have your people set up regular patrols in the grounds, just in case another dimensional door opens up. We can't afford to be caught napping again. When you've done all that, then you can come back here, and I'll find something else for you to do."

"That's telling him," said a voice from the floor.

"Shut up, you," I said.

The Sarjeant had been nodding reluctantly all through the Armourer's tirade, but now he stopped and fixed him with a cold gaze.

"There is one other thing we need to discuss, Armourer. In case of another attack, and things not going quite so well. We need to discuss the extreme option: Alpha Red Alpha."

"What?" I said. "What was that? And why have you suddenly gone all pale and thoughtful, Uncle Jack?"

"Alpha Red Alpha is our security strategy of last resort," the Armourer said slowly. "For use only when all else has failed . . . We have a dimensional door of our own, buried deep under the Hall. Power it up, and the device can rotate the Hall and its immediate environs right out of our world and into another reality. The idea being that we could stay there until the danger was past. Unfortunately, this particular device has never been tested. We might survive the journey, and we might not. And we might be able to get back again, or we might not." He looked steadily at the Sarjeant. "Put the thought right out of your mind. Things would have to get a bloody sight more serious than this before I would even consider activating Alpha Red Alpha."

"Am I to take it that this is another of those things that no one thought fit to tell me about, back when I was running this family?" I said.

"You didn't need to know," said the Armourer. "No one does."

I had to smile. "You mean it might upset the family, if they learned they were living above such a thing?"

"People panic far too easily," the Armourer said airily. "I'm almost certain it's entirely safe, as long as no one goes too near it. Panicking . . . Try working down here every day, surrounded by enthusiastic lab assistants, with too much imagination and no moral compass. You'd wear out your adrenaline gland before the first tea break. Sarjeant. You are still here. Why? Get back out into the grounds! For all we know, the whole open assault could have been just a diversion, to distract us from something else! Move!"

"I want a full transcript of the interrogation," said the Sarjeant, moving reluctantly away.

"Yes, well, it's nice to want things," said the Armourer, waving him away. "And don't forget to check for tunnels!"

"I'm still down here, you know," said a voice from the floor. "It's bad enough I'm dying, but do I have to do it in a cold draft?"

I knelt down beside the mercenary and undid the leather straps, while the Armourer wandered off in search of something. The mercenary wasn't any threat, just skin and bones and a face like a road map. I'd never seen a man look so old and not be laid out in a coffin. His skin had shrunk right back to the bone, his mouth was just a thin slit, but his eyes were still clear and knowing. It was hard to think he'd been a young and vigorous man, just a few hours before. I checked him over quickly for wounds, but he didn't seem to have taken any serious damage. His black and gold uniform hung baggily around him, as though it had been meant for a much larger man. The mercenary just let me get on with it, grunting occasionally with pain when I moved him too roughly. I did my best not to care. He was a hired killer, and he would have killed all of us, if he could.

The Armourer came back lugging an oversized metal chair, with cables hanging off it. He let it slam down on the floor, grunting with the effort, and then leaned on it for a moment while he got his breath back. He straightened up slowly, massaging the small of his back with both hands.

"I am too old, too talented and too necessary to be doing heavy lifting," he said flatly. "If I put my back out again, everyone's going to suffer. All right, Eddie, help me get him into the chair."

I looked the chair over. "Are we going to electrocute him?"

"I'd really rather not be electrocuted," said the voice from the floor.

"Shut up, you," said the Armourer. "Of course we're not going to electrocute him, Eddie. Dead men tell no tales, except under very specific conditions. I got this from the hospital ward. It's a diagnostic chair. Plug him into it, or possibly vice versa, it's been a while since I did this . . . then we hook the chair up to my computer, and we can see everything that's happening inside him on these display screens. If he even thinks about lying, alarms will go off all over the shop. The chair should also help stabilise his condition, keep him alive long enough for us to get something useful out of him. Provided I know what I'm doing. I'm almost sure I know what I'm doing."

"I demand a second opinion," said the voice from the floor.

We got him into the diagnostic chair easily enough. The dying Accelerated Man hardly had any strength left, but he did his best not to cooperate, for his pride's sake. I tightened various straps around him, as much to hold him up as hold him in place, while the Armourer attached various sensors. One by one a series of display screens lit up above and around the chair, showing everything from heartbeat and electrolytes to brain activity. The mercenary sniffed loudly.

"Wonderful. Now I can watch myself dying in detail. Hold everything; what are you going to do with those tubes?"

"Nothing you'll enjoy," the Armourer said cheerfully. "I'm just going to plug them into you, here and there. I'd look away, if I was you."

And he proceeded to do quite uncomfortable and intrusive things with the colour-coded tubes, while I looked away and the mercenary protested bitterly. I assumed this was all part of the softening-up process, before we started the interrogation. I'd never been involved with an interrogation before. I have beaten the odd piece of information out of the occasional scumbag in my time, when lives were at stake and there just wasn't time to be civilised . . . but that had always been in the heat of the moment. I'd never done anything as cold-blooded and premeditated as this promised to be.

"Normally I'd give the patient a local anaesthetic," said the Armourer, working away briskly. "But one, I don't have the time. Two, other people need it more than you. And three, you came here to kill my family, so I don't care."

"There's a fine line between interrogation and torture, Uncle Jack," I said.

"Not if you do it right," said the Armourer. "Do you really give a damn, Eddie?"

"Yes," I said. "Yes, it matters. We don't torture, because that's what they do. We're supposed to be better than them. We have to be, or they've already won."

"Too late," said the Armourer. "I've started, so I'll finish. And stop whining, you. Be a big brave mercenary. It wasn't that bad."

"Yes, it was! I'm dying, remember?"

"Not anymore," said the Armourer. "Those tubes I've just introduced to various parts of your anatomy are now feeding you a whole series of things that are good for you, and working hard to neutralise the last traces of the Acceleration Drug in your system. Have you stable before you know it."

"For how long?" said the mercenary.

"For as long as I choose to keep you alive. So, feeling chatty, are you? Splendid. Tell me things I need to know."

"My name is Dom Langford," said the ancient man in the chair, with what dignity he had left. "The Drug isn't in my head anymore. I can think clearly. I'm me again."

"The chair can only do so much," said the Armourer. "You're still dying. The human body was never meant to handle such superhuman stresses. So earn yourself some good karma in the time you've got left, by telling us what we need to know."

"You've got a really lousy bedside manner," said Dom.

"There isn't time for politeness and false hopes," said the Armourer. "Talk."

"I don't remember much of what I did, when the Drug had me," Dom said slowly. "Just . . . horrible, nightmare images. I know I did . . . unforgivable things, and would have done worse if I'd got inside the Hall. But I swear, that wasn't me. That was the Drug."

"You killed a lot of good people out there," I said. A part of me still wanted to be harsh with him, but he looked so small now, so pathetic.

Dom tried to smile. "I'm a mercenary, soldier for hire. Killing's what I do. But before this, I was always a professional. The Drug changed all that. We were lied to, all of us. No one said the Drug would turn us into monsters. I don't owe those bastards loyalty anymore. Not after what they did. Ask me anything."

"Where did Doctor Delirium get so many people to dose with the Acceleration Drug?" said the Armourer. He didn't sound so harsh, anymore. I think he had been ready to coerce the dying man, if he had to, but Dom Langford was so clearly bitter and betrayed, and so clearly at death's door, that the Armourer just didn't have the heart. He fussed over the chair's controls, trying to make the mercenary as comfortable as possible, for what time he had left. I watched the information on the display screens steady some more, as the tubes delivered painkillers and sedatives. The mercenary seemed to settle a little more easily in the chair.

"Doctor Delirium's been raising a new mercenary army for years," said Dom. "Had us set up in several different bases dotted around the world, just waiting, so we'd be ready for the big score when it came. Some of us had been waiting so long we'd begun to wonder if the call would ever come. Or if he just liked having us around, as a status symbol. You're no one in the mad scientist game, if you haven't got your own private army. We'd taken his money, so we just lounged around, treated it like a vacation . . . But when the call finally came, it wasn't like anything we'd expected. We'd be fighting Droods, they said, so we'd need a little extra. Something to make us as good as Droods, maybe even better. That was the first time we heard about the Acceleration Drug. The Doctor made it sound wonderful. We were all going to be superhuman, and live lifetimes. Should have known it was too good to be true."

"Who was giving the orders?" I said. "Was it just Doctor Delirium?"

"No. He had his partner with him, by then. A rogue Drood, called Tiger Tim. So full of himself you wouldn't believe it. But it was the Doctor who betrayed us. None of us ever trusted Tiger Tim; we'd all heard the stories. But the Doctor had always done right by us, till then—good pay, and the best of everything. That all changed . . . He changed, after he acquired that bloody Door."

"The Apocalypse Door," I said.

"Yeah. He brought it back from Los Angeles, and within a few hours he was a different man. He abandoned his old base in the rain forest without warning, and suddenly our base was the new centre of operations. And don't ask me where we were; I haven't a clue. We were brought in on planes with no windows, and put up in underground barracks. Could have been anywhere; we were never allowed outside. Most of us were glad when the Doctor arrived; extra security meant something to do, at last. But right from the beginning, it felt wrong . . . The Doctor locked himself away in his private office, and wouldn't talk to anyone. Just sat there, with the Apocalypse Door, talking to it, and listening to what he thought it said to him."

I looked at the Armourer. "Could the Doctor really be talking to it?"

"We don't know enough about the Door," said the Armourer, frowning. "Given what's supposed to be on the other side of it . . . Who knows?"

"William was supposed to be digging up some more information on the Door," I said.

"Haven't heard anything from him . . . Arthur! Front and centre!"

A long, gangling type in a messy lab coat nowhere near big enough for him lurched forward out of the crowd, and swayed to a halt in front of the Armourer. He had a broad open face, wide owlish eyes, and a general air of bruised innocence that had no place in the Armoury.

"What have I done now?" he said, in a tone of voice that suggested he'd said that many times before.

"For once, nothing obvious. Arthur, contact the Librarian, in the Old Library, and ask him what he's turned up about the Apocalypse Door."

"I already tried, sir, just before the incursion. There was no reply. But that's not unusual, for the Librarian. Do you want me to try again?"

"Rafe's probably convinced William to take some rest at last," I said. "I'll pop down and have a word with him later."

The Armourer dismissed Arthur, and we turned back to Dom Langford. He started talking immediately, as though he needed to talk to someone.

"I saw the Apocalypse Door, once. I'd been sent to the Doctor's private office, with an urgent message. He wasn't answering his phones again. When I got to the office the door was open, but he wasn't there. I thought I'd better wait. They wanted an answer to the message. So I went in, and waited. The Apocalypse Door was there, standing upright on its own, right next to the desk. I walked around it; it looked like just an ordinary, everyday wooden door. But . . . the office was hot. Unbearably, unnaturally hot. I could hardly breathe. And it felt like the Door knew I was there. That it was looking at me, watching me with bad intent. I didn't want to look at it, but I didn't dare turn my back on it. I started shaking. I was in a cold sweat all over, despite the heat. I edged closer to the Door, and listened. Put my ear right next to the wood. I couldn't hear anything, but suddenly

I was *terrified*. There was something there in the office with me, some huge awful presence . . .

"I panicked. Turned and ran out of the office, dropping the message on the floor. I'd never panicked on a battlefield, never turned and run in any firefight; but I ran then. I never went back. No one ever said anything. But the Doctor was in there with that Door all the time! No wonder he changed. Being around that Door would change anyone."

"What about the rogue Drood, Tiger Tim?" I said. "Did you ever see him with the Door?"

"Tiger Tim gave everyone their orders, on the Doctor's behalf," said Dom. "Because the Doctor couldn't be bothered with everyday matters anymore. Tiger Tim more or less took over operations, and we all went along, because he seemed to know what he was doing."

"And he put together the army that attacked us today?" said the Armourer.

"Took every man the Doctor had, and more," said Dom. "Word had got out on the circuit, in all the recruiting markets: good pay, and I mean really good pay, and a chance to try out a new drug that would make you superhuman. New men kept turning up all the time. And a lot of them didn't answer to Doctor Delirium or Tiger Tim. They represented someone else. Someone with really big pockets, to foot the bill for so many mercenaries.

"They didn't tell us we'd be attacking Drood Hall until the very last moment. And by then we'd taken the Drug, and we didn't care anymore. We'd fight anyone, kill anyone, do anything . . .

"The things I did, the things we all did . . . That wasn't us! We were soldiers, professionals, not butchers! Not monsters . . . The Drug turned us into monsters. I don't remember most of what I did; just enough to make me glad I can't remember the rest. I'm not like that. I'm not. They poisoned our souls . . ."

His head slammed back against the chair suddenly, and his whole body convulsed, straining against the straps. The display screens were going wild. Dom Langford aged horribly, years gone by in seconds, collapsing in on himself before our eyes, looking desperately at us all the time for help we couldn't give. The last of his strength had run out. The Armourer rushed back and forth, injecting drugs into the tubes, working the controls of the diagnostic chair, doing everything he could think of to try and save the man who'd been his enemy only minutes before. But there was nothing he could do. Dom Langford died with the face of a man hundreds of years old, his body little more than a hollow shell. He looked at me pleadingly, right up to the moment when the light went out of his eyes. He thought I could save him, because I was a Drood, and Droods can do anything.

I held his hand, at the end, but I don't know if he could feel it.

"We should have taken him to the hospital wards," the Armourer said finally. "He might have lasted longer there . . ."

"They didn't have the room, and we didn't have the time," I said. "We needed his information. And we didn't kill him; they did, when they introduced him to the Acceleration Drug. So, are you going to make a scarecrow out of him, like the others?"

"Of course," said the Armourer. "Waste not, want not."

But I could tell his heart wasn't in it. The Armourer gestured for some of his people to take away the chair, with the withered body hanging loosely in the straps.

"I need to ask you something," I said. "How did the Accelerated Men get their hands on strange matter guns? You told me you only ever made the one, for Uncle James, and you had that destroyed."

"There was only ever one," insisted the Armourer. "And I gave it to one of my lab assistants to destroy. Very capable young man. Raphael. Went on to be Librarian, you know. Before William came back, and took over."

I had a sudden terrible suspicion.

I called up the Merlin Glass, made it form a doorway into the Old Library, and hurled myself through it. I looked around, and there was Rafe, packing ancient and important-looking books into a travelling bag. As though he was preparing to leave, in a hurry. He froze where he was when I appeared through the Glass, and his eyes shot to one side. I followed his gaze, and there was William, lying unconscious on the floor in a pool of his own blood. Someone had cracked his head open, from behind. I looked back at Rafe. He hadn't moved. He watched me silently as I went over to kneel beside William. The old man was still breathing, though his pulse was faint and thready. I straightened up and looked at Rafe, who flinched back despite himself.

"What have you done, Rafe?" I said.

He didn't move a muscle, studying me carefully. "He shouldn't have tried to stop me leaving."

"He was your colleague. He was your friend. He trusted you!"

"He trusted Rafe. And I'm not Rafe. He never mattered to me. He's not one of us."

"One of you," I said, sick to my stomach. "An Immortal."

"Exactly. If you're wise, you won't try to stop me leaving. My work here is done."

"Over my dead body; traitor."

"My plan exactly," said Rafe.

There was a gun in his hand. A large bulky pistol of a kind that sent a chill through me.

"Yes," said Rafe. "The gun that fires strange matter bullets. This is the actual original, that the Armourer made for the Grey Fox. The one he trusted me to destroy. Of course, I couldn't do that. Far too useful. And I have a sentimental attachment, to anything that can kill Droods. I got this to my people, and they used it as a template, to make more. Though it took our scientists years to work out its secrets. The Armourer does good work. He really does have a first-class mind, for someone who isn't an Immortal. Step aside, Eddie. You don't have to die here. Just disappear back through your useful little toy, and you can come back again for poor William when I'm gone. And you'll never see me again."

"I've faced a far better man than you, with that gun," I said. "And I'm still here."

"Oh, Eddie," said Rafe. "You never met a man like me. I'm an Immortal."

"And I'm a Drood. Anything, for the family. Remember?"

I was ready to jump him. I knew the odds weren't good, knew that even if I could get my armour up in time, the strange matter bullets would punch right through it, but I didn't have a choice. I couldn't let Rafe get away with it. I just couldn't. I was bracing myself for the jump when Ethel suddenly materialised in the Old Library. A fierce red glare filled the air—a heavy overwhelming presence, like a never-ending clap of thunder. Rafe

cowered away from it, and then cried out and threw his
gun away, steam rising from his hand where the gun had
burned it. The red glare concentrated around the gun,
and it faded away to nothing.

How dare you! said Ethel, her voice so large it roared
inside my head. It must have been worse for Rafe; he
clapped both hands to his ears, as though he could keep
it out. *You stole my substance from me, my very existence in this world! You took it by force!*

"I'm sorry, I'm sorry," said Rafe.

*Sorry isn't enough! Give back your torc. You are not
worthy of it.* There was a pause, and then Ethel spoke
again, in her usual tone of voice. *Eddie, this is rather
odd. I can't take his torc, because he doesn't have one.
That thing around his neck is a fake.*

"He's not a real Drood," I said. "He just looks like
one."

Rafe turned to run, and immediately I was upon him.
I clubbed him to the ground with a single blow, and he
hit the floor hard. I kicked him in the ribs, and all the
breath went out of him. I kicked him again, just because it felt so good. Rafe cried out, and curled around
his pain. I reached down, grabbed his shirt front, and
pulled him up so I could stick my face right into his.

"Where's Rafe? What happened to the real Rafe?"

"You'll never know," said Rafe. His voice was sharp
and defiant, but he couldn't meet my gaze.

"Search the Hall, Ethel," I said. "See if you can find
any more of these bastards with the false torcs. If you
do, tell the Sarjeant; let him deal with them. Go."

The harsh red glare shut off in a second, and the usual
calm golden glow of the Old Library returned. I let go
of Rafe, and he slumped back onto the floor.

"You're too late," he said. "They're all gone."

"Well," I said. "You would say that, wouldn't you?"

Rafe suddenly stopped being all beaten and broken, and lunged forward across the Library floor. He knelt over William's unconscious form, pulled the head back and pressed a knife against the Librarian's throat. I'd started after him, but stopped abruptly as I saw a thin trail of blood trickle down William's throat, as the knife's edge just parted the skin.

"Get out of here, Eddie," said Rafe, smiling again. "And tell everyone else to stay out, until I'm safely gone. Or you'll have no Librarians left at all."

"I can't let you go, Rafe," I said steadily. "Or whoever you really are. You're a clear and present danger to the whole family."

"I'll kill him!"

"He'd understand. Anything, for the family."

We looked at each other, both of us ready to do what we had to; and then Rafe looked round sharply. He saw something, and shrank back horrified, the knife falling away from William's throat. Rafe's face was horribly pale, his eyes focused on something so terrible, something so bad he had no thought for anything else. He scrambled backwards away from William, making low whimpering noises.

I looked where Rafe was looking, and couldn't see a damned thing. Just the books on the shelves, and the steady golden glow of Library light. Rafe's back slammed up against a stack, and he cried out miserably when he realised he couldn't retreat any farther. His wide eyes were locked on something, and he was making a high whining noise now. I moved forward, to put myself between Rafe and William, but Rafe no longer cared about either of us. He threw his knife away, and made pitiful, childish *go-away* motions with his hands.

I raised my Sight and looked hard, but I still couldn't See anything.

"Can't you see?" said Rafe, in a harsh, strained voice. *"Can't you see that? It's coming for me! Do something! Don't let it get me!"*

I could feel all the hackles rising on the back of my neck, in response to the stark terror in Rafe's voice. He was definitely seeing something, and given what the sight of it was doing to him, I was glad I couldn't see what he was seeing. I moved cautiously forward, grabbed up the knife from the floor, and Rafe scrabbled quickly behind me, putting me between him and whatever he saw coming for him. William had been convinced there was Something living down here in the Old Library with him; Something that watched him, or watched over him. Rafe clutched at me like a frightened, desperate child.

"Don't let it get me," he said, in a small broken voice. "Please. I'll tell you anything you want to know."

"Come with me," I said. "I'll get you out of here. But you give me any trouble, and I'll just walk away and leave you here."

"Yes. Anything. Please; *I can't stand it* . . ."

I stood up straight, and addressed the space before us. "I am Edwin Drood. I speak for the family. Who's there?" There was no response. The light didn't flicker, and the shadows were just shadows. I still couldn't See anything. Rafe stopped whimpering suddenly, the sound cut off in his throat. I looked back, and saw him turn his head slowly, as though watching Something move across the Library and then disappear behind the stacks. He collapsed, shuddering with relief.

"What was it?" I said. "What did you see?"

Rafe shook his head. He didn't want to say, as though

just naming or describing it might be enough to summon it back. Finally, he whispered one word.

"White . . ."

I left him sitting huddled up against a stack, clutching his knees to his chest, looking around with wide, shocked eyes. I used the Merlin Glass to summon medical help for William. A doctor in a blood-smeared white coat came through, and examined William quickly but thoroughly. He ran gentle fingers over William's broken head, while shooting me an accusing glance.

"I do have other patients to attend to, you know. Other people who need my help. This is nothing serious. Bad, but fixable. Upstairs, we're so packed we're running triage, sorting out the saveable from the hopeless. The Librarian can wait."

"No he can't," I said flatly. "You give William top priority. He knows things no one else in the family knows. Take him up to the hospital wards through the Glass, and make sure he gets to the front of the queue. Don't make me come looking for you."

The doctor sighed. "Go ahead, bully me! That's what I'm here for." He called through the open Merlin Glass for stretcher bearers, and then peered across at Rafe, still shuddering and staring. "Want me to take a look at that one too? Though I'm pretty sure I can diagnose shock from here."

"He stays with me," I said. I wasn't ready to say we had an Immortal in the family. Not just yet.

They took William away, still unconscious, and I took Rafe back to the Armoury. He clung to me like a child. I told the Armourer everything that had happened, and he looked at Rafe with cold, angry eyes. He pulled Rafe away from me and thrust him into the diagnostic chair, tightening the restraining straps around him with almost brutal efficiency. He then attached all the sensors, checked the display screens, and put the tubes in place. Rafe jumped and flinched a few times, but didn't say anything. Away from the Old Library, he was quickly regaining his old composure and self-control. He looked at the Armourer and me with a cold and thoughtful gaze. The Armourer finished his work, stepped back to look at the display screens, and then scowled fiercely.

"Wait a minute, that can't be right . . ." He checked all the connections again, fiddled with a few things, and even gave his computer a warning slap; but when he checked the display screens again he still didn't like what he saw. "These readings . . . they're just *wrong*. They're barely human. Half of what I'm looking at makes no sense, and the other half . . . Whatever the Immortals are, Eddie, they're a long way from anything we'd call human."

"Of course," said Rafe, sitting calmly and at ease in the diagnostic chair, as though he'd chosen to sit there. "We're better than human. We don't have your . . . limitations."

He had all of his poise and arrogance back, the same superior attitude he'd shown me with his knife at William's throat. He surreptitiously tested the restraining straps, and smiled slowly.

"A diagnostic chair," he said easily. "One of the few things that might actually hold me. You can't tie down an Immortal with ropes and chains. But, it'll take me a while to break free from this, so off you go, Eddie; ask me your questions. I might answer them. I might even tell you the truth."

"You even look like you're trying to escape," said the Armourer, "and I will have the chair do really quite appalling things to your central nervous system."

"So you're the Drood torturer, now?" said Rafe. I knew that wasn't really his name, but it was hard to think of him as anyone else, even when the look on his face had nothing to do with the young Librarian I'd thought I'd known. He sneered at the Armourer. "I don't think so. You Droods don't have it in you to be really ruthless. Not like us."

The Armourer punched Rafe in the face. A sudden, vicious blow, with all of the Armourer's strength behind it. I heard Rafe's nose break, and saw blood fly on the air as the force of the blow whipped Rafe's head around. The Armourer studied Rafe calmly. He wasn't even breathing hard. Rafe sat stunned in the chair, blood coursing down his face. I didn't know which of us was more startled by what had just happened: Rafe or me. I'd never seen my Uncle Jack do anything like that before. Certainly not with a defenceless prisoner. Rafe looked at me.

"Are you going to just stand there, and let him do that?"

"Sure," I said. "I might even join in. I like William."

"We all like William," said the Armourer.

And he hit Rafe again, right in the eye. It was a hard, solid blow, and the sound was loud and unpleasant. People around us hesitated, decided quickly it was none of their business, and got on with their work. Rafe strained briefly against his bonds, breathing hard.

"I can keep this up all day," said the Armourer. "You can't. Traitor."

"I am not a traitor," Rafe said thickly. He spat out a mouthful of blood. "I'm not a Drood. I never was. I'm an Immortal. You can't treat me this way."

"People forget I used to be a field agent," the Armourer said easily. "And those who do know, prefer to forget the kind of things field agents had to do, in that coldest of wars. Hard men, for hard times. We were men, in those days, making hard necessary decisions, to do hard necessary things, to keep the world safe. I haven't been that man for some time, but I still remember how to get things done."

"What happened to the original Rafe?" I asked the man in the chair.

He spat out some more blood. "Removed and replaced, long ago."

"How long ago?"

He smiled. "Before you came back. You never met the real Rafe."

"Is he dead?"

"Of course," said the Immortal, smiling easily. "We detest loose ends. Never leave anything behind that might come back to haunt you."

He shook his head sharply, back and forth, back and forth, and then the Armourer and I fell back a step as flesh rippled all across Rafe's face. The cheekbones rose and fell, the chin lengthened and the nose narrowed, and just like that, a whole new face stared back at us. Completely different features, with an unbroken nose and an unsmashed mouth, fierce green eyes that shone with a cold intelligence. A whole new person was sitting in the diagnostic chair, staring at us with unbridled arrogance.

It was the face of a teenager, with ancient eyes.

"All of us can do this," said the young man who used to be Rafe. Eerily, he was still using Rafe's familiar voice. "All of us Immortals. See, Armourer: no broken nose, no blood. You don't scare me, because you can't hurt me."

"Don't put money on it," said the Armourer. "I've

spent twenty years in this place, learning how to damage people in new and inventive ways. About time I got my hands dirty again."

Probably only someone who knew the Armourer as well as I did would have been disturbed as I was. Uncle Jack had played up to the mercenary, Dom Langford, to put him in the right frame of mind. But the Armourer wasn't playing a role anymore. He was deadly serious. And I . . . didn't know what to think. The thing in the chair was seriously freaking me out. It was one thing for the display screens to imply he wasn't human, and quite another to see it demonstrated right in front of you.

"Talk," I said. "Tell us everything you know."

"Or?" said Rafe.

"Or I'll take you back down to the Old Library," I said. "Lock you in, and leave you alone with whatever it is that doesn't like you."

The Armourer looked at me. "William was right? There really is Something living down there?"

"Oh yeah," I said. "Big time. We're going to have to do something about that, when we've got a spare minute. Though when I say we, I mean someone a damned sight braver than I am."

The teenager squirmed unhappily in the chair, the tubes clattering quietly around him. He was breathing hard, and he didn't look nearly as certain as he had. The Armourer glanced at the display screens.

"He's not faking it. If I'm reading the screens right, he's seriously traumatised . . . What the hell did you see down there, Eddie?"

"Ask me later," I said. I leaned in close, to glare right into Rafe's face. "What's your name? Your real name?"

He smirked. "Call me Legion, for we are many."

"You want another slap?" said the Armourer. "This

is taking too long, Eddie." He held up a hypodermic needle big enough to frighten a horse, and shot a thin stream of clear fluid out the tip. "I have truth right here, in liquid form. I don't care what the screens say, he's close enough to human for this to work. Slide the needle past his eyeball and into the forebrain, and he'll tell us things he doesn't even know he knows. Of course, a certain amount of brain damage is inevitable. So, Rafe, tell us what we need to know. And the first time you don't answer, or the screens tell me you're lying, in goes the needle. I don't care how many doses I have to deliver. You can't have too much truth, can you?"

"All right, all right!" Rafe took a moment to compose himself, and then fixed me with his cold arrogant gaze. "It doesn't matter what I tell you. It won't help. We're always ten steps ahead of you. I've been plundering the Old Library of useful items ever since you rediscovered it. I was put in here, years ago, to work as an assistant in the Armoury. To get a good look at new weapons before they were put into the field, so we'd be ready for them. Pure luck put me in charge of the Library—all of the Droods' secret knowledge, under my control! And then, the Old Library, with all its forgotten secrets and treasures . . ."

"How long did you work for me?" said the Armourer. "Did I ever know the real Rafe?"

"Oh, I think I'll let you work that out for yourself. The Old Library . . . I've been systematically removing anything that even mentioned the Immortals, their history and practices, along with anything else we didn't want you to know about. When I'd finished with that, I started removing any books we didn't have: unique editions, original manuscripts and folios, that sort of thing. It wasn't difficult to keep William from noticing; he's always been easily distractible. Any time he did spot a missing volume, I just blamed Zero Tolerance fanatics. I did slip a few in Truman's direction, for Manifest Destiny, so I could point the finger if necessary, but never anything important. We were quite happy for him to keep you busy, but we never trusted him. He could have been dangerous, if only his viewpoint hadn't been so terribly limited. I also removed certain Books of Power, that were weapons in their own right. You can never have too many weapons, and besides, you wouldn't have appreciated them."

"Having established that you're a thief as well as a traitor," I said, "let's get to the important stuff. Have the Immortals joined forces with Doctor Delirium and Tiger Tim, to exploit the Apocalypse Door?"

Rafe hesitated. The Armourer leaned in, and showed him the horse needle.

"Of course we're working together! We're big, big enough to take in anybody, to get what we want. We would have taken the Door for ourselves, in Los Angeles, if you hadn't interfered. But we always look forward, never back. So we made a deal, with Doctor Delirium and the rogue Drood, offering them our resources in return for access to the Door."

"What do you want with the Apocalypse Door?" I said. "Are you really going to risk the Doctor opening it?"

"It's more complicated than that," said Rafe. "You have to understand; there were only ever twenty-three original Immortals. The man who first made contact with the Heart, and his immediate family and friends. Though there have of course been many long-lived offspring, down the years. Immortals can't breed with each other, so children can only ever be half-breeds. You'd recognise the names of some of them. Important people, movers and shakers. We can be anybody we want to be. We've been a lot of famous people, down the centuries. Kings and kingmakers, philosophers and generals, heroes and villains, great artists and celebrities. Sometimes for power and glory, sometimes to protect ourselves, but mostly just for the fun of it. We do so hate to be bored. The Immortals are everywhere, ensuring that the world goes the way we want it to go. We're on both sides of every argument, every conflict, every war. Sometimes for profit, mostly just to watch you dance to our tune.

"Of the twenty-three original Immortals, only nine remain. We can die. We were made Immortal, not invulnerable. But we are a large family, larger by far than you Droods. Thousands of offspring to serve the Elders, who serve the Leader, the man originally touched by the Heart. Oh yes; he's still with us. And even more serve us throughout the world, knowingly and unknowingly. We own the world. We own you. We're your worst nightmare; an organised extended family of Anti-Droods. The real secret rulers of Humanity. You Droods only thought you ran the world. We just let you handle all the dull, boring bits. You worked for us, and never knew it."

"All right," I said steadily. "What's changed? Why are you ready to reveal yourselves, over the Apocalypse Door?"

"I told you, it's complicated," Rafe said sullenly. "The Elders now believe that immortality isn't necessarily all it's cracked up to be. Are they, in fact, missing out on something? As in, the greater experiences and possibilities of an afterlife? Don't look at me like that. Don't be so limited in your thinking. They've lived for centuries. They've exhausted all the pleasures of this world, and now they lust after new adventures in the next world.

Heaven. Paradise. Why settle for anything less? But, they're afraid of Hell. After all the things they've done. They believe the Apocalypse Door can be . . . turned. Reversed. Made over, into a Paradise Door. So they can open it and go straight through into Heaven. After Doctor Delirium and Tiger Tim have served their purposes, we'll take the Door away from them, turn it around, and then all the Elders will go through into Paradise, and explore all the pleasures that may be found there."

He smiled at the Armourer, in a silly sort of way. "I don't know why I'm telling you all this. You slipped me a dose of your truth drug, didn't you?"

"Right into the main feed tube," said the Armourer. "You were so busy boasting you never even noticed."

"Bastard."

"Keep talking," I said. "What happens to the Immortals, after the Elders pass on?"

"Well, to start with, everyone else moves up one place. Promotions all round! The eldest remaining offspring will take control, and the Immortals go on. Forever and ever and ever. We may not be technically immortal, like the Leader and the Elders, but we still live many lifetimes. Some of us are quite keen for the Elders to go through the Door, so we can take over and run things the way we think they ought to be run. It's our time now, and we'll make the world jump . . ."

"Don't you want to go to Paradise?" I said.

Rafe sniffed loudly. "The Elders might believe in the Door; the rest of us have more sense. They're old and tired, they've lost their appetite for life. We want to make the world dance to our tune, and eat it all up with spoons. Oh, the plans we have . . . You're really not going to like them."

He giggled happily.

The Armourer and I moved away from the Immortal in his chair, so we could talk quietly together. As a Drood, you learn to believe ten impossible things before breakfast, and have a plan ready to deal with them by lunchtime. But this . . . was a bit much.

"Is this even *possible*?" I said to the Armourer.

"Storming Heaven, and forcing your way in?" said the Armourer. "I doubt it. Theologically flawed, at best. But who knows what living for thousands of years has done to these people's minds? The point is, if they believe it, they could open the Apocalypse Door and let loose all the hordes of Hell, while thinking they were doing something else entirely."

"I can still hear you, you know," said Rafe. "The Elders dictate policy, and leave us poor bastards to carry it out. The Door is a supremely powerful artefact, and that's all that really matters. We will master it, as we have mastered everything else that has come into our possession. We will uncover its true nature and capabilities, and use it to make us even more powerful. Because that's what we do. If the Elders disappear through it—fine. After they've gone, we'll use the Door to blackmail everyone. The governments of the world will do anything, give us anything, as long as we promise not to open the Door."

"I thought you already ran the world," I said.

"Indirectly," said Rafe. "The Elders always believed in keeping to the shadows, lest the world discover just how few of them there were. They ruled by pulling strings; a lot of us youngsters yearn to be more hands on. And get our hands *dirty*."

He giggled again, while I looked at the Armourer.

"How much more do you think we can get out of him?"

"Don't look at me," said the Armourer. "I haven't used this truth stuff since nineteen sixty-two. I'm surprised it still works. I was just bluffing, to put him in the right frame of mind. It'll take me a couple of days to whip up another batch. And I've no idea what repeated use might do to him. He could tell us everything he knows, from his childhood on, or his brains could start leaking out his ears. Not that I care, after everything he's done. Arrogant little shit. But, I'd ask your questions now, if I were you. While he's still feeling talkative."

I turned back to Rafe. "What other traitors are there, inside the Droods?"

"Wouldn't you like to know?" said Rafe, grinning widely. "Lots and lots . . . Probably. Not just Immortals, either. We're not the only ones who understood the advantages of having a man on the inside . . ."

"That could be merely an opinion," murmured the Armourer. "Just because he believes it's true, doesn't mean it is. I can't believed we're riddled with traitors and informers. I'm sure we'd have noticed . . ."

"How many Immortals are there, posing as Droods!" I said to Rafe. "I want names!"

"I don't know! None of us know! We're all only ever told what we need to know, just like your field agents." He studied the Armourer, with something of his old cold arrogance back in his face. "Basic security measure. You can't be made to tell what you really don't know."

"Did you kill my mother?" said the Armourer. "Are you responsible, for the murder of the Matriarch?"

"Were you responsible for the death of my Molly?" I said. "Or Sebastian, back during the Hungry Gods War?"

He tried to shrug inside the restraint of the straps. "Not me personally, but yes . . . that was all down to us. Don't ask me why. I don't know. Not my mission. I was just told to take advantage of the chaos, grab as much as possible, and then get the hell out of Dodge before my cover was blown."

"Molly," I said. "Tell me about what happened, to Molly."

"Ah yes," said Rafe, smiling unpleasantly. "They did tell me about that. We wanted to see what Doctor Delirium's addition to the Acceleration Drug would do to the Droods, on its own. So one of us dropped a little into the air-conditioning system. It's amazing what people will do, what they're capable of, if you give them just a little push in the right direction. Even goody little two-shoes Droods can be made to run wild, if you push the right chemical buttons in their brains. Shame it didn't last longer . . . but then, you can't have everything."

"You killed my Molly," I said, leaning in close. "You Immortals. I will kill you all, for that. I will cut you down and trample you underfoot, and make you extinct."

Rafe looked at me, but though he met my gaze steadily enough, he had nothing to say. The Armourer took me by the elbow, and pulled me gently away so he could talk to the Immortal.

"How were you able to masquerade as Droods?" he said bluntly. "How could you pretend to have torcs, and armour?"

"Because we did, for a long time," said Rafe. "The Heart remembered the Immortals, and indulged us. I think we amused it. We've been inside the Droods, working both for and against you, for centuries now. Of course, that all changed after the Heart was destroyed. A definite setback there, thanks to you, Eddie.

Who knew one man could make so much trouble for everyone?"

"It's a gift," I said. "But flattery will get you nowhere. What did you do, after Ethel gave the family new torcs and new armour?"

"We learned to fake it," Rafe said easily. "We've had centuries to learn how to hide in plain sight. Our scientists produced new torcs, good enough to hide us from Ethel, unless she looked really closely, and why should she? We made it easier on ourselves by only substituting Droods who would probably never be called on to armour up."

"But we're a family," I said. "We're all so close, living on top of each other in the Hall. How could you fool everybody? How could we not notice?"

"Because we've been doing this forever, and we're really good at it. We can fool anyone, because deep down you want to be fooled. You don't want to believe that the high and mighty Droods could ever be infiltrated, and played for fools. It's not difficult to replace a Drood. Just catch one on their own, pose as someone they trust, then abduct and kill them, and replace them before anyone even knows they're missing. And taking on a new face, even a whole new body, is never a problem. We're flesh dancers. Shape-changers. Just one of the many arcane abilities we've acquired down the centuries. We can look like anyone . . . and we do! We can be your friend, your mother, your child . . . you'll trust us right up to the point we stick the knife in, and twist it. Look around you. Anyone could be an Immortal. And if we live a little too long, and people start noticing, we can always fake our own death and come back as our own bastard offspring. Always lots of Drood bastards turning up . . ."

"Like Harry, and Roger," said the Armourer, frowning.

"Exactly!" said Rafe. "Isn't paranoia wonderful? A game for the whole family!"

"You're everything we exist to fight," said the Armourer. "Heartless, soulless, all the evil in the world in one place."

"Evil is such a subjective term," said Rafe, yawning widely. "So . . . situational. Immortals see the long game. Compared to us, all Humanity, and yes that includes you Droods as well, are just . . . mayflies. Come and gone in a moment. You're just there to be used because, after all, you're not around long enough to make any real difference in the world." He stretched slowly, within the chair's restraints. "I've had enough of this. My superior flesh has metabolised your stupid drug. I don't need to justify myself, to the likes of you."

I drew my Colt Repeater from its holster, and pointed it at Rafe's face. "Tell me where the Headquarters of the Immortals is located. Tell me where to find you. Or I swear I'll shoot you in the head. Right here, right now."

Rafe looked at me, and saw I was completely serious. He tried to shrink back in the chair away from my gun, but the chair wouldn't let him. I centred my aim on his left eye.

The Armourer cleared his throat. "I don't think we should kill him, Eddie. Not when there's still a lot more we could get out of him."

"Nothing else matters," I said. "Except this. Did you think I was joking, Rafe, when I said I'd kill you all? After what you did to my grandmother, and my Molly?"

Rafe looked past me at the Armourer. "You can't just stand by and let him shoot me in cold blood!"

"There's nothing cold about my blood," I said. "All I have to do is think about my Molly, and how she died, and my blood is blazing hot. Where do I find the Immortals? Where are Doctor Delirium and Tiger Tim and the Apocalypse Door?"

Rafe couldn't meet my gaze, so he concentrated on the Armourer. "You're a Drood. This isn't what Droods do! Stop him!"

"Most Droods don't do things like this," said the Armourer. "That's why we have field agents. He's all yours, Eddie."

"Is it any easier to die, having known centuries?" I said. "Or is it harder, knowing you could have had centuries more? You have so much more to lose than us mere mortals . . ."

"All right, all right!" said Rafe. There was sweat on his face, for the first time. "I'll tell you, but only because it won't do you any good. You can't get in. No one can get in, who isn't an Immortal."

"Tell me anyway," I said.

"We live in Castle Frankenstein," said Rafe. "The real one, the original thirteenth-century fortress, set atop a great hill overlooking the River Rhine. The Baron Georg Frankenstein killed a dragon there, in fifteen thirty-one. These days, another castle stands in for the original; they've made it over into a hotel for tourists who love the legend, and the films. We took over the original facilities at the end of the nineteenth century, after the infamous Baron Viktor von Frankenstein went on the run. He was never one of us; we just liked the irony. The Baron hasn't been seen since, but various of his offspring and his creations keep turning up, looking for knowledge, or revenge, or closure. The hotel takes them in, gives them the grand tour, and sends them on their way. No one ever bothers us. I told you. No one can get in, unless you're one of us."

I made him give us an exact location, and the Armourer checked his computer. He nodded briefly.

"Any more questions?" said Rafe.

"No," I said. And I shot him in the left eye. His head slammed back against the chair. He kicked once, and then slumped in the restraints, and was still. I shot him twice more in the head, because I wanted to be sure. Above the chair, the display screens went out, one by one.

"For Rafe," I said. "The real Rafe." I looked at the Armourer. "See that this piece of shit is cremated. And then scatter the ashes in the grounds, just in case."

CHAPTER NINE

Here Comes the Bride

The Armourer threw a sheet over Rafe's body, and then we both turned our backs on it. The noisy hustle and bustle of the crowded Armoury went on around us, as though nothing unusual had happened. As though I hadn't just shot a defenceless man in the head. The Armourer's lab assistants are a tough crowd to shock. I slipped the Colt Repeater back into its holster with a steady hand, and looked at the Armourer. He shrugged.

"Some of my people will take care of the body," he said. "When they're not so pushed."

"I'm going to break into the Immortals' base," I said. "Right now, while they're still trying to figure out what's happening. One agent on his own has a far better chance of getting in, uncovering the necessary information and getting out again, than any larger force. And it has to be me, Uncle Jack. I'm the only one the family can spare. The rest of you have to concentrate on making the Hall and grounds secure again. Just in case there's another assault on its way."

"That isn't why you want to do this," said the Armourer. "It's still all about revenge. Didn't I teach you better than that? Never take it personally. You weren't the only one who was lied to, and taken in."

"But I'm the only one who can do something about it."

The Armourer shook his head. "You always were good at finding reasons why you should be allowed to do something you'd already decided to do anyway."

"This needs doing, Uncle Jack, and it needs doing now!"

"I'm not arguing," the Armourer said mildly. "If anyone can take on the Immortals where they live, it's you. I just don't want you going in there in the wrong frame of mind. That gets more field agents killed than anything else. Come over here, Eddie, and let's take a look at the place."

We pulled up chairs before his main workstation, and he put his whole computer network online. Screens lit up one after another in a long row, and the Armourer cracked his prominent knuckles noisily as he bent over the main keyboard. It took him only a minute to lock on to a Chinese surveillance satellite, and task it to cover the exact location Rafe had given us. (I still thought of him as Rafe. Even though he wasn't.) A remarkably clear image appeared on the screen before us, but the image was that of a ruin, fallen down and beaten into submission by the erosive forces of time and rough weather. A few stubby stone towers, some crumbling inner walls, and a bunch of uneven stone boundaries half buried under ivy. Desolate and destroyed, open to all the elements, it was clear no one had lived there for centuries.

"He lied to us!" I said. "If the Immortals ever were there, they moved out long ago."

"Not so quick, not so quick," said the Armourer, checking the information on his other screens. "Rafe couldn't have flat out lied to us—not after everything I'd pumped into him. This is the right location, and it matches what we have on file for the infamous Castle Frankenstein. So let me try a few things here . . . slip in a few filters . . . Ah. Now that's more like it. I'm picking up major energy spikes, and definite traces of scientific and magical protections. Layer upon layer of the things . . . not unlike Drood Hall, actually. We're looking at a carefully designed and maintained illusion; the same kind of thing we use to hide the Hall from prying outside eyes. Yes, very professional work. But not good enough to keep me out."

"Can you slip in past these defences, without setting off any alarms?" I said, leaning in for a closer look.

"Teach your grandmother to suck oranges," he said absently, his hands flying over the keyboard. "It's all about matching resonances and reversing the polarity . . . Look, Eddie, you wouldn't understand it if I did explain it to you. Just trust me when I say this is going to be very tricky, and don't disturb me while I'm working." He gave all his attention to the computers, and I sat back and let him get on with it. The side screens were going crazy displaying cascades of incoming information, and the computers were making a series of high-pitched noises I was sure couldn't be good for them. I tend to forget that my Uncle Jack doesn't just make things with his hands; he makes them with his mind and his computers. He finally sat back in his chair, grunting loudly with satisfaction.

"All right, that's taken care of the scientific protections: the force shields, the intelligence systems, the subspace generators. The magical protections . . . are pretty straightforward, actually. Just what you'd expect. They're all based on existing pacts and treaties, backed up by the usual Objects of Power. All very potent and respectable, but nothing out of the ordinary. They'd keep out anyone else . . . but we are Droods, which means we have our own pacts and treaties, and even more powerful Objects of Power. You know, I don't think the Immortals have updated their protections in years, maybe even centuries. Could be arrogance, or complacency. Either way, they haven't got a damned thing I can't deal with."

The image of the ruin on the main screen disappeared abruptly, and something altogether different took its place. I leaned in close again, for my first look at the real Castle Frankenstein. A huge, grim, overpowering medieval edifice, a fortress set on a cliff overlooking the River Rhine far below. Tall towers, high stone walls with crenellated battlements, and massive doors heavy enough to stand off an invading army. All kinds of light blazed in the windows, from clear and clean electric light to the kind of murky glares you normally see only underwater. There were eerie glows and unhealthy illuminations, that flared up briefly and then sank down to flickering glimmers. Dark shadows crawled slowly across the towering stone walls. But there was no sign anywhere of human activity, and not a single human guard in place.

"I'm impressed," said the Armourer. "Damned good illusion, behind powerful protections. Would have fooled anyone else. And now this . . . of course, they're bound to have improved the place since the Baron's time. Amazing, when you think of what that man achieved, with the limited knowledge and resources of his time. All right, the Baron was undoubtedly ten parts crazy to ten parts genius, and he ran away from his responsibilities every chance he got, and he had the moral compass of a deranged sewer rat, but still, you have to admit . . . he did it. He brought the dead back to life, right there in his laboratory."

"I know," I said. "I've talked to some of his creations. Most of them weren't at all happy about it."

"Yes, well," the Armourer said vaguely. "That's progress for you." He stopped, and looked at me. "Eddie, what are you thinking?"

"Frankenstein defeated death," I said slowly. "Out of all the stories, and all the legends that have grown up around him, that's the one thing we can be sure of. He took dead bodies and made them live again. And I'm wondering . . . if his knowledge is still there, somewhere, preserved by the Immortals."

"No, Eddie," the Armourer said firmly. "That's not a road you want to go down. Whatever Frankenstein's techniques might bring back, it wouldn't be your Molly. Or my mother. All that bastard ever really did was make the dead stand up and walk around, and I don't remember anyone ever thanking him for it. There's nothing in that Castle or anywhere else that can help us. Dead is dead, Eddie, even in our world. Because all of the alternatives are worse."

"I know, Uncle Jack. I know."

"Stick to what you can do," the Armourer said kindly. "The good thing about our work is that it never ends, so we always have something to distract ourselves with. Now, there's no way you can teleport directly into Castle Frankenstein. Not through all those shields. Whatever got through would eventually arrive as a small pile of steaming red and purple blobby bits."

"The torc couldn't protect me?" I said. "Not even if I went through in full armour?"

"That's the problem," said the Armourer. "The shields would let you through, but stop the torc. Your body would pass through . . . probably piece by piece. And no, you can't use the Merlin Glass, either. If an artefact that powerful were to come tap tap tapping on the Castle's shields, it would set off every alarm in the place. You can't sneak past defences like these."

"All right," I said. "Let's see what the Glass can do."

I summoned it into my hand, and had it show me a view of Castle Frankenstein. But all the mirror could manage was an aerial view, from fairly high up. I winced.

"Forget it," I said. "I am not falling for that again."

The Armourer's ears pricked up. "Again?" he said innocently.

"Don't ask," I said. "No, I mean it. Don't ask. Glass, zoom in and give me the closest image you can."

The image in the hand mirror loomed swiftly up before me, and then slammed to a halt still some way out. The image flickered back and forth between the real Castle Frankenstein and the Immortals' illusion, and then the Merlin Glass abruptly shut itself down, and I was left with just a mirror in my hand, showing me my own confused reflection. I shook the mirror hard a few times, and tried half a dozen different command words, but faced with the Immortals' levels of protection the Merlin Glass had given up, and was now clearly sulking. I sent it back to its subspace pocket to think things over.

"Okay," I said to the Armourer. "Defences strong

enough to defy the Merlin Glass? I am seriously impressed."

"Well, don't forget, the Immortals are older than Merlin," said the Armourer. "However, they might have the experience, but we are more up to date. Give me a few weeks, and I could put together a package that would let you stroll right through those shields."

"We don't have a few weeks," I said. "I'm going to have to get as close to the Castle as the Glass can get me, and cover the rest of the distance on foot."

"Only an Immortal can pass safely through the defences," said the Armourer. "That's what Rafe said."

"And Rafe is going to get us in," I said. "Because Rafe is going to make me into an Immortal. Remember those clever little cuff links you gave me, Uncle Jack? The Chameleon Codex?"

I went back to the diagnostic chair, and flipped back the sheet to reveal Rafe's damaged head. Half of it had been blow away by my bullets, but the face was still mostly there. Blood was still dripping from his chin, and his remaining eye stared at me with cold accusation. Like I gave a damn. I looked at Rafe dispassionately for a moment, and then ran my right cuff link swiftly down one side of his face. Didn't get a single blood spot on my cuff. I covered him up again, and when I looked, there wasn't any blood on the cuff link either. It had eaten it all up, the necessary DNA information now stored and ready for use.

"You're getting cold, Eddie," said the Armourer. "I don't think I like that. Not in you."

"Molly's gone," I said, looking at him steadily. "I was going to be free, and have a life, with her. She was going to save me from my family. Now she's gone, and all I have left is duty and responsibility. And revenge. It's not much . . . but it's something."

"The family's not such a bad thing, Eddie," said the Armourer. "It means you're never alone. I lost my mother today, and my only son a long time ago, but I still have the family. I have you, and you have me."

"The Immortals took away my hope when they took away my Molly, Uncle Jack. I will make them pay for that; make them pay in blood and suffering. I had a life and a future, and now all I have is the family, and what it means to be a Drood. A life in service, to a war that never ends. A cause that consumes you, and an early death for reasons you'll probably never understand. Well, I can live with that, if there's revenge to be had along the way. Let's get to work, Uncle Jack. It's all I've got now."

"There's one obvious dropping-off point," said the Armourer, his face and his voice all business again. "The fake Frankenstein Castle—now just called ... the Castle Hotel. The tourist trap, remember? Only a mile and a half down the road from the real thing, next to a small village. You could be just another tourist, attracted by the name and the legend. They must see enough of those. Hmmm. Wait a minute ..." He searched quickly through several drawers, muttering to himself, and finally came up with a slim folder. "This should do you nicely. Standard field agent's package, for sudden intrusion into foreign climes. All the paperwork you'll need: passport, visa, travel documents, credit cards ... the usual. I always keep a few basic sets handy. What name do you want to use?"

"Shaman Bond," I said. "He has a reputation for just turning up anywhere."

The Armourer grunted, and quickly customised the necessary documents. He passed them over to me, and I settled them here and there about my person. Nothing like a bunch of fake documents to make you feel like a real field agent. The Armourer fixed me with a firm stare.

"You probably won't need most of them, but it would be stupid to get yourself picked up by the locals over something so routine. And use the credit cards sparingly, we're on a budget. And get receipts, if you want to claim expenses."

"Shaman Bond's a good cover," I said. "I'm comfortable being Shaman. I'll book into the hotel, spy out the lay of the land, and if it looks clear I'll head straight for Castle Frankenstein. And then I'll use the cuff links to turn me into Rafe, and walk right in."

"You'll need a cover story as Rafe," said the Armourer. "To explain your escape from us. They must know we captured him by now."

"Easy," I said. "I'll just say I stole the Merlin Glass, and stepped through from the Hall to the Castle. They'll be so overjoyed at the prospect of getting their hands on such an unexpected prize, they won't even think to challenge my version of events until it's far too late."

"You can't actually give them the Glass, Eddie! Once it's out of your possession, there's no guarantee you'd ever get it back! I don't even want to think what the Immortals could do with the Merlin Glass!"

"Will you relax, Uncle Jack? Breathe deeply, and unclench. I have done fieldwork before. Promising them the Glass is one thing, delivering it quite another. I have no intention of handing it over to them; I'll just say I have it stashed safely somewhere nearby. You know, standard operational bullshit. I'm very good at bullshit."

"I've always thought so," said the Armourer. He looked at me thoughtfully. "Do you think you'll find Doctor Delirium and Tiger Tim with the Immortals? Could they have the Apocalypse Door at Castle Frankenstein?"

"I don't know," I said. "Dom Langford said he saw the Door at one of the Doctor's bases. But, who can be sure of anything, where the Immortals are concerned? Dom never actually saw where he was . . . But at the very least, I should find information on its location at the Castle. The Immortals will know."

"Information is what we need, first and foremost," the Armourer said sternly. "Revenge can wait. Let's put a stop to the immediate threat of the Apocalypse Door, and save the world; and then we can decide how best to drop the hammer on the Immortals."

"Of course," I said. "Information first. I understand."

"But, Eddie, if you get a chance . . . And I mean a *real* chance . . ."

"I will wipe them out down to the last man," I said. "Burn down their Castle, and piss on the ashes."

"Good man," said the Armourer. And then he hesitated. "Eddie . . . I need to ask you something. A personal favour. If you should find the rogue Tiger Tim at the Castle . . . If you should find Timothy Drood . . . Eddie, he's my son. My only child."

I could only gape at him for a moment. We're a big family, and I'd been away from the Hall for a long time. "Tiger Tim, Timothy . . . I knew the name, but I never made the connection. But, he nearly killed you, trying to persuade you to open the Armageddon Codex!"

"He lost his mother at an early age," the Armourer said steadily. "And I wasn't there for him. Afterwards, well, perhaps I tried too hard. I never was father material. You of all people should understand someone driven to rebel against family discipline . . ."

"Well, yes, but I was never a rogue," I said. "Not even

when Grandmother said I was. I turned on the family, not on all Humanity. The things he's done, Uncle Jack, you don't know . . ."

"I know," he said. "I've made it a point to know. But . . . he's all I've got left, that's mine. He can still be saved, Eddie. I have to believe that. Please, if you can, don't kill him."

"I'll do what I can," I said. "But he may not give me any choice."

The Armourer nodded stiffly, and turned away. I wondered if he really knew all the awful things his estranged son had done, and planned to do. If he knew about what Tiger Tim had done at Doctor Delirium's Amazon base. And if it would have made any difference, if he had known. I've never found it easy to lie to my Uncle Jack. But I gave it my best shot when I said I'd try not to kill Tiger Tim.

Some people just need killing.

I coaxed the Merlin Glass back out of subspace, and had it open a doorway through to the Castle Hotel in Germany. I stepped through into a cobbled courtyard, and the Glass immediately disappeared again. If I hadn't known better I would have said it was frightened. After this was all over, I'd have to give it a good talking-to. Preferably where no one else could see me doing it.

I have to say, I wasn't that impressed by the Castle Hotel. To start with, it wasn't a Castle—and never had been—just a larger than usual manor house in the old European style. Five stories, half-timbered frontage, gables and guttering but no gargoyles, and three different satellite dishes. Pleasantly old-fashioned but with the clear promise of modern amenities. Warm, welcoming lights shone from the ground floor windows. On the whole, the hotel looked like it had stepped right out of one of those old Universal monster movies, from the thirties. Probably quite intentionally. Nostalgia for old fictions is the strongest nostalgia of all.

I looked around me. No one about, to notice my arrival. A dozen or so parked vehicles, scattered across the adjoining car park. Not many guests, then. Off season, no doubt. So if nothing else, the hotel should be grateful for an extra guest. It was early evening, cold with a cold wind blowing, and very quiet. There was no passing traffic, and the lights of the nearby village were a good half mile away. Dark ominous clouds were already covering half the evening sky, spreading long shadows across the bleak countryside. I shuddered suddenly, for no reason, and headed for the Castle Hotel's brightly lit entrance.

The lobby turned out to be warm, cosy and inviting, and gave the impression of being an old family business. A real fire blazed in an oversized fireplace, lots of wood panelling and beams in the ceiling. The walls were covered with framed photographs. I wandered over for a closer look. They were all head and shoulder shots of actors who'd played Baron Frankenstein and his monster. Colin Clive and Boris Karloff, of course, and Peter Cushing and Christopher Lee. All of them personally autographed. A whole bunch of familiar faces, from dozens of European films that at the very least, tried hard. The most recent photos were of Kenneth Branagh and Robert De Niro. Boy, had Branagh got his film wrong. There was nothing romantic about the Frankenstein story. Ask any of his creations.

There was just the one photo of Elsa Lanchester, as the Bride of Frankenstein. I nodded respectfully to her. Absent friends . . .

Someone had made a recent effort to tart up the lobby with various items of Gothic chic, including lots of black crepe paper and a few rings of garlic flowers. (Wrong films there, I thought, but didn't say anything.) I strode up to the reception desk, and smiled briefly at the receptionist—a determinedly cute lady of a certain age, in a traditional black-and-white uniform, with peroxide white hair, too much makeup, and a knowing look. She welcomed me to the Castle Hotel with a wide smile and a bright eye, and I made a mental note to be careful around this one. She looked like the sort who'd ask if you wanted *extras* . . . and then turn up to supply them personally.

I booked in as Shaman Bond, and explained I was on a walking holiday, and just happened to be in the area . . . I speak enough conversational German to get by. All Droods are taught several languages from an early age, because the whole world is our concern. Almost the first thing the receptionist did was to ask for my passport and credit card. Score one for the Armourer. I'd always been field agent for London; I wasn't used to gallivanting around in foreign parts. I watched unconcerned as the receptionist carefully entered the details into her computer. They'd pass; my family has connections everywhere. And then she asked about my luggage. Well, you can't think of everything when you're planning a mission in a hurry.

"It's with my friends," I said smoothly. "They'll be along later."

"And how long will you be staying, sir?"

"Two, three days," I said. "Is there a shortage of rooms, just now?"

"Oh no, sir. We have many vacancies at the moment; it is the time of year, you understand? If it weren't for the Convention . . ."

"Fans of the films?" I said.

"Oh yes! We have many such gatherings here, sir. They do so love the old stories, and the legends. This week we have"—she stopped, and looked about on the desk for a brochure—"there are so many of them . . . Ah yes. The Spawn of Frankenstein. Not a group I'm familiar with, and I know most of them—all part of the hotel training, you understand. They've been arriving all day; nice people, very good makeup . . . Here are your keys, sir. We do a traditional breakfast, from seven thirty sharp. Don't be afraid to ask, if there is anything you require. Is there anything more I can do for you?"

She gave me a certain look. I smiled blankly back at her, and headed quickly for the stairs.

I had to take the stairs, all five stories of them, because there weren't any elevators. The Castle Hotel might have adopted most modern conveniences, but apparently elevators were a step too far. All to do with authenticity, no doubt. I was seriously out of breath by the time I reached the top floor. It hadn't been that long since I had been fighting for my life on the Hall grounds, and my resources were only slowly coming back. My real metal key opened a real metal lock, no electronic tags here, and I let myself into my room. And locked the door very firmly behind me.

I went over to the window and looked out, and off in the distance were the ruins of Castle Frankenstein, half silhouetted against the lowering sky. The illusion looked entirely convincing. I turned my back on it, and considered my room. Pretty good, actually; reasonably large, cosy and comfortable. I sat down on the bed, sinking into the goose feather mattress, and bounced up and down cheerfully. Little pleasures . . . I wondered if they did room service. I could just do with a bite. But

I decided I'd better not risk it. The last thing I needed was the receptionist turning up at my door, asking if I fancied something spicy. I sat still on the bed, suddenly tired. That was the kind of joke I would have shared with Molly. I desperately wanted to just lie down on the bed and sleep, and not have to think about anything. But I had work to do.

I got up off the bed, and then paused, thoughtfully. I had the distinct feeling I was being watched. I raised my Sight and looked casually round the room, and immediately half a dozen surveillance cameras revealed themselves to me, all craftily hidden, along with over a dozen traditional listening devices. Between them they had the whole room covered, in sound and vision, without a single blind spot anywhere. I had to consider—was the whole hotel riddled with them, so the Immortals could keep an eye on everyone who booked in, or was this just one of the rooms reserved for people who arrived suddenly, with no luggage? I had wondered why I'd been given a room on the top floor, when there were supposed to be so many vacancies.

Just how paranoid were the Immortals?

It didn't make any difference, of course. My torc could hide itself from even the most sophisticated devices, and maintain my disguise as just another tourist. Still, I'd have to be careful what I said and did, in this room. Maybe I should steal a few items, just to seem normal. I could use a few good fluffy towels . . . Maybe later.

I washed up, took a good long pee on the grounds it might be ages before I could hit the facilities again, and took my time descending the five flights of stairs, so I wouldn't be out of breath when I got to the bottom. A man has his pride . . . At the foot of the stairs was a new

sign, in German and English, saying THE CASTLE HO-
TEL IS PROUD TO WELCOME THE SPAWN OF FRANKENSTEIN.
MAIN BALLROOM. TICKETS ONLY FOR SPECIAL BANQUET. I
decided I might as well take a look, while I was there,
so I wandered over to the main ballroom. Just to take
a peek. And the first person I met at the open door was
the Bride of Frankenstein. The real one.

She was tall, a good seven feet. All of the Baron's first
creations had to be big, so he could fit everything in.
The skin on her face was very pale and very taut, like
someone who's had too much plastic surgery. But hers
had always been that way, and always would. She had
huge dark eyes that didn't blink often enough, a prominent nose, and her mouth was a deep dark red without
benefit of makeup. She would never be beautiful, but
she was attractive, in a frightening sort of way. She wore
her long jet black hair piled up on her head in a beehive,
like Amy Winehouse, and she wasn't bothering to dye
out the white streaks anymore. Or use makeup to cover
the familiar scars that stood out on her chin and neck.
She wore flowing white silks, with long sleeves to cover
her wrists, a tight blouse that showed off a lot of cleavage, and knee-length white leather boots.

She recognised me immediately, and flung her arms
around me. I braced myself for her embrace; she'd never
known her own strength. Up close, she smelled of attar
of roses, and maybe just a hint of formaldehyde. She
released me, and clapped me hard on the shoulder with
one heavy oversized hand.

"Shaman, my dear! So long since I have seen you!"
Her voice was a rich contralto, full of life. "What are
you doing here?"

"Little bit of business," I said solemnly. "You know
how it is . . ."

She laughed easily. "Of course. If there is a profit to be made, or trouble to get into, there you will find Shaman Bond! If you should find yourself in need of an alibi, or someone to stand bail for you . . ."

"I'll bear you in mind. I see you're not covering up the scars anymore. Or is that just for the Convention?"

"No . . . I have come out of the living dead closet, my dear. I am who I am. I'm almost fashionable, these days . . . And more and more I think, the best place to hide is in plain sight."

The Bride and I first met at the Wulfshead Club in London, that well-known gathering place and watering hole for the strange and unnatural. We soon warmed to each other. Shaman Bond is always very sociable because you never know when it might come in handy down the line. We fell into one of those easy friendships where you're always popping in and out of each other's lives. We even worked together on a few cases. Always with me as Shaman Bond; the Bride had no idea I was a Drood. The last job we'd done together had turned out rather messy. We'd been asked to stamp out the Cannibal Priests of Old Compton Street, who worshipped the insides of people, and not in a good way. Still, fire purifies. And even when it doesn't, it's still a damned good way to destroy evidence.

The Bride has been around. She's worked with pretty much every unorthodox organisation there is, including the Droods, but she's always been her own person. She prefers to work with a partner, though given who and what she is, she tends to either wear them out or outlive them. The Bride specialises in the most dangerous of cases, on the grounds that she has so much less to lose than most.

She's a very feminine creature; she works hard at it.

Her latest companion was the current Springheel Jack, latest inheritor of the title, and the curse. Apparently she quite literally stumbled over him in the middle of a case, when it was all new and horrible and he didn't understand what was happening to him. So she took him under her wing, showed him the ropes, and the padded handcuffs, and they've been inseparable ever since.

"He's isn't at all put off that I am very much the older woman," she said cheerfully. "And the scars aren't a problem at all. He likes them! And I always was a size queen, so . . ."

"Hold it right there," I said. "We are rapidly approaching the point of too much information. Where is Jack?"

"Off seeing the sights," she said. "These gatherings aren't for outsiders. They are reserved only for those who have known the benefits, and otherwise, of the Baron's methods. For those who belong dead."

"Got it," I said. "The Spawn of Frankenstein."

"A gathering of all the various creations, creatures and by-products of the Baron's admittedly amazing surgical gifts. We like to get together once a year, for self-help groups, companionship, and the pursuit of closure. We all have abandonment issues, after all. We end each meeting by cursing the Baron in his absence, wherever he may be."

"I did hear he was dead . . ."

The Bride snorted loudly. "He's cheated death so many times they don't even bother screwing the lid down anymore. No, he is still out there, practicing his ungodly arts on those who cannot defend themselves, bringing new and awful life into the world. And hiding from us, his forsaken children."

"What would you do?" I said. "If you ever did track him down?"

"I don't know. Call him Daddy. Have sex with him. Kill him. It's a difficult kind of relationship. Complicated . . . What would you say, if you came face-to-face with your creator? Ask him why you were made to suffer so much? I think I have a better chance of getting a straight answer out of my creator, than you have from yours."

"Mine might have had better motives," I said.

"But can you be sure?" The Bride chuckled quietly. "I'm afraid I cannot ask you in, Shaman, my dear. You understand how it is."

"Of course," I said. "Family only."

I did take a quick glance through the open door, and the Bride didn't object. There were enough of them to fill the ballroom, standing around like any group, talking and drinking and nibbling dubiously at finger snacks provided by the hotel. Hidden speakers dispensed inoffensive classical music, the only safe bet when those present come from so many times and cultures. There were all kinds on view, from those who could pass for normal, with a little help, to those who never would. Not all of the Baron's children were monsters, but they were all marked by the obsessions of their creator. Everyone in the room had started out dead, and it showed. In the eyes, in the voices, and in their image, which could be disguised but never forgotten.

Some of the more extreme cases displayed their differences openly here, among the only people who would understand. Men and women with two pairs of arms, or legs with too many joints. Gills on the neck, bulbous foreheads, bulging chests that contained specially designed new organs. Feathers, fur and even scales. The Baron had grown more adventurous as his work progressed. They talked easily together, bastard offspring of a bastard science. All they had in common was their scars, and their pain; but sometimes, that was enough.

I looked thoughtfully round the crowded room. Something was nagging at me. Something I'd seen or sensed, but not understood. So I raised my Sight, and looked again. And just like that I saw the one person present who didn't belong in this group. Oh, he had the look down pat. A tall bulky chap, in black leathers with studs and dangling chains, with prominent scars at his wrists, and a ragged line across his bulging forehead. But he had an aura. No one else in the room had an aura. Revenants of whatever kind may have a mind, and even a soul, but they never have an aura. That's reserved for the living, and the Spawn of Frankenstein were the living dead. So whoever this guy was, he definitely wasn't one of the Baron's creations. I pointed him out to the Bride, and explained why, and she swore viciously.

"I should have known! He said all the right things, dropped all of the right names, but the scar on his forehead was just too ragged. The Baron, for all his faults, always did neat work. How dare he! How dare he intrude on such a strictly private gathering? The one place where we can be honest and open, without fear of condemnation . . . This could put some people's therapy back months! He is probably a reporter, from some squalid little tabloid . . . I will take his hidden camera and shove it so far up him he'll be able to take photographs through his nostrils!"

And she stalked forward before I could stop her. I had a pretty good idea of who and what he was, and it wasn't any kind of journalist. I watched from the doorway as the Bride marched right up to the only living man in the ballroom, spun him around and stabbed him hard in the chest with one long bony finger. I winced, but he didn't.

"Who are you, and what are you doing here?" demanded the Bride, towering over the intruder. "You are not one of us!"

The room fell quiet, all the conversations stopped dead. Everyone turned to look at the intruder, and the expressions on their faces would have scared the crap out of anyone else. Death was in the room, cold and angry. The man I'd pointed out realised immediately that there was no point in continuing his pretence, and he smiled easily about him with calm, practiced arrogance.

"I am an Immortal," he said. "The real thing; not a botched scientific experiment, like you. And I am here because Immortals go where they please, to learn what they need to know. Get on with your little party. I'll see myself out."

But the Bride still blocked his path. She stabbed him again in the chest with one long thin finger, hard enough to rock him back on his feet, and this time he did wince.

"This is a private gathering of gods and monsters, of men and women who have sworn never to be victims again. You insult us by your very presence, and we will have an apology."

"I don't think so," said the Immortal, and his tone of voice was a slap in the face to everyone present.

All the features on his face suddenly ran, like melting wax. The underlying bone structure rose and fell, and then everything snapped back into place, and the intruder had a whole new face. He was now a middle-aged man with a broad square face, fierce dark eyes and a cruel mouth. It was a face I'd seen before, in a number of portraits from the nineteenth century. The Bride fell back a step, and a slow murmur ran round the ballroom.

The Baron . . . It's the Baron . . .

"Bow down before your creator," said the Immortal.

In the doorway, I felt like covering my face with my hands. Bad idea, Immortal, really bad idea. The Bride punched the Immortal so hard in the face, I half expected her fist to come out the back of his head. The false Baron staggered backwards, his features already moving again, trying to become someone else. The Bride went after him, and every one of the living dead in the ballroom closed in, looking for their own little bit of vengeance and payback, if only by proxy.

"We are the Spawn of Frankenstein, little man," said the Bride. "And you should not have come here."

The crowd fell upon the Immortal like a pack of savage beasts, hammering him with oversized fists, slicing at him with clawed hands, and hacking at him with all kinds of blades. The Immortal took a terrible punishment, that would have killed an ordinary man, but he just soaked it all up and stubbornly refused to fall. His features settled into yet another face, proud and disdainful, and he struck out at those creatures nearest him with more than human strength. Bodies flew threw the air, slammed into walls and furniture, and took their time about rising again. The Immortal raged through the crowd, striking them down with cold purpose, but still the living dead pressed forward, determined to get their hands on him, driven by more than one lifetime's rage.

I stepped quietly inside the ballroom, and pulled the door shut behind me. Someone had already thoughtfully turned up the music, so if the receptionist did hear anything, hopefully she'd just think it was more than usually enthusiastic dancing. In the meantime, I stayed by the doors. It wasn't my place to get involved. First, it would have been presumptuous, implying I thought they couldn't handle this themselves. And second, I didn't see what I could do, without armouring up and revealing myself a Drood. Which could be bad, for any number of reasons. So I stood my ground, and watched, and winced as the Immortal threw the Spawn of Frankenstein around like they were children.

They were hitting the Immortal from every side at once, but he was still standing, and more and more they weren't. I was starting to feel really glad we'd strapped the false Rafe down while we had the chance. The Immortal lashed about him with both fists, beating his attackers down with contemptuous ease. But the Spawn were learning, cutting at him with their claws and blades and then darting back out of reach. He was losing a lot of blood, and the strength in his blows wasn't what it was. So he pulled his next trick.

His whole body shuddered, and bone plates rose up out of his flesh to cover his chest, arms and skull. Pale, gleaming bone, the plates turned aside blades and claws and took no damage. Spikes and spurs of bone rose up from his hands, and his fingertips lengthened and hardened into vicious claws of his own. *Flesh dancing,* Rafe had called it. I was impressed; the Immortals had developed their own armour.

The Immortal tore into the living dead with recovered energy, and blood and other fluids flew on the air. (Not all of the Baron's creatures had blood in their veins.) But they could all take a lot of punishment, and they were used to pain. They pressed forward just as eagerly as before, hitting the Immortal with everything they had, and still they couldn't bring him down. He stood his ground, ripped through their pale flesh, hammered them to the floor, and trampled them underfoot. One by one they fell back from him, nursing their wounds and struggling for breath, still surrounding him, still searching for something else to try. And then the Bride came forward to stand before the Immortal. She towered over him, and showed him the spiked silver knuckle-dusters on both her hands. She smiled a cold and deadly smile, and even the Immortal could see the power in her.

"Let's dance," said the Bride.

"Let's," said the Immortal.

They slammed together like crashing cars, all strength and fury. Clawed hands versus spiked silver knuckle-dusters. The strength of the flesh-dancing Immortal, set against the inhuman vitality of the living dead woman. There was no skill or strategy in what they did; they just stood their ground and hammered at each other, both refusing to give an inch. They each took terrible punishment, but neither of them cried out. But in the end, the Immortal had flesh that healed itself, and an energy that simply wouldn't give out, and he just wore her down. He beat her to her knees, and then grabbed her by the throat with one heavy hand, and squeezed. The Bride clawed at his face with her long arms, even as her breath was cut off. Death had no fear for her. She'd already been there. The Immortal throttled the life out of the Bride, and looked around him disdainfully.

"Don't think you're anything special. You're just an ugly bunch of failed experiments. My family throw away better things than you in our laboratories every day. How many of you do I have to kill, before you get the message? *Know your place.*"

And that was when I hit him in the face with the punch bowl. It was a good throw. The heavy glass bowl shattered over his head, and the industrial strength alcohol filled his eyes, blinding him. He cried out with shock and pain, and let go of the Bride so he could claw at his face with both hands. I knew I shouldn't have intervened, but there's some shit I just won't put up with. I was looking around for more things to throw, when the French windows suddenly blew open and there, silhouetted against the night, was a tall dark shape. All of Frankenstein's creations turned to look, and then as one they fell back, opening up an aisle between the newcomer and the Immortal. I nodded slowly, smiling. I'd been wondering when he'd show up. The Immortal cleared the last of the noxious punch from his eyes, and glared at the man in the French windows. The newcomer advanced slowly on the Immortal, with a calm, elegant bearing. He was wrapped in a long black cloak that swept about him like batwings, and wore an old-fashioned top hat. From his pale face, he was barely my age, but his eyes were very old and very cold, and he was smiling a most unpleasant smile.

"Get away from my Bride," he said, in a cool and really quite disturbing voice. "Or you'll be resting in pieces before you know it."

The Immortal looked at him incredulously. "Who the hell are you?"

"Ah, that's the question, isn't it? Sometimes I think one thing, sometimes I think another. But unfortunately for you, right now I'm Springheel Jack."

The Immortal lashed out at him with a bone-spurred hand, and Springheel Jack jumped lightly into the air, high enough to trail his fingertips across the ceiling. The Immortal lurched forward and almost fell on his face, as his blow whipped through the air where Jack had been only a moment before. He stepped quickly back, and Jack dropped lightly to the floor again. But now he had two brightly shining straight razors, one in each hand. He smiled mockingly at the Immortal, and then jumped right over him. He somersaulted over his enemy's head, landed elegantly behind him, his legs absorbing the impact as though it was nothing, and then he spun round and hamstrung both the Immortal's legs at once. Blood spurted thickly, and the Immortal cried out in agony; and then he collapsed to the floor as his legs failed him, both leg muscles sliced completely through. Springheel Jack looked down at him, thrashing helplessly on the bloody floor, and then stepped elegantly forward to stand before his Bride.

"You all right, love?"

She caressed her throat briefly, but her smiled never wavered. "All the better for seeing you, my sweet."

"I know you," the Immortal said harshly, from the floor. "We all know you. We keep killing you, and you keep coming back!"

"It's a gift," said Springheel Jack. He grabbed the Immortal's head and jerked it back to expose the throat. A straight razor pressed against the taut skin, and a thin runnel of blood trickled down, as the steel edge nicked the skin.

"Say good night, Gracie," said Jack.

"No!" said the Bride. Springheel Jack looked at her.

"No?" he said, politely.

"I'm not in a mood to be merciful," said the Bride.

Springheel Jack considered this, and then nodded. He hit the Immortal a vicious blow on the top of the head with his elbow, and the Immortal slumped unconscious to the floor. Jack stood up, and took his Bride in his arms. They embraced, laughing, and then she crushed him to her. And since she was a good foot taller than he was, his face disappeared into her cleavage. He didn't seem to mind. She finally released him, still laughing, and he smiled happily around him. The straight razors were gone from his hands. He looked down at the unconscious form at his feet.

"Who is he, anyway?"

"An Immortal," I said. "Shaman Bond, at your service."

"Ah," said Springheel Jack. "The Bride has spoken of you, in a quite annoyingly approving way. If I weren't so secure, I might be jealous. But I'm not. Thanks for throwing the bowl."

"Least I could do," I said.

"Yes," said Jack. "That's what I thought. Still, an Immortal, you say? One of those terribly up themselves long-lived creeps, from the real Castle Frankenstein, up the road?"

"They think we don't know," sniffed the Bride. "Of course we know! We all remember where we were born."

Springheel Jack considered me carefully. "What do you know of Immortals, Shaman?"

"I'm just here to do a favour for a friend," I said. "You know how it is . . ."

"Of course," said the Bride. "If there's anything . . ."

"I'll let you know," I said.

"And if you should by any chance find a way into the Castle . . ."

"I'll let you know."

I bowed to them all politely, and headed for the open French windows. Just in case the receptionist was listening at the door and wondering why it had all gone quiet. I was just stepping out into the dark of the evening when I heard the Bride say, "An Immortal, who claims to be our superior? I think not. I think . . . we'll make him one of us. Jack, fetch me my scalpels!"

Some monsters are scarier than others.

I moved quickly across the cobbled yard, putting some distance between me and the Hotel. I looked up the long narrow road that led to the real Castle Frankenstein, but it was hidden from view behind the rising hill. I had to wonder if perhaps Rafe had got some kind of warning off, before we grabbed him. In which case, they knew I was coming. Was that why the Immortal had been sent down to the Hotel? But there is caution, which is useful, and paranoia, which is mostly not. Not everything is about me. I was here to do a job, and it was time I got on with it. I started up the road. There was still no sign of any passing traffic. The evening had gone dark, and the last of the light was going out of the day. A storm was gathering.

Perfect atmosphere, for an assault on Castle Frankenstein.

I walked up the middle of the road, pacing myself. It was a fair walk to the Castle, and I didn't want to miss anything interesting along the way. There were no streetlights, no markings on the road, and as the Hotel vanished behind a curve in the road, it felt like I was walking back into the Past, into a more primitive time, where the peasants in the small village I'd left behind me had reason to be afraid when the lightning flared, and strange lights shone at Castle Frankenstein.

There were no more signs of civilisation, just the rising hill and the darkening sky, and the road winding away before me. It wasn't even much of a road. A nearly full moon rode high on the sky, just enough to see by. I would have liked to use my torc, to call up some golden glasses to see through, but I didn't dare, this close to the Castle. The torc could hide itself, but my armour would stand out like a beacon in the dark. It wasn't as though there was much to see, anyway. It was all black basaltic rock and shifting scree, rising up increasingly on the one side, and the dull sounds of the River Rhine far below, on the other. No life, no vegetation, not even the usual hardy shrubs. And then, not nearly far enough off, I heard the sudden howling of a wolf. At least, I hoped it was a wolf. In this kind of territory, you never knew. I checked my Colt Repeater was secure in its holster, so I could be sure I had access to silver bullets.

First the Bride of Frankenstein, and now werewolves in the night. It was liking walking through one of the old Universal monster movies.

Cool.

But even as I kept a cautious eye on my surroundings, it dawned on me that I hadn't seen anything moving, anything living, ever since I left the Hotel behind me. Which was . . . unusual. I raised my Sight, and then stopped dead in my tracks. The world around me was completely empty, and that never, ever happens. There's always something: ghosts from the Past, elementals, otherworldly entities . . . they're everywhere. Part and parcel of the Hidden World, that most people don't even know exists. The unnatural world, of which the natural world is only a part, like the tip of the iceberg. But, not here.

And then finally my Sight showed me something, something I'd overlooked simply because it was so very big. The hill was alive, and it was watching me. I couldn't make out any actual eyes, even with my Sight, but I could feel their regard. The whole hill . . . either was something, or covered something, very huge and very old. The steady gaze didn't feel particularly dangerous, or menacing. Just . . . interested. So I faced the hill, bowed politely, and raised my voice on that empty silent night.

"Good evening. I am Edwin Drood. May I inquire, whom do I have the honour of addressing?"

The answering voice rolled around inside my head like a long crash of thunder, ancient and powerful, but strangely . . . wistful.

Drood . . . Yes, I know that name. Though it has been long and long since any of that name came to talk with me. I am a dragon, Edwin Drood. Or at least, a dragon's head. Cut off long ago, by the Baron Frankenstein. Left here to rot, as a warning to others. But I am a dragon of the old blood, and we do not die easily. I did not rot. I watched him with my eyes, and I cursed him with my voice, and eventually he had his people cover me over with earth and stone, and I became a hill. And so . . . I remain, slowly dying, slowly passing from this world of men.

"All right," I said. "That . . . is just unfair. I have business with the current occupants of Castle Frankenstein, but after I've dealt with them . . . Would you like to come home with me? You'd be welcome at Drood Hall, for whatever time you have left."

I couldn't tell you why I made the offer. I never met a dragon that didn't deserve killing on general principles, like the one at the Magnificat . . . but I felt sorry for this one. Just left lying here, alone and ignored, fading away down the years . . . It didn't sit right with me. I know; it's stray dog syndrome with a vengeance, but . . . the family could learn a lot from talking to a dragon. We don't normally get the chance.

Home . . . Yes, Drood. I think I would like that. The

world is very quiet here, and empty. I would enjoy having something new to look at.

"I've noticed that," I said. "Where is everything? What happened to all the inhabitants of the Hidden World?"

They killed them. Killed them all. From the greatest to the smallest, from the most dangerous to the most insignificant, they wiped them all out. In the space of one long bloody night.

I didn't have to ask who they were. The Immortals had protected their privacy and their security by destroying everything that surrounded them. Just because they could. And I thought my family was ruthless . . .

"I have business with those murderous sons of bitches," I said. "When it's all over, I'll send a message to my people, and we'll see about getting you out from under this hill. Talk to you later."

Good-bye, Drood. It is a kind offer, and I wish you good fortune. But honesty compels me to inform you that in my experience, no one comes back from Castle Frankenstein.

I followed the increasingly rough road up the side of dragon hill, and finally came to a halt atop a tall bluff, looking down at the ruins of Castle Frankenstein. Even this close, the illusion was perfect. Just a couple of stumpy stone towers, a few tumbledown walls, crawling ivy and dark shadows; all of it standing starkly against the dark sky. It would have been convincing . . . but even without my foreknowledge of its true nature, I would have known something was wrong. There was no trace of any of the wildlife that would normally have infested such a ruin. I couldn't See a single life sign anywhere. No rats, no wild dogs or feral cats, not even a single bat.

And that . . . was a real giveaway. I looked the ruins over carefully with my Sight, but couldn't See a single gap or weakness anywhere in the illusion. Which meant I was going to have to do it the hard way.

I started down the steep crumbling path that led to the Castle, wincing every time I dislodged a few small rocks, but I hadn't got far before I had to stop abruptly. The way was blocked by the Immortals' first line of defence: a simple but incredibly powerful force field. It hung on the air before me, invisible, intangible, but carrying enough energy to fry me on the spot if I so much as touched it with a fingertip. There was a built-in avoidance ward, a basic *go away nothing to see here* influence, enough to keep out the tourists; but I was concentrating so hard on not making any noise that my Sight only caught it at the last moment. I'm pretty sure my torc would have saved me by automatically armouring up, but that would have set off God alone knew how many alarms. So I stood very still, feeling the cold sweat bead on my face, as I realised how close I'd just come to blowing my whole mission.

Time to use the Chameleon Codex. I touched a single fingertip to the silver cuff link, muttered the activating Words, and the stored DNA data rushed into my system, rewriting me from within. My flesh crawled, surging and rippling all over my body, like a terrible itch I couldn't scratch, and then I swayed on my feet as everything suddenly snapped into place. I held up my hands, turning them back and forth, but in the gloom they looked just the same. Hard to tell with hands, really. I started to call up the Merlin Glass, so I could study my new face in its mirror, but again stopped myself just in time. Just the proximity of such a powerful artefact would undoubtedly trigger its own set of alarms. I had to trust that I was Rafe now, right down to his Immortal DNA.

And people say their lives are complicated.

I walked forward, into the force field, and it opened up before me, its subtle energies trailing across my bare face like caressing fingers. And then I was through, and moving on, and Castle Frankenstein lay open and defenceless before me.

CHAPTER TEN

Assault on Castle Frankenstein

could have just walked up to the main entrance, banged on the door and demanded to be let in, but somehow I just didn't like to. There had to be more to getting into Castle Frankenstein than just having the right face. So I made my approach slowly and cautiously, sticking to the shadows wherever possible. I wasn't used to sneaking up on things without the benefit of my armour to fall back on, if things went seriously wrong in a hurry. The Castle seemed to grow bigger and bigger the closer I got, its vast stone face looming over me, impossibly tall and foreboding. Lights burned fiercely in all the many windows, though here and there unhealthy glows seeped past the outlines of closed shutters. And still, not a sign of a human guard anywhere. Not up on the high crenellated battlements, not peering out of any window, not even standing guard outside the main entrance. Did the Immortals really feel that safe, that secure? I suppose if no one's dared attack you where you live for centuries, you just come to assume no one ever will. Especially if you've got the kind of protections in place that can keep out gods and monsters and Droods. But after the failed attack on Drood Hall, and the rout of the Accelerated Men, they should have been expecting some kind of response, or counterattack . . . Could they really be that arrogant, that complacent?

First rule in the field: when events seem too good to be true, they probably are too good to be true.

Still, the Castle's quite remarkable protections had failed only because I had access to the false Rafe's DNA, and that was a very recent development. Even the best of protections need regular updating. I kept checking around me with my Sight raised, looking for new levels of protection, disguised booby traps, land mines or trapdoors, but there was nothing. It was almost completely dark now, the only light shining down from the Castle's long rows of windows. Which left me plenty of shadows to take advantage of, right up to the Castle itself. But the approach to the main door was sharply illuminated, with harsh white electric light. Presumably backed up by modern surveillance systems, because nobody's that secure. I kept well away from the lit door, and sneaked along the front wall, my shoulder pressed hard against the cold rough stone. I kept my head well down, ducking under each of the lit windows, listening carefully.

The night was eerily silent, but through the closed windows I could hear conversations, raised voices, laughter. They sounded just like ordinary people, not the evil murdering bastards they were. But I suppose even monsters aren't always monsters, when they're at home. Did they plot to murder my Molly, in one of these bright and cheerful rooms? I had to stop for a moment, as a cold hand closed around my heart, and squeezed. Not now. Not now . . . I'd mourn my love later, when I had time. I made myself move on, darting from window to window, until finally I came to one where there was no sound at all. I crouched there a while, motionless, until I was sure the room was deserted. And then I held my right hand up before me, and studied the golden ring gleaming on my finger. The Gemini Duplicator. It was time to try out the Armourer's new toy. I pressed hard against the ring with the fingers on either side of it, and just like that there were two of me.

And the duplicate was standing on the other side of the wall, inside the room. I'd spotted that possibility early on, when the Armourer first explained the ring's extended range to me.

At first, being two of me felt *really* freaky. All my senses were registering in duplicate, in a weird stereo effect. I was in the light and in the dark, in the cold and in the warm, inside and out. I swayed on two sets of feet, unbalanced in a whole new way, and concentrated fiercely until I could separate out the two sensory streams. I found the trick of it surprisingly quickly; like patting yourself on the head while simultaneously rubbing your stomach. I'd always known that talent would come in handy one day. At first, my consciousness kept switching back and forth from one head to the other, but I soon learned to keep both sets of thoughts going at once, holding one set in the foreground while pushing the other back.

Still; *really* freaky.

I pushed down the outside me and took a good look around the room I was in. (While thinking, Was the one outside the original me, with the one inside a duplicate?

Or had the Gemini Duplicator projected me where I needed to be, while generating a duplicate to stay outside? And, where did all the extra mass come from, to make a whole second body?) My heads started to hurt. When this was all over, and I got back to Drood Hall, I was going to have to sit the Armourer down, and ask him a whole bunch of seriously pointed questions.

I concentrated on the room I was in. It was cheerfully lit with perfectly modern electric lighting, comfortably appointed, and no one was home. I padded quickly over to the door, eased it open a little, and listened. A few people were coming and going, talking quietly. I waited till they were gone, gave it a few more moments just in case, and then opened the door and slipped out into the main hall.

Pretty impressive, at first look. Old style Baronial, all eighteenth-century features carefully preserved, parquet flooring and exposed stone walls, and a really high ceiling with half a dozen cut glass and diamond chandeliers. Probably draughty as hell, and a pain to heat in the winter. I grew up in Drood Hall; I know about these things. I thought wearing long underwear most of the year round was normal. I hurried over to the main door, and then hesitated, and studied it thoughtfully. Fashioned from a single huge slab of some dark wood, reinforced with steel bands, but . . . no hidden surprises that I could See. Just a perfectly ordinary brass lock, and two sets of heavy bolts, top and bottom. The bolts weren't even in place, and when I checked, the door wasn't even locked. Arrogant, complacent, and stupid . . . Some people deserve everything that's coming to them. I pulled open the heavy door, and there I was, waiting for me.

Freaky, weird and very disturbing. My consciousness

ricocheted back and forth between my heads, me seeing me seeing me, and the only coherent thought I could manage was, *Is that really what I look like?* I concentrated, bearing down hard, and then it occurred to the me looking in from outside that I had to be the original because I was still wearing the Gemini Duplicator ring. I held up my hand to prove it, and the me standing inside held up my hand. We both had rings. I decided enough was enough, and both of me squeezed my fingers against the ring. And just like that there was only me, standing in the open doorway. Air rushed in to fill the vacuum where the other me had been standing just a moment before, like an explosion in reverse. I rocked on my feet, struggling to reconcile two sets of memories from the same period, but it all came together surprisingly easily. I hurried forward, and closed the door quietly behind me.

I put my back to the door and scowled at the long empty hall stretching away before me. My skin crawled in anticipation of sudden alarms, but there was nothing. I couldn't quite believe how easy they were making this for me. Powerful protective shields are all very well, but you can't beat the human touch when it comes to spotting intruders. In the end I just shrugged, and allowed myself to breathe a little more easily. I might not be able to call up my armour here, but my torc's basic nature should still be enough to hide me from any and all inner surveillance systems. The Immortals might or might not have had systems in place to detect the presence of old torcs, but I was betting they didn't have anything that could deal with the new strange matter torcs. The Immortals might have infiltrated the Droods, but they didn't understand Ethel.

Nobody did.

I pulled up my collar a little, to hide the torc from a

casual glance, and strode down the long hall like I was thinking of renting it out. When penetrating an enemy stronghold, confidence is everything. Look like you belong there, and no one will challenge you. So far, Castle Frankenstein was everything it should be: old stonework, marvellously carved and ornate; standing suits of armour, burnished to within an inch of their lives; elegant medieval tapestries and hanging cloths; and rows of dark frowning portraits. Old Frankensteins or old Immortals, I didn't know or give a damn. It was all very Gothic, apart from the electric light chandeliers and the hidden central heating, the benefits of which I was currently enjoying after so long in the cold, cold night.

The Castle so far reminded me a lot of Drood Hall. Of long and not forgotten history, held over into the modern day. The Immortals were as old as we were, and the two of us had a lot more in common than I liked to admit. Two ancient families, their present still dominated by their past, who never threw anything away. The Immortals were the one thing we'd always feared the most, our darkest nightmare: the Anti-Droods. Everything we could have been, if not for our role as shamans, defenders of the Human tribe. Be sure your nightmares will find you out . . .

I stopped, some distance down the hall, and looked thoughtfully about me. It had just occurred to me that everything in the hall was perfectly clean, polished, and waxed . . . For all the Gothic look, there wasn't a cobweb in sight. And I had to wonder about that. Surely the Immortals wouldn't allow humble cleaning staff to enter their secret sanctorum? Who could they trust, to come in and do for them? They couldn't employ the local townspeople as servants; like everyone else, the locals had been programmed to see Castle Frankenstein as nothing more than ancient ruins. And surely the great and secret masters of the world wouldn't lower themselves to get out the bucket and mop and do it themselves?

A quiet, subtle sound caught my attention, and I looked sharply round. And there behind me was a short, squat creature, almost as broad as it was tall, wearing simple blue overalls, with a bucket and mop . . . slowly but thoroughly cleaning up the trail of scuffed muddy footprints I'd left behind me. (I couldn't believe I'd done that. *Footprints?* I was far too used to my armour looking after me.) I recognised what the cleaner was; I'd seen his people at work, in and around London. This was a kobold, one of the underfolk, from under the ground. Ancient inhabitants of the Hidden World, like Pixies, Brownies, Trolls. Mostly gone now, to other more hospitable realities, like the Elves. But the kobolds I'd encountered before had been proud, hardworking creatures, always paid the best rates because they were the only ones brave enough to do the really hard work. So what was a kobold doing here, working as a cleaner for the Immortals?

I strolled back to the creature, smiling on it in what I hoped was a friendly and not at all threatening way. It looked up from its work, but didn't stop, slowly and methodically removing all traces of my presence. Up close, it looked more like a Neanderthal than anything else: brutal but still basically humanoid, heavy browed and heavy boned, with a wide face, no chin, and sharp crafty eyes. It nodded briefly to me.

"You shouldn't be here," it said, in a low growling voice. "Come to take on the Immortals, in their own place of power, have you? Be welcome, fool. Try to die well, with honour."

"I'm a Drood," I said calmly. "Other people do the dying."

The kobold looked at me sharply. "Then you should know better than to be here. You might stand a better chance than most, but you're still a damned fool to break into Castle Frankenstein. And a doomed one. Doomed . . . No one can beat the Immortals. They go on forever, because they can."

"Everything comes to an end eventually," I said, with a confidence I wasn't entirely sure I felt. "You're a kobold, aren't you? What are you doing here, working for the Immortals?"

"Kobold. Yes. Very old people. We were here before the Immortals. Before this Castle. We were miners, then. Digging deep, deep under the earth. Left to ourselves, and liked it that way. We stayed on after so many of the other underfolk left, because no one bothered us, down in the depths of the earth. There was still a lot of gold left, and we like gold. They built a Castle above us, and we didn't care. Until he came. The one everyone talks about. The Frankenstein, the living god of the scalpel. He discovered us, brought us up into the light, made us his servants. And after he left the Immortals moved in, and they made us their slaves. Put these yokes upon us."

He lifted his head to show me the cold iron collar around his throat, etched with runes. He was careful not to touch it.

"The Immortals own us now. Generations of kobolds have been born in this cold stone tomb, never to know the comforts of the dark, and the earth, the mines and the gold. Once there were thousands of us, then hundreds, now less than one hundred. We do not belong in this world. And we were never meant to be slaves."

"I can rip that yoke right off you," I said. "If you want."

"No, you can't. The yoke will kill me, rather than let me go. The Immortals never let go of anything they own."

"Then I will bring down the Immortals," I said. "And make them free you. All of you."

"Why should you?" said the kobold. "Why should you give a damn about the underfolk? You're human."

"Because I'm a Drood," I said. "And that's what Droods do."

The kobold leaned forward, fixing me with its cold, bright eyes. "Kill them all, Drood. They've earned it."

I walked the whole length of the hall, looking vaguely around for a map of some kind, or a floor plan of the Castle. Preferably something set out neatly on a wall, with YOU ARE HERE, and all the important areas clearly marked. But of course, there was nothing like that. The people who lived here didn't need a map, and they actively discouraged tourists. I had no idea of what I was looking for, and where I should be going; that's what happens when you plan a mission in a hurry. All my thoughts had centred around how I was going to get in, and not enough about what I'd do afterwards. We should have got more specific information out of Rafe, but I was too impatient. Now I was here, I wanted information, which meant records, which meant computers. While I was standing at the foot of a long sweeping set of stairs, at the end of the hall, looking vaguely around in search of inspiration, a side door opened, and out came a teenager with long floppy hair, in sweatshirt, jeans and trainers. He stopped abruptly, and looked at me.

I smiled and nodded easily, secure behind my Rafe face. The teenager glared at me, and opened his mouth to shout a warning. I sprinted forward, crossing the

space between us in a few moments, and hit the teenager a savage straight finger jab under his sternum. All
the air shot out of his lungs before he could shout a
single word, and the force of the blow sent him staggering backwards. All the colour dropped out of his face
as he struggled to get his breath. I hustled him quickly
backwards into the room he'd just left, checked it was
empty and then closed the door behind us. The teenager reached out to me with a shaking hand, perhaps
to grab me, maybe just to ask for help. I hit him once,
expertly, and he slumped forward into my arms, unconscious. The whole scuffle was over in a few moments,
hardly long enough to qualify as a fight. I dropped him
into the nearest chair, and considered him thoughtfully.

Why hadn't my disguise worked? Why hadn't he accepted me as an Immortal? Maybe . . . they didn't keep
track of all the people they replaced. He was young,
maybe he didn't have access to information like that. I
arranged him in his chair so he looked like he was just
dozing, and then paused as another thought struck me.
Rafe's face might not be familiar here, but this teenager's had to be . . . So I used the Chameleon Codex
again, and suffered the shudders that ran through my
flesh, as I became him.

I did consider changing clothes with the teenager—
but there are limits.

With all the changes I was putting myself through, I
was in danger of suffering a real identity crisis, but that's
business as usual for an agent in the field. I considered
the unconscious teenager in his chair. He looked so
young, to be part of such a family of monsters. Given
how hard I'd hit him, he shouldn't wake up for ages, but
who knew what his shape-changing flesh was capable
of? He could wake up any time, and sound the alarm.

The sensible and prudent thing to do was kill him, and put an end to the problem. Part of me wanted to kill him. For what his people had done to me, to Molly, and Rafe, and all the Droods who'd fallen to the Accelerated Men. But I couldn't bring myself to kill him in cold blood. I'd executed Rafe without a second thought, but this was different.

I am an agent, not an assassin.

So I left him, apparently sleeping in his comfortable chair, and went back out into the hall, shutting the door carefully behind me.

I trotted up the long sweeping staircase, which gave out onto the next floor, and strolled down the wide passage. And almost immediately I started bumping into people, Immortals coming and going, and every single one of them was a teenager. They were dressed in a curious mixture of fashions and styles, from the past to the present: everything from Elizabethan ruffs and tights to Edwardian dandies to seventies punk. A little thought suggested that this was because they were all most comfortable in the periods they grew up in. They all had the same arrogant poise, the same aristocratic ease, an almost palpable sense of entitlement. And they were all teenagers because . . . that was when the Immortal genetic inheritance kicked in, and they stopped aging. No wonder the one downstairs hadn't accepted me. Rafe was too old.

I nodded and smiled perfectly casually to the people I passed, and they just smiled and nodded back to me. Because I was acting like I had a perfect right to be where I was, they all just assumed I had. I must be one of them or I wouldn't be there. Attitude can get you a long way, as a field agent. I studied them all carefully, behind my borrowed teenage face. They didn't look like monsters. But they didn't exactly seem like teenagers, either. There was something *wrong*, in the way they moved, and talked, and acted. They had none of the usual teenagers' awkwardness or high energy; instead, they all moved with a certain cold confidence, presumably the result of living lifetimes. And in their eyes I caught a glimpse of more experience than anything human should ever have.

I got to the end of the corridor without anyone shouting out or pointing at me, and then I looked about me, wondering where to try next. Or whether I should pick one Immortal out from the pack, drag him into an empty room, and beat the information out of him. I was getting impatient again. And then I saw another kobold, peering round a far corner. It gestured to me urgently, and I set off towards it as though I'd meant to go that way all along. The kobold was indistinguishable from the one I'd met downstairs, wearing the same blue overalls.

"Drood," it said, in the familiar low growling voice. "You have come to free us."

"Well, I'd like to," I said. "But I have to complete my mission first. I need information. Records, computers . . . you know computers?"

"Of course I know computers," it growled. "I'm a slave, not stupid. We keep informed, up to date. How else could we serve our hated masters efficiently? You want the computer rooms, down in what used to be the dungeons. Better for the machines, down there. Temperature controlled. I know all about computers. I read *Wired* magazine. Every month."

."Sorry," I said.

"Follow these back stairs, all the way down. Watch out for the guard on duty. And the alarms. Did you really break in here, without first doing some reconnaissance?"

"I was in a hurry," I said, with as much dignity as I could muster.

It gave me a long hard look. "And you're our great hope for liberation. I think I'll go and have a little lie down."

It sniffed loudly, pointed out the back stairs with quite unnecessary thoroughness, and shuffled off. Almost immediately, a door to my right swung open, and a whole crowd of teenagers rushed out, talking loudly. I stood back to let them pass, and although they all did so, several of them looked at me oddly, as though I hadn't said or done something they expected. One of them actually paused and looked back at me, the look on his face clearly suggesting that he thought something was wrong, but he couldn't quite put his finger on it. I couldn't get past them to the back stairs, so I just turned casually away and made a point of going into the room they'd just come out of.

It turned out to be some kind of common room, with more teenagers standing around in groups, sitting in comfortable chairs, drinking and talking. There was a bar in one corner, manned by yet another kobold. I drifted over to the bar and acquired a Beck's in a bottle, and the kobold actually slipped me a sly wink as it served me. God save us all from amateur conspirators. Even if they did have one hell of a gossip network. I was a bit concerned I might be promising the underfolk more than I could deliver. I was here for information to take back to my family, not to start a revolution of the downtrodden. If I found the kind of information I was looking for, I might have to grab it and run. My duty to the family came before anything else. I fully intended to come back, sometime, preferably at the head of a large army of armoured Droods, and bring down the Immortals in blood and fire. And then, of course, we'd free all the kobolds. But that wouldn't be today or tomorrow. Might even be years. The Immortals were the deadliest and most devious enemy we'd ever faced; any attack would have to be carefully planned. And there was still the problem of the Apocalypse Door, and the end of the world. I had a lot to do, before I could even think about freeing the kobolds.

But it still didn't feel right, to take their help under false pretensions.

I wandered round the common room, sipping from the bottle when anyone got too close, nodding and smiling and listening in on as many conversations as possible, without seeming like an eavesdropper. Everyone in the room was a teenager, fifteen or sixteen years old at most. And they all had the same cold, ancient eyes, as though they'd seen everything there was to see, and put their mark on it. None of them were particularly handsome, or beautiful; striking would be a better word. Long experience had put its stamp on their faces, but not in wrinkles or sagging flesh; more in their expressions, and the way they held themselves. They all had perfect skin, perfect teeth, and not a blemish among them. They all looked to be in good shape, though that could be flesh dancing. None of them would need to be fat for long, and they could just grow what muscles they needed . . . or that terrible bone armour I'd seen down in the Hotel. They could be anything, so why hadn't they made themselves attractive? All of these *teenagers* were defiantly ordinary.

All the better to walk among you . . .

The common room itself had the air of a peculiarly

old-fashioned Gentleman's Club; nothing like a teenage hangout. It was all very calm, and ordered, and tidy, and no one raised their voice. They all seemed very relaxed, and comfortable in their own skins, and there was a basic ease you get only among people who've known each other forever. And maybe they had . . . That was why I was still getting glances. I wasn't acting like one of them. I didn't immediately recognise faces, or say someone's name; I didn't know catchphrases and familiar gestures established over long years. I sat down in a chair in the corner, away from everyone, and did my best to radiate *I want to be alone* with my body language. I was wasting time here, but I was fascinated by the Immortals. Know thy enemy . . .

Two teenagers sat at a chess board, the pieces flying back and forth at incredible speed. Half a dozen more were playing some complicated game with human knucklebones. Others were playing a word game that made no sense to me at all. There was a huge widescreen television on one wall, tuned to a twenty-four-hour rolling news channel, and no one was watching it. And all through the room I heard a dozen different languages spoken simultaneously, along with others I didn't even recognise. Dialects and special patois so obscure they sounded almost alien. Could it be that the Immortals remembered and still used languages that had actually died out in the outside world?

But even as I listened in, while pretending to sulk in my chair, I slowly realised that everything I could understand was just simple social chatter. Nothing about world events, or the great things they'd done or were planning to do, nothing about the recent attacks on my family . . . It was all just gossip. Who was with who, who'd fallen out with who, who was two-timing who and what would happen when everyone found out . . . All the Immortals cared about, was themselves. Because the world might change, but the Immortals went on forever. So they were the only things that mattered.

I looked up sharply as a young woman marched right up to me. From the glare she was giving me, it was clear she knew the face I was wearing, and not in a good way. Which meant I had to know her. She was tall and blond, dressed to the height of nineteen thirties fashion. She folded her arms and glared at me, clearly waiting for me to say something. Other people were starting to pay attention. I rose to my feet and gave her my best disdainful glare.

"I'm not talking to you," I said flatly, stuck my nose in the air, and brushed past her as I strode from the room. Knowing laughter followed me, so it seemed I'd struck the right note. At least she didn't try and follow me. I decided I'd pushed my luck quite enough, and headed straight for the back stairs, and the computer rooms below.

The corridor was completely empty, with no sign of Immortals or kobolds. I clattered down the back stairs, still marvelling at the complete lack of security guards. These people were asking for it. The back stairs went on and on, falling away, descending into the depths under the Castle. Given the bare stone walls and the rough stone steps, I guessed this wasn't a route used by the Immortals very often. They would have put in a handrail, and maybe even carpeting. This was more likely a maintenance way, for the underfolk. The hard stone steps slammed against my feet all the way down, and when I finally got to the bottom, it was just one long cavern, dug out of the bedrock. The dungeons themselves were gone, replaced by simple offices and storerooms, and as I made my way cautiously forward, even my quietest steps seemed unnaturally loud, carrying on the still air. Harsh electric lighting filled the long cavern from end to end, leaving no shadows anywhere. I felt more exposed here than I had above.

So I marched down the cavern like I was there on inspection, and soon came to the two large glass cubicles at the end. One was quite clearly the computer room, while the other was a communications and security office, with a single guard. He wasn't even looking in my direction. An Immortal, of course, because they couldn't trust an important task like this to the underfolk, but quite clearly one very bored Immortal. He was sitting in his chair with his feet propped up on his desk, sulking, because he'd been lumbered with this job he didn't feel was necessary. No one could ever get into the Castle, never mind all the way down here ... He was slowly flipping through the pages of a magazine, and from the look on his face I had a pretty good idea of what kind of magazine it was. I couldn't believe he hadn't heard me approaching, but when I got closer I could see he had phones in his ears. He was listening to music on his iPod. While he was on guard. Some people just deserve every bad thing that happens to them.

I stayed back, pressed against one wall, out of his direct line of sight. I used the Gemini Duplicator to make another me, and once again I was thrown by the sudden doubling of my senses. I quickly pulled it back under control, and the two of me looked at each other closely, studying our new teenage face through two sets of eyes. I gestured for me to stay put, while I strode down the cavern to the glass-walled security booth. The guard didn't look up until I was almost on top of him, and even then he didn't get out of his chair. He just glared at me sullenly, and reluctantly pulled the phones out of his ears. I gestured imperiously for him to leave the booth and come out to talk to me. He acquiesced to my assumed authority, but made a big deal out of putting aside his mucky magazine and slouching out to join me. He'd probably been instructed never to leave the booth without checking first, but boredom can be a terrible motivator. He glared at me.

"What do you want?"

"Look who's come to see you!" I said brightly, and gestured down the cavern.

The other me stepped out into the clear light, and waved cheerfully. The guard gaped at the second me, and while he was doing that I slipped in behind and got him in a choke hold. After a few moments, I dragged his unconscious body back into the booth, and arranged him neatly in his chair so it looked like he was dozing. I was getting quite good at that. I hurried down the cavern to join me, and we both looked around the security booth. Neither of us talked about killing the guard, though it was on both our minds. I'd already had this conversation with myself.

"I'm going into the computer room," I said. "You go back down the cavern and keep watch."

I scowled back at me. "Who put you in charge?"

"I did. You did. What does it matter, I'm the original, so . . ."

"You don't know that. You can't be sure. I have all the same memories you do."

"I can't believe I'm arguing with myself. I get to go into the computer room because I'm nearest. Now go!"

"All right, all right! God, I can't believe I'm this bossy . . ."

I hurried back down the cavern, while I turned my

attention to the door into the computer room. I concentrated on bringing my thoughts to the front, while keeping my duplicate's in the background. It was easier when I wasn't talking to myself. I took out the skeleton key the Armourer had given me. One ordinary-looking key, but fashioned from old yellowed human bone. The door between the booth and the computer room had a complicated electronic lock, with a numbered keypad. I just pressed the skeleton key against the pad, and it cycled quickly through its functions and opened the door for me. Skeleton key. The Armourer does like his little jokes. I waited for an alarm to go off, but there was nothing. I strode into the computer room, pulled up a chair and sat down before the main terminal.

It all looked pretty straightforward. Of course, I didn't know any of the passwords, or file names, but that shouldn't be a problem. I was just starting to armour up, so I could use the golden fingertip trick that Luther taught me, when I remembered and stopped myself. I couldn't use the armour here. That would quite definitely set off every alarm they had.

So I took out the skeleton key again, and waved it vaguely back and forth in front of the computer, hoping it might act like a Hand of Glory, but it didn't. The computer just stared back at me, smugly mute. I looked at the bone key. Since it was a key, perhaps it needed to be inserted and turned . . . I pushed the key against the computer, and it sank into and through the plastic casing. The surface just seemed to soften and open up, and the key disappeared inside, almost sucked in. I was so startled I almost let go of the key and lost it inside the computer. But I held on, until my hand was pressed right up against the computer casing. It felt disturbingly warm, almost organic . . . I turned the key, and the computer started up. The monitor screen turned itself on, and all kinds of passwords and secret protocols flashed on and off. I gingerly withdrew the key, but the computer just kept going, all but rolling over on its back and showing me all it had. Records going back centuries, trivial and ultrasecret, were all right there at my fingertips.

First things first: where were Doctor Delirium and Tiger Tim, and the Apocalypse Door? The computer didn't even hesitate: all three were now located at Area 52, in the Antarctic, out past the McMurdo Sound. I grimaced, despite myself. There were harder places to get to and get into, but not many. Area 51 has always been a government joke, a public distraction, all smoke and mirrors to hold the world's attention, while all the real secret research goes on in Area 52. That's where America keeps all the dangerous and exotic weird stuff it's accumulated down the years, trying to reverse engineer something useful out of it. Far and far away from anywhere civilised, of course, so that if something does go wrong . . . they can always blame it on global warming. Of course, they never get their hands on the really dangerous stuff. We always get there first, and grab the good stuff for ourselves. Droods aren't big on sharing. But we let America find enough to keep them happy, and occupied. And who knows, maybe one day they'll create something really neat. And then we'll probably step in and steal it. Droods aren't big on playing well with others, either.

I found an attached and encrypted file that looked interesting, so I opened it. Turned out to be a recent communication between Tiger Tim and the Immortals, in the form of a video recording. So I set it running, and sat back to watch it. The screen showed Tiger Tim, sitting at ease in an office I didn't recognise. So this had to have been sent after he left the Doctor's Amazon base. The rogue Drood looked very relaxed, and almost indecently pleased with himself, like the cat who's just licked cream off the caged bird. He smiled casually at the camera.

"Hello, my secret masters. My hidden partners. Or whatever you see yourselves as this week. As far as I'm concerned, you just exist to get me what I want, and don't you forget it. If you choose to think you're in charge, that's fine by me, but don't get uppity. My family, the high and mighty Droods, thought they were in charge of me, right up to the point where I decided to prove them wrong. Anyway, you asked for an update, so here it is.

"Dear Doctor Delirium is still in the dark about our relationship. He still thinks he's in charge. Though he doesn't do much of anything, anymore. Just sits there in his very private office, weirding out over the Apocalypse Door. Won't let anyone else near it. They say he talks to it, but until it starts actually answering him, I don't think I'll worry. I'm having him carefully watched, round the clock, just in case he suddenly decides to try and open the Door ahead of schedule. In which case my people will jump on him with heavy boots on.

"On your orders, oh my masters, I persuaded him to move everyone here to Area 52, and we're settling in nicely. Taking control meant using up most of our remaining Accelerated Men, but that was to be expected. I've got my people running everything now. Everyone else is dead. The Doctor ordered them dumped outside in the ice, so he could use them for experiments later, but his heart wasn't in it. He only really cares about his precious Door, these days. So I just have a few bodies brought in, now and then, for snacks.

"The Doctor did show some interest in the wide variety of strange and unusual objects stored in the Area Armoury. He was like a kid with new toys there, for a while. I kept an eye, just to make sure he didn't press the wrong big red button. However, the Doctor now seems convinced that he's found something he can use to keep himself safe and protected, after he opens the Apocalypse Door. So he can be King of the Earth, with all the hosts of Hell at his command. I am not convinced. He won't let me see what it is, so I can't be sure of what he's found, or indeed if it exists at all outside of his increasingly addled mind. While we're on the subject, take a look at this."

The image on the screen changed abruptly, to show surveillance coverage from a presumably hidden camera in Doctor Delirium's office. The mad scientist was dancing in front of the Apocalypse Door, which stood quietly upright on its own. The Doctor stopped abruptly and railed at the Door, waving his hands about. His voice was loud and harsh. I hit the pause button, and then zoomed in on the Door itself. I'd never seen it before. It did look quite remarkably ordinary, and everyday, except for the fact that it stood upright entirely unsupported. But given what just simple proximity had done to the Doctor . . . I started the message running again, and listened to the Doctor rant.

"It didn't have to be like this! It didn't! I was just going to blackmail all the governments of the Earth, and have them all bow down to me, and give me everything I ever wanted, but not now. Not now! You showed me. You were right all along. They laughed at me. They laughed at me! Never took me seriously! Well, now I'm mad as hell and I'm not going to take it anymore! No. No. I will open the Door of Hell, smash all the locks and break all the bolts and the dead shall come forth to take their revenge on the living. Oh yes! And all the peoples of the Earth shall be outnumbered by the damned . . . Yes. People. Why should I care about people? What did they ever do, but laugh at me . . ."

He disappeared, his image replaced by Tiger Tim, slouched almost bonelessly in his comfortable chair. "See what I mean? Loony tune, big time. It's a wonder to me he can still dress himself. Do we really need to indulge him anymore? Can't I just kill him? As long as I don't actually do it in front of his people, they'll carry on taking orders from me. I don't know why you're dragging your feet on this. It's not like we need him for anything . . . Except as a possible scapegoat, in case the Door turns out to be a dud, and we all need to disappear hastily into the background . . ." He smiled suddenly. "No. It's real. The Door is very definitely everything they say it is. You can't be around it for more than a few moments, and not know that. You can feel it, right down in your bones, in your soul. I'm quite looking forward to the opening. Let loose the Dogs of Hell, rain darkness down upon the Earth . . . Cull Humanity back to a more manageable level, just as I always wanted. And unlike the dear Doctor, I will be in control of the Door. I've done my research, quite separate from the Doctor's. It should be simple enough to reverse the process, and have all the devils and all the damned just sucked back through the Door into Hell. And then I will slam the Door shut in their faces, and laugh at them. All right, yes, I admit it, that is just a theory. But then everything is, where the Apocalypse Door is concerned. But it all seems straightforward enough. As though whoever originally created the Door intended for it to be easy to use."

And all the time I was thinking, *You fool. You bloody*

fool. Easy to open and easy to close? That's what the Door wants you to think.

"We have to do something soon," said Tiger Tim. He was suddenly quite serious, and all business. "The American military has to know that something's gone wrong at their precious Area 52. All communications are down, and all the security protocols have been compromised. But they can't know exactly what's happened, so they're going to be cautious. They'll take their time looking us over, before they try and break in. But you can bet their best military units are already on their way here. They've got a lot of golden eggs locked away in this place that they won't give up without a fight. I'd say we've got twenty-four hours at most, before someone comes banging on our door. So we've got to be prepared to open the Door before that, or be ready to move it somewhere else. Your call, Immortals."

The screen went blank.

So. I had a new deadline. I had to get this information out of Castle Frankenstein in a hurry, and then use the Merlin Glass to transport me straight to Area 52. Someone in the family would know exactly where it was. We know where all the secrets are buried. Still—Area 52. In the Antarctic. I should have dressed warmer.

I reached out to my duplicate at the far end of the cavern, and immediately his sensory input crashed into prominence. I was standing at the foot of the back stairs, watching and listening, but so far no one had come down. I could feel my other self calling me, and immediately I was back in the computer room. I concentrated, and called my dupe back into me. I just had time to grab hold of the desk to steady myself, and then the two of me slammed back together. The two sets of memories were harder to reconcile this time. The longer two of me existed, the more different we inevitably became. Gradually, my mind settled down again. My head hurt viciously, and I had to struggle to remember what I meant to do next. I was going to need a hell of a lot of downtime, when this was all over.

But for now, I'd had enough sneaking about. I had the computer download all its secrets onto a number of discs, and slipped them into pockets about my person. Centuries of knowledge, secrets and essential information. The Drood archivists would be studying this for years. Maybe even centuries . . . Time to go. Time to get the hell out of Castle Frankenstein, and head for Area 52. Busy, busy, busy. I laughed briefly, subvocalised my activating Words, and my armour slid smoothly into place around me.

Immediately, every alarm in the world went off at once. Bells and sirens and flashing lights; not just down here in the cavern, but up above as well, from the sound of it. Steel shutters slammed down all around me, covering the glass walls and closing off the only door. I was locked in. I snorted, inside my golden mask. It would have worked on anyone else. I smashed my way out in a few moments, tearing the heavy steel shutters like paper napkins. I stepped out into the cavern, and headed for the back stairs. I did some damage along the way, just to show I'd been there. The Immortals needed to take the Droods more seriously. There was still no sign of any security guards. What did I have to do, to earn their attention? No doubt the Immortals upstairs were still arguing about whose turn it was to do something. They'd grown soft and complacent in their Castle refuge, never dreaming anyone would dare to break in and menace them where they lived.

I ran up the back stairs, taking them three steps at a

time, and burst back onto the second floor. The alarms were more muted here, so as not to upset anyone. But there was no one around. No one running, or panicking, or shouting orders. I moved swiftly along the passage, looking curiously about me and listening at doors, but there was nothing, nothing at all. Until I came to one door that was standing just a little ajar. I heard raised voices. Curious, I eased the door open a little and looked inside.

It was a massive lecture hall, packed full of hundreds and hundreds of Immortals. Every single one of them, for all I knew. They were giving their full attention to one teenager, standing alone on a raised dais in the middle of the room, addressing them all in a calm, reasonable and only slightly mocking voice. Everyone else sat in circles of seats, surrounding the dais, radiating out to the sides of the hall. Given how many Immortals were here, this had to be seriously important. Especially if they were ignoring the alarms. So I armoured down, revealing my fake teenage self, eased the door open and slipped inside. I stood at the back of the hall, and concentrated on what the Immortal in the centre was saying. I knew I should be getting out of the Castle and heading for Area 52, but . . . I was curious. I had been sent here to get information, after all . . .

The teenager on the raised dais stared calmly about him, and spoke commandingly to his audience. It took me only a moment to understand that this was, this had to be, the Leader of the Immortals. The oldest of them all, who'd first made contact with the extra-dimensional Heart, when it first descended into this world all those years ago. It was the way he stood, the way he held himself, and in every word he spoke. You couldn't take your eyes off him.

He didn't look like much. Just another teenager,

wearing a T-shirt and jeans. The T-shirt bore a simple
message: EAT THE WORLD. He was short and squat,
barely five feet tall. Broad shouldered and well muscled,
with dark shaggy hair, a broad face, dark eyes and a
quick wolfish grin. He had the look of a man who'd be
able to bargain with a god fallen to earth.

I tore my gaze away from the Leader and studied the
teenagers sitting in circles around the dais. Those in the
closest circles looked the most like the Leader. These
would be the Elders, all that was left of the Leader's family and friends of that time. As the circles spread farther
out, the genotype grew more diluted, spreading through
generations of children bred with non-Immortals.

"Call me Methuselah," the Leader said smoothly.
"The old jokes are always the best, aren't they? I am the
oldest of us all. I met the Heart as a teenager, and made
my deal with it, and here we all are. Forever. Or as near
to forever as makes no difference."

I glanced around the packed lecture hall. The Immortals were all sitting very still, hanging on his every
word.

"I remember everything," said Methuselah. "Every
year, every century, every day since I made my way
slowly and disbelievingly through miles of burned and
shattered trees, across blackened earth and through
smoke-filled air, treading past the bodies of blown-
apart animals and birds that had fallen dead from the
heavens. It was early morning, and the sky had changed
colour. I thought it was the end of the world. Just a
teenager then, but already a man as far as my tribe was
concerned, because no one lived long in those days. I
pressed on when no one else would, when no one else
dared, because I was too fascinated to be properly
afraid. Centuries ago . . . but only yesterday to me.

"I found the Heart. It was still deciding on a shape then, and what I saw made my eyes bleed and my head hurt. I should have taken it for a god, or some great being fallen from the starry sky, I should have fallen to my knees and worshipped it, but I was a contrary soul even then, and had problems with authority figures. So I just stood there, watching it twist and turn in the great crater it had made, and it talked to me. I think . . . I amused it.

"Later, the Drood ancestors came and found it, and asked it to make them shamans and protectors of the Human tribe. The Heart gave them their wonderful armour, in return for sanctuary and sacrifice. The Droods never knew I got there first. And I didn't want to be anyone's protector. I wanted to live forever, along with some of my family, and a few friends. So the Heart made us Immortals. The Droods got to be shepherds, and we got to be lords of all we surveyed. Can't help thinking we got the better deal.

"And so we survived and prospered, down the ages. Discovering along the way that if you live long enough, you can learn to do all sorts of amazing things with your body. Make your flesh do anything, become anyone. Change your face, change your shape, change your identity. Become a man, become a woman, an old man or a young girl, anything you can imagine."

His face shifted suddenly, his features slipping and sliding across his bone structure, until abruptly he looked just like Doctor Delirium. His audience laughed, and applauded. His face changed again, all the details of his flesh rising and falling, until suddenly . . . he looked like me. Eddie Drood. The audience really liked that one. Methuselah let them enjoy it for a while, and then took back his own face again, and continued with his speech. I wasn't sure where he was going, what this was all about. And, why was his audience so intent?

"We are everywhere," said Methuselah. "We are everyone. Or at least, everyone who matters. We supply a word here and a push there, and the world goes the way we want it to. Always remember the Creed I gave you. Words to live forever by. Greed is good. Contempt is good. Hate is good. The crushing of the weak and glorying in their plight is good. Anything that profits us is good. Because we . . . are all that matters. No one else lasts long enough to matter. They come and they go but we go on. Everyone else in the world is just there to serve us, or for us to play with. They are mayflies. We are Immortals. Now, my special guest tonight is the man you've all been waiting for . . ."

He gestured to one side, and suddenly Tiger Tim was there, standing right beside Methuselah. He was still wearing his Great White Hunter outfit, down to the tiger-skin band on his bush hat. He smiled and waved condescendingly to the assembled Immortals, as though he was slumming just by joining them. They rose as one from their seats and booed and hissed him, hurling abuse and angry words. The sound was deafening, but it didn't bother Tiger Tim in the least. Methuselah let it go on for a while, and then gestured sharply at his audience, and they all fell silent and sank back into their seats again.

"Hush," he said, with just a hint of mockery. "We must all be very grateful to this rogue gentleman, who has done such good work for us. He may be a Drood, but he is our Drood. He set us on our present course, when he saw the potential in the Apocalypse Door, and brought it to our attention. He is our inside man at Area 52. We can't put one of our own in there; Doctor Delirium has seen to that. So I want you all to listen to what Tiger Tim has to say. Because we are very near the point of no return, when with a single act, I shall change the world forever."

"Why have I been summoned here?" Tiger Tim said bluntly. "You know I hate teleporting; it always makes my fillings ache. I have to get back to Area 52 soon, before I'm missed. Not by Doctor Delirium; he's still obsessed with the Door. But some of his people are getting seriously suspicious about me. Some have actually started questioning my orders, and I can't kill them all. Rumours are beginning to circulate about what happened to the people left behind at the Amazon base. I get the feeling that when the truth finally comes out, these people won't see the funny side."

"You're here to listen, while I explain the grand scheme to everyone," said Methuselah, just a bit sharply. "I felt you deserved that honour, after all you've done for us. Once I've finished here, you can return to Area 52 and kill Doctor Delirium. Take control of the Apocalypse Door, destroy any of your people who cannot be controlled, and then drop all the protections and let me in. It's time to put this show on the road."

"That's it?" said Tiger Tim. "I'm not standing around listening to anyone. There's work to be done."

And he disappeared, gone in a moment. The Leader of the Immortals shrugged easily, and turned back to face his children.

"Some people have no sense of drama. Mayflies get so impatient . . . Anyway, I thought you should see him. The rogue Drood who made all this possible. Yes, I thought you'd enjoy the irony . . . As soon as he's carried out his orders, and he will for all his impertinence . . . I shall go to Area 52, along with all those who choose to accompany me. And once there I shall dispose of our dear rogue Drood, since we won't need him anymore, and then I shall take control of the Apocalypse Door and transform it. And for the suspicious among you, yes, I do have the power to do that. The answer, once I'd thought about it for a bit, turned out to be surprisingly simple. A Hand of Glory, properly prepared, can open any door, any lock, even potential ones. Of course, it would have to be a very special Hand . . ."

He was teasing them now, dealing out little titbits of information, and we were all lapping up every word. This was what it was all about. Methuselah smiled calmly upon us all, and then suddenly produced and held up a large mummified Hand. Its skin was so white it blazed, and the long tapering fingers were still intact, though they'd been made into candles, with wicks protruding from the fingertips. Even at the very back of the lecture hall, I could still feel the incredible power and presence radiating from the thing. It beat on the air, like the wings of a great captured bird, fighting in its rage to be let loose. Those Immortals nearest the dais shrank back in their seats from it. Methuselah held the Hand high, enjoying the shocked gasps and protests all around him. It was all I could do to stop myself armouring up, fighting my way through the crowd, storming the stage and taking the Hand from the Leader. I thought I knew what he'd made his Hand of Glory from. His blasphemous Hand.

"There was an angel war in the Nightside, not so long ago," said Methuselah, when all was quiet again. "Agents of light and darkness, angels from Above and Below, raged against each other in that place where the night never ends . . . and against the morally dubious powers that live there. Some angels fell, struck down,

and had their heads impaled on spikes. Dangerous
place, the Nightside. Dangerous people . . . I was there,
going about my private business, when I found one of
the destroyed angels. I cut off its hand, and took it away
with me. And eventually I made a Hand of Glory out
of it. Because I just knew it would come in handy some
day. Do I hear the word blasphemy? Abomination? An
outrage against Heaven and Hell? What better way to
overpower and transform the Apocalypse Door, and
make it over into what I want it to be?"

He looked around, clearly anticipating applause and
acclamation from his audience. Instead, they sat there
silently, looking at each other. There was a general sense
of unease, and even blank disbelief. No one thought any
part of this was a good idea. Finally, someone roughly
halfway through the circles stood up, urged on by many
around him.

"Yes?" Methuselah said sweetly, with only a hint of
danger. "You have a question, perhaps?"

"Not everyone here believes in this," the younger Immortal said bluntly. "And even among those who do,
not everyone here wants to do this. You want to pass
through this Door in search of Heaven? Fine. Off you
go. We'll all stand here and wave you good-bye. Most
of us have a good life, and no intention of giving it up."

"You don't have to," Methuselah said patiently.
"Once I've turned the Door, and reversed its nature, I
shall open it. And then those who wish can follow me
through, and enjoy all the pleasures that can be found in
Paradise. None of you will be forced through. Heaven is
not for the timid. I offer you all a gift, a chance, for those
who've earned it through long service to the family."

He looked about him, more impatiently now; he
could tell he hadn't convinced them. They either didn't

understand him, or halfway understood and wanted no part of it. Only a few of the Elders, in those circles nearest the dais, were nodding slowly. Methuselah sighed loudly.

"Very well! One more time, for the hard of thinking! I have been searching for the Apocalypse Door for centuries. I first read about it in an illuminated manuscript, a piece of apocrypha recorded by the Venerable Bede. Then again, in a sixteenth-century manuscript that turned up during Henry VIII's dissolving of the monasteries. I almost got my hands on the Door during the Great Fire of London, but it disappeared in the general confusion. Imagine my surprise when it finally reappeared in the Really Old Curiosity Shoppe's auction catalogue, in LA. Of course, I couldn't risk being outbid, so I sent in a few of my more deniable people to pick it up.

"All would have been well, if Doctor Delirium hadn't turned up with his people, and not one but two Drood field agents. Some days things wouldn't go right if you twisted their arm. Ever since dear Eddie reorganised the Droods, it's been very difficult to get reliable information out of Drood Hall."

"Why don't we just kill Edwin?" It was the same younger Immortal, on his feet again. There was a loud murmur of agreement.

"We're working on it," said Methuselah. He gave the other Immortal a hard look, until he sank back into his seat again. Methuselah continued. "We will take care of Eddie, the moment a decent opportunity presents itself. For the moment, he and his family are preoccupied with digging out all the doppelgangers we placed inside Drood Hall. We knew this was inevitable, the moment Eddie started reorganising things, that's why I ordered the Matriarch murdered, and tried out the Acceleration Drug's addition on them. Always such fun, spreading chaos among one's enemies. The witch's death . . . was unfortunate. It's made Eddie more dangerous than ever. But, assaulting the Hall with Doctor Delirium's Accelerated Men distracted them all nicely, and killed a satisfying number of Droods along the way. And that is the most we can hope for, for now. Strike directly against Eddie, or those closest to him, and they will strike back. That can be your problem, for the future. Once I, and whoever chooses to join me, have passed through the Door . . . you can choose a new Leader, and a new direction, if you wish. The family will be yours to run and shape."

The young Immortal was back on his feet again, waving a hand angrily to be acknowledged. It was clear Methuselah was growing angry with this open challenge to his authority, but he still kept his calm, and finally gestured for the Immortal to speak.

"What if Doctor Delirium opens the Door before you get there, and all Hell is set loose on the world? Why are you waiting?"

"This is Area 52 we're talking about," Methuselah said flatly. "The most secure, and most heavily guarded, military base on the planet. All of its security measures and protections are still very much in place, along with Doctor Delirium's personally designed anti-Immortal measures. If we even try to break in through brute force, you can bet Doctor Delirium will open the Door, if only to spite us. We have to wait to be invited in, by our man on the inside.

"Once Tiger Tim has assassinated Doctor Delirium, he will shut down all the defences, and we can just stroll right in and take what we want. Starting with our dear rogue Drood's head. Never trust a traitor, even when he's your own. Perhaps we'll send his head back to Drood Hall; I understand they can be terribly sentimental about such things. Of course, once I've turned the Door, and passed through it, all of you who choose to remain behind can help yourselves to whatever goodies lie hidden away in Area 52's forbidden armouries." He smiled briefly. "You see how good I am to you? New toys to play with! Won't that be nice?"

"But how soon are you planning to go?" the younger Immortal said stubbornly.

"Eight hours, maximum," said Methuselah. "So you'd all better prepare yourselves, hadn't you?"

Eight hours . . . it seemed I had an even tighter deadline than I'd thought.

"Any more questions?" said Methuselah, just a bit pointedly. "Any other little thing I can do, to put your Immortal minds at ease? I swear, it's like working with a bunch of whiny little children. I should have kicked you all out of the nest long ago, and let you learn to fly the hard way. You've got soft, all of you. Soft and complacent, and stupidly arrogant! The world is yours; get out there and trample all over it! I can't hold your hands forever! I swear, it's youngsters like you, with no real ambition, that will make me glad to leave all this behind . . ."

Someone else in the audience stood up, an Immortal from a circle closer to the stage. "You haven't been a real leader in years, and you know it. You've let our plans for world domination lapse, excused yourself from all the strategy meetings, just so you could concentrate on your damned Door, and your dreams of Paradise. You're abandoning us, to chase your own fantasies!"

"So?" said Methuselah. "Choose a new leader, make

new plans. It'll be your world, once I'm gone. Make of it what you will. Use it up, eat it up, spit it out. It's all yours to play with. While some of us go on to better things."

And that was when the door behind me burst open, and the Immortal I'd knocked out and replaced staggered in. He was unsteady on his feet and his eyes were still somewhat dazed, but sheer rage kept him moving. It was strange to see his face, after I'd been using it for so long. He clung to the door and yelled almost hysterically at the faces turning to look at him.

"We've been infiltrated! Someone's got into the Castle!" He saw me then, looking back at him with his own face, and he almost went into meltdown with sheer outrage. He pointed at me with a shaking finger. "There! That's him! He's made himself look like me, but he's not one of us! He's a Drood! A Drood!"

That's what you get for being merciful. Ungrateful little scrote. I jumped up, punched him out, leapt over his falling body, and raced out of the lecture hall while the general cry of outrage from within was still building. I ran down the hallway, and already doors were opening everywhere, with angry Immortals spilling out. I could hear more of them fighting each other to get out of the lecture hall and get after me. They sounded like they wanted my blood, and weren't too fussy how they got it. I pounded down a side corridor, and Immortals appeared from everywhere, in front and behind me. So I squeezed the ring on my finger, and made a duplicate of myself. And then both of me squeezed my rings, and there were four of me.

The sudden rush of extra sensory input would have been overwhelming, but all I had to concentrate on was running. And every time I came to a corner, or a turning point, all of me chose different directions. I couldn't keep track of who was who, or which had been the original me, so I just kept on running. It seemed like every Immortal in the Castle was after me now, numbers beyond counting, so every time I came to a corner or a change in direction, I made more of me. Soon there was a crowd of me, running and running full pelt, back and forth, up and down the Castle. It was all just a blur of stone walls, narrow corridors, and screaming angry faces wherever I looked. I ran and ran, lost in the crowd of me, losing all track of where and who I was. Dozens of me, running endlessly, running blindly, swamped by too many details, maddened by my own chattering thoughts and impulses, driving me in a hundred different directions at once.

I ran on, lost in myself, everywhere at once, unable to concentrate on anything. Immortals jumped me, hit me, dragged me down, over and over, and I fought back, lashing out at everyone who wasn't me. I couldn't think, couldn't plan, lost in the horror of endlessly branching possibilities, lost in the crowd, lost . . . I panicked, and called all of me back into myself.

Suddenly there was just me, alone in my head, and it felt good, so good. I stumbled to a halt, as I struggled to assimilate a whole host of conflicting memories. I leaned against a cold stone wall, breathing harshly, sweat running down my face, trembling from exhaustion, and other things. A terribly personal nightmare, to be drowning in a sea of you, your very identity diluted by duplication . . . I shuddered, and forced the memories back until I was just me again. I looked around, and found I was back down in the dungeons under the Castle, outside the computer rooms.

Presumably because it was the one place I thought I knew best. I shook my head. I'd been so confused I hadn't even thought to armour up, and protect myself from the various attacks my various selves had experienced. Though I had to wonder . . . each of me must have had a torc, but what would have happened if I'd tried to call up so much strange matter at once, enough for dozens of suits of armour? This was all getting really complicated . . . and quite definitely a problem for another day. I had eight hours to stop Methuselah from getting to Area 52, then get there myself and stop anyone from opening the Apocalypse Door.

I checked myself for damage, but I didn't seem to have taken any, even though I could clearly remember being hit and attacked any number of times . . . I could only assume the sheer number of me I'd made had diluted the effects, when they all slammed back into me. Could have been worse; I could have ended up with all the damage that all of me had taken, expressed in the one body. Nasty.

I smiled slightly as I took in the state of the computer room, with its torn steel shutters and kicked-out door. I really had made a mess of the place, the last time I was here. The guard I'd taken out was still slumped unconscious in his chair. But, I couldn't hide out here for long. I had a lot to do . . . The mission was escalating wildly out of control, so many players . . . Doctor Delirium, Tiger Tim, Methuselah, all with their own different plans for the Apocalypse Door . . . All I could be sure of was that I had to get to Area 52 in a hurry, before somebody did something we'd all regret.

I heard footsteps approaching. So I slipped into the security booth, and knelt down beside the unconscious security guard, hidden in the shadows. The footsteps kept coming, just the one person, calm and unhurried. Not someone chasing me. But once they saw the state of the trashed computer room, they'd know I'd been there. I'd have to wait for the right moment, then jump out and strike them down before they could cry out. I raised my head cautiously, and looked down the corridor.

And there, coming towards me, was Molly Metcalf.

I stayed very still, crouched in the shadows, and watched silently as Molly came to a halt before the computer room. She looked at the damage, and her mouth twitched briefly, in a smile I knew all too well. Undamaged, unhurt, utterly perfect, my Molly. My heart hammered in my chest, and I couldn't move, paralysed by surging emotions. Wanting to believe, not daring to hope. My chest was hitching silently, and tears burned in my eyes. It could be her, she could be . . . I wanted to run out and run up to her, and hold her in my arms and never ever let her go, but I didn't. I couldn't. Because in this rotten and corrupt Castle, not everything was always as it seemed, and not everyone was who they seemed to be. You couldn't trust a face. Not here. This could be an Immortal, pretending to be my poor dead Molly, to bring me out into the open. After all, how could Molly, my Molly, have survived such terrible wounds? I saw the blades slam into her, again and again, saw her blood spill . . . My hands were clenched so hard they hurt, and I could hardly get my breath, but I couldn't look away.

I stayed where I was, and watched her silently as she stepped casually over the torn steel shutters, entered the computer room and looked around her. Even though I ached to go to her, I held myself still, because I had a duty to my family. I couldn't afford to get caught, not with the safety of all Humanity riding on me, and yet . . . I had to be sure. I needed to be sure. Molly pulled up a chair and sat down before the computers, still open and running from where I'd left in a hurry. It occurred to me that I was still wearing the face and body of a teenage Immortal . . . So I stood up abruptly, and strode into the computer room. Molly glared at me, without getting up.

"What do you want?" she said. It was her voice, it was . . .

"Shouldn't that be my line?" I said. "What are you doing here?"

She gave me a hard withering stare that would have worked on anyone else. "Stay out of this, and don't get in my way. I have work to do. And I'm just in the mood to kick the crap out of any Immortal who gets in my way."

I took a chance. "You're not one of us," I said. "You're not an Immortal."

"Damn right I'm not," said Molly Metcalf, and my heart leapt in my chest. She looked me over, and sniffed loudly. "I wouldn't be a teenager again for all the chocolate in the world. I'm here on my own business, and if you're wise you won't interfere. I'm looking for records of the deal I made with you people, all those years ago, when I was making all kinds of unwise agreements, in return for power. I'm here to destroy all the files with my name on them; my little way of saying I wash my hands of the whole pack of you. I'm a good girl now, and I can't have any evidence to the contrary left in unfriendly hands."

"You were never one of us?" I said. "Never worked for us? You knew nothing about the infiltration of the Droods?"

"Of course not! I wouldn't work for scum like you; hell, I haven't exchanged two words with any of you since we made our deal. I do have standards. And all the promises I had to make, in return for power, were all used up years ago. I don't owe you scumbags anything, especially after you nearly killed me in the Hall. Oh yes, I know that was you. I should kill you all, for what you've done. But I don't have the time, right now. So run away, little Immortal, before I turn you into something distressing."

"If it's all over," I said, "what do you care about your files? You're not here to destroy them; you're here to destroy all the computer records, to strike back at the Immortals."

"Oh hell," said Molly. "A bright one. What were the odds? Too bad for you . . ."

She got up to face me, and she'd never looked more beautiful, or more dangerous.

"The Drood was here before you," I said. "Edwin. Too stupid to get what he needed from our computers."

"Don't you talk about him," she said. "Don't you talk about my Eddie! He's a better man than all of you put together!"

"I know," I said. "But it's good to hear you say it." I used the Chameleon Codex to change my shape, and took on my own face and body again. I smiled at Molly. "Hi, sweetie. Miss me?"

"You bastard," she said, and her gaze and her voice had never been colder. "You bloody bastard Immortal. How dare you take on my Eddie's face? I'll kill you for that!"

"Wait a minute, wait a minute," I said, retreating rapidly as she advanced on me. "It's me, Molly; it's really me!"

Something in my face and voice stopped her. She looked at me for a long moment, with a cold, unwavering and quite deadly gaze.

"Prove it."

"You're convinced your left tit is smaller than your right one, even though I keep telling you they're the same."

"It is you! Eddie!" She stepped forward and slapped me hard across the face. "That's for pretending to be someone else, to test me! Oh Eddie, my Eddie . . ."

I took her in my arms and we hugged each other tightly, clinging together like we'd never let each other go, like the whole world couldn't pull us apart, now we'd found each other again. She buried her face in my shoulder, and I hid my face in her hair. We were both breathing hard, as though we'd run a long way to get here, to this moment. Our bodies pressed tight together, as though we wanted to touch every part of each other at once.

"I thought I'd lost you," I said finally. "Oh God, Molly, I wanted to die. I didn't want to go on living, without you."

"I'm sorry," said Molly. She pulled back a little, so she could look me in the eye. "I'm so sorry, but I couldn't let you know I was still alive. I had to keep you in the dark, for your own protection."

We let go of each other, but still stood close together, face-to-face. I could feel her breath on my mouth, and her gaze was like a caress.

"How?" I said finally. "How did you survive, Molly? I saw the blades . . . and the blood . . ."

She put her fingertips on my mouth to stop me talking. "I did tell you once, but you clearly weren't paying attention. I'm a witch, Eddie. We all keep our hearts separate from our bodies, safely stored and hidden in a protected place. As long as they don't actually cut my head off, I can survive anything. I always come back. Isabella got me out of the Hall, and then watched over me while I slowly healed myself."

"But . . . why didn't you come back to the Hall?" I said. "Why couldn't you at least contact me, tell me you were still alive?"

"I had a lot of time to think, while my body was repairing itself," said Molly. "Everything that had happened only made sense if the Droods had been infiltrated. And the only ones who could do that, were the Immortals. And that meant I couldn't trust anyone, anymore. It was safer for both of us if our enemies thought I was dead. So I came here, to break into their computers and search out a list of everyone they've replaced inside your family."

"Hold everything," I said. "You knew about the Immortals? Why didn't you ever say anything?"

"You never asked. I know all kinds of things, Eddie."

"We will come back to that, at a later date," I said. "For now, how did you get into the Castle?"

"I made a deal with these people, remember? And while I was here, I was allowed to come and go as I pleased; so I took the opportunity to set up my own little back door teleport. Just in case I needed to come back again, without their permission. It never even occurred to the smug little bastards that I might not be as completely taken in by them as they thought I was. How did you get in?"

I smiled. "The Armourer makes the very best toys."

She grinned back at me. "I should have known you'd been here before me. Look at this mess. You never were the most subtle of secret agents."

"Don't know what you're talking about," I said loftily. "I am a thing of mists and shadows."

"How were you able to look like one of the Immortals?" she said abruptly. "That wasn't an illusion; I would have Seen through that."

I explained to her about the Chameleon Codex, and the Gemini Duplicator, and she grinned wickedly.

"So . . . you can make two of yourself, or even more? You can change to look like anyone at all . . . Including celebrities? Male and female? Oh, Eddie . . . we are so going to give these toys a workout in your bedroom when we get back!"

"How well we know each other," I said.

The computer made a polite noise, to let us know it was done doing what Molly had told it to do, and we both looked round, and leaned over the monitor to study the long list of names scrolling down on the screen.

"You don't look happy anymore, Eddie. In fact, you look like you want to kill someone. I know it's a lot of names, but is it really that bad?"

"So many names," I said. "Past, and present. People I've known all my life. Trusted faces. I can't believe we were infiltrated this badly, and never knew. And from *outside*. We should have spotted them, we should have noticed something . . . But we were too arrogant. We just couldn't believe it was possible . . ." And then I saw one particular name. "Damn. I know now. I know who killed the Matriarch. I know who murdered my grandmother, and how."

"Who?" said Molly, peering past my shoulder at the screen. "Who was it?"

I set the computer to downloading the list onto a disc, and turned away from the screen. "It doesn't matter now. That's family business. It can wait. We have work to do, Molly. I don't know if you've been keeping up with everything that's happening here, but we only have eight hours or less to get to Area 52, and deal with the Apocalypse Door, before some poor fool opens it."

"Damn right," said Molly. "The old team, back in action again! I've missed you, Eddie."

"I missed you, Molly. More than life itself."

"All right, you're pushing it now . . ."

We hugged each other again, but broke apart almost immediately as we heard a whole crowd of people approaching, at speed. Molly grabbed the disc with the list, and tucked it away about her person.

"Must have set off a silent alarm, this time," I said. "You've got better long-range senses than me. How many are coming?"

Molly concentrated briefly, and then frowned. "At a conservative guess, I'd have to say . . . all of them. If I'm reading the signs right, and I am, every Immortal in the Castle is up in arms, loaded for bear, and headed this way with vengeance on their minds. All right, Eddie, what have you done this time?"

"Why is it always my fault?" I said innocently.

"Because it is always your fault!"

You can't argue with logic like that. "How far to the nearest exit?"

"Eddie, they've blocked off every exit, including half a dozen I didn't even know existed until now. And I'm very thorough about things like that."

"So," I said. "You and me, up against the whole family of Immortals. Not good odds . . ."

"Can't you just open a doorway for us, with the Merlin Glass?"

"It won't work inside the Castle's protections. Nothing living can pass through their defences. What about your teleport spells?"

"Same problem," said Molly. "We're going to have to fight our way out."

"Works for me," I said. "Don't suppose you happened

to bring any really nasty and powerful magical weapons with you, by any chance?"

"I don't normally need them," said Molly. "I take it you can at least armour up?"

"Oh yes. Ready to rock and roll."

"Oh good. I was almost worried there, for a moment."

"Here they come," I said. "Don't hold back, Molly. They won't."

"The thought never even crossed my mind."

"Of course. Don't know what I was thinking of. Now, let us go forth and smite the ungodly with malice aforethought."

"Let's," said Molly. "I can do malice. I am just in the mood to do appalling things."

"Never knew you when you weren't," I said. "You're a bad influence on me."

"And you love it."

We left the computer room and headed down the stone corridor to the back stairs. I was still sort of hoping the Immortals might have overlooked them. I didn't want to fight down in the dungeons if I could help it. Not enough room to manoeuvre. But by the time we'd got to the foot of the stairs, I could already hear a host of angry voices hurrying down towards us. They sounded really quite upset about something. I smiled, and I could feel it was not a very nice smile. Now they knew how it felt to be infiltrated, violated, where they lived. I armoured up, gleaming golden strange matter sweeping around me in a moment. I felt stronger and faster and more focused, more alive. I was a Drood, in my armour and in my fury, and the Immortals were about to learn what that meant. I extended golden spikes from my knuckles, and took up a position blocking the foot of the stairs. I didn't want anyone getting past me. I wanted them blocked in, only able to come at Molly and me a few at a time. Molly moved in beside me, disturbing energies already spitting and crackling around her hands, waiting to be unleashed. I reached inside my armour, and drew my Colt Repeater. I like to think of myself as an agent and not an assassin, but sometimes the enemy just doesn't give you any choice. The first Immortals came charging round the corner and down the stairs, and I opened fire.

The first few were thrown back by the bullets' impact, but you can't kill an Immortal with lead. The fallen were already healing as the next few jumped over them, to get at us. They flesh danced in midair, growing their thick bony plates, and my bullets ricocheted away harmlessly. I tried silver bullets, to no better effect, and then called on cursed ammunition, and that did the job. The cursed bullets punched right through the bone protection, and the Immortals cried out in pain and horror as the curse took root in their Immortal flesh. Their skin cracked and burst apart, the meat beneath corrupting and rotting from the inside out, eating them up. The Immortals died horribly, screaming, and the ones coming next hesitated. I raised my Colt, but when I pulled the trigger nothing happened. I called for more bullets, for any kind of ammunition; but nothing came. The Immortals had found a way to block the Colt, so its bullets couldn't reach it. Clever Immortals. I put the gun back inside my armour, and grew long golden blades from my fists. The Immortals found their courage again, and came forward, howling ancient war cries.

And Molly and I waited for them with death in our hands.

We hit the first few hard, striking them down and trampling them underfoot. My golden blades sliced and chopped through Immortal flesh, my armoured strength slamming the blades through skin and bone with equal ease. Blood spurted, staining the stone walls and running thickly down the stone steps. Immortals died screaming, and behind my featureless gold mask I was smiling a cold, cold smile. Let them die. Let them all die for what they had done to the world, and Humanity, and my family.

Crackling energy bolts flew from Molly's upraised hands, blasting heads and bodies apart, exploding bone and flesh with bad intent. The Immortals were used to striking from hiding, from behind trusted faces; they weren't used to going head to head and hand to hand, even with overwhelming odds on their side. The ones at the front hesitated, and even tried to back away, but the press of eager bodies behind wouldn't let them. So they came at Molly and me with every kind of weapon, guns and blades, ancient and modern, scientific and magical, and none of it did them any good.

I pushed forward with Molly at my side, forcing our way up the stairs over the bodies of the dead and the dying. I punched a golden blade right through a bony chest plate and into the heart, twisted once and then withdrew, hauling the falling body out of the way so I could get at the next Immortal. Molly grabbed a man by the chin and ripped his face right off. And while he was screaming through the crimson mess, she blasted a fireball down his throat. Molly always did fight dirty. Side by side, step by step, we fought our way up the narrow stairway, and there was nothing the pack of Immortals could do to stop us.

Molly blasted them with Words that hit like shrapnel, tearing through flesh and ripping out eyes. She sent lightning bolts dancing among the packed bodies before us, and the stench of burning meat was thick on the close air. I cut the bastards down, and crushed their skulls with casual blows. And if I always seemed to position myself so that I stood between Molly and most of the attackers, that was my business. She would have been furious if she'd noticed, but I couldn't, I just couldn't risk losing her again.

The Immortals came at us with swords and axes, in a dozen styles out of history, their blades glowing brightly, reinforced with terrible magics and sparkling plasma energies. Most of them rebounded harmlessly from my armour, and I dodged the rest. I could be hurt, even inside my marvellous armour, though it took a lot to do it. And if anyone could come up with a supernatural can opener, it would be the Immortals. Molly blew the more dangerous-looking weapons apart with a quick gesture, before they could get anywhere near her. Some of the Immortals had guns, firing bullets and explosive charges and all kinds of fierce energies. None of them could penetrate my armour, though the deadlier energies crackled around me like malevolent ivy for a worryingly long time, before falling reluctantly away. Molly had her own shields, magical protections established so long ago they kicked in automatically.

One Immortal hid behind others, and jabbed an Aboriginal pointing bone at me. The magic slammed against my chest, hitting me like a cannonball, stopping me dead in my tracks. The Immortal cried out in triumph, and stabbed at me again. The magic crashed against my armour, made a sound like the striking of a great golden gong, and then rebounded. The bone exploded in the Immortal's hand, driving hundreds of bone splinters into the ruined flesh. The woman behind him hauled him back out of the way, ignoring his ago-

nised screams, and smiled nastily at me as she held up
a Hand of Glory. My heart missed a beat as I remembered Methuselah showing us all the Hand he'd made
from an angel's flesh, and then I breathed again as I realised this wasn't that. It was a Hand of Glory all right,
made from a dead man, with the fingers lit like candles,
and presumably she thought she could use it to unlock
my armour. She really should have known better. She
thrust the dead Hand at me, and its fingers writhed
briefly, and then it turned around, grabbed her by the
throat and throttled her to death. She should have done
her research.

The next Immortal pushed past her, making no attempt to help her, and trained on me the biggest machine gun I've ever seen, complete with trailing bands
of ammo. I was frankly amazed he could even lift the
thing. He sprayed me with bullets, trying to force me
back so he could get at Molly. I stood my ground, and
the armour absorbed every single bullet. Molly shel-
tered behind my armoured form until the shooting
stopped abruptly, as the Immortal ran out of bullets.
And then she just peeked past me briefly, snapped her
fingers, and where the Immortal had been there was
now a rather surprised-looking toad. It's a neat trick,
and not one Molly can do often, as it takes a lot out
of her; but the psychological effect on the enemy is always outstanding. The Immortals at the front turned
and fought those behind them, refusing to be pushed
forward to a fate worse than death. They jammed together in the narrow stairway, and Molly and I cut and
blasted our way through them like lumberjacks through
virgin forest.

We pressed forward, forcing our way into and through
the Immortals, stepping over bodies and splashing

through blood. I cut them down and hauled them aside, and plunged on again, with nothing in my heart for them but a terrible coldness. For all the things they'd done, and for all they intended to do, there could be no quarter, no mercy. And after a while I hardly heard the screams, and the pleas, and the horror.

It was still slow, hard, bloody business. They fought us every inch of the way, with all kinds of weapons, and they took a lot of killing. And for a family built on treachery and striking from the shadows, they weren't cowards. They could fight, when they had to. I was glad of that. It made killing them easier. Less like butchery. More like execution than slaughter. Molly pressed in close beside me, when she could, when there was space enough, and threw energy bolts and vicious magics from behind me when she couldn't. She was having to change her spells more frequently now, as she used up her reserves. There were limits to what even she could do, though she went to great pains to hide that from people. Her magic was running out, and by the time we made it to the top of the stairs she was breathing hard, and blood was seeping from her eyes, from the strain of what she'd done to herself.

I paused in the doorway, looking quickly around the open space before me. The wide corridor was packed with howling Immortals, crying out for our deaths, and if Molly and I moved forward, it would leave us open to attack from all sides at once. We had to get off this floor, and down into the hall below, with a chance at the main door. But there were hundreds, maybe even thousands of Immortals between us and the great stairway. I might make it, protected by my armour, but Molly almost certainly wouldn't. She had to see the situation as clearly as I did, but she didn't say anything. She was waiting for me to come up with a plan, and then she'd back me up, whatever it was. The Immortals were waiting too, grinning and yelling mockingly at me, daring me to step out from the protection of the doorway, so they could fall on Molly and me like the pack of wolves they were. But I had no intention of fighting my way through that crowd to the great stairs. I had a better idea.

Well, better, relatively speaking. I looked at Molly.

"Trust me?"

"Always."

"Good."

I grabbed her round the waist, held her tightly to my side, and using all my armoured strength I leapt right over the crowd of Immortals, over the balcony, and out into open space. Everyone fell silent. Molly and I fell through the air, and the hall lay below us, a very long way below us. Molly whooped with enthusiasm as we dropped to the floor below. We hit hard, the parquet flooring exploding under my armoured feet. My armoured legs absorbed most of the impact, and I didn't fall back a step. Molly took the sudden stop rather harder, all the breath knocked out of her, her head snapping back on her neck. I held her up as the strength went out of her legs. I looked quickly to the front door, at the far end of the long hall.

There were still a lot of Immortals down there in the hall, between me and that door. And more spilling out of adjoining rooms, and plunging down the main stairs. I had only a few moments before battle would be joined again. From all sides, now. But . . . I could feel something. There was a sense of . . . pressure, of something pressing hard against the Castle's shields with growing, resolute strength, fighting its way towards me. The power of the Immortals might be ancient and forbidding, but what was coming had been made by Merlin Satanspawn himself, and it would not be denied. I called to it, and the whole Castle seemed to cry out, as something primordial and inviolate suddenly shattered, broken by something greater than itself. And just like that I held the Merlin Glass in my golden hand.

Not all my luck is bad.

Molly finally stirred, got her feet under her, and pushed herself away from me. Her face was pale, and she was breathing hard, but her eyes were tracking and she knew what was happening.

"Okay, mind the first step, it's a bastard. Next time, a little warning, perhaps?"

"If I'd told you what I was going to do, you wouldn't have let me do it," I said reasonably.

"True. Can you get us out of here through the Glass?"

"Not as such, no. The Glass broke through the main shields to get here, but my armour's telling me the remaining protections are still functioning. No living thing can pass through them, either way. But, I think I've got an idea."

"Should I go and stand somewhere else?"

"No, trust me, you're going to like this one. I think I can get us some reinforcements. Very special reinforcements."

I held the Glass up before me. A few Immortals shouted out, as they recognised it. But none of them were worried. No living thing could pass through Castle Frankenstein's shields. But we live in a big world, and it contains far more than just the living. I used the Glass to make an opening between the hall and the Castle Hotel, and the Merlin Glass leapt out of my hand, growing rapidly to provide a door between me and the Castle Hotel ballroom. The Spawn of Frankenstein were still partying. They all stopped abruptly and looked round, as the door appeared out of nowhere in the midst of them. The Bride stepped forward, and then bowed respectfully as she recognised my armour.

"Who calls on us? What can the Spawn of Frankenstein do for the mighty Drood family?"

I couldn't call on her as Shaman Bond; no one must ever know he was a Drood. Luckily the mask disguises my voice.

"Eddie Drood, at your service. And it's more what I can do for you. I'm speaking to you from inside Castle Frankenstein. Yes, the real one, currently occupied by the Immortals. I've opened a door between here and you; no living thing can pass through the Castle shields, but you're not living, are you? If you'll come through, and fight alongside me against the Immortals, the Droods will give you Castle Frankenstein for your own. The whole place will be yours, along with whatever secrets you can find here."

Give her credit, she didn't hesitate, not even against the terrible Immortals themselves.

"Deal," the Bride said crisply. "Stand back and give us some room; we're coming through."

She charged through the doorway, all seven foot of her, spiked silver knuckle-dusters gleaming on both hands again. And right behind her came Springheel Jack, with his cloak and top hat and gleaming straight razors. And behind him came all the Spawn of Frankenstein; all the creatures and creations, ready to fight for the home they'd never known, and the secrets of their creation. Not the living but the living dead, come to fight the Immortals on their behalf as well as mine, laughing as they came, because death held no terror for any of them. They'd been there, done that, and were all too ready to hand it out to those who'd kept them from their ancient home for so long.

The Immortals cried out in shock and horror as the monsters came surging out of the doorway I'd opened, realising at last that their hidden retreat was no longer inviolate. They opened up on the Spawn with all kinds of weapons, but most of those had been designed to work on the living, not the living dead. The Spawn fell on their hated enemies, and blood and horror filled the hall.

The Bride paused briefly to look at me. "How can we best serve you, Drood?"

"Hold these bastards off, till I can get to the front door," I said. "I've had another idea."

"Wonderful," said Molly.

The Bride threw herself at the nearest Immortals like a wrecking ball, sending bodies flying this way and that with the unnatural strength of her long slender arms. She just strode right into them, lashing about her with casual grace, her spiked silver knuckle-dusters ripping off faces and smashing in skulls. She towered above them, her black beehive hair clearly visible at all times, her face stark and cold with years of fury. The Immortals fought back as best they could, and could not hurt her dead flesh. The Bride threw them all back, with contemptuous indifference.

Springheel Jack was at her side and at her back, hopping and leaping, and sometimes jumping right over the heads of his enemies, somersaulting in midair. His razor-filled hands struck out with inhuman speed, never missing a target, and blood spurted everywhere. Immortals fell to the ground, clutching at new crimson mouths in their throats, or pawing feebly at where their eyes had been. Springheel Jack danced among them

with deadly grace, spinning and pirouetting, his glowing razors shining with supernatural brilliance. The Immortals were the enemy of his Bride, so he was their
enemy too.

The rest of the Spawn spread out to form a protective
barrier between me and the Immortals, so Molly and
I could head for the front door. The Immortals were
trying desperately to block my way. They didn't trust
their shields to protect them anymore. The Spawn held
them back easily, tearing and clawing, biting through
centuries-old flesh, or just smashing in heads with blunt
grey fists. If nothing else, the Baron had made sure his
creations would always be able to protect themselves.
The Spawn also opened fire with a surprisingly large
number of really quite appalling weapons they just happened to have about their person. When you're a Spawn
of Frankenstein, the thought of mobs with pitchforks
and flaming torches and modern firepower is never far
away. And they've been trying to find or force their way
into Castle Frankenstein for many years—centuries, for
some of them. They didn't hold their annual meeting in
the Castle Hotel out of sentiment. They'd always hoped
their day would come, and now they were delighted for
this chance to bestow years of frustrated fury on their
old enemy, the usurpers of Castle Frankenstein.

The Immortals came flooding into the hall from all
directions, filling the long hall from wall to wall, flesh
dancing desperately to make them strong enough to
take on the Spawn of Frankenstein. They writhed and
twisted, flesh rippling across bones and exploding into
wild new shapes as they became ogres; with massive
slabs of muscle, terrible fangs and claws, all their vulnerable parts hidden behind bony armour. They became gargoyles, and lizards, and even weird abstract

shapes, as they struggled to find some form strong and vicious enough to match the Spawn of Frankenstein. Who, if anything, became even more furious, believing the Immortals were mocking them, becoming monsters to fight monsters. The Spawn fell on the Immortals with angry cries, tearing them limb from limb with their more than ordinary strength. And though their dead flesh took awful wounds, they did not bleed, or hurt, or cry out. They were beyond such things.

Molly and I fought our way down the long hall, heading for the front door. Molly was almost out of magic now, her protective shields flickering on and off. Only her pride kept her back straight as she staggered exhausted beside me. She held a glowing witchblade in one hand now, and enough basic viciousness to make her dangerous. Inside my gleaming armour, I was deathly tired too. I'd been on my feet and fighting for a long time now, moving from one battle to another with never a chance to rest. Every movement was difficult, every muscle ached, and sweat ran down my face behind my golden mask. The armour is only ever as strong as the man inside it. But still Molly and I pressed forward, striking our enemies down and kicking their bloody corpses out of our way. I'd lost count of how many Immortals I'd killed, men who should have lived forever; but it seemed like there were always more.

I hadn't seen Methuselah anywhere, and tired as I was I was still alert enough that his absence worried me.

A group of maybe twenty Immortals, savage teenage men and women with ancient eyes and powerful guns, blocked our way, standing between us and the front door, determined not to be moved. The guns were energy weapons, alien by the look of them, and I lurched to a halt so I could study the situation. If those guns were what I thought they were, I could be in real trouble. Energy weapons of that design could blast the armour right off me, like a steam hose blasting paper off a wall. Even strange matter has its limitations, in this material world. And while I was still struggling desperately for something I could do that didn't involve running or hiding in a corner, Molly drew herself up from where she'd been standing slumped against me, glared at the Immortals blocking our way, brought up both her hands, and slammed them together in a single almighty clap. The impact blew the Immortals away like a storm wind, sending them flying through the air to the left and to the right, slamming them into the walls on either side so hard that the walls cracked. The Immortals fell, and did not rise again.

For the moment, there was nothing between us and the front door. I grabbed Molly as her legs started to buckle, threw her over one golden shoulder and sprinted for the door with all the speed I had left in me. I ignored her muttered *Eddie, you bastard,* and yelled for the Bride and Springheel Jack to guard my back. I didn't look back to see if they'd heard me. All of my concentration was fixed on that door. I got there in a few moments, grabbed the heavy door with both hands and ripped the bloody thing right off its hinges. I threw it to one side, and charged out into the night.

I put Molly down, and she sank into an exhausted heap, too tired even to curse me properly for offending her dignity. Outside the Castle, the cold fresh air seemed to revive her some. I knelt down before her, and she fixed me with bleary eyes.

"What? What do you want, Eddie? Because I am really very tired right now. I am running on fumes."

"This Castle is surrounded by protective shields," I

said urgently. "Even outside the front door. But when you made your deal with the Immortals, you were given a free pass to come and go. It was never revoked. That's how you got in here. I need you to channel that invitation through the Merlin Glass, and open a door between here and Drood Hall. Can you do that, Molly?"

She looked used up. She looked like death warmed up and allowed to congeal. But she managed one of her old wild grins for me anyway.

"Of course I can do it. I'm Molly Metcalf."

I helped her stand up, and then she pushed herself away from my supporting arm. I called the Merlin Glass into my hand again, and held it up before us. Molly glared around at the Castle's shields as though she could see them, and maybe she could. She always had more of the Sight than I did. She thrust out a hand, the fingers splayed, and spoke aloud a single Word that shook her whole body. The Glass flared brightly against the night, and I felt rather than saw a great powerful force rush through it, blasting a hole right through the Castle's protections. The Merlin Glass leapt from my hand, growing into the biggest door it had ever made. And through that doorway I could clearly see the Armoury, in Drood Hall.

All kinds of alarms went off, and lab assistants came running towards the opening I'd made with all kinds of weapons in their hands. They stopped when they saw me in my armour, and gaped at Molly, who was sitting on the ground beside me, resting her head on her drawn-up knees.

"It's Eddie!" I yelled. "Get the Armourer! Now!"

I looked behind me. The Bride and Springheel Jack stood together in the gap where the front door had been, holding back any number of Immortals with a merry, vicious fury. I looked back through the Glass, and there was the Armourer, and the Sarjeant-at-Arms.

"Come on through!" I yelled to them. My voice was harsh, ragged. I barely recognised it. "This is Castle Frankenstein, home to the Immortals, and I've opened a door for you, right through all their shields! This is your chance to take out the Immortals, once and for all."

The Armourer turned to his assistants. "Grab every weapon you can find, and follow me! Sarjeant, gather the family and bring them after us! All of them, every damned Drood who can stand and fight! Death to the Immortals!"

He charged through the Merlin Glass, armouring up as he came, and after him came thirty or forty lab assistants, also in full armour, carrying deadly and disturbing weapons.

"The Spawn of Frankenstein are on our side!" I yelled at them as they passed. "The Immortals are all teenagers! And if you see any kobolds, leave them alone! And above all, for God's sake don't mess with the Bride and Springheel Jack!"

I was shouting at golden backs. The first Droods had already shot past the pair defending the door, hammered into the waiting Immortals, and were doing terrible things to them. They had guns that melted people, or froze them from the inside out, and made their blood run out through their pores. The Armourer had his Kirlian gun again, and people exploded wherever he pointed the ghastly thing. And they all wore the armour of the Droods, against which the Immortals could not stand. The ancient teenagers fell back, scattering, running and screaming and shouting confusedly. They had never thought this could happen; to be invaded and attacked in their most private redoubt, by those who had most reason to hate them.

And then the Sarjeant-at-Arms came through the Merlin Glass, followed by an army of hundreds of armoured Droods, and the real slaughter began.

I got Molly up on her feet again, and helped her back through the empty doorway of Castle Frankenstein. I knew she'd want to see the end of the Immortals. The Bride and Springheel Jack were back fighting in the hall again, alongside the Spawn and the Drood. We were a terrifying sight, and the Immortals broke and ran before us. Their confidence had been shattered, destroyed, their ancient arrogance and certainty broken for the first time, and all they wanted to do now was run. But after everything they'd done, even that simple mercy could not be allowed to them. I saw one of the Spawn tear an Immortal apart like a chicken at the table. I saw a Drood rip off an Immortal's head, and use it as a flail to smash in other skulls. I saw the Bride tear a glowing sword from an Immortal's hand and run him through with it. I saw Springheel Jack dance among the screaming Immortals, doing awful, unforgivable things with his flashing razors. One by one, the Immortals died, their long lives ending in blood and fear and horror. For what they'd done. They screamed in agony, begged for help, pleaded for mercy, and no one listened. Because they had never listened, never cared, for all the suffering they'd caused.

We didn't get them all. There was a teleport ring set up in an adjoining room, and maybe half a dozen got out before we found the ring and shut it down. There were a few hidden doors and secret passageways, and maybe a few got out that way, before we sealed them off. But that was it. We could hunt them down later, because no one would give a fallen Immortal sanctuary. The family of Immortals was destroyed, from the youngest to the Eldest. We cut them down and piled up the bodies, and moved on, searching through the Castle from top to bottom.

At the very end, one of them ran up to me, and sank to his knees before me. He was a teenager, like all the others. I didn't recognise him. He could have just joined the family, or been one of those originally made immortal by Methuselah. I had no way of telling. There was blood on his face, and his eyes rolled wildly. He babbled tearfully on his knees, begging me for mercy. He tried to grab my legs, but his hands couldn't get any purchase on my armour. I looked down at him, as the Bride and Springheel Jack stood watching. The Immortal was promising me anything, everything, money and hidden weapons, all the secrets of the Immortals and their plans for the future, if only I would spare him.

"I'm sorry," I said. And I was, in a way. "I'm sorry, but we could never trust you."

I took his head between my two golden hands, and twisted it hard. His neck broke and I let go, and he fell away, dead at my feet.

"Typical Drood," said the Bride. Her voice was cold and flat, and she could have meant any number of things.

I showed her my featureless golden mask, and she stirred uneasily.

"Would you have done anything else?" I said.

"Probably not." She shrugged and turned away, draping one long arm companionably over Springheel Jack's shoulders. "Come on, Jack. Let's take a walk around our new home."

"If you hadn't killed him, I would have," said Molly Metcalf. She was standing a little straighter now, absorbing strength and magic from the air around her. "Are you all right, Eddie? You should be happy. Rejoice; your greatest enemy has been defeated and destroyed."

"I'm an agent," I said. "Not an assassin. But sometimes . . . your enemy just doesn't give you any choice."

"I know," said Molly. "I know."

"Anything, for the family."

"I know."

Some of the remaining Immortals flesh danced, trying to pass themselves off as Droods, but we could always tell. And some tried to surrender, even though they must have known by now that we were taking no prisoners. It didn't come easy to any of us, to kill the defenceless, but we did it anyway. Because we had to. Because we could never trust them. The Sarjeant-at-Arms came over to join me.

"You're holding back, Edwin. This is war. They have to be stamped out. Because they're not human; they prey on humans. We're fighting for the safety and security of the human species. For our freedom, from our secret overlords. We can be sentimental later, when the work's done."

"What good does it do us to win?" I said. "If we have to act like Immortals to do it?"

The Sarjeant shrugged and turned away, and went off to finish his bloody work. I armoured down. Molly moved in close beside me, slipping an arm through mine.

"You're a good man, Eddie, in a bad world. The Immortals made themselves into monsters, by their own choice. Look at the Bride, and her people. Made to be monsters, they chose to be people. Think of all the things the Immortals could have done, could have achieved, with all the years and experience and knowledge they acquired. They could have made a Golden Age for all Humanity, but they chose to be teenagers forever, and never grow up. We were their playthings, and they played with us till we broke, because there were always more. I love it that you care, Eddie, but I don't. You kill monsters because you have to, because they don't give us any other choice. People can change, but monsters will always be monsters."

The hall was quiet now. Droods and Spawn moved slowly around, making sure none of the bodies were faking it by cutting off their heads. The last time I saw so many bodies piled up, it was at Drood Hall, after the incursion by the Accelerated Men. The air was so full of the stench of blood I could taste it in my mouth. The Armourer came over to join me, picking his way carefully through the bodies. He'd armoured down, and was beaming happily.

"Eddie, there you are! I found these wonderful little people, emerging from their hiding places! Slaves to the Immortals . . . They say they know you."

"We are not little people!" said a kobold, peering suddenly out from behind the Armourer. "We are underpeople! Are we free now?"

"Yes," I said. "To stay or to go, as you please. Your masters are dead. I'm afraid I had to promise the Castle to the Spawn of Frankenstein . . ."

"Our tunnels are waiting," said the kobold. "Still, they're going to need people, to help them settle in. We can do that. For gold . . . We like gold."

"I'm sure we can negotiate a fair agreement between you and the Bride," said the Armourer, still beaming happily. "It's a big Castle; I'm sure there's room for everyone."

The Sarjeant-at-Arms came striding over to join us,

also armoured down. He was frowning, which is never a good sign.

"There's no sign of the Immortal Leader," he said flatly. "We've checked all the bodies, and he's not there. He could have got out through the teleport ring, before we destroyed it."

"The ring," I said. "He's gone to Area 52, to get his hands on the Apocalypse Door. I have to go after him."

"Me too," said Molly. "I am never leaving you alone again."

"Yes!" said the Armourer. "It is good to see you alive and well, Molly. May I ask, how exactly did you . . ."

"Later," I said. "Oh, Uncle Jack . . . While I'm off saving the world one more time, there is something I need you to do for me. There's something rather special living under the hill, on the road leading up from the Hotel. I promised him he could come back to the Hall, and live with us. Could you take care of that for me?"

"Of course," said the Armourer. "No problem. Why are you smiling like that?"

CHAPTER ELEVEN

Knock Knock Knocking on Heaven's Door

"So," I said. "Molly and I have to get to Area 52, the most heavily shielded and guarded military base in the world, stop Doctor Delirium or Tiger Tim from opening the Apocalypse Door and unleashing all the horrors of Hell upon the world, and also stop the Immortal leader Methuselah from transforming the Door into the Paradise Door, so he can open it and go through to take Heaven by storm."

"And give everyone present a good kicking, just on general principles," said Molly. "And then afterwards, I thought we might have a little light supper, with some of that nice peach brandy you like."

"I could eat," I said wistfully. "Seems like ages since I had the chance to sit down and tuck in. But, needs must when the Devil's peering over your shoulder and sniggering. The Merlin Glass can't take us directly into Area 52; the place has far too many shields and protections. But I think I've persuaded it to drop us off close to a main entrance. So, let's do it. Busy, busy, busy, and never a moment to rest."

"You can't just run off and leave me to deal with transporting a dragon's head the size of a mountain!" said the Armourer, just a bit shrilly.

"Of course I can," I said. "Watch me."

I moved over to one side with Molly, while the Sarjeant-at-Arms did his best to restrain the Armourer. We both knew he'd cope; this was just his little way of telling me not to take him for granted. I summoned up the Merlin Glass, and instructed it to show me the hidden entrance it had found for Area 52. But when I looked into the hand mirror, all I could see was an endless vista of snow and ice, without a single structure or a living thing for as far as the eye could see. I gave the mirror a good hard shake, but the view didn't change. At least it wasn't an aerial view this time. Either the base was invisible behind its shields, or it was underground, or this was just as close to the entrance as the Glass could get us. I shrugged, and commanded the Merlin Glass to open a doorway.

It leapt out of my hand, and then hung on the air before me, growing rapidly in size until it was big enough for Molly and me to walk through. And then the door opened, connecting here with there, and brilliant light shone out, throwing back the darkness of the German night. I had to look away for a moment, dazzled, and then shuddered suddenly as a bitter cold wind came howling out of the doorway, shot through with snow and ice crystals. Molly squeezed in close beside me, and with our eyes narrowed against the Antarctic light, we stepped through the doorway.

The terrible cold stopped me dead in my tracks,

piercing my flesh and sinking into my bones. The wind cut me like a knife, and my lungs filled with razor blades as I tried to breathe the frozen air. Snow swirled around me, driven this way and that by the blustering wind. I armoured up, and cried out in relief inside my golden mask as my armour shielded me from the bitter cold. It took me a moment to stop shaking and clear my head, and then I looked quickly around for Molly. Who was quite happy, inside a personal shield so powerful I could actually see it shimmering on the air around her. She stood hands on hips, looking about her with an infectious grin.

"Isn't this the most spectacular thing you've ever seen, Eddie?"

She had a point. We'd come a long way from the grim surroundings of Castle Frankenstein. The sky was a sharp, almost painful blue, and the sun burned like a demon's eye. Snow fields stretched away for miles, rising and falling, capped to one side by a jagged range of snow-covered mountains. The heavy winds lifted sudden clouds of snow off the mountain peaks and threw them this way and that. Not a single living thing moved anywhere on the icy panorama, for as far as the eye could see. For all its snow and ice and cold, the Antarctic was really just another desert.

Molly stretched slowly, as unselfconscious as any cat, grinning widely. "Now this is more like it! There's a whole load of local magic here for me to draw on, and replenish my batteries. Pretty much untapped, as far as I can tell. I guess not many people get out this far."

"Most people have got more sense," I said. "What are you picking up from the Hidden World?"

"Oh, there's lots going on round here, but nothing to do with people, or Area 52."

I raised my Sight and looked around me, and discovered the empty Antarctic scene was anything but. Huge semitransparent snakes the size of subway trains writhed and curled slowly through the snow deep below us, vast blind creatures following their own unknowable instincts. The sky above us was full of wind-walkers, air elementals the size of blue whales, swimming languidly through the coruscating aurora, far too big to take any notice of the tiny mortals watching from below. And off in the distance, standing inhumanly still on the horizon: dim and vaguely humanlike shapes. Hundreds of them, just standing, and watching. There was something vague and insubstantial about them, as though they weren't totally solid or completely real. Images out of Time, perhaps, from the Past or even the Future. There have always been legends of another tribe of Man, another species, waiting patiently in the empty places of the world, ready to come forward and take over, should Humanity fail. Our replacement, if things should go very wrong.

I'm not sure whether I find that comforting or not.

But even with my Sight I still couldn't make out any sign of Area 52, or the entrance we were supposed to be near. *Really* well shielded. So I lowered my Sight, and breathed a little more easily. (You can't See too much of the world as it really is, for too long. It wears you out.) The Merlin Glass had disappeared, immediately after dropping us here, as though ashamed. I called it back out, and it slipped almost apologetically back into my hand. I told it to show me the way to Area 52's entrance, and the mirror immediately presented me a whole new view of unbroken snow and ice. I swept the Glass back and forth, and it tugged insistently in my hand in one particular direction, like a hound on a scent. So I set off into the snow and the cold, following the mirror, and Molly moved happily along beside me, merrily singing an old song called "Eskimo Nell."

I ploughed through the deep snow, my armoured legs sinking in deep with every step, until finally I was trudging along in a low trench of my own making. The weight of my armour pulled me down, but its strength enabled me to blast right through the packed snow as though it wasn't even there. Brief flurries of snow shot up into the air, flying left and right, as I stomped and kicked through the snow, forcing my way through by sheer brute force. Common sense told me that Doctor Delirium and Tiger Tim wouldn't do anything with the Apocalypse Door until Methuselah showed up, and we had to be close on the Immortal's trail. But I wasn't sure I believed common sense. There was a feeling in the air, in the atmosphere, a sense of imminence. Of something terrible and implacable and horribly irreversible, getting ready to happen.

The Door. The Apocalpyse Door. *I shall break the bolts and shatter the locks, and unleash Hell upon the Earth, and the dead shall outnumber the living, and the damned shall take their vengeance on the innocents . . .*

Molly floated serenely along beside me, hovering a good foot or so above the snow on the ground, hardly exerting herself at all as she just drifted along. Every now and again I made a point of flinging some snow in her direction, but somehow she was never there when it arrived. At least she'd stopped singing that damned song. I'm sure she made up some of the verses herself.

After a while it occurred to me to reshape my armoured feet into snowshoes, even if they did look rather like golden waffles. They spread my weight more easily and allowed me to walk on top of the snow. I made much better speed, with far less effort. Molly said nothing, in a loud sort of way.

The landscape didn't seem to change much, as we pressed on. The jagged mountains took up half the horizon now, rising high into the fierce blue sky, sunlight reflecting painfully bright from their snowy sides. The snow fields rose and fell before us, and brief flurries of snow still blew this way and that, never really amounting to anything. Every now and again I'd stop and raise my Sight, hoping for some glimpse of Area 52 in the distance, or at least its entrance, but the base remained stubbornly elusive. Strange energies flared up and collapsed, dancing on the high mountain peaks, but never to any purpose or effect I could understand. And sometimes I'd See strange creatures scurrying in the distance, or burrowing deep in the snow. Some had shapes so abstract I wasn't sure whether they were real or not, or just manifestations of some unknown phenomenon. As we drew closer to one particular mountain, I Saw within it an entire city, engulfed and entombed by millennia of snow and ice. Huge and alien, made up of monstrous shapes and weirdly made structures that my mind tried to grasp, and failed. They were too big, too strange, and possessed far too many angles for any truly solid shape. Nothing human had gone into the making of this ancient monstrous city, never meant for human eyes or sensibilities. I had no idea at all of what kind of creature could have lived in it, without going utterly mad.

I hadn't realised I'd stopped to stare at it, until Molly moved in close beside me, and waved a hand in front of my mask.

"We really don't have time for sightseeing, Eddie."

"I know! I know, but . . . look at it. I've never seen

anything like that. Ugly as sin and twice as old. When we're finished with Area 52, and assuming we and the world are still around, we have got to come back here. Get the family archaeologists on the job."

"I wouldn't," said Molly. "You might wake what's in there."

I looked at Molly, and then back at the frozen city. "Ah . . . You mean that's . . . Hmm. I think I'll ask the Armourer if he's got any of those thermonukes left."

Maybe half an hour later, I walked right into an invisible force shield, bounced off, and fell backwards onto my arse in the snow. Molly laughed so hard she hurt herself, and ended up curled into a ball, turning slowly in midair. I got to my feet with as much dignity as I could muster, and prodded the air with a golden fingertip. I could feel the shield but not see it, even with my Sight. And it didn't take me long to figure out that the field extended a long way in every direction, presumably surrounding Area 52 completely. The shield was entirely scientific in nature, as far as I could tell. My Sight wasn't showing me any magics, and when Molly finally got her giggles under control, she confirmed it. She did blast the shield a few times, with various nasty spells, just to please me, but everything she threw at the shield just slid off. Magic and science really don't get on. Most of the time they just pretend the other doesn't exist.

So, when in doubt, hit it. I retracted my snowshoes, planted my golden feet firmly in the heavy snow, reared back and hit the invisible force shield with all my strength. I gave it everything I had, everything the armour had, and the force shield didn't react in the least. I hit it again and again, summoning up all the strength in my armour and delivering it through one heavy golden fist, and the shield began to resonate, like a struck gong. Great ripples spread out across the snow, digging themselves deeper and deeper with every blow, until finally . . . I just stopped. I wasn't tired, and my hand didn't hurt, but it was clear I wasn't getting anywhere. I growled and shook my head, and took a moment to get my breath back.

"Very therapeutic, I'm sure," Molly said kindly. "But that was never going to work. Also, I feel I have to point out that such a blatant attack on the shield is almost certainly going to tell everyone in Area 52 that we're here."

"They know we're here," I said. "Methuselah will have told them by now. But if my armour can't break this shield, and your magics can't even touch it, how the hell are we going to get through?"

"We could tunnel under it," Molly said brightly. "Or rather you could; I don't do manual labour."

"You don't even do dusting," I said. I looked thoughtfully at where the field should be. "Has to be a way in . . . We didn't come all this way just to be stopped by a stupid force shield."

"Right," said Molly. "So do something, Eddie!"

"I'm thinking!"

I pulled out the Merlin Glass. It nestled comfortably into my armoured hand, still showing a snowy scene very different from the one before me, and still subtly urging me on. I weighed the Glass in my hand, and then stepped forward and slapped it hard against the force shield. The Glass hung in midair, shaking and shuddering, and then it grew suddenly in size to a doorway, breaking through the shield by making itself part of the shield. I took Molly by the hand and led her through, and then the doorway slammed shut behind us and the Merlin Glass shot back into my hand, like an obedient dog. I put it away, and set off again, with Molly just a few steps behind me.

"You're so sharp you'll cut yourself one of these days," she said finally.

"I'm sure you'd have thought of it," I said generously. "Eventually."

We headed on across the great plateau of snow and ice, stopping occasionally so I could take out the Merlin Glass and use it like a compass, to make sure we were still heading in the right direction. Still no sign of Area 52, or anything like an entrance. We'd been walking for almost an hour now, though I had to check my armour's internal clock to be sure. With so few real landmarks, it was hard to be sure of space or time. I was growing dangerously tired. I'd done so much today, and there was still so much more to do. And then I stopped suddenly, and looked sharply about me. Molly hovered beside me, her eyes bright and alert.

"You feel it too," she said. "We're not alone. I can't See anything, but I can feel it, in my bones and in my water. Something else is here with us, and it knows we're here. It's watching us."

"Guard dog," I said flatly. "Has to be. If you had a secret base set up here, you'd invest in a guard dog or two, wouldn't you? But what kind of creature could survive on its own, in this environment? Without my armour and your protections, we'd have been dead within minutes of arriving. So whatever it is . . . would have to be seriously tough and nasty, able to survive where nothing else could. Feel free to disagree with me, Molly, because I am starting to depress myself . . ."

"Wendigo?" said Molly, looking quickly about her. "Giant polar bears? Didn't Superman have some of those guarding his secret fortress in one of those films? Or did I just dream that?"

"I did once send a Russian werewolf here," I said thoughtfully.

"You've lived, haven't you, Eddie?"

And that was when the robot guard dog erupted from under the snow right in front of me, a huge steel shape with glowing red eyes, snapping steel teeth and flailing steel claws. It hit me hard in the chest, throwing me backwards, and I had to struggle to keep my feet under me. It was bigger than me, and heavier, a huge steel hound with moving parts showing clearly through its latticeworked steel hide. It clung to me, scrabbling at my shoulders with its forepaws, whilst its lower paws came up to claw at my belly, trying to disembowel me. Steel claws scrabbled uselessly against my golden armour, while steel teeth shattered and broke on my golden throat. I grabbed the guard dog by the forearms, and forced the snapping steel jaws away from my face.

Molly darted back and forth around me, trying for a clear shot, and yelling what she thought was helpful advice. I concentrated on forcing the killer robot dog away from me, until finally it hung helplessly in my grasp, the lower legs still scrabbling for something to attack. And then I tore the dog apart, first limb from limb, and then piece by piece, until there wasn't enough left of it to function. It lay scattered across the snow, just so many intricate steel parts and glimmering tech, still moving and twitching as the last of its energy ran out. The red glowing eyes took a long time to fade away. I knelt down and studied the mess thoughtfully, while Molly floated at my side.

"This wasn't just some stupid robot," I said finally. "There was definitely intelligence at work. Primitive AI. I should have tried to communicate with it."

"Like what?" said Molly. "Down, boy? Stop trying to kill me? Good dog?"

"How long was it lying here, under the snow?" I said. "Waiting patiently in the dark, for months or maybe even years . . . For something, anything, to come along? And when someone does turn up, all its programming will allow it to do, is attack. Was it lonely, do you think? Poor thing. Poor doggie."

"Poor doggie?" said Molly. "It would have quite happily ripped us apart, and probably pissed machine oil on our bits and pieces afterwards. Honestly, Eddie, you can get sentimental about the strangest things."

I stood up. "I'm surprised there aren't more of the things. Who bets all their money on a single guard dog?"

Molly shrugged. "Too expensive, probably. Did you see that tech? Alien derived. I'm betting they found the original and then reverse engineered it into a guard dog."

"Poor doggie," I said. "When this is all over, I think I'll come back and collect up the pieces. The Armourer will have a great time putting it back together again. He's always wanted a pet that didn't die easily."

Molly rolled her eyes at the heavens. "Look—all of this is just slowing us down. We have to move faster than this!"

"All right," I said patiently. "What have you got in mind?"

"Oh right, put the pressure on me! Leave it to me to come up with something to save the day!" She scowled heavily. "There's any number of magics I could use here, or at least tap into, but I can't help feeling I'm going to need every nasty spell I've got, once we're inside Area

52. That business at Castle Frankenstein took a lot out of me, and I'm nowhere near back to full strength."

"What about what happened at the Hall?" I said carefully. "Are you fully recovered from that?"

"It's sweet that you worry about me, Eddie, but stop it or I will slap you. I'm fine. Really. In fact, I can't wait to get this all over and done with, so I can get you back to our bedroom and show you just how fine I am."

I grinned. "You do know how to motivate a man." And then I broke off and looked sharply around. "Hold everything; I think it's time for round two."

A mist formed around us, grey tendrils coalescing out of the cold air, thickening into a grey sea of churning, roiling mists, that cut us off completely from the rest of the world. Sounds became increasingly distant and diffuse, as though we were underwater. Or as though the world was drifting farther and farther away. Molly and I moved instinctively to stand back to back, searching about us for some sign of an enemy. The thick grey fog had an unnatural chill to it, that made me shudder even inside my armour.

"Unnatural," I said, just to show I was keeping up.

"Very," said Molly. "Look! You see that?"

I did. Dark shapes were moving in the fog, circling slowly, keeping their distance for the moment. Their movements were awkward, strange, not human, for all their basically human shape. I tried counting them, but the number always came out different, as though they were fading in and out. Over a dozen, certainly, maybe twenty. There was something horribly abstract about them; their details kept changing, like the menacing shapes we see in dreams, or just briefly out of the corner of an eye. My skin crawled under my armour, and sweat ran down my face. I could hear Molly breathing heavily behind me, feel her back shaking where it pressed against mine. The shapes circled faster and faster, closing in on us from every direction at once.

I struck out at the first dark shape to come within reach, but my spiked golden fist shot right through without touching anything. I stumbled forward, caught off balance. And the shape grabbed me by the shoulders with two dark hands, lifted me up and threw me a good thirty feet. I shot through the air, tumbling ungracefully, and then hit the packed snow hard, half burying myself. I lay still for a moment, getting my breath back. I hadn't expected that. I wasn't used to being physically dismissed that easily. I shook my head hard, rolled over onto my side, and forced myself up onto my feet again. My armour had protected me, but I was still shaken. But then I saw Molly, blazing brightly in the fog, surrounded by fast-moving dark shapes, and that was all I needed to get moving again. I charged forward, ploughing through the snow at speed, sending it flying left and right in sudden flurries.

Molly threw spitting fiery magics at the dark shapes, attacks so powerful they crackled and roiled on the freezing air, but none of it did any good. Magics powerful enough to crack open mountains passed through the shapes without affecting them in the least, as though they weren't really present in our world. Except when they chose to be. Molly's magics were keeping the things at bay, for the moment, but they were pressing in closer all the time. Snow exploded several feet beyond the shapes as the magics passed harmlessly through, blasting out deep craters and leaving them full of steaming water.

The dark shapes swarmed around Molly, reaching out with dark hands to drag her down, but they couldn't touch her either. Her protective shields flared up viciously whenever dark hands came near her, and the shapes fell back, thwarted. But Molly's shields were only powerful enough when she gave them her full concentration, when she was facing the shapes attacking her. Which meant she had to keep turning, circling, twisting sharply this way and that, frustrating one attack after another, never able to relax her concentration for a moment. The dark shapes were packed around her now, crowding in, reaching out with dark eager hands.

I slammed into them at full speed, sending some of them flying. I lashed about me with my golden fists, but they were quickly gone again, as insubstantial as the fog that thickened around us. I flailed about me, desperate to drive them back from Molly, and then one of the shapes grabbed me from behind, lifted me up and threw me thirty feet in the other direction. I turned over and over in midair, trying desperately to get my feet under me, and then I hit the packed snow hard, much harder than before.

I had to dig my way out, throwing great handfuls of snow in all directions, and then went charging back again. I wasn't hurt; hell, after that fall into the Amazon rain forest, I didn't think any fall would ever worry me again. But I was angry, and worried, because every time I was thrown away it left Molly to fight on her own.

I couldn't let her be hurt again. I'd die before I let her be hurt again.

This time I thought it through. I slowed to a fast walk as I approached the crowd of jostling shapes, and when one turned to face me I thrust out one arm, tantalisingly, and when the shape grabbed it I grinned inside my mask. Because that meant the shape had made itself solid. I punched it hard in the face with my other hand, and my golden fist sank deep into its head. I pulled my hand out, and it was like pulling back toffee, with streamers of dark stuff following my hand. The shape fell apart, slumping into a dark sticky mess at my feet.

The other shapes forgot about Molly, and turned on me. They hit me from all sides at once, their fists very real and very solid, hammering me with a terrible unnatural strength. I hit back, but they were never where my fists were. I staggered back and forth in the snow, lashing about me but never connecting, while they beat me viciously with a strength and ferocity I'd never encountered before. I spun round and round, keeping my shoulders hunched and my head well down, because I could feel every blow, inside my armour. I had no doubt it was still protecting me; those dark shapes would have beaten me to a pulp in a minute without it. But I'd never been hit so hard before, and there were so many of them . . . and there was nothing I could do to protect myself. I had to wonder if the strange matter of my armour had finally met its match, and if it might actually split and crack and break open under such a relentless assault, such never-ending punishment.

I raised my head for a moment, and saw Molly hovering desperately on the outer edge of the dark shapes.

"I can't call up enough power to hurt them, without dropping my shields!" she cried out to me.

"Don't do it!" I yelled back immediately. "That's what they want!"

Their attack intensified, heavy fists crashing into me from all sides at once, and I was driven down onto one knee. I could feel blood trickling down my face under my mask, feel its bad copper taste in my mouth. I don't think I cried out, but as I reared up again, flailing savagely about me, I saw the shimmer on the air disappear from around Molly, as she dropped her shields. Immediately, all the dark shapes spun around, ready to go for her. But I realised that I could see Molly more clearly than before. The mists were thinner where she was, away from the shapes. And the dark shapes had only appeared after the fog materialised . . .

"It's the fog!" I yelled to Molly. "Disperse the fog! That's what gives them a hold on this world!"

Even as a dozen of the dark shapes fell upon her, Molly raised both hands and blasted the fog with a sheet of blisteringly hot flames. The fog was blown away in a moment, consumed by the intense heat, and along with the fog went all of the dark shapes. The air was clear and distinct and utterly empty, and Molly and I were left alone on the snowy prospect.

I sat down hard. I couldn't tell how badly hurt I was without lowering my armour, and I wasn't about to do that and expose myself to the cold. I hurt all over, but it didn't feel like anything was broken. I flexed my fingers and my toes, and tried to probe my ribs through my armour, but had to stop that because it hurt too much. Molly came crashing through the deep snow to join me. She wasn't hovering anymore, from which I deduced that the fight had taken a lot out of her too. I forced myself up onto my feet again. We stood facing each other, like two fighters fresh out of the ring, trying to hide how hurt we were.

"You okay?" I said finally.

"Down, but not out," she said. "You?"

"Shaken, but not stirred. What the hell were they?"

"Beats the hell out of me," said Molly. "Some kind of demon. Clearly someone at Area 52 didn't place all their faith in science."

"Magical attack dogs," I said. "Hate to think what Area 52 paid for their services . . ."

"Come on," said Molly. "We have to get out of here. There's always the chance the fog could re-form, and then the demons would be back again."

"Moving right along," I said. "Moving right bloody along."

Finally, at a point in the snowy landscape that looked just like every other, the Merlin Glass appeared in my hand without waiting to be summoned, and shook and shuddered like a divining rod in the presence of an underground lake. I held it firmly, and the scene in the hand mirror exactly matched the scene before me. Molly peered over my shoulder into the Glass, and sniffed loudly.

"I'm starting to think that thing's alive."

"Funny you should say that," I said. "The Armourer thinks there's someone trapped inside the Glass, hiding in the background of its reflections."

"Okay, seriously creeping me out now," said Molly. "As long as it doesn't turn out to be a young Victorian girl with long blond hair."

"I said that!"

"You would."

I put the Glass away, and studied the scene before me with my Sight. And there, buried deep under the snow, was a circular steel door, maybe ten feet in diameter. I pointed it out to Molly, and she whooped loudly as she confirmed it. I dug away the snow with great handfuls, and then looked back to see Molly watching me.

"You could help, you know," I said.

"I just like watching you work," she said. "Or maybe I just like the thought of you all sweaty."

"Oh good," I said. "I knew there had to be a reason. Want me to build you a snowman, when I'm done here?"

"Did you bring any carrots?"

"Damn," I said, clearing the last of the snow away. "Knew I forgot something."

"Why did they bury the entrance so deep?" said Molly, coming in close for a better look. "It's like no one's used it for years."

"From the look of it, this was never intended for use as an entrance," I said. "This has all the appearances of an emergency exit. For getting out of Area 52 in a hurry, when the brown stuff is hitting the revolving blades."

I crouched down in the hole I'd made, and studied the steel door carefully. Molly pressed in close, peering over my shoulder. The door was solid steel, inches thick, with a really complicated locking system. Reminded me very much of an airlock.

"I could probably smash through this," I said finally. "It's only steel. But given the sophistication of the locking systems, I'd bet good money that any break in the door's integrity would result in a complete shutdown of the access systems. Not to mention setting off all sorts of alarms and security systems. Which means . . . either we figure out how to open all those locks, or we don't get in."

"When in doubt, cheat," Molly said cheerfully. "Lend me that Chameleon Codex thing of yours, for a minute."

I reached through my golden armour at the wrist, carefully undid one of my cuff links by touch, brought it out and handed it to Molly. I watched interestedly as she pressed the cuff link carefully against the various sensors, picking up the latent DNA traces left by whoever touched them last, preserved, hopefully, by the snow and the cold. She then held the cuff link up, muttered over it for a while, and suddenly a small cloud of dust motes was flying around her hand. They leapt up and coalesced into a vaguely human shape, becoming gradually clearer and more distinct as Molly shaped

them with her muttered Words. She was putting together what we in the trade call a smoke ghost: a mind-
less, soulless re-creation of a human body, made from
discarded DNA, skin flakes and other human remnants,
mixed with whatever happened to be floating about in
the air at the time. Not real, not even the memory of
a person, just a flimsy spectre created from what men
leave behind them. They don't tend to last long, but you
can do all kinds of interesting things with them.

Molly's first few attempts at smoke ghost sculpting
weren't too successful—deformed and misshapen, bits
missing or wildly out of proportion ... but eventually
she put together something that would pass. It crouched
in the hole with us, bent over the steel door, made of
shades of grey so fine it was hardly there. It had no sense
of presence, of anyone actually being there with us,
which was actually quite disturbing. I gestured sharply
for Molly to get a move on, and the smoke ghost moved
jerkily as Molly moved it with her mind. It presented
its grey eye to the retina scanner, touched the finger-
print lock with a grey fingertip, and even managed a few
words for the voice recognition circuits. And then it collapsed, returning to the dust from which it was made.

"Freaky," I said.

"Lot you know," said Molly. "I knew this guy who
used to put together smoke ghosts just so he could have
sex with them ..."

"Far too much information," I said.

The steel door revolved slowly beneath us, making
low grinding noises, and then fell away, revealing a bleak
steel chamber below. A light snapped on, illuminating the
chamber. It had no details, no controls, just a single red
button on one wall. Molly drew back, shaking her head.

"No way. There is no way on this good earth that I am

trusting myself to *that*. I mean, come on; it looks like a coffin!"

"Emergency escape capsules are not usually noted for their frills and fancies," I said patiently. "It's the only way in, Molly."

She scowled. "Damn thing hasn't been used for years. Suppose it gets stuck halfway down? Or we can't open the door at the other end?"

"Then you'll just have to teleport us the rest of the way."

"Jump blind? In a base crawling with all kinds of shields and protections? *Are you crazy?*"

"I was hoping for a rather different response," I said. "Look—this is the only way into Area 52 that we know of. And time, as you have already pointed out, is getting tight."

"I *really* don't want to get into that thing," muttered Molly.

"I'll hold your hand," I said. "You'll be fine. Come on, be a brave little soldier and you can have a sweetie afterwards."

"You want a slap?"

We helped each other down into the steel chamber. It was big enough to hold maybe half a dozen people, if they were all on really friendly terms. It was the lack of details that made it so claustrophobic; this wasn't a place people were supposed to be in, unless they absolutely had to. I pressed the red button firmly, and the heavy steel door lifted back up into place, revolved a few times, and was still. For a worryingly long moment nothing happened, and then the chamber descended slowly into the depths. There was no sound of any motor, no sense of speed, only the sense of falling into an unknowable pit.

The descent went on for rather longer than was comfortable, and I had to wonder just how deep they'd buried Area 52, under the concealing snow and ice of the Antarctic. Just what were they hiding here, that needed to be imprisoned so deep in the earth? Were they worried about something getting in, or something getting out?

"They built this place *deep*," said Molly, echoing my thoughts.

"Well, wouldn't you?" I said reasonably. "Given some of the truly dangerous things they're supposed to have stored away here?"

"Like what?" Molly said immediately. "Come on; you're the one who's read all your family's files on this place; what exactly are they sitting on here?"

"Ah," I said. "Nothing too important or frightening, of course, because we always get to those first. But they are supposed to have squirreled away a fair collection of very interesting pieces . . ."

"You don't know!" said Molly. "You haven't got a clue what's down here, have you?"

"Be fair," I said. "No one in my family has even been to Area 52 before. Never felt the need, until now. We've always relied on reports from people on the inside. But don't worry, sweetie, I'm sure we'll find something nice you can take home as a souvenir."

The steel chamber finally came to a halt deep underground, and a door opened that I would have sworn wasn't there a moment before. I stepped quickly out and looked around, ready for any response. Molly was right there with me; but the shining steel corridor was completely empty. The door slid shut behind us, and then the corridor was utterly still and silent. Fierce electric light meant there were no shadows, and there wasn't even a whisper of air-conditioning. Nothing moved.

The steel corridor stretched away in both directions, empty and deserted.

"You know, I thought for sure someone would be expecting us," said Molly. "I had some really unpleasant transformation spells lined up, just waiting to be unleashed on the wicked and deserving."

"I thought those took a lot out of you," I said.

Molly smiled. "The look on people's faces makes it all worthwhile. Your trouble is, you just don't know how to have fun."

"I have a really bad feeling about this," I said.

"You always have a really bad feeling," said Molly.

"And I'm usually right."

Molly looked up and down the long steel corridor. "So, which way do we go?"

"I don't know," I said. "Your guess is as good as mine. I told you—no one in my family has ever seen the inside of this place. Even the floor plans in our files are years out of date. And the regular reports we get usually just consist of *Everything's fine, nobody panic*. I have to say, I'm not entirely sure we're getting value for money there."

"And there's no one here to ask," said Molly. "Funny, that. There ought to be somebody around. Especially as we've just arrived out of nowhere, riding an emergency exit in reverse. You'd have thought someone would have noticed that."

"Yes," I said. "Spooky, isn't it?"

I armoured down. There was always the chance Doctor Delirium, Tiger Tim, Methuselah, or any of the base's security people might be able to detect the presence of strange matter. I turned to look at Molly, and she actually gasped, her hands rising to her mouth.

"Oh Eddie, what have they done to you?"

I looked at my blurred reflection in the steel wall. Even in that distorting surface, I looked pretty bad. I raised a hand to my face, and winced as I touched swollen eyes and nose, and a pulped mouth. When I took my hand away, there was blood on my fingers. As though seeing made it suddenly real, my whole face pulsed with pain. Those dark shapes really had done a number on me, even inside my armour. Suddenly it was all I could do to stand up straight, as the pain kicked in; all the damage, from torn muscles to cracked ribs, the sharp aches flaring up from a hundred injuries, inside and out. Molly must have seen something of it in my bloodied face, because she stepped forward and placed a gentle hand on my chest.

"My hero," she said. "My knight in shining armour. Sometimes I forget how brave you are, Eddie. Because you try so hard to seem as strong and invulnerable as your armour. Look at what they've done to you . . ."

"Don't fuss," I said. "I've had worse. Comes with the job, and the territory."

"Not while I'm around," said Molly. "Hush. Hush, my darling."

She pressed her hand hard against my chest, and a subtle thrilling energy ran through me. I cried out despite myself as the pain blazed up, and then was suddenly gone. I could move without wincing, breathe without hurting, and when I put my hands to my face all the damage was gone.

"There," said Molly. "All better now."

She produced a clean handkerchief and dabbed at the blood on my face. But her voice hadn't been entirely steady, and neither was her hand, and there was a grey cast to her face that hadn't been there before. The healing had taken a lot out of her.

"I know," she said, before I could say anything. "But

it's my choice to pay the price, instead of you. If I'd told you what it would cost me, you wouldn't have let me do it, so I didn't ask. You can be too bloody noble for your own good, sometimes."

I just nodded, kissed her briefly, chose a direction at random and set off down it. Molly bounced along beside me, smiling happily, quite ready to lash out at someone she didn't know and do terrible things to them. After a while the corridor branched out into junctions and side turnings, and I just kept changing directions at random. But even as we penetrated deeper and deeper into Area 52, we never saw another living soul. The whole base gave every indication of being deserted, abandoned. No sign of any struggle, or violence, nothing to suggest any sudden emergency. It was as though everyone had just . . . walked out. Except there was nowhere to walk out to—just the bitter and unforgiving cold of the Antarctic above. So where had everybody gone?

I remembered Tiger Tim boasting that all the Base personnel were dead; but where were Doctor Delirium's people?

We found a canteen. The door was wide open, and when we looked in the long tables had all been set out for a meal. Plates and cutlery, jugs and glasses of water; but no food. And no one there to eat it. We kept on walking, pushing open doors along the way that led to offices and living quarters, and there was every sign of life except people.

"This whole base has gone *Marie Celeste*," said Molly. "Spooky . . ."

"Déjà vu all over again," I said. "And not in a good way." I filled her in quickly on what I'd found at Doctor Delirium's Amazon base. On what Tiger Tim had done there. Molly shook her head in slow disbelief.

"What a bastard. All right, no way are we taking him in alive."

"No," I said immediately. "You have to leave him to me, Molly. He's family. That makes him my responsibility."

"Okay, I'll take the Doctor and the Immortal."

I had to smile. "Self-confidence has never been a problem for you, has it?"

Some time later, we came to the Area 52 Armoury. Carefully sign-marked, with a whole bunch of not at all veiled warnings and threats, about not opening the Armoury door without all the proper instructions and authorisations, and a whole army of heavily armed security to back you up. The massive door was the kind you usually only find in banks, in maximum security vaults.

"Just a quick look," pleaded Molly. "Come on, Eddie; you know you want to. We can get in there, no problem."

"Yes," I said. "We probably could. But . . . later. We've work to do first, and we can't let ourselves be distracted."

But just down from the Armoury we stopped again, at a door labelled simply RED ROOM. The signs surrounding the door were just as ominous, just as self-important; but here the heavy bank vault door was hanging half open. And since I had never even heard of a Red Room in Area 52, I thought I had a duty to at least take a quick peek inside. So Molly and I squeezed through the gap, and went in. Into the Red Room.

At first, I couldn't figure out what the place was for. White-tiled walls, bright electric lights, clean as clean could be. And then I noticed the runnels in the floor, to carry away liquids to the drains at the side, and the sharp astringent smell of antiseptic. There were long steel tables, bolted to the floor, with trays bearing surgical instruments. Some of the tables had heavy restraining straps.

"It's a dissecting room," I said, and my voice came out cold and flat in the white-tiled room. "They cut things up here. And I don't think everything that came in here was dead to begin with."

"But . . . why, for God's sake?" said Molly. "What did Area 52 want with a dissecting room?"

"I don't know," I said. "But I can guess. Area 52 was all about getting at secrets. Whatever it took. I didn't know about this, Molly. I swear no one in my family knew; or we would have come here in force and put a stop to it. There wasn't supposed to be anything here like this."

"You're right," said Molly. "Look . . ."

She was looking around a corner at the end of the room. I went forward to join her, so I could see what she was seeing.

The long hall stretched away before us, lined with rows and rows of tall transparent tubes, lit from within. Display cases. Inside the tubes: aliens. A hundred different species of aliens, cut open and investigated in the Red Room, and then brought here as specimens to be studied. There were other, smaller containers, holding alien organs, limbs, other items of interest. I walked slowly down the hall, between the illuminated display cases, Molly moving quietly along beside me.

"I know most of these species," I said. "None of them are threats to the Earth! None of them were any danger! Some are our allies, with pacts and treaties going back generations. And those . . . they're just tourists! None of them did anything to deserve being cut up like this . . . Some of them, if their worlds ever find out what happened here . . . No. That can't be allowed to happen, for all our sakes. We're going to have to burn this whole place out, destroy the evidence, and then bury the ashes deep. Make the whole thing never happened."

"The people who did this must be punished," said Molly.

"I'm pretty sure that's already happened," I said. "Oh no . . . Oh Molly, look at this."

In a tall refrigerated tube, lit with a merciless light that allowed for no shadows, hung the gutted corpse of an elf.

"If the Fae Court ever hears about this," I said.

"They'd probably find it funny," said Molly.

"True. The Fae are seriously weird. But we don't want to start giving them ideas."

I made myself turn around and walk back through the rows of the dissected dead. Molly had to hurry to keep up with me.

"We've allowed ourselves to be distracted," I said. "We're here for the Door."

I called up the Merlin Glass, and ordered it to show me where Doctor Delirium, Tiger Tim and Methuselah were, right then. An image formed immediately in the hand mirror, showing all three standing together in the same room; all of them careful to maintain a respectful distance from each other. I opened a door with the Glass, and Molly and I stepped through into the room, to face the three men we'd come so far to stop. And, if need be, kill.

They were arguing heatedly when Molly and I arrived, but they all broke off instantly to stare at us with varying degrees of surprise. Doctor Delirium was so wide-eyed and startled he actually fell back a few steps, so he could stand protectively beside the Apocalypse Door. The Door stood still and upright and absolutely unsupported in one corner of the room. Tiger Tim nodded easily to me, one professional to another, but he did a definite double take as his gaze fell on Molly Metcalf. And Methuselah, the oldest of the Immortals, just folded his arms across his chest and looked at me with typical arrogance and disdain.

I took a moment to look around. We were all standing in a comfortable lounge, with easy furniture and a deep pile carpet, potted plants and relatively tasteful prints on the walls. It could have been anywhere. The only thing out of place was the Apocalypse Door. Even on the far side of the room, tucked away in one corner, I could still feel its presence. It was as though there was another person in the room with us, watching and waiting. The carpet at the base of the Door was blackened and charred, and there was a definite smell on the air, of blood and sour milk and sulphur. The stench of Hell. An unbroken chain of gold links circled the base of the Door, augmented here and there with delicate crystal technology. A teleport ring. No wonder Doctor Delirium was able to move the Door around so easily.

"What are you doing here?" he demanded hotly. "You shouldn't be here! You'll spoil everything! Get out! *Get out!*"

"What's up, Doc?" Molly said easily. "Visiting hours over?"

"Don't tease the good Doctor," said Tiger Tim. "He's just crazy. So, Eddie . . . how goes it, cousin?"

"Your father sends his regards," I said.

Tiger Tim smiled broadly. "I very much doubt it. But then, he always was a better Armourer than a father."

"Hold everything," said Molly. "Your father is the Armourer? That sweet old man produced a turd like you?"

Tiger Tim looked at her coldly. "Why aren't you dead?"

"I got over it," said Molly.

I gave my full attention to the former Leader of the Immortals, Methuselah. He was looking far too calm and collected for my liking.

"I'm pretty sure I already know the answer," I said, "but how did you get here ahead of us?"

"A teleport circle, back in Castle Frankenstein," said Methuselah. "The moment I realised my home's integrity had been compromised, I went straight to the circle and came here. Nothing can be allowed to interfere with what I have planned for the Door, and myself."

"You ran out on your family?" said Molly.

"The strong will survive," said Methuselah. "The rest don't matter."

"You came here alone?" I said. "You didn't even wait for the rest of the Elders? The ones who believed in you?"

"They know where the teleport circle is. It's up to them to use it."

"So that's what immortality does," said Molly. "It makes you a selfish little prick."

"Let me fill you in on what happened, after you ran away," I said. "I brought my family into your Castle, and the Droods went head to head with the Immortals. Your family is dead and gone."

"All of them?" said Methuselah. "Not one of them got away?"

I shrugged. "Maybe half a dozen. They ran, like you. And I'm sure there are still a few out in the world, somewhere, pretending to be other people. It doesn't matter. We'll hunt them down and kill them."

"Don't," said Molly. "Don't smile like that, Eddie. Don't gloat. It doesn't become you."

"It doesn't matter," said Methuselah, and his voice

and his face were as calm as ever. "I'm moving on. I would have left them behind anyway."

"I gave you that teleport ring," said Doctor Delirium. "I created it. I've always been a lot smarter than anyone ever gave me credit for. I put it together originally so I could get into the Magnificat. And then I gave it to Tiger Tim, so he could attack Drood Hall with his new Accelerated Men. It kept him quiet, so I could concentrate on the Door. It's given me so many good ideas . . ."

"It had to be you," I said, looking at Tiger Tim. "Only you knew the secret codes and passwords that would shut down most of our defences, to make the attack possible. Have you any idea how many good men and women died in that attack, fighting your Accelerated Men?"

"Not enough, clearly," he said. "You're still here."

I looked at Doctor Delirium, and he paled at what he saw in my eyes. "It serves you Droods right," he said defiantly. "For all your interference. Why couldn't you just leave me alone?"

"There will be judgement," I said. "There will be justice."

"You can't touch me!" said the Doctor. But he didn't sound very sure about it.

"You are a lot smarter than we ever thought," I said. "As a scientist. Otherwise, you're really a bit dim, aren't you? Or you'd never have put your trust in a rogue Drood and a selfish Immortal."

"I don't trust anyone," said Doctor Delirium.

"What about the Apocalypse Door?" said Molly. "Do you trust the voices you hear, talking to you from beyond the Door? Do you believe the promises they make, and the lies they tell you?"

"You think I don't know whose voice I'm listening to?" said the Doctor. "Of course I know. The voices tell me everything they think I want to hear; but in the end I'm the only one who can open the Door from this side. I'm the only one who can give them what they want, and I won't, until I can be sure I'm going to get everything I want." He glared at Tiger Tim. "I'm not crazy. I know what I'm doing. You're just jealous because the voices only speak to me."

"Ladies and gentlemen of the jury," murmured Tiger Tim. "The defence rests. Now hush, there's a good Doctor. The big boys are talking." He turned his back on the Doctor, so he could smile at me. "I have to say I'm impressed, Eddie. Still here, still hot on my trail, even after all the things I've thrown at you to slow you down. Tell me, how many of our family died at the hands of my glorious Accelerated Men? I want numbers, I want names, I want details. Was my father among the dead, by any chance?"

"You betrayed your family," I said. "You put at risk the one real power that stands between Humanity and the darkness!"

"Why not?" said Tiger Tim. "What have they ever done for me? I thought you of all people would understand, Eddie. They made you a rogue too, just for wanting to be different. Of course, you weaselled your way back in. You probably even think you can save them. But the Droods are really no different from the Immortals, when it matters. All these generations of golden men and women—we should have been ruling the world by now, worshipped and adored! Why settle for being shepherds, when we should have been lords of all we surveyed . . . I'm tired of hiding my light under a bushel, Eddie. I want the throne that's rightfully mine."

"God, you Droods love the sound of your own voices!" said Molly. "Okay, everyone step away from the Door, before I decided to turn you into something small and squishy."

"But you haven't heard the best bit yet," said Tiger Tim. "Haven't you wondered why we're here, in this particular room?" He snapped his fingers loudly, and one whole wall disappeared, replaced by a virtual view of an outside scene, of the snow and ice surrounding Area 52. The image was flawless; it could have been a window. I could almost feel the cold.

"We're here," said Tiger Tim, just a bit grandly, "because this room has the best view of what's going to happen. Out there is where we're going to place the Door and then open it by remote control. And then we can stand here and watch, as all the hordes of Hell break out, into the world of men."

"The Door chose those particular coordinates," said Doctor Delirium. "I confess I'm not entirely sure why. Sentimental value, perhaps? Did something important happen here long ago, before the poles shifted, and snow and ice came to cover everything that was here? It doesn't matter. I would have chosen the centre of some great city, for maximum shock and maximum slaughter, but then, that's just me."

"Think what you're saying!" said Molly. "Mass murder? Death and suffering and the slaughter of innocents? You're just a mad scientist with a thing for rare postage stamps; when did you ever care about things like that?"

The Doctor paused, uncertain. "I have changed. I know that. I had to grow up. Become . . . cold. Because I couldn't get the revenge I wanted so badly, if I stayed my old soft-hearted self. I never really wanted to destroy the world, before. It was all about power; about threatening the governments of the world with my wonderful plagues, just so that they would be forced to acknowledge my genius. But that was then, this is now. I will have my revenge. It's all I've got left."

Tiger Tim beamed happily at the virtual view before him. "Nothing like a ringside seat, for the end of the world."

I advanced on Doctor Delirium, and then stopped as he put one hand on the Apocalypse Door. The room felt distinctly warmer, the smell of Hell more distinct. The Door's presence seemed to beat upon the air like great membranous wings. The light was fading, slowly but surely, as darkness pressed in around us. Molly glared about her uncertainly, but none of the other three seemed to have noticed anything. Perhaps because they'd spent too much time in the presence of the Door.

"Is this really what you want, Doctor?" I said. "It's not too late to turn away from the destruction of the whole world."

Doctor Delirium drew himself up to his full height, and glared at me; but close up, more than ever he looked like a child playing dress-up. Not a mad scientist and supervillain, just a small podgy man in a grubby lab coat, standing next to something far more evil than he could ever hope to be.

"Typical Drood," sneered the Doctor. "Still trying to save the world, even when it's far too late. Why? It's not like the world's worth saving. It's rotten, corrupt, and it doesn't care. Let it burn. I wasn't always Doctor Delirium, you know. I had a real name once, a real life in the real world. I was hired right out of college, given all the best equipment and really good money, and all I had to do was make bio weapons for the Government. Nasty new diseases, with which to smite our enemies.

"I wanted to work on cures, but it was made very

clear to me that there were no resources, no money, for that. I wanted to achieve great things, but my government just wanted me to be a mass murderer. And I went along with it . . . Until a lawyer told me my uncle had left me a fortune, a secret base and a private army. I quit that very day, and chose a new name for myself, a new identity. And then I set out to make the world respect me, as it never had before. I wanted to be Louis Pasteur; but it was bullies like you Droods that made me Doctor Delirium.

"I gave my life to that cause. I gave up friends and family, all hope for love and happiness, in pursuit of my revenge. It's all I've got left, and I will have it."

"Who was this uncle of yours?" I said. "We never could work that out."

"Oh, that was us," said Methuselah.

"What?" said Doctor Delirium.

"Just standard meddling," said the Immortal. "We regularly locate and identify useful embittered people, and give them funding. Just to see what will happen. I suppose it's our equivalent of poking an ant's nest with a stick . . ."

Doctor Delirium stared at him incredulously. "You started all this? You pushed me into this life? When I could have been happy? Then I suppose it's only fitting that you should be here for the end. I could kill you; I do want to. But what's coming will be far worse than anything I could do to you. Hell is coming, Methuselah, and all its horrors . . . And you will grovel at my feet and beg for mercy. And I'll say no."

Methuselah shrugged. "There's just no pleasing some people."

"Nasty little man," said Tiger Tim.

I moved as close to the Apocalypse Door as the Doctor would allow, and studied it thoughtfully. Tiger Tim tried to join me, but Molly moved quickly to block his way. Methuselah stayed where he was, watching us all calmly. Up close, the Door's presence was disturbing. It seemed more real, more *there*, than the rest of us . . . I could feel the Door watching me, studying me as I studied it. I started to raise my Sight, and then stopped. I didn't want to See what lay beyond the Apocalypse Door.

The teleport chain lying in a circle around the Door looked familiar. I'd seen that crystal tech before, and there was nothing human about it. Doctor Delirium might claim he invented it, but his genius was with germs. More likely he'd adapted the ring from some alien leftover.

The Apocalypse Door dominated the room, just by being there. Like a ticking bomb, or a murderer with a fresh blade in his hand.

"Where is everybody?" I said, looking in particular at Tiger Tim. "Where are your scientists and soldiers, the mercenaries and the security guards? Why haven't I seen a single living soul in this entire base, apart from you three?"

Methuselah smiled. "You didn't really think we'd share this sublime moment with anyone else, did you?"

"We cleaned house," said Tiger Tim. "Just like in the Amazon, only not as messy. We didn't need anybody else, anymore. They'd only have got in the way."

"Really quite a subtle organism," said Doctor Delirium. "I released it into the base's air supply, and it ate them all up. Flesh and bone and even their clothing. Hungry little bug, and very industrious. The Door gave me the idea. Of course, I took pains to inoculate myself and Tiger Tim in advance, just in case any of the bug happened to hang around after it was supposed to have dispersed."

"And I don't need any inoculation," said Methuselah. "I am an Immortal and a flesh dancer; after all these years my immune system produces white blood cells like wrecking balls. Though I have to say, given that there could still be a few traces of the nasty thing floating about, for all your protestations, Doctor, I'm surprised you and the witch are still here, Drood."

"I have my torc," I said.

"And I'm Molly Metcalf. The most powerful witch you'll ever meet."

"Witch," murmured Tiger Tim. "Not quite the word I had in mind . . ."

"Don't push your luck, Timothy," I said.

Molly went back to glaring at Doctor Delirium. "You killed everyone here? Your own people?"

"Why not?" said Tiger Tim. "We didn't need them anymore, and who knows, they might have tried to stop us opening the Door."

"They never cared about me," said Doctor Delirium. "All they ever cared about was my money! They weren't loyal. Mercenaries are never loyal; I've always known that. And they would have died anyway, after I opened the Door." He giggled suddenly, a shockingly childlike sound. "Maybe I'll see them again, running and leaping among the hordes of the damned . . . I don't care. They were just people. And what have people ever done, but laugh at me? Do you hear anyone laughing now?"

Molly looked at me. "Total bugfuck weirdo, and nasty with it."

"Was there ever any doubt?" I looked at Methuselah. "What about the other Elders, the ones who believed in you? Aren't you going to wait, just in case any of them turn up? It's always possible we missed a few."

"No more waiting," said Methuselah. "I never was big

on sharing. I was the first Immortal, so I suppose it's only fitting that I should be the last. And the first again, to transcend this appallingly limited world. I shall become glorious, and know pleasures beyond belief."

"Another loony tune," said Molly. "I'm starting to feel like the only sensible one here, and I'm not used to that."

Methuselah ignored her, staring out at the virtual view. "I suppose I'll be sorry to say good-bye. For all its many problems and imperfections, it has been a pleasant enough world, I suppose. You mayflies don't appreciate it.

"The things I've seen, since the Heart made me Immortal, all those centuries ago. The wild boars and hairy mammoths running wild in the primordial forests of Olde Englande. The pyramids up beyond Hadrian's Wall, (although the Sceneshifters made them never happened, the bastards). I danced at Louis' Court at Versailles, sat with the first Queen Elizabeth, laughing at a production of Marlowe's *Doctor Faustus*, complete with fireworks. I've talked with Genghis Khan, Hitler and Pol Pot. All of them surprisingly good company. Though they all had a taste for peasant's food. I've met great poets and painters, actors and authors, and lent most of them money. I've seen wonders and marvels, abominations and atrocities, and applauded them all. I never fought in a war, but I've profited from most of them. They all had their moments, as spectacle, if nothing else."

"But you never got your hands dirty," I said. "Never the hero or even the villain, just a voyeur."

"Do you interfere in a dogfight?" said Methuselah. "Or intervene in a war between two anthills? I've seen it all, done it all, and I'm bored. Time to move on, to trade up, to leave this grubby world behind in search of fresh new pleasures and indulgences."

"Were you ever at Camelot?" Molly said suddenly. "Did you ever visit the Court of King Arthur? I've always been fascinated by that period."

"No," said Methuselah. "By the time I realised just how important Arthur was going to be, Merlin had already got his claws into him. And relatively young as I was then, I still had enough sense not to get up against Merlin Satanspawn. I did get to meet Mordred, though. Very ambitious, in a single-minded sort of way. Completely dominated by his mother, of course."

"You wasted your life," I said, and the harshness in my voice brought his head jerking round. "All the things you could have done, all the things you might have achieved . . . and you wasted your years, your lifetimes, because you didn't know what to do with them. No great causes, no great achievements, because you didn't have it in you. You could have made a better world, you could have been greater than Arthur and Merlin, built a Camelot that would have endured for centuries, but all you cared about was yourself. You could have led Humanity out of the darkness, but you couldn't be bothered. And when you're finally gone, you'll leave nothing behind but a bad taste in the mouth of history."

I turned back to Doctor Delirium. "Give it up, Doctor. You've been lied to and used, all along. Timothy Drood is here to betray you, just as he betrayed his own family. He has his own plans for the Apocalypse Door. So does Methuselah."

The Doctor sneered at me. "Yes, well, you would say that, wouldn't you?"

"Oh Eddie," Tiger Tim said sadly. "Always putting

your faith in the truth, when a lie can be so much more liberating."

"And you can wipe that smug smile off your face, Timothy," I said. "I'm taking you back to the family to stand trial at Drood Hall for all the evils you've done."

Tiger Tim laughed softly. "Dear Daddy got to you, didn't he? Asked you to go easy on me . . . Sentimental old fool. You're not taking me anywhere."

"I have the armour," I said. "And you don't."

"Funny you should say that," said Tiger Tim. "You'll never guess what I found, locked away in the vaults of Castle Frankenstein." And he opened the top of his shirt to show me the golden torc around his neck. "I don't know how the Immortals got their hands on this originally. Perhaps an Immortal murdered and replaced a Drood, and took the torc . . . Or maybe the old Baron himself cut it off one of his victims . . . Don't suppose we'll ever know. The point is, this torc had been locked away inside a box inside a vault, under the wrong description. No one even knew it was there, until I came across it quite by accident, while looking for something else. Isn't that always the way? I took the torc for my own, because I just knew the Immortals wouldn't appreciate it. And it settled around my throat quite happily, like it was coming home, like it belonged there."

"You might have asked," Methuselah said reproachfully.

"No, I couldn't. You might have said no. I didn't want to put you in an awkward position. And besides, who has a better right to it, than me?"

"Knew I should have killed you when I had the chance," said Methuselah.

"You never had the chance," said Tiger Tim. He

looked at me and smiled suddenly, a happy, anticipatory smile. "I haven't had a chance to try out my new torc; been a bit busy, you know how it is. And I was just a bit concerned that your armour might be able to detect mine, once I put it on. But now, all bets are off. We've come to the end of the line, Eddie, where it's just you and me, armour to armour, man to man. To the death."

"Wouldn't have it any other way," I said.

He armoured up, and so did I. And just like that there were two gleaming golden figures in the room, facing off against each other. Doctor Delirium cried out, and hid behind the Apocalypse Door, peering round the edge with wide eyes and an uncertain mouth. Methuselah fell gracefully back to a safe distance; and Molly moved quickly out of our way to give us room to fight. Her eyes were shining as she urged me on. It must have looked like a fair match and a fair fight, but I knew different.

Timothy Drood had the old armour, and I had the new.

I raised up a golden fist, and grew a set of heavy spikes from the knuckles. And then I concentrated, and extruded razor-sharp blades all the way up my arms to my shoulders. I reshaped my mask into a grinning devil face, complete with curling horns. Tiger Tim stood very still. He didn't know how to make his armour do any of those things. In fact, he'd been away from the family so long he probably didn't even know such things were possible now. I wondered if he was afraid, biting his lip behind his featureless golden mask. I hoped so. I was too angry to be afraid.

He lunged at me, striking out with a golden fist. I stood my ground, blocked the blow with a raised arm, and then we went head to head, battering each other fiercely with all our unnatural strength. The sound of armour beating on armour was deafening as we slammed each other all over the room, kicking the furniture out of the way, the floor cracking under our stamping feet. But neither of us could hurt the other, for all our strength and fury. The armour protected us. But my armour was strange matter, provided by the other-dimensional entity now known as Ethel. Tiger Tim's armour derived from the destroyed entity once known as the Heart.

I cut at Tiger Tim with razored fists, and the unnaturally sharp edges opened up long cuts and furrows across his chest. Which should have been impossible. The furrows healed quickly, filling themselves in, so I cut him again, and again, harder each time, gouging deep scars into his mask and chest, and they took much longer to heal. I wondered if he was bleeding, inside. I pressed him hard, determined to tear open his armour and drag him right out of it.

We hammered each other back and forth across the lounge, fists rising and falling with inhuman speed, while the others scattered hurriedly to get out of our way. Because we were both so caught up in the fight that we had eyes only for each other. Both of us moving so swiftly it seemed like everyone else was moving in slow motion. If any of them had got in our way, I think either one of us might have swept them aside without thinking, our heads were so full of rage and fury. I would have been sorry afterwards, of course, but right then . . . Timothy Drood seemed to be responsible for all the evils I'd encountered since this all began, and I wanted him dead more than anything else in the world.

I don't think I've ever been that angry before. Because he was a Drood.

Tiger Tim broke off, and backed away. He couldn't match my strength and speed, and he knew it. He had nothing with which to meet my armour's versatility. So he picked up heavy furniture and threw it at me. I slapped them away effortlessly, and laughed out loud, full of the exhilaration of my armour. Tiger Tim picked up the heavy couch and brought it sweeping down in an overhead blow. I put up a golden arm to block it, and the couch broke in two across it. We were moving like superhumans now, in a world made of paper, and things just broke when we touched them.

But we never went near the Apocalypse Door. We could both See it clearly now, and neither of us could bear to look at it.

In the end, Tiger Tim broke. He reached out and grabbed Molly, moving so swiftly she didn't even know what was happening till he had her in his golden arms. She started to struggle, and he crushed her briefly, driving all the breath from her lungs. Her legs sagged, until he was all that was holding her up. I stood very still, knowing he could kill her easily before I could reach him.

"Armour down," said Tiger Tim. "Or I'll kill the witch. I'll crack her bones and crush her insides, and then I'll rip her head right off her shoulders."

"Don't hurt her," I said. "This is between you and me."

"Knew I'd find a way to hurt you eventually," said Tiger Tim. "There's always a way."

I was thinking furiously, but I couldn't see any way out. I had no doubt he'd kill her. I was just starting to subvocalise the activating Words that would send my armour back into my torc, when Molly laughed suddenly.

"Come on, Eddie. You know I don't do the damsel in distress bit."

Crackling energies surrounded her in a moment, coruscating in vivid flashes and boiling magics, blasting Tiger Tim's arms away from her. She moved quickly to one side, and yelled at me to get him, but I was already moving. I'd thought I'd been angry before, but it was nothing to the rage that moved me now. Now he'd threatened to kill my Molly again.

I fell upon him with all my strength and speed, my golden hands locking onto his golden throat. He fell backwards, tripped, and measured his length on the lounge floor. I followed him down, my grip on his throat never loosening for a moment. I knelt over him, forcing my hands closed with all my strength. He struggled and kicked and tried to throw me off. He grabbed my wrists with his hands and tried to break my stranglehold, but he couldn't. I saw my Molly, stabbed through again and again, dying at the hands of Droods maddened because of Timothy Drood. I saw good men and women dying on the grounds of Drood Hall, at the hands of his Accelerated Men. I saw him talking calmly of throwing Humanity to the wolves of Hell. I saw him threatening to kill my Molly, again, right in front of me. And there was no room left in me for anything but the need to kill.

I concentrated on my armour, moulding it with my will, and my fingers became impossibly sharp, cutting through the armour round his throat. I forced my hands through the gap I'd opened up, and my bare hands closed around his bare throat. I throttled him to death, inside his own armour.

After a while, I realised he wasn't breathing, wasn't moving. I pulled back my hands, releasing my hold on his armour, and it disappeared back into his torc. Tiger Tim stared blankly upwards, seeing nothing. There was a little froth around his distorted mouth. I knelt over him for a while, getting my breath back, and then I extruded a blade from one hand and cut his head off. So I could take the torc back to my family, where it belonged.

Doctor Delirium cried out as blood flooded across the lounge floor. He wasn't used to bloodshed. He always did his killing from a safe distance. Methuselah allowed himself a mild moue of distaste. I looked at Timothy's severed head, and wondered what I should tell his father. I would have brought his son back alive, if things had gone differently. I'm almost sure I would have. Though whether that would have been a kindness, in the end . . . I could tell the Armourer that his son had died fighting bravely. Or that Tiger Tim had somehow got away, and was still out there, somewhere. But I'd never been able to lie to my Uncle Jack.

I armoured down, and rose slowly to my feet. I felt horribly weary; bone deep, soul deep. Molly came over and held me carefully, as though I was fragile, and might break. She understood what I was feeling; she understood about family. But she also knew there was still work to be done, so she let me go and stood at my side. I looked at Doctor Delirium, still half hidden behind his Door. He flinched away from my gaze, but I just stood where I was, and beckoned for him to come out.

"You don't dare touch me!" he said, his voice high and shrill. His eyes kept going to Tiger Tim's headless body, and then jerking away. "You'd better not even get too close! I've infected myself with every deadly disease known to man, and several I made up specially. I'm the universal carrier, for everything from typhoid to Ebola, from the black death to green monkey fever. Doesn't affect me at all, but all I have to do is concentrate in a certain way, and my pores will sweat poison, releasing all the deadly germs into the air!"

I looked at Molly. "Does that even sound likely to you?"

"Doesn't matter," said Molly. She strode right over

to Doctor Delirium. "I have been to Heaven and Hell and back again, and walked on alien worlds. You really think you've got anything that can touch me?"

As she moved in close the Doctor suddenly whipped out a spray aerosol and blasted its contents right into her face. Molly fell back a step, wiping at her face with a hand, while the Doctor crowed triumphantly.

"That was the Acceleration Drug! Full strength, with all the wonderful new extra ingredients! And you breathed it in! It's running through your system now, speeding you up, faster and faster till it burns you up from the inside out! You'll live a whole lifetime in just a few minutes, and I'll watch you die of old age right in front of me!"

Molly swept the last few tears from her eyes. Doctor Delirium fell suddenly silent as he realised she was laughing.

"You need to get out and about more," she said cheerfully. "I'm Molly Metcalf! I take nastier stuff than that for fun!"

"Don't laugh at me," whispered Doctor Delirium. "Don't you laugh at me!"

Molly reached out and grabbed him by an ear. She hauled him out from behind the Door and walked him back to me. I looked at her, and she let go of his ear.

"Don't be afraid, Doctor," I said. "I think there's been enough killing. It doesn't always have to end in blood. Forget the Door, and its voices. They lied. It's what they do. Give up on your revenge; what did it ever get you, except a life on your own? Come back with me to Drood Hall. Put your genius to work for us. Use our labs to create all those cures you used to believe in. Be the good man you originally wanted to be, before Methuselah gave you money, and made you into the kind of man he wanted you to be. Come with me, Doctor. It's not too late."

"I won't give up the Door," said Doctor Delirium. "It's mine. It's my revenge on you all. I can't give that up. It's all I've got." He looked at Molly, and his face was utterly empty. "You shouldn't have laughed at me."

And he went for her, lunging forward with a knife in his hand. Molly snapped her fingers hard, and Doctor Delirium disappeared. A very warty green and yellow toad fell to the floor, and crouched there, looking around in a bemused kind of way. Molly nudged it with her foot, and it hardly reacted.

"He can go back to the Amazon rain forest," Molly said briskly. "Where he'll feel right at home." She came over to join me, and prodded me in the chest with one finger. "Offering to take Tiger Tim back for trial? Offering the Doctor a job at the Hall? After everything they've done, and meant to do? You're getting soft, Eddie."

"There's been enough killing," I said. "I'm sick of it. I saw you die, and I have avenged you. But I never want to feel this way again."

"I know," said Molly. "I know. My knight in shining armour." She caressed my face with one hand, and her touch was very gentle.

"How very sentimental," said Methuselah. "You should have dealt with me first, you know. I always was the most dangerous."

And when Molly and I turned to look at him, he was gone. And so was the Apocalypse Door in its teleport ring. Molly pointed abruptly at the virtual view on the wall, and there he was, standing in the snow and ice, one hand resting possessively on the Door.

"Oh shit," said Molly.

"Can't take your eyes off the bastard for a second," I

said. "Quick, Molly, teleport us after him before he can open the Door."

"How?" said Molly. "I've no idea where that is! It's just a view from a hidden camera; what we're looking at could be just outside the base, or somewhere miles from here! I can't jump blind!"

"Oh shit," I said.

"The Glass!" Molly said quickly. "Remember how it got us through the invisible force shield?"

I grinned. "I always said you were the smart one."

I called up the Merlin Glass and slapped it flat against the virtual view. The hand mirror clattered fiercely against the image, and then grew suddenly in size to make a doorway. The Glass was apparently a great believer in lateral thinking. Which I would have found worrying if I'd had the time, but I didn't. I could feel the freezing cold rushing through the open door. I grabbed Molly by the hand, and we rushed through the door, back into the freezing Antarctic air.

I armoured up, and Molly raised her shields. I couldn't help noticing they didn't look as strong and certain as they had before. The Apocalypse Door was standing firmly upright, in a circle of steaming melted snow. Methuselah stood before the Door, holding up the awful Hand of Glory he'd made from the severed hand of an angel. The dead white skin glowed fiercely, brighter than the sun itself, and as the Immortal chanted something in a tongue so old I didn't even recognise it, the candles made from the Hand's fingers ignited one by one. Somehow I found the time to wonder whether that was the language the Immortal had originally spoken, when he bargained with the Heart for eternal life.

"Where the hell did the Hand come from?" said Molly. "He didn't have it before. I would have noticed."

"He must have a subspace pocket, like me," I said.

"Oh, I want one of those . . ."

Methuselah let go of the Hand and backed away, and the brightly shining Hand hung on the air before the Door. Its fingers moved slowly, flexing through a series of mystical gestures, significant and compelling. It hurt just to watch them, as though they were moving through more than three dimensions.

"He's preprogrammed the bloody thing!" said Molly. "All he has to do now is say the right Words, and it's all over! From the Apocalypse Door to the Paradise Door, in a series of easy gestures. I think I'll believe that when I see it, but . . . Look; you take the Immortal, I'll take the Hand. I don't care what it's made from, it's magic, and that puts it in my territory. If it's magic, I can work my will on it. That's what being a witch is all about."

"Who are you trying to convince?" I said. "You or me? Just how much magic do you have left, after everything you've done?"

"Enough! Now be a good boy, and go hit the Immortal."

"Love to."

Molly charged forward, skipping lightly over the snow as though she was playing hopscotch. She grabbed the gesturing Hand of Glory with both of her hands, and tried to stop the fingers from moving. When that failed, she tried to pull the Hand away from the Door, but it wouldn't budge so much as an inch. So she forced one of her hands inside the Hand, and arm-wrestled it. The brightly glowing Hand slammed shut, crushing Molly's hand inside it. I heard the bones crack and break, saw blood fly on the air; but although Molly's whole body convulsed, she never made a sound.

I charged forward, ploughing through the deep snow

and sending it flying. The Hand of Glory slowly opened, and Molly fell to her knees on the snow, cradling her injured hand against her chest. Blood dripped steadily from her broken fingers, onto the accepting snow. I could hear Methuselah laughing. I moved quickly to put myself between Molly and the Hand, and knelt down beside her. She was breathing hard, her eyes wide with shock and pain. She hadn't healed herself, and that told me all I needed to know about how much magic she had left.

Molly glared at me. "All right, you deal with the Hand. I'll deal with Methuselah."

"Works for me," I said.

I heard heavy footsteps slamming through the snow, and looked round to see the Immortal coming right at us, wielding a glowing blade he hadn't had earlier. Molly raised her good hand, and snapped her fingers fiercely. But though Methuselah flinched at the sound, it didn't stop him. Either Molly had used up all her magic, or as an Immortal and a flesh dancer, he was immune. Either way, he was a lot closer now. So I rose up and went to meet him. I lashed out at him with a golden fist, but somehow he dodged it at the last moment. And while I was caught off balance, he lunged past me and ran on. It took me a moment to turn around in the heavy snow, and when I did, it was just in time to see Methuselah run Molly through with the glowing blade. It slammed in under her sternum, and punched out her back. Blood shot out of her contorted mouth. And then she grabbed the Immortal's extended arm with both her hands, and broke it in two. The sound of the bone breaking was sharp and crisp on the still air. Methuselah screamed, and fell backwards into the snow. Molly grabbed the glowing blade, pulled it carefully out of her, and threw it away. She looked up to see me watching, and glared at me.

"How many times do I have to tell you? He can't kill me! Now deal with the bloody Hand!"

Methuselah clutched his broken arm and gaped at Molly. "Cheat!" he said shrilly. "You're all cheats!"

I ran through the snow towards him, and he scrambled back onto his feet again. His arm wasn't broken anymore; the wonders of flesh dancing. He still backed away rather than face me. I knew I should be going after the Hand, but he'd tried to kill Molly. I hit him in the face with my golden fist, with all my strength behind it. The bones of his face collapsed inwards, and blood exploded out, steaming on the cold air. He didn't fall, so I hit him again and again, until finally he did fall, into the blood-soaked snow. He glared up at me, eyes shining fiercely through the bloody mess I'd made of his face.

"It's not fair! I've won, I've won! Look at the Door, you see? You're too late! My Hand has done it!"

I turned and looked. The Door didn't seem any different. Methuselah seized the moment to scramble back onto his feet, and run raggedly towards the Door. I went after him. And the Hand of Glory drifted slowly, almost thoughtfully, forward; and then knocked three times on the Door. The sound was impossibly loud, and carrying, reverberating on the air. And then the Hand closed, and fell out of the air like a dead bird. The Door started to open. It didn't actually move, as such, but I could *feel* it opening. I put on a burst of speed, and ran right past Methuselah, sending snow flying in every direction. I slammed up against the Door, and put my golden shoulder against it. I dug my feet in, and strained against the Door with all my armoured strength. I could feel a growing pressure on the other side of the Door.

None of the disturbing heat, or the voices Doctor Delirium had heard, just an increasing sense of pressure. Of something on the other side, moving slowly, relentlessly closer. Wanting *out*. I threw all my weight, all my strength, against the Door. I was a Drood, shaman to Humanity, and I would hold against all the hoards of Hell, or die trying.

And then Methuselah called my name. I looked around, and he was back with Molly. Only this time, he had the glowing blade pressed against her throat. He was grinning broadly, his eyes wide and no longer entirely sane.

"Get away from the Door!" he yelled. "Even a witch will die, if you cut off her head! Doesn't matter where she keeps her heart then, does it? Get away from my Door, or watch your witch die, right in front of you."

"She wouldn't want me to do that," I said.

"Yes I bloody would!" said Molly. "It's all right, Eddie. Do as he says."

"What?"

"Trust me, Eddie. You can't stop the Door opening. So let Methuselah have what he wants."

There was something in the way she said that. I looked at her closely, and she dropped me the briefest of winks. *Okay,* I thought, *she must know something . . .* So I pushed myself away from the Door, and backed away from it. Methuselah waited till I was a safe distance away, and then headed for the Door, dragging Molly along with him, the blade still pressed against her throat. He hesitated by the Door, clearly wondering if he could cut Molly's throat and get away with it, but in the end he just threw her face forward into the snow, grabbed up the fallen Hand of Glory, and pronounced one final, irrevocable Word. I ran forward, grabbed

Molly, and hauled her away from the Door. She struggled fiercely in my arms, so I put her down, and we both turned to look at the Door.

"I've done it!" yelled Methuselah, dancing hysterically before the Door. "I've turned it, I've transformed its nature, it's the Paradise Door now! I will take Heaven by storm, and know pleasures beyond bearing! Paradise is mine!"

The Door opened, just the slightest crack, and a brilliant light blasted out, so pure and blindingly brilliant that Molly and I both cried out, wanting to turn our gaze away but held where we were. The light incinerated Methuselah where he stood, reducing him to ashes in a moment. The Door closed, and all that was left of the Immortal was a few final ashes, spiralling slowly to the snow below. And then the Door just disappeared, turning in a direction my eyes could not follow—gone forever, leaving nothing behind but the crater of steaming water it had been standing in.

"Well," I said finally. "The light of Heaven is not for mortals. And . . . somebody really doesn't like gate-crashers."

CHAPTER TWELVE

Taking Care of Loose Ends

Afterwards

Back at Drood Hall, I paid a visit to the Infirmary. One of the closed-off wards, where we keep the lost causes. For those Droods injured or damaged beyond all hope of recovery, but somehow still alive. Because out in the field, a bullet can be the kindest threat an agent has to face. We never give up on them, because they're family. And because every now and again, we win one. Alistair had a small private room all to himself, befitting his status as husband to the late Matriarch, my grandmother. He wasn't my real grandfather; that had been the Matriarch's first husband. Which might have been why I never cared much for Alistair.

He lay quietly on his bed, still wrapped from head to toe in bandages, even after all this time. Surrounded by the very latest medical equipment, apparently helpless to do anything more than monitor his condition. They made pleasant, efficient sounds at regular intervals, and lights made impressive patterns on their displays, but still Alistair lay there, held somewhere between life and death. He slept most of the time, I was told, waking up just often enough to take nourishment through a straw. He breathed slowly, evenly, without any help.

He'd been like this for months, ever since he tried to protect the Matriarch from me. He used a forbidden weapon, a witch-killing gun called the Salem Special. It fired flames called up from Hell itself, according to legend. I couldn't let Alistair use it on Molly, so I made it backfire. I can still remember the way he screamed, the stench of his burning flesh, as the flames ate him up.

Nurses and doctors had given me hard looks as I headed for his room. They couldn't deny me some time with the man, even though they blamed me for his condition.

I pulled up a chair, and sat down beside the bed. The heavy smell of antiseptic in the room bothered me obscurely, until I made the connection with the Red Room in Area 52, and pushed the thought from my head. I looked Alistair over. His bandages covered every visible part of him, the rest covered by a single light blanket. They were clean, white, spotless even, which suggested they were being regularly changed, at least. His face was as blank as any Egyptian mummy's, with only dark holes for the eyes and mouth. He breathed slowly, not moving, and if he knew I was there, he gave no sign.

"Sorry I haven't been to see you before," I said. "But I never had a good enough reason, till now. All the Immortals at Castle Frankenstein are dead. They're still dragging out the bodies, and piling them up. There are still some Immortals out in the world, scattered here and there, living their various lives as other people. But we'll hunt them all down eventually. We have their computer records, and the Armourer swears he's almost ready with a device that will always identify an Immortal, no matter how well they hide themselves. Isn't that good news?

"The Matriarch is dead. Martha Drood, my grandmother, your wife. Murdered in her own bed, by someone she thought she could trust. But of course, you already knew that. Because you killed her. Whoever you are, inside those bandages. When did you make the swap? After the bandages, presumably, when no one could tell the difference. Who would ever suspect a helpless invalid like you? Did you kill Alistair, before you took his place, or had he already died from his injuries? I'd like to think you were responsible for his death, not me. Because he did try to be a good man, at the end.

"You had the perfect disguise here, and the perfect place to hide. Easy enough for you to reprogramme the machines when no one was watching, so they wouldn't recognise your occasional absences. Were you planning on a miraculous recovery, at some point? It doesn't matter. The moment I saw the name Alistair on the computer's list of Droods who'd been replaced by Immortals, I knew you'd killed my grandmother. Who else would she trust, long enough for you to get close enough to stick a knife in her?

"There are so many things I could ask you. Things only you Immortals could know, about the infiltration of my family. I don't suppose you'd care to volunteer which of you was responsible for the summoning of the Loathly Ones? No? It doesn't matter. I have my list. One of you will talk."

The bandaged head turned slowly on the pillow to look at me. I shot him twice in the head, with the Armourer's special gun, that fired strange matter bullets. I needed to be sure. Who was he, really? It didn't matter. Blood from the massive exit wounds had soaked the pillow. The machines fell silent, replaced by an alarm bell. I got up, and left the room.

For you, Grandmother. And you, Alistair. One last duty, one last service.

Later, in the Sanctity, I met with the rest of the Council. We were, after all, supposed to be running things in the Matriarch's absence. The Armourer was there, the Sarjeant-at-Arms, even William the Librarian, though he seemed even more distracted than usual. Harry was there, with his partner the hellspawn Roger Morningstar. No one objected to his presence, or to Molly's. With the Matriarch gone, we were all allowing ourselves a little more freedom from the old restrictions. I was relieved to see that Molly had recovered enough magic to mend her broken arm and crushed hand, though she still looked a little fragile to me. She was currently stuffing herself with mushroom vol-au-vents at the standing buffet.

Ethel's familiar red glow filled the Sanctity, but the once refreshing and revitalising energies of her manifestation now seemed distinctly weakened.

"Ethel?" I said. "You seem a little off colour. Is everything all right with you?"

I don't know, she said. *Is it really over, Eddie?*

"Pretty much," I said. "It's just down to mopping up, now. Taking care of the loose ends."

There were traitors and murderers right here in the Hall, and I never knew . . . The Droods are under my protection. I failed you.

"We can all be deceived, Ethel. Happens to the best of us."

I never knew humans could be so . . . deceitful. I'm going to have to think about that.

I left Ethel thinking, and headed for Molly and the buffet, only to be intercepted by Harry. We nodded to each other, warily. He pushed his owlish wire-rimmed glasses into place with a fingertip, and considered me thoughtfully.

"We're going to have to talk soon, Eddie," he said, in his most reasonable voice. "About who's going to replace our dear departed grandmother. Someone has to take control of the family."

"We'll organise an election as soon as the family's recovered from its various traumas," I said. "We've all been a little busy, in your absence."

"An election?" said Harry. "Yes, well, I suppose that's one way of doing it."

He drifted away to join Roger Morningstar at the buffet, where they kissed briefly before taking turns to feed each other delicate little rolls of sushi. I saw the Armourer standing on his own, staring suspiciously at something palely loitering on a cocktail stick. I braced myself, and went over to join him.

"Uncle Jack . . ."

"You killed him, didn't you?" said the Armourer, not looking up.

"Yes," I said. "He didn't give me any choice."

The Armourer sighed briefly. "No. He wouldn't." He looked at me directly. "Tell me he died well."

"As well as could be expected," I said. "He stood his ground, and fought to the end."

The Armourer shook his head slowly. "I thought that would mean something, but it doesn't." He popped the thing on a stick into his mouth, and chewed fiercely.

404 ° Simon R. Green

"We took the dragon's head out to the old north barrow, and buried it there. Apparently it had got quite used to being covered, and felt . . . exposed, in the open air. Took a dozen men a whole day to manage it, but then, that's what lab assistants are for. Healthy exercise, I'm sure. Right now, our best historians are taking it in turns to sit and talk with the dragon, and take notes. That dragon has seen an awful lot of history in its time, before and after it was beheaded. A surprisingly amicable creature, I found, for a dragon. Spending centuries as just a head under a hill, winding down but unable to die, did a lot to mellow it. Now it's just glad for some company." He looked at me sternly. "But you can't keep bringing home stray pets, Eddie. The thought does you credit, but we just don't have the room." He brightened abruptly. "On the other hand, theoretically speaking, it does seem possible that we might be able to grow back the rest of its body! And stick it back on, of course. We could really hold our heads up, with our very own personal dragon! Even those snotty London Knights don't have their very own personal dragon! If only it hadn't been dead for so long . . . Still, that just makes it a little bit trickier. I do so love a challenge . . ."

"Speaking of which," I said, "how are you getting on with the Hand of Glory, and the remains of the robot dog?"

He positively beamed on me. "You're spoiling me, Eddie. You don't usually bring me back such wonderful presents. The Hand in particular has real possibilities . . . It seems to have exhausted all its magical properties, but it is still the hand of an angel."

I gave him a hard look. "Tell me you're not thinking of trying to grow a whole angel from the Hand."

The Armourer smiled innocently. "It is tempting, isn't it? But no, the last thing we need round here is another plague of frogs. I'll just lock it away somewhere safe, until Someone turns up to ask for it back. And thanks for the robot dog. I love jigsaws. And I've always wanted a dog. I used to have one, a long time ago. But it exploded. Poor little Scraps."

"Well," I said. "As long as you're happy."

"I still want my devices back," said the Armourer. "The cuff links and the ring. I want to run a whole series of tests on them; see how they stood up to use in the field."

"In a while," I said. "Molly and I have it in mind to run a few special tests of our own."

"Ah, yes . . ." The Armourer gave me a knowing look. "I had the same idea. Ran some very interesting tests, with the assistance of four of the more open-minded female lab assistants."

I could feel my jaw dropping. "You didn't . . ."

He grinned. "You young people think you invented sex."

He started to turn away, but I stopped him with one last question.

"Uncle Jack, why did Timothy call himself Tiger Tim? Was it something to do with Africa?"

"No," said the Armourer. "Tiger Tim was his favourite character, when he was a child. I used to read to him from some old children's books, in between rushing off to save the world in the Cold War. He always liked the Tiger Tim stories the best."

We both looked round as the Sarjeant-at-Arms strode over to join us, chewing enthusiastically on a chicken leg. He nodded briskly to the Armourer, and to me.

"I've just put together a team of our best field agents, to track down the remaining Immortals. Wherever or whoever they are. You'd better get that detecting device finished, Armourer; the computer files from the Castle are far from complete. They're still dragging bodies out of Castle Frankenstein, you know. That was a good night's work. Not often you get to smite the ungodly in such great numbers."

"And the team I had you send to Area 52?" I said, just to get a word in edgeways.

"They have blown up, burned out, and utterly destroyed every last bit of it," said the Sarjeant. "The American government has made all the expected protestations, but I got the distinct impression that they were actually very relieved. It would appear previous administrations had rather let things get out of control."

"Tell me your people thought to empty out the armoury before they blew the place up," said the Armourer.

"Of course," said the Sarjeant. "Acquired some very interesting pieces."

I left them deep in discussion over their new toys, and slipped in beside William, standing at the buffet table staring at an empty plate. The Librarian seemed even more lost and distracted than usual. We'd found him a new assistant, a keen young chap called Iorith, and he was hovering beside the Librarian, ready to be of use at a moment's notice. But William didn't even seem to know he was there. I said a few kind words to the new assistant Librarian, and he brightened immediately.

"I do try to help," said Iorith. "But I think he's still getting used to me. Used to me not being Rafe, I mean. He still calls me by that name, now and again." He looked at me thoughtfully. "Can I ask you, is it true, what they say? That there's Something . . . alive, in the Old Library? I haven't seen anything myself, but . . ."

"There's definitely Something there," I said. "But don't ask me what. I was right there when it stopped the false Rafe from killing the Librarian, and I still couldn't tell you what it is. But it does seem very keen on protecting William and the Old Library, so I think we should just let it be, and try very hard not to upset it."

"I wonder what it is," said Iorith. "Or perhaps who . . ."

William stirred suddenly, and looked at me directly. "I trusted him," he said. "Rafe. I trusted him. He looked after me, and I was teaching him how to be a good Librarian . . . I liked him. Was the Rafe I knew always an Immortal? Did I ever know the real Rafe? We have to find him, Eddie. The real Rafe, I mean. Find him, and bring him home . . ."

"It's in hand, Librarian," I said. "We have people working on it. We never give up on family. You know that."

"Yes, of course," said William. He seemed to suddenly realise he was holding an empty plate, and put it down. He turned away, and headed for the door.

"Come along, Rafe."

Iorith nodded quickly to me, and hurried after the Librarian. And having done my duty, and spoken to all the people I should have, I was now free to join my Molly at the buffet table. She grinned at me, mopping her mouth with a napkin.

"Family . . . Doesn't it just give you a wonderful sense of security?"

"Don't start," I said. "I can't wait for this nonsense to be over, so I can take you back to my room . . ."

"You have still got the cuff links, and the ring?"

"Of course. And then afterwards, I think I'd like to just lie down and snooze quietly for several weeks."

"After what I've got in mind, you'll need to."

"Delightful wench. There's still a lot of work to be done, you know. There are still some Immortals out there, hiding in deep cover. We'll never feel properly safe until they've all been found and dealt with. And we still need to find out just how badly this family's been infiltrated. The list we found in the computer said it was complete, but I don't think I trust it."

And that was when the Sanctuary doors burst open, and Isabella Metcalf came storming in.

"Molly! I know who killed our parents! And yours too, Eddie!"

I stepped forward to hear what she had to say, and I was so caught up in the moment I didn't see the knife in her hand until she buried it deep into my chest. I staggered backwards, blood gushing down my front. All the strength went out of my legs, and I sat down suddenly. I hit the floor hard but I didn't feel it. I looked stupidly at the hilt of the knife sticking out of my chest. Blood bubbled around it. I could feel the pain, but it seemed very far away. I couldn't seem to get my breath. I wanted to pull the knife out, but I still had enough sense not to. There was a lot of shouting going on. The Armourer was kneeling beside me, holding my shoulders, talking urgently, but it didn't seem important.

I was looking at the Sarjeant-at-Arms, as he hit Isabella in the head again and again. Her head whipped round, blood flying on the air, and then she slumped to the floor. Harry and Roger were suddenly there. They grabbed an arm each, and hauled her up, and suddenly she wasn't Isabella anymore. A teenage boy struggled in their grip, laughing breathlessly. He saw me looking at him, and laughed even harder.

"I got you! You killed my family, but I got you!"

Molly thrust her face into his. "Speak to me, you bastard Immortal! Where's Isabella? What have you done to her?"

The Immortal laughed in her face. "You'll never know."

He bit down hard, and dark blood frothed around his contorted mouth. He fell backwards, convulsing so hard Harry and Roger couldn't hold on to him. He was dead before he hit the floor.

"Poison tooth," said the Sarjeant. "Hell with him. Where's the doctor?"

Molly came running over to kneel before me. Her face was white with shock, as she made desperate magical gestures over me.

"Must have been poison on the blade too," said the Sarjeant, looking over her shoulder. "He's going fast."

The Armourer was crying, as he held my shoulders gently in his strong engineer's hands. "Hold on, Eddie. Help's coming. Hold on . . ."

"Get a doctor in here!" screamed Molly.

She gave up on her magics, and held both my hands in hers. I couldn't feel them. It hurt to keep trying to breathe, so I stopped. I looked at Molly. Tears streamed down her face. I tried to say something, but all that came out of my mouth was blood. I tried to smile for her. I felt cold. Colder than I'd ever been in the Antarctic. Darkness closed in, and the last thing I saw was Molly's face.

Voices. I could hear voices.

"I'm sorry, Molly." That was the Armourer. "I'm sorry. He's gone. Eddie's dead."

"He can't be!" That was Molly. "He can't be! Eddie . . . !"

"I'm sorry. There's no pulse. No heartbeat. He's not breathing. We've lost him."

"Then I'll just have to go after him. And bring him back."

And then—